GHOST TOWNS

GHOST TOWNS

Edited by Martin H. Greenberg
and Russell Davis

PINNACLE BOOKS
Kensington Publishing Corp.

www.kensingtonbooks.com

PINNACLE BOOKS are published by

Kensington Publishing Corp.
119 West 40th Street
New York, NY 10018

PUBLISHER'S NOTE
Following the death of William W. Johnstone, the Johnstone
family is working with a carefully selected writer to organize and
complete Mr. Johnstone's outlines and many unfinished manu-
scripts to create additional novels in all of his series like The Last
Gunfighter, Mountain Man, and Eagles, among others. His story
in this anthology was inspired by Mr. Johnstone's superb story-
telling.

All Kensington titles, imprints, and distributed lines are available at special quantity discounts for bulk purchases for sales promotions, premiums, fund-raising, educational, or institutional use. Special book excerpts or customized printings can also be created to fit specific needs. For details, write or phone the office of the Kensington sales manager: Kensington Publishing Corp., 119 West 40th Street, New York, NY 10018, attn: Sales Department; phone: 1-800-221-2647.

The stories in this book are works of fiction. Names, characters, businesses, organizations, places, events, and incidents either are the product of the author's imagination or are used fictitiously. Any resemblance to actual persons, living or dead, events, or locales is entirely coincidental.

PINNACLE BOOKS and the Pinnacle logo are Reg. U.S. Pat. & TM Off.

ISBN-13: 978-0-7860-4235-7
ISBN-10: 0-7860-4235-4

First printing: July 2010

10 9 8 7 6 5 4 3

Printed in the United States of America

First electronic edition: July 2010

ISBN-13: 978-0-7860-2506-0
ISBN-10: 0-7860-2506-9

Contents

Contents

Introduction
Russell Davis

My memory isn't quite what it used to be, but I think the year was around 1977, perhaps 1978. My mother and father took me on a family vacation to Colorado and I have three very distinct memories from that particular journey. The first is of my father pushing my mother into the hotel swimming pool with all her clothes on. The second is of discovering mica—a type of sheet mineral that can slide apart in paper thin pieces and has the ability to cut like a razor. And the third . . . the third is of taking a Jeep tour of several ghost town sites.

The tour itself was pretty neat, but what made it truly memorable was how many things went wrong just as we were trying to reach that last ghost town. The "best one" the guide said. The Jeep broke down on a narrow, steep mountain track. It began to rain. And the rescue Jeep sent for us ran over the toes of my right foot. Nothing broken, but I suspect that was more luck (the road was soft, my feet were small) than it was anything else. We never did make it to the last ghost town. To the "best one."

From my earliest exposure to the idea of ghost towns—especially *western* ghost towns—I've been hooked. As I've traveled throughout the West, I've visited many places that were once booming and are now empty places that often feel haunted to me. The idea for this anthology came from those visits and from suspecting—deep down, where I try not to look too often—that even places like Tombstone, Arizona, and Virginia City, Nevada, are haunted by the spirits of those people who lived (and died) there during those early days of westward expansion.

The invitation for the authors in this anthology was simple: write a story about a ghost town (real or fictional) and, if they so desired, the story *could* have elements of the supernatural. Most of them, to my surprise, decided to go with it and wrote tales of ghosts and other supernatural events. Being surprised is one of the great pleasures of putting together a project like this. And I don't want to ruin the surprise for you, so I'll let you travel these pages on your own, without too much forewarning of what you may find.

Some people say that the western is dying; I say it is changing and evolving, but still very much alive. In this book, you'll find a story from Steve Hockensmith—who is best known for his western mystery series that began with *Holmes on the Range,* a tale from *New York Times* bestselling author Margaret Coel, and even a ghost story from Elmer Kelton, whose career has been a shining example of brilliance and originality in the western field. Most of the authors have won Spur Awards or Western Heritage Awards (or both); many have been on best-seller lists and have a great many readers who look forward to each new work with anticipation. It should come then, as no surprise to you, that the stories you are about to read are, as they say, "good 'uns."

I believe that stories should be shared—some of these would make fine tales to be told around the campfire, preferably to young kids who've just tried to visit a ghost town and strange events kept them from ever seeing it. I believe that stories, especially stories about the West, are durable—like the men and women who first crossed into the frontier to discover that only the strong survive. And, finally, I believe that well-written stories take on a life of their own . . . that they leave the page and enter the imagination of the reader, almost like a ghost, whispering in the ear from the inside of the mind, rather than the outside.

As always, I suggest and hope that you share this anthology with your family and friends. Western literature in all its forms can and will survive, but only when the stories are shared, when they are durable, and when they take on a life of their own, reaching more people and, in particular, those who have yet to read a real western.

Some might say that because many of these tales contain an element of the fantastic, they aren't *real* westerns. This is nonsense, of course. The American West is a place of the fantastic. It was tales of the fantastic and the unimaginable that drove people to reach out and attempt to tame the frontier. It was tales of the fantastic that led people on the search for gold, and tales of the fantastic that created so much fear about the native peoples of this land. And now, so many years after the first frontiersmen came here, the American West is still a place of the fantastic.

I know this to be true because I live here . . . and I've seen wild mustangs appear and disappear in the blink of an eye during the sunrise, walked the ruins of an abandoned mine and found the claim paper in an old coffee can tied to a post, and ventured through the graveyards that no one tends or even visits anymore, yet somehow the stones remain and the occasional bundle of flowers appears.

And so, I invite you to turn the pages and discover these stories and share them with anyone who might be willing to discover them too. Because, in the end, the Western story is about the fantastic, about discovery, and about places that still exist.

The West is not gone, nor even a ghost. It is still here, ghost towns and thriving places, working mines and abandoned claims, haunted saloons and taverns teeming with life. The West has changed in many ways, but if one looks—in the stories and in the places—the *real* American West remains and always will.

Northern Nevada, Autumn 2009

GHOST TOWNS

The Water Indian

Steve Hockensmith

Mr. William Brackwell
c/o The Sussex Land & Cattle Co.
Somerset House
London, England

Dear Mr. Brackwell:

I trust your journey back to Merry Old was a smooth one, and you met with fewer of the, shall we say, surprises that were so commonplace during your stay in Montana. (By "surprises," of course, I mean dead folks.) I do hope you won't let the carnage you witnessed at the Bar VR color your view of the American West. Such goings-on are hardly the norm, no matter what your experience (or the dime novels) might lead you to believe. I mean, here my brother and I are in Utah, and we haven't witnessed a murder in *minutes!*

Not that our travels have been boring. Nope, that would hardly do it justice. Tedious—now that hits closer to the mark. Monotonous, wearying, and mind-numbing too.

Except for when it was bloodcurdlingly, hair-raisingly, pants-fillingly terrifying, that is. And for about twenty-four hours up in the Rocky Mountains, that's exactly what it was.

When we parted ways a couple months back, you asked that I keep you apprised of whatever progress we might make toward my brother's goal. But I didn't bother writing before now, as there was no progress to report. And there's still not. In lieu of news, though, let me present you with this: something you can trot out the next time you're in need of a spook story to entertain your friends of a dark, stormy evening by the fire. You can tell them one of your American cowboy pals passed it on to you, and such men aren't given to balderdash or exaggeration. Ever. Any of them. Why, the last time a drover was caught in a lie was 1876, and the scoundrel was immediately stripped of his spurs and sent east to become a banker.

Anyway—on to the yarn.

As you'll recall, Old Red and I planned to hit the trail in search of jobs as Pinkertons. *And we've succeeded!* In hitting the trail in search of jobs as Pinkertons, that is. As for actually *finding* jobs as Pinks . . . there we've utterly failed. Believe it or not, when a couple dusty saddle-bums stumble into a Pinkerton office intent on joining the payroll, they are *not* received with open arms. (Though when one of said saddle-bums tries to explain that he's actually a "top-rail deducifier" thanks to all the Sherlock Holmes stories he's studied on, the pair is greeted warmly indeed—with gales of laughter.)

As if this wouldn't be tiresome enough, it took us days and sometimes weeks to reach each fresh humiliation. Hailing from Kansas Grangers as we do, we were raised to view the Southern Pacific as Satan, the Union Pacific as Lucifer, and the Central Pacific as Beelzebub—different names for the same great evil—and my brother refused to bankroll the bastards with even a penny from our meager kitty.

Conscience rarely comes without a cost, though, and in this case it was paid mainly by our backsides. After leaving the Bar VR, we journeyed first west across Montana, then southeast through Idaho, all of it on horseback. By the time we were skirting around Bear Lake into Utah, my saddlewarmer was bruised black as an anvil.

Now, this wasn't just Utah Territory we were riding into—it was Mormon territory. And given the clashes of years past, a couple drifting Gentiles like ourselves could hardly assume we'd be welcome . . . or even tolerated. So we kept to ourselves as we wound down through the Bear Lake Valley, steering clear of the main towns thereabouts.

I didn't mind missing out on the saggy, smelly, lice-infested boardinghouse beds we'd have no doubt found in places like Pickleville and Fish Haven. Once you've been on a few cattle drives, camping out seems like a positive luxury when there's no night herding to do and no belly cheater waking you at the crack of dawn banging a stew pot over your head. And the Bear Lake Valley made "roughing it" none-too-rough, what with its well-worn trails, ample trees for shade and tinder, and teeming cutthroat trout practically fighting each other for the honor of gracing your frying pan.

In short, the place was Eden without the serpent . . . or Eve. Or so it seemed.

Our first clue that all was not paradisical came as we rounded the southwestern corner of the lake. Just off the trail was a rotten, falling-down fence and, beyond it, what might have been a field of alfalfa before weeds and grass were allowed to overtake it. It wasn't long before we spotted an abandoned farmhouse—and then another soon after with its own fields choked with wildflowers and thistle.

This was beautiful country, good for grazing cattle or raising crops either or, and it was a puzzlement to me that farming folk should ever give it up.

"There ain't never been no Indian troubles up thisaway . . . have there?" I asked my brother, eyeing the tree line nervously.

Of course, the only "Indian troubles" these days are suffered by the Indians alone, and they run to starvation and disease rather than raiding and killing. Yet the bloodshed isn't so far behind us that the thought of braves on the warpath can't still chill the blood.

"Nothin' but Shoshone and Ute 'round these parts . . . provided you could still find 'em. Friendly ones, they are." Old Red leaned out from his saddle and spat. "Too friendly for their own good, I expect."

"Well, then . . . where'd everybody go?"

"What you really mean is *why'd* they go. And you know what I say to that."

I did indeed. I'd heard him say it often enough. "It is a capital mistake to theorize before you have all the evidence"—my brother's favorite quote from his hero, your famous countryman, Sherlock Holmes. Most drovers want to be Charles Goodnight or

Buffalo Bill Cody if they have any ambition at all, but Old Red's always been a contrarian (or just plain contrary, anyway). The Holmes of the Range—that's what he's set out to be.

We were to rendezvous with ol' Holmes shortly, as it turned out . . . and be in need of his particular brand of wisdom, as well.

As we were passing our third deserted farm, the sun was sinking below the mountains behind us, and my brother made a most sensible (though not entirely welcome) decision. We would spend the night in the abandoned homestead visible just off the trail.

It felt a little like a violation, a desecration even, settling into someone else's house. They hadn't been gone long—no more than a couple years, Old Red judged by the cobwebs and dust and dry rot—and they'd left some of their furniture behind. A table and chairs hewn from local pine, a bed with a finely crafted headboard of mahogany, even a battered foot-pump organ. I half-expected the rightful occupants to barge in any minute, slack-jawed to find a couple presumptuous cowpokes lighting up kindling in their fireplace,

Yet I might actually have welcomed the intrusion, provided nobody felt the need to shoot us. Old Red's far from the chattiest man around—very, *very* far—and whatever topics of conversation we had to chew over had been gnawed down to the bone weeks before. Fresh company would've been mightily appreciated. As it was, we had to rely on the old, dog-eared variety: my brother's stack of Holmes stories.

Old Red requested a rereading of *A Study in*

Scarlet, no doubt because it takes as its backdrop a bloody feud betwixt Utah Mormons. I obliged him, like I always do (my brother, you'll recall, being unable to tell A from Z unless they're in a cattle brand).

Round about the spot in the story where Doc Watson gets to writing about "The Country of the Saints," my brother interrupted me—with his snores. So I put down the magazine I'd been orating from and closed my eyes myself.

Even stretched out there on the floor by the hearth (for the bed frame had no mattress) I was more warm and snug than I'd been any night in weeks. Yet sleep didn't come. I still had that creepy feeling we didn't belong there and that someone might come along to confirm it, loudly and forcefully, at any time.

After what seemed like hours, I finally drifted off to the Land of Nod—only to be yanked back to the Land of Here and Now by a noise outside.

Something was moving in the woods a stone's throw from the front door. And not just *moving* in it. Crashing through it and tearing it down, by the sound of things.

"Hey," I groaned groggily.

"I hear it," my brother said, sounding so crisp and alert he might've been polishing off a pot of coffee at high noon.

We lay there a moment, listening to the creaking of tree limbs and the *shush-shush* of movement through the brush.

"Big," I said.

"Yup."

"Bear?"

"Maybe." Old Red sat up, ear cocked. "Horses ain't spooked."

There was a *snap* outside, loud.

"Yet," I said.

My brother reached down for the Winchester lying next to him on the floor.

"Better have us a look."

Together, we crept to the nearest window and peeked outside warily, careful not to create silhouettes against the ember-glow from the fireplace. Mighty good targets, those would make. And if what we were hearing outside was horses—from a party of the faithful come to root out Gentile squatters, let's say—targets we could well be.

Our own ponies were stabled in a dilapidated barn about a quarter mile off, and that's where we directed our squints first. My brother and I were safe enough from bear, puma, or wolf long as we stayed inside, but we couldn't just cower there while something big and hungry made a midnight snack of our mounts. We might yet have to venture out for a face-to-face with who-knew-what.

There was just enough moonlight to make out a shimmying in the trees near the barn, branches dancing in the half-darkness. The movement was high up—nine or ten feet off the ground. Beyond it, a single star flickered in the nighttime sky.

Only it couldn't have been a star. It was too low on the horizon, not in the sky at all.

Then I saw the *other* star—another perfect pinprick of yellow light, right beside the first. And that's when I knew what they were.

Glowing eyes, at least a foot apart. Eyes that were staring straight at us.

"Sweet Jesus," I gasped. "If that's a hoot owl, it's got a wingspan as wide as Texas."

"Ain't no owl," Old Red growled, and he moved to the door, threw it open, and stepped outside.

I came out behind him, Colt in hand, as he took aim.

The lights jerked downward, then disappeared entirely. There was another rustle of quick movement in the trees, and then . . . nothing. No eyes, no motion, no sound for the next two minutes.

"Well," Old Red finally sighed, "we'd best pass the rest of the night out with the horses. Just in case."

I looked back wistfully at our cozy spots by the fire.

"Can't we bring 'em in here with us?"

My brother just went inside and started gathering up his bedroll.

We split the hours till dawn into watches, but we needn't have bothered. *You* try sleeping with only a few planks of knotty, warped barn wood between you and some monstrous whatsis stalking around in the dark. Not that we ever heard the beast come back. But one visit was more than enough to keep me jumping at every cricket chirp all the way to daybreak.

"Well?" I said as my brother and I finally stepped out into the orange-yellow light of early morning.

"Well, what?"

Old Red moved off toward the trees, eyes down, scanning the ground.

"Well, what was that thing?"

"I have no earthly idea."

"You got an *unearthly* one?"

My brother glanced back just long enough to

shoot me a scowl. "You know I don't believe in spooks."

"Me neither . . . usually. And last night sure as hell wasn't usual."

Old Red knelt and picked a broken branch out of the underbrush. It was maybe three feet long and still studded with fresh, green pine needles. One end was splintered, and in the middle was a notched groove cut into the bark, as if the branch had been torn down by one powerful, clutching claw.

My brother looked up, then pointed at something above him.

A broken stub stuck out from a pine tree a dozen feet up.

"Spooks don't tear down tree limbs."

"All right, granted," I said. *"So what does?"*

"'It is a capital mistake to—'"

"Oh, for chrissakes!" I spat. "You wanna make a capital mistake? Quote Sherlock Holmes to me after I spent the night lyin' around waitin' to be eaten by the bogeyman."

Old Red put down the branch and moved farther into the brush. "Ain't no such thing as . . . hel-lo."

He stopped cold.

"What is it?"

"Tracks."

"What kind?" I asked, already feeling relieved. If it steps with paw, hoof, or foot, my brother'll know what it is. I've seen him identify not just a cow's breed but its age, weight, and brand from one long stare at the pies it left behind.

"Never seen the likes of this," Old Red announced.

He started off again, still crouching low. "Bogeyman tracks, maybe."

"Har har. Thanks a lot," I grumbled, following him into the forest to have a look for myself. I assumed he was guying me . . . till I laid eyes on those tracks.

There were two footprints pressed into the soft, mossy sod beneath the tree, right where we'd spotted those eyes shining in the night. They were side by side, a right and a left, plain as day. What wasn't plain, though—not plain at all—was what could have made them.

Whatever it was, it had big pads and claws, like a bear. But there was something stretching from toe to toe, mashing the earth down into little humps. Webbing, it looked like, as one might see on a duck or frog or beaver—a water-critter.

"There's more over thisaway," Old Red said. "Coming and going."

He stopped, but his gaze kept on moving along the forest floor, following a trail I was blind to. Soon he was staring straight into the sun streaming down through the trees.

To the east. Toward the lake.

Old Red started off again.

"Uhhh . . . shouldn't we be movin' along?" I called after him. "Salt Lake City ain't gonna come to us, y'know."

"Salt Lake City ain't goin' nowhere," my brother muttered.

I sighed, then started after him—but only after dashing back to the barn to collect the Winchester.

It was a comfort having it at hand, for the deeper we went into the woods, the stronger the feeling grew that we weren't alone. And we weren't, of course: There were chipmunks and squirrels and songbirds all around us. But they went on about their business in their usual jumpy, oblivious way, whereas the presence I sensed was steady, quiet, watchful.

And purely imaginary . . . or so I tried to tell myself.

It wasn't long before the lake came into view ahead of us. I hadn't spied much more than the occasional dimple in the sod or trampled twig after the first set of prints, but that changed but good as we approached the shoreline. There were tracks in the bank so deep and well-defined even a bottom-rail, bat-blind sign-reader like myself couldn't miss them.

One set led one-two, one-two straight into the water.

The other led *out* of the water.

"You know what I just realized?" I said.

"What's that?"

"Whatever made them prints . . . it walks on two feet."

Old Red shook his head sadly, as if—through my keen powers of observation and deducification—I'd just surmised that mud is brown and water wet.

"You don't say," he mumbled.

The tracks ran parallel to a big, rotten cottonwood that looked like it had toppled into the lake a half dozen years before, and my brother stepped up onto the trunk and walked along it, using it as a pier. The water was crystal clear back toward the bank, but the farther out Old Red went, the more it deepened and darkened until you couldn't see what might be beneath the surface.

The tree dipped under my brother's weight, tilting farther forward with his each step until the water was swirling over his feet.

"You wanna know what else I just realized?" I said.

"Yeah?"

"I wanna get the hell outta here."

"What are you still doing here, then?" a voice boomed out behind me.

I jumped so high I was wearing the sky for a hat.

"Easy," the voice warned when my feet touched ground again. "Put the rifle down and turn around . . . *slow.*"

I did as I was told and found myself facing a big-boned, potbellied man of perhaps fifty-five years. He had a long, white, wild beard and even wilder eyes, which were glaring at me, incidentally, over the leveled barrels of a scattergun.

"You," he said to Old Red. "Keep your hands where I can see 'em."

"Ain't got nothin' to do with 'em anyways," my brother said.

We'd left our gun belts back at the barn.

"Listen, mister—you wanna do us all a favor?" I said. "Point that cannon of yours at the water. Cuz you won't be gettin' any trouble out of me and my brother . . . but that there lake I ain't so sure about."

Rip Van Winkle didn't oblige me. He was about thirty yards off—far enough that a shotgun blast might not kill me outright, but close enough that he couldn't miss if he tried.

"Oh, ho. Seen something, have we?" he said,

and for the first time I noticed a hint of brogue in his voice.

"We seen *something,* all right—something that come outta the lake, from the look of things."

"You got a notion as to what our something mighta been?" Old Red asked. He was still balanced precariously on the end of that log with dark water lapping up around his ankles.

"At the moment, I'm more interested in who *you* are," Rip told him.

"Amlingmeyer's the name," I said. "Otto and Gustav—Big Red and Old Red to our friends." I grinned as genially as a preacher passing out how-do-you-dos at an ice cream social. "That could include you, provided you point your artillery some other direction."

The old man tightened his grip on his shotgun. "Your kind and my kind can never be friends."

"Now, now—let's not be so hasty," I said (hastily). "I've known cats and dogs that come to be bosom chums, by and by."

"Which 'kind' is it you're thinkin' of, mister?" my brother asked.

"What do you think? Gentiles and Mormons."

"Oh. *Those* kinds." I did my best to look guileless. "And which might you be?"

Rip narrowed his eyes. "Which are *you?*"

Never in my schooling days (all five years of them) had I ever faced a quiz as weighty as this. Stand up and spell "danger" with a j, and the worst you'll get is laughed at. But answer wrong now, and the punishment might be a bellyful of buckshot.

I peeked over at my brother, hoping he'd Holmesed out which faith it was Rip seemed to hold so dear. As you so well know, it's amazing the things Old Red can tell about a fellow from little more than a quick glimpse and some careful cogitation. A man's trade, his home life, his hopes and fears—my brother can see it all in a hangnail and a dirty collar. I've often told him he could clean up as a sideshow fortune teller if only he didn't have his heart set on detecting.

And yet all I got from him now was a shake of the head.

I couldn't bullshit our way out of this. I'd have to gamble on honesty.

I hate when that happens.

"I suppose we'd be Gentiles, as Mormons reckon it. We was raised Lutheran, but ain't neither of us seen the inside of a church in a coon's age." I looked heavenward, palms pressed together as in prayer. "Sorry 'bout that. No hard feelin's . . . I hope."

Apparently, He was in a forgiving mood: Rip lowered his scattergun and favored us with a grin wide enough to spy even through the white thicket of his beard.

"Well, then—welcome to Kennedyville, boys!" he said. "I'm Kennedy."

There were handshakes all around (my brother having been allowed at last to come ashore) while Kennedy made apologies for the less-than-hospitable way he'd originally greeted us.

"Me and my kids, we're the last Gentiles left around here. The other families pulled up stakes after the valley got to overflowing with Mormons. I've just been waiting for the day the Brethren turn up to claim all the old homesteads. And when they do . . ."

His grin actually grew wider, though there was no amusement to be seen in it. It almost looked like he was a-baring his fangs.

"So what brings you two through these parts?"

I laid out a judiciously expurgated account of our travels, saying only that we were out-of-work drovers headed south in search of jobs. The truth of it—that we'd set out to become sleuths—tends to get folks eyeing you like you're foaming at the mouth.

"Cowhands, are you?" Kennedy asked, seeming pleased. "So you've worked on ranches."

"Ranches, cattle drives, farms," I said. "We've had dealings with animals about every way you can without joining the circus."

Old Red cleared his throat. He'd opted for his usual greeting when shaking hands—a grunt—but now he had something to say.

"Speakin' of animals . . ."

He nodded down at the peculiar tracks leading into and out of the lake.

Kennedy nodded, his expression turning grim.

"Oh, yes. We'll talk more about that."

Then he brightened again—and I did too when I heard what he said next.

"Why not over breakfast? I can have the girls whip up hotcakes and bacon."

Hotcakes, bacon . . . *and girls?* God had most definitely forgiven me.

I rubbed my hands together and tried to keep from drooling on my shirt.

"Lead the way, Mr. Kennedy."

And so he did, cutting back through the woods to

a spread no more than a quarter mile from the farmhouse we'd stayed in the night before. As we tromped past rows of summer-gold wheat, Kennedy and I chatted amiably about his daughters, Fiona and Eileen. ("Pretty as a picture, the pair of 'em," he boasted. "If there was anything but Brethren around here, they would've been married off ages ago.") Old Red remained silent, though, his gaze darting from side to side as if he might catch a glimpse of our giant, web-footed friend out for a morning stroll.

"Wait here for a minute while I run ahead," Kennedy said as we approached a tidy little cottage. "The girls would never forgive me if I brought home gentlemen callers without giving 'em a chance to pretty up first!"

He scuttled on into the house, leaving me and my brother out front with the chickens strutting to and fro hunting for grubs.

"Mighty hospitable feller, once he decides not to kill you." I eyed the henhouse nearby. "Say . . . when's the last time we had us some eggs, anyway?"

"That all you can think about? Food?"

"Nope," I said. "I'm mighty anxious to meet them gals too."

Old Red rolled his eyes—then turned them back toward the forest.

"You're wastin' your time, Brother," I said. "Bogeymen don't get around much afore dusk."

Yet I was feeling it too for all my tomfoolery. That presence again, lurking, watching, waiting.

There were patches back in those trees where the thicket and leaves left it black as night at highest noon. Who knows? Maybe that'd be darkness enough for a bogeyman to do his prowlings, even though the sun might still shine.

Neither Old Red nor myself were superstitious men. But, then again, it's not a superstition if something's *real*. And those tracks sure weren't an old wives' tale.

Something was out there. Something . . .

I forced myself to turn toward the henhouse again.

"Back to more important questions," I said. "Such as 'scrambled or fried?'"

"Scrambled, I reckon," Old Red sighed. "Like your brains."

"Oh, no, Brother—*you're* the egghead of the two of us, remember?"

Kennedy stepped out of the house and gave us a pinwheeling wave of the arm.

"Come on in, boys! It's time you met the best cooks in Kennedyville!"

Fiona and Eileen proved to be the prettiest girls too—and might have been even if they weren't the only ones. Willowy, raven-haired, bright-eyed, and smiling, they were visions of loveliness such as a drover carries with him for a thousand miles. By the (alluring) look of them, they fell in age somewhere between myself and my brother—in their midtwenties—and though they teetered on the brink of what some would call old maidhood, their charms had not faded but rather deepened with time.

Then again, I always have been partial to older women.

And younger ones.

And skinny ones, plumps ones, and all the ones in between.

Oh, hell—let's just face it. I'm gal crazy.

Old Red, on the other hand, is crazy about women in his own way, which is crazy-scared. I doubt if that whatever-it-was in the woods could spook him half as much as a wink from a pretty lady. The more Fiona and Eileen fawned over us— taking our hats, pouring us coffee, asking (huzzah!) how we'd like our eggs—the more Old Red lived up to his handle by blushing as scarlet as a pimpernel.

(I will admit to you here, Mr. Brackwell, that I don't know what a "pimpernel" actually is. I gather from my readings that some come in scarlet, though.)

"You are a lucky man, Mr. Kennedy," I said, slathering butter over a stack of flapjacks that stretched halfway to the roof. "Having two such daughters to look after you here."

Kennedy nodded, his obvious pride slowly giving way to sadness.

"Lucky, I am . . . though I'd think myself luckier if their mother was still with us."

Eileen was hurrying past with a pitcher of milk, and she stopped behind him and put a hand on his shoulder.

Kennedy reached up and smothered her fingers under his big paw.

"She died bringing my youngest into the world. It's been just the three of us ever since."

"I'm sorry," I said.

Kennedy gave his daughter's hand a squeeze, then let go.

"Oh, we get along fine. It's only in the last few years things have turned lonely."

"With the other families leavin', you mean," Old Red said. "So . . . there any reason they cleared out other than the Mormons movin' *in*?"

Kennedy gave my brother a somber nod. "There's another reason, all right. One I gather you two know about firsthand."

My mouth was stuffed full of griddle cake and bacon, but that didn't stop me from offering a reply.

"Well, there weren't no hands—nor *claws*—involved, thank the Lord. But yeah, we saw something mighty strange last night. And then there was them tracks we was followin' when you, uhhhh . . . stepped out and introduced yourself."

"What's goin' on around here, Mr. Kennedy?" Old Red said.

The old man took in a deep breath. He looked reluctant to speak, and once he got to going I figured I knew why. He was afraid we'd take him for a madman.

"I suppose the simplest way to put it is this," he said. "We've got us a monster."

Kennedy's daughters stopped their bustling in the kitchen, listening along with my brother and me as their father told his tale.

"The Utes called it a Pawapict—a Water Indian. A spirit that lives in the lake. A lonely, ghostly thing, they said. Coaxes you in, then never lets you go. They can come to you as a snake, a baby, even a beautiful woman . . . or so the legend goes. I never put any stock in it myself. Redskin twaddle, that's all I took it for. But then those Latter Day heretics swarmed in, and before long they were claiming the Indians were right. Some of the Brethren

started saying they'd seen a sea serpent up near
Fish Haven. The Bear Lake Monster, they called it.
Of course, it was obvious what they were trying to
do—scare us 'Gentiles' off our land. But we just
laughed . . . until we started seeing the thing ourselves. A giant with great, glowing eyes prowling
around our farms, frightening our women and children. Well . . . first the Mormons, and now *this*? It
was more than most people could take. Argyle—
that's what the town called itself then—it just
drifted away, scattering like dandelion seeds on the
wind until it was all gone."

Now, if we'd heard such a windy as this around
some cattle-drive campfire, I know how Old Red
would've received it: he'd snort, roll his eyes, and
quickly compare it to the fresh little mounds dot-
ting the ground all around the cows bedded down
for the night.

My brother heard Kennedy out quietly, thoughtfully, though. He wasn't quaking in his boots over
that "Water Indian," yet he wasn't cutting loose with
any sneers, either.

"Argyle ain't *all* gone, though . . . is it?" he said.

Kennedy shook his head and chuckled. "No. Not
so long as Kennedyville's still here. And here it'll
stay. Here *we'll* stay."

"Why?" I asked. "I mean—you got a nice spread
and all, don't get me wrong. But it must be awful
lonesome up here with all your old neighbors gone."

Over in the kitchen, behind their father's back,
Eileen and Fiona exchanged a little look. Raised
brows, widened eyes, tight lips.

The question I'd just raised—"Why stay?"—

seemed to be one they'd done some thinking on themselves.

Eileen caught me watching, and I beamed a grin at her, turning my attentions into something flirtatious.

"And I can't say I care much for your one new neighbor, from what we've seen of him," I said. "I don't guess you'd be too happy should *he* come a-callin'."

"Oh, I don't know," Eileen replied, her voice, like her father's, honeyed with just a drop of brogue. "We're grateful for whatever company we get."

"Very grateful," her sister added, mooning at Old Red.

My brother felt the sudden need to re-butter his hotcakes.

"Lonely or not," Kennedy said sternly, going stiff-backed in his chair, "we won't abandon our land. Not to the Mormons, we won't."

Old Red peeked up from his pancakes.

"And not to a monster?"

"Ah! That's all the more reason to stay." Kennedy leaned forward toward my brother. "I'm going to catch the rascal!"

That was enough to slow even *my* chewing.

"You aim to catch a 'Water Indian'?"

"Why not? Whatever it really is, it's solid enough—you've seen the tracks. Why shouldn't a trap catch it the same as any other animal? And Mr. Barnum . . . he'd pay thousands for such a thing, wouldn't he?"

"Maybe he would've," I said. "But ol' P.T.'s been dead goin' on two years now."

"Oh. Well." Kennedy shrugged. "Some other

huckster, then. It hardly matters who. Get your hands on a living, breathing monster, and the showmen'll line up for the chance to buy him. We'll be *rich*."

I tried for another sneaky peep at the women to see what they thought of their father's beast-wrangling scheme. But they were ready for me this time with faces as blank as a fresh-wiped chalkboard.

"Of course, it's not easy without any help." Kennedy slumped and shook his head. "It's hard enough to manage the farming, just me and the girls. There's not much time for tracking or trapping. Still, I've come close to catching the big devil. More than once, I have. And one day . . ."

Kennedy slapped a palm on the table.

"But look at me!" he boomed, suddenly jolly. "Keeping guests from their feed with all my blather. Eat up, boys! Eat up! Then, when you're done, I'd like to show you around the place, if I may."

Right on cue, Fiona and Eileen hustled over to re-heap our plates with steaming-hot grub, and when my brother and I stood up fifteen minutes later, my belly sagged out over my belt like an over-filled sandbag. Yet somehow I found the strength to drag my newfound girth around after Kennedy as he gave us a tour of his spread.

He had plenty to be proud of there: acres of wheat, garden vegetables growing in neat rows, a small but hearty assortment of livestock. And the pens, the barn, the water pump—all of it in good repair.

I was amazed one old man and two women could manage so well on their own. But then I learned of the toll it took, and it seemed to make a little more sense.

Behind the barn, in the midst of a small stand of firs, was a single grave marker. Kennedy noticed us eyeing it as he led us past.

"My wife," he said.

Old Red moved closer to the lonely little family plot. Kennedy and I followed him.

When we reached the cool shade of the trees, we all stopped and doffed our hats.

"A good woman," Kennedy said. "Been gone many a year now."

But not as many as I would've thought. Carved into the dark, knotty old wood were these words, which I read aloud for my brother's benefit:

ABIGAIL KENNEDY
BELOVED WIFE & MOTHER
DECEMBER 1, 1847—MARCH 15, 1875

Which meant Eileen wasn't three or four years my elder, as I'd reckoned. If her mother died birthing her, she was three years *younger* than me. Pretty though she still was, at the rate she was going she'd be a bent-backed, snaggle-toothed crone by the time she hit thirty.

The Kennedys may have been surviving as a trio, but to thrive they'd need to be a quartet or quintet, at least. If the Water Indian didn't kill them, the drudgery would.

Well, the only decent thing to do was help out in whatever way we could. It was Old Red who volunteered us, actually, though I'd been just about to do so myself. Kennedy tried to look surprised, but it

was plain he'd been hoping all along we'd offer to
take on some chores. "No need for that" gave way
to "You could nut a couple bull calves for me" in
two seconds flat.

The rest of the day passed as so many once had
for me and my brother. Collecting prairie oysters,
milking cows, slopping hogs, chopping wood—it
was our childhood all over again, right down to the
womenfolk. Instead of our dear *Mutter* and sisters
toiling away beside us, though, it was Eileen and
Fiona. Wherever we were, whatever we were doing,
they were somewhere nearby, chattering, singing
songs, bringing us cool water and warm smiles.

Hard though the work was, it felt comfortable.
Right. Seductive, you might even call it. I'd thought
farming was about the last thing I ever wanted to
do—all sodbusting ever brought our family was
aches, pains, and early graves. But the Kennedys
did their best to make it seem pleasant.

And pleasant it was except for the flutter in my
stomach, the itch at the back of my scalp, the
creepy-crawly feeling that kept pulling my gaze to
the woods.

Something's out there.

The thought stayed stuck in my mind like a bit of
gristle in your teeth you keep worrying with your
tongue.

Yet Old Red didn't seem edgy in the least. Even
more unlike him, he appeared to be enjoying himself, hotfooting from chore to chore with such
cheerful obliviousness I almost expected him to
start skipping and whistling. Knowing my brother
as you do, you might doubt me more on this than
on my sighting of the lake creature, but I swear I

saw it with my own eyes. At one point, he approached Fiona—not just voluntarily, but *smiling*—and offered to help her hang out the washing.

Soon after that, Kennedy invited us to stay the night. It was an offer we all knew was coming, as the sun was practically down in the treetops, and the shadows from the forest were stretching out ever longer and darker. My brother and I had already brought our horses over to be watered and fed, so there was nothing to it but to say yes.

Kennedy seemed pleased—ecstatic, almost—and he immediately set his daughters to cooking up a regular feast. When us men came in at dusk, we found the kitchen table laden with baked ham, mashed yams, green beans in butter, and fresh bread.

I felt a mite guilty about the sumptuousness of it all, these being folks who probably made do with vegetable stew and squirrel meat, most nights. Yet declining such hospitality would be a grievous insult, I told myself. Good manners dictated—nay, *demanded*—that I stuff myself like (and with) a pig. Which I did my utmost to do.

Yet my utmost, for once, wasn't up to the task. My stomach was already full . . . of butterflies. A whole swarm of them, it felt like, all of them a-flapping and a-fluttering and generally giving me the collywobbles. What I did get down my gullet, I barely tasted.

"You don't like the food?" Eileen asked me from across the table.

I looked up—realizing only then that I'd been staring out the window—and found her pouting at me prettily.

"Like it? Nope." I popped a forkful of ham into my mouth. "I *love* it! Why, with you two here to work the stove for him, it's a wonder your pa don't weigh a thousand pounds."

"I'm getting close!" Kennedy chortled, and he leaned back in his chair and gave his big belly a playful pat.

"So I noticed," my brother shot back with (for him) uncommon impishness. He'd just been picking at his vittles, like me, though for him this was the norm. Most days, Old Red doesn't eat enough to put fat on a consumptive flea.

"You're one to talk!" Kennedy joshed him. "You look like you're about to dry up and blow away. What you need is a good woman cooking for *you* like this every day."

Fiona was seated next to him, across from my brother, and she turned and gave the old man a swat on the arm.

"Dad. . . ."

She peeked over at Old Red and batted her eyes.

"I'm just saying," her father went on, "our friends here should settle down. Drifting from town to town, job to job—that's all well and good for a young buck, but a *man* needs more. Sooner or later, you have to put down roots."

"We used to have roots," I said. "Then the whole danged family tree up and died on us."

"We'll put us down some new roots one day," Old Red added, looking at me—almost making me a promise, it seemed. He shifted his gaze back to Kennedy and Fiona. "But the thing about roots is, they don't just hold you steady. They hold you still. Almost like—"

Chains, I think he was about to say. He amended himself at the last second, though.

". . . an anchor."

"Ahhh, but there's nothing wrong with dropping anchor when you've found calm waters," Kennedy said. "Stormy seas, my younger days were. Up here I finally found safe harbor."

"Safe harbor? With your Mormon troubles and your . . ."

I couldn't quite bring myself to say "monster," so I jerked my head at the door—and the blackness beyond it.

". . . exotic wildlife."

Kennedy chuckled in a dismissive sort of way.

"Oh, well, as much as I might complain about the Brethren, the worst of those troubles is long past. And as for the Water Indian, whatever it is, it's never harmed anyone. It's frightening, yes. But dangerous? That I haven't seen."

"There's a first time for everything," I said.

"Not for *everything*," Kennedy replied. "Not if I can't catch the thing. Then there's no way to know what it's really like . . . or what it's really worth." The old man cocked his head to one side, his eyes flashing so fiery bright it's a wonder his puffy white eyebrows didn't burst into flame. "But if I were to have some help . . ."

I couldn't stop myself—I jumped. Not that the old man's words were so shocking. It was the dainty foot stroking my calf under the table that startled me.

"Something the matter?" Eileen asked, all dewy-eyed innocence even as her foot snaked its way up toward my thigh.

I blocked her with clenched knees. Flirting's all

well and good, but even I'm not dumb enough to let a gal toe-tease me when her father's five feet away and a shotgun's nine.

"'Scuse me." I gave my chest a little thump. "Hiccups."

And then I jumped again—as did everyone else.

Outside, twigs were snapping, branches creaking, leaves shushing.

Inside, I was quivering.

"Set out another plate, Eileen," Kennedy said, his voice hardly more than a whisper. "We've got more company."

Eileen didn't move.

"All we have to do is wait," her sister said, voice a-tremor. "It'll go away eventually."

"We'll be fine as long as we stay inside," Eileen added, so straight and stiff in her chair she could've been carved out of wood herself. "In the light."

"That's right. The nighttime's his," Kennedy said. "But we can track him tomorrow, when the sun's out. With three of us to look, maybe we could finally find his lair. And once we've got that, we've got *him*."

"Oh, please," Old Red snapped. "That's bunk, and you know it."

The old man, Fiona, Eileen, *me*—we all gaped at him.

"Excuse me?" Kennedy said.

"You're really just scared to face that thing, ain't you?" my brother sneered at him. "Well, I'm not. Now's our chance, and I'm gonna take it."

Old Red pushed his chair back from the table and came to his feet, his expression a scowling jumble of fear and anger and defiance. There was a wildness in his eyes I'd never seen before. In any other man, I would've called it bloodlust.

He stomped to the nearest window and peered out through glass so black it could've been a mirror dipped in pitch.

"'His lair'? 'His *lair*'?" Old Red barked out an incredulous laugh. "His lair's at the bottom of the damned lake. Ain't no way we could ever . . . a-ha!"

He jabbed a finger at the window. Even from my spot at the table, I could see what he was pointing at: twin pinpricks of light glowing in the darkness high in the trees outside.

Old Red whirled around to face us.

"I don't care what kinda critter that is," he growled—and he marched over and snatched up Kennedy's scattergun. "Two barrels in the gut'll kill it quick enough."

"No, no, no," the old man spluttered. "We need it alive, remember? To sell."

"I think we oughta listen to the man, Brother," I said.

But Old Red was already striding off again.

"Can't sell it if we never catch it," he said without looking back. "And a body'll fetch a pretty penny too."

He threw open the front door and stepped out onto the porch.

Kennedy hurled himself from his chair and stumbled after him.

"Noooooo!" he howled.

Old Red took aim.

Fiona and Eileen screamed.

Out in the darkness, the lights dropped downward, then disappeared.

Old Red pulled the triggers, and the shotgun spat fire into the night . . . but not where the lights had been. At the last second, my brother had jerked the shotgun up, spraying buckshot at the stars.

When my ears stopped ringing, I heard a new sound: whimpering. From the women and from somewhere out in the forest too.

"Mr. Kennedy," Old Red said coolly, all trace of his killing frenzy suddenly gone, "why don't you tell your boy to stop playin' games and come on inside?"

"My . . . boy . . . ?"

"Your son, sir." Old Red turned back toward the woods. "And bring them special moccasins of yours with you! And your rig for the candles! Y'all owe us a look at 'em, I'd say!"

And with that, he handed Kennedy the shotgun, sauntered inside, and retook his seat at the table.

"That was a cruel thing to do!" Eileen spat at him.

"Oh, I'm sorry. Did he frighten you?" I shot back, matching her venom with acid. "Not a pleasant sensation, is it?"

I still didn't know all the hows and whys, but the *what* was plain enough. The clan Kennedy had taken my brother and me for fools. And, alas, they'd been half right.

Fiona and Eileen glowered back at me, sullen and silent.

"Keeley! Keeley, boy! Are you all right?" the old man called out from the porch.

A sniffling "I'm fine" drifted from the darkness of the trees, and then the Water Indian himself emerged from the shadows—a slender, slouching teenage boy. As he and his father shuffled inside, I saw that the kid was carrying a length of rope. Tied to it was a wooden rod sporting a snuffed candle on each end.

"Take those ridiculous things off," Fiona muttered at the boy. She waved a hand at his feet, which were encased it what looked like Goliath's furry bed slippers. "You're not going to track mud all over my clean floor."

Keeley nodded glumly, wiped his nose on his sleeve, and shuffled back out to the porch.

"Make those yourself?" Old Red asked as the kid kicked off "those ridiculous things."

"Yes sir," the boy said, managing a sad little smile. He held up his fuzzy fake feet, both embarrassed and proud. "Bear paws and rawhide."

"Neat bit of workmanship—you might have a future as a cobbler," I told him. "Providin' your career as a confidence man don't pan out."

The boy slinked over to the table and took the last empty seat—the one to my left, at the head of the table opposite his father. The rope and rod he put on the table next to the ham.

"Well, isn't this cozy?" I said. "Y'all got any more kin out scarin' the bejesus out of strangers? Cuz if you do, may as well bring 'em on in. There's still plenty of eats to go around."

"We're sorry, all right?" Eileen snapped. She pointed dagger-eyes at her father. "It wasn't our idea."

The old man had slumped into his seat so limp he could've been a scarecrow stuffed with pudding. But his daughter's spiteful tone brought him up ramrod straight, and he met her glare head on.

Eileen's backbone slowly lost its starch until at

last *she* was the one hunched in her chair looking wilted. It was as if her father's gaze had sucked the life right out of her.

Kennedy turned to my brother.

"Tell me. How did you know?"

"Well, sir . . . usually I make it a point not to have any prejudices and to just let the facts lead me where they will," Old Red said, paraphrasing a line from You Know Who's latest adventure in *Harper's Weekly*. ("The Reigate Puzzle," should you care to look it up.) "But it turns out I've got me one preju-dice I can't shake. I don't believe in spooks and monsters. So that's what's been leadin' me today."

My brother looked at the other end of the table, at the boy.

"Led me to notice how them tracks of yours just happened to go in and out of the lake next to a big ol' log—which somebody could use to climb out of the water without leaving more footprints on the shore. And led me to notice a notch in a broken tree limb where the 'Water Indian' had been skulkin' around." He nodded at the rope coiled up on the table. "The kinda notch *that* might make if it was thrown over and used to shake the branches way up high. Or to dangle something up there. A couple candle 'eyes,' let's say."

The boy nodded, looking awestruck. Old Red hadn't shot wide of the target once.

My brother turned back to the old man.

"Course, it didn't have to be y'all playin' bogey-man. At first, I thought it might be someone tryin' to scare *you* off—some of 'the Brethren' hopin' to clear out Kennedyville for good. But when you run on ahead this morning to tell your family we was comin'? Seemed like a good time to cook up some flimflam. And when you told us your wife died birthing your youngest . . . and then the gravestone said she passed in 1875?"

Old Red threw Eileen a quick there-and-gone glance.

"I'm sorry, miss, but there just ain't no way you're eighteen."

Eileen perked up just enough to shoot him a hateful scowl.

"So I volunteered to help you hang out the washin'," my brother went on, turning to Fiona. "Pinned up some shirts and britches a big, bluff man like your father'd bust at the seams. Looked like clothes for a smaller feller. Younger, maybe. Like eighteen, perhaps."

"My, my . . . you're smarter than you look, aren't you?" Fiona said, something like admiration peeking out from behind weary bitterness. "But I bet there's still one thing you haven't figured out."

"That's right," Old Red said. "Why?"

Fiona jerked her head at her father.

"Because the king of Kennedyville commands it, that's why."

Then more words spilled out of her, coming so fast, in such a flood burst, she couldn't even take the time to breathe.

"At first, he sent Keeley out to scare you off. That's what he does whenever any Mormons try to stay the night around here. But when he found out you were Gentiles, he thought we could trick you into *staying*. Permanently. As part of the family. Keeley would have to keep out of sight for a while, but that wouldn't last long—just until my father could catch one of you in the act."

"Catch us—?"

"—in *what* act?" I'd been about to ask. But then suddenly I knew, and all I could whisper was, "Oh, my."

Catch one of us with one of them, she'd meant. With her or her sister.

I couldn't help myself then: I shivered. When it comes to sheer blood-freezing terror, a lake monster's got nothing on a shotgun wedding.

"You know," Old Red said, "if y'all are this desperate to, uhhh . . . expand the family, I'd say it's time you moved on to greener pastures, courtin'-wise."

"Don't you think we know that?" Eileen cried out, her voice quavering, on the verge of becoming a sob. "Don't you think that's what we—"

"*No!*"

Her father slammed down a fist with such force every plate on the table jumped an inch in the air.

"I was here before those bloody Mormon heathens, and I'll still be here after they're gone! This is my home! My land! My town! My family! And I'll never give any of it up! *Never!*"

When Kennedy was done, Fiona, Eileen, and Keeley were all looking down, silent and still, like worshippers in church competing to seem the most pious. Hate the man as they might—and I suspected they did—a little blustering and table thumping and they were utterly in his thrall.

"Well," Old Red said quietly, "I think we best be leavin'."

The old man blinked at him.

"What? You can't leave now. It's dark out."

"Oh, don't worry about us," I said. My brother and I stood and started backing away from the table. "We've done plenty of night herding. We won't break out necks."

"Look . . ." Kennedy tried out an unconvincing smile. "I'm sorry about the tricks. The lies. Let us make it up to you. A good night's sleep indoors and a hearty breakfast before you hit the trail. What do you say?"

I say you're insane, I thought.

For obvious reasons, I kept this to myself.

Kennedy's smile went lopsided and slowly sank. "You can have your pick of spreads. . . ."

The old man stood and took a staggering step after us. He stopped next to the spot where he'd left his shotgun propped up against the wall.

"Your pick of *wives.* Just stay. Please. You won't regret it."

We kept backing away.

Kennedy took another step toward us. Beyond him, his daughters and son just watched from their seats, unmoving, unblinking, glassy eyed. They seemed strangely sleepy, as if what they were seeing was merely a dream they'd had before and would no doubt have again.

Old Red and I reached the door.

"Don't go," Kennedy said, his voice half-pleading, half-demanding. "We need you here. *I* need you. . . ."

"Good-bye," my brother told the old man.

"And good luck," I said to his children.

And then we were outside in the gloom.

We saddled up quick as we could by lantern light. I kept expecting Kennedy to come out and tell us again to stay . . . or try to *make* us. Yet when it came time to swing up atop my mount, I found myself lingering, waiting.

Old Red horsed himself without pausing a jot.

"They ain't comin', Brother," he told me.

He knew what I was thinking. Maybe the boy or one of the women would dart out after us, beg to be brought along. And we could—maybe should—help them out. After all, we knew what it was like to be trapped on a farm, tied down by obligation and expectation. And Old Red, at least, knew what it was like to escape.

He hit the cow trails at eighteen and never saw the family farm again. And in a way, I felt like he was running from the old homestead even still. You can't get much further removed from the dreary toil of sodbusting than a gentleman deducifier cracking mysteries in well-appointed drawing rooms.

Old Red had freed himself from the past—or was trying to, anyhow, which maybe amounts to the same thing. So if he looked at Fiona and Eileen and Keeley and didn't see the strength there to do like-wise, I suppose it wasn't there to be seen.

I pulled myself up into my saddle.

"Think they'll ever get away from here? The gals? Or the kid?"

"Not till the old man's dead." My brother gave his pony his heels. "Maybe not even then."

The horses ambled slowly out toward the trail, finding their way by memory as much as moon-light. It could have been a short journey—all we had to do was head north fifteen minutes and bed down in the same abandoned farmhouse we'd been in the night before. But Old Red and I agreed to push south a ways instead. More than

ever since we'd begun our travels, we both felt the
need to *move on*.

I looked back just the once. All I could see was
the dull yellow glow from the cottage windows
aflicker through the trees like a sunset shimmering
on dark, rippling water. Then a turn in the trail
blotted it out, and the last of the light was swallowed into the black depths of the forest.

Should you ever make it to America again, Mr.
Brackwell, I'd urge you to visit the Bear Lake Valley.
It's beautiful country, and friendly too. Lord knows
they like their visitors.

If it should be ten years before you pass that way—
heck, a *hundred*—I feel like you'd find "Kennedyville" there still, utterly unchanged.

Population: Four . . . but always room for more,
if you're of the right frame of mind.

> Yours faithfully,
>
> O. A. Amlingmeyer
> Logan, Utah
> July 4, 1893

The Ghosts of Duster

William W. Johnstone
with J. A. Johnstone

"All I'm sayin' is that I never promised to marry the gal. Hell, you know me better'n that, Bo! Do I look like the sort o' fella who'd want to get himself tied down by apron strings?"

Bo Creel glanced over at his best friend and said, "You look like a fella who's damned lucky to be alive. That lady's brother had a shotgun, you know."

Scratch Morton grinned. "I know. For a minute I figured I'd be pickin' buckshot outta my backside until next week."

The two men rode along the base of a ridge in West Texas, being careful not to skylight themselves. They had lived long, eventful lives on the frontier and knew that although most of the hostiles were either on reservations or had gone south into Mexico, it was still possible to run across a band of renegade Apaches in this vast, rugged area west of the Pecos.

Bo and Scratch were of an age and had been best friends for decades, ever since they'd met as youngsters during Texas's war for independence some forty-odd years earlier. They'd been on the drift for almost that long. They didn't think of themselves as saddle tramps; they were just too restless by nature to stay in one place for too long. Although they had been just about everywhere in the West, they liked to wander back to their home state of Texas every now and then. Once a Texan, always a Texan—born, bred, and forever.

Scratch was a handsome, silver-haired dandy in a fringed buckskin jacket and cream-colored Stetson. The twin Remington revolvers on his hips had ivory handles. Bo, on the other hand, looked like a preacher in a sober black suit and flat-crowned black hat. His Colt had plain walnut grips.

The weapons were similar in one respect, though: they were well used. Bo and Scratch had a habit of running into trouble. Scratch was just a natural-born hell-raiser, and Bo couldn't help but stick up for folks who were outnumbered and outgunned.

They were in El Paso when Scratch made the acquaintance of a comely maiden lady. One thing led to another, and although the lady was still comely, she wasn't quite a maiden any longer. She hadn't made any complaints about that change in her status, but her proddy, overly protective older brother did, so Bo and Scratch had left the border city rather hurriedly.

Since then they had spent a couple of days riding east and were still a long ways from getting anywhere. This part of Texas took awhile to ride across. Bo had done pretty well in a poker game before their hasty exit from El Paso, so they had enough money to buy supplies. The problem was finding a settlement where they could pick up some more provisions.

"If I remember right," Bo mused, "there's a little town not too far from here. Name of Duster, I think. We ought to be able to buy a few things there."

"I hope so," Scratch said. "Otherwise we're gonna get mighty tired of eatin' jackrabbit by the time we get to San Antonio."

"Tired of it, maybe, but at least we won't starve to death."

The ridge was to the north, on their left hand. Beyond it rose a range of jagged mountains, the sort of peaks that jutted up out of the desert with little or no warning in this part of the country. To the south swept a vast, brown, semiarid plain that ran all the way to the Mexican border. A few water-holes were located along the base of the ridge, Bo recalled; otherwise this was mighty dry country.

They rode on, and as it became late afternoon, Scratch asked, "How far'd you say it was to this Duster place?"

"Ought to be there any time now," Bo replied.

"Then shouldn't we be seein' smoke from the chimneys?"

Bo rubbed his jaw and frowned. "Yeah, you'd think so. Maybe no one's cooking right now."

"I was hopin' for a nice hot supper, followed by a cold beer."

"Well, don't give up hope just yet. Maybe I'm wrong about how far it is. I've never been there, just heard hombres talking about the place."

A few minutes later, though, the settlement came into view. Bo and Scratch reined their mounts to a halt and stared at it in surprise.

Or rather, at what was left of it.

Some sort of catastrophe had happened here, that much was obvious. A number of the buildings had been reduced to flattened, scattered piles of lumber and debris. Other structures leaned at crazy angles. Only a handful of buildings were upright and relatively intact. At the northern edge of town, nearest the ridge, was a huge mound of bricks and lumber. It looked like a large building had collapsed in on itself.

"Good Lord A'mighty," Scratch said. "What in blazes happened here?"

Bo's eyes narrowed as he studied the landscape both north and south of the ruined settlement. "Look yonder," he said, pointing. "Below that notch in the ridge."

The roughly V-shaped gap he indicated had a deep gully below it, running arrow-straight toward the town. Scratch frowned at it and then said, "That ain't natural, is it?"

Bo shook his head. "I don't think so. Looks to me like there must've been a mighty big thunderstorm in the mountains. The rain all washed down behind that ridge and busted through at a narrow place. That was like a dam breaking. The flood carved out that gully and came thundering down until it smashed right into the settlement."

Stretch gave him a dubious glance. "You sayin' it rained enough to do that, here in West Texas? Hell, this is one of the driest spots east of . . . well, east of hell."

"Most of the time that's true," Bo agreed. "But every now and then it comes a big cloud. I've heard more than one story about folks drowning in the desert in flash floods."

"Yeah, but only when they was dumb enough to make camp in an arroyo or some place like that."

Bo pointed again. "When that ridgeline crumbled, the water *formed* an arroyo, and it was just like pointing a gun at Duster. I don't know if everybody in town was killed in the flood. Seems unlikely. But the survivors must've packed up and left, because I sure don't see anybody moving around."

"No, the place looks to be deserted, all right," Scratch admitted. He let out a groan. "So much for buyin' supplies here."

"Maybe we can find some the citizens left behind."

"If we do, they'll likely be rotted from bein' waterlogged. Folks probably took anything that was any good with them when they pulled up stakes."

Bo knew that Scratch was probably right about that, but it wouldn't hurt to have a look around. He said as much and jogged his horse into motion again toward the settlement.

Scratch rode alongside him and asked, "What do you reckon that pile o' bricks was? Don't see too many brick buildin's out here. Mostly adobe and some lumber."

"I don't know, but it was a good-sized building. I'm surprised it collapsed. Looks like it should've been sturdy enough to stand up even to a flood."

"Maybe a cyclone come along and flattened it later."

"Maybe," Bo said. "We'll ride over and take a closer look after we—"

He stopped short and jerked back on the reins as a ragged scarecrow of a figure dashed out from behind one of the leaning buildings and ran toward them, screaming.

Scratch cursed and slapped leather, filling his hand with the butt of an ivory-handled Remington. But as the gun came up with blurring speed, Bo reached across with matching swiftness and clamped a hand around the barrel.

"Don't shoot," he snapped. "That hombre's not attacking us."

It was true. The man was too scrawny to constitute a threat anyway, even if he had been hostile. As he loped forward and waved his sticklike arms over his head, his pitiful screeches became words that the two drifters could understand.

"Are you real? Oh, dear Lord, are you really there? Please be real!"

"Please be real?" Scratch muttered. "What in blazes does he think we are, ghosts or somethin'?"

Bo glanced around at the abandoned, devastated settlement. "Good place for it, don't you think?"

Scratch couldn't argue with that.

The scarecrow man stumbled and fell to his knees as if the last of his strength had deserted him. He pawed at the dust of the street, then threw his head back and howled. "Oh, Lord, take me! Spare me from these tormenting phantasms!"

"What'd he just call us?" Scratch asked with a frown.

"I don't think he's talking about us," Bo replied as he swung down from the saddle. He handed his reins to Scratch. "Here. Hang on to my horse while I see what I can do for the old-timer."

It was rare for the two of them to run into anybody *they* could call "old-timer." This man, who appeared to be the sole inhabitant of Duster, fit the bill, though. He looked to be in his seventies, with long, tangled white hair and a ragged beard that reached down to his narrow chest. He was so skinny a good wind would blow him away. Filthy rags flapped around his emaciated form. Bo thought the duds had once been a brown tweed suit and a white shirt. The man wore no shoes or boots; his bare feet were scarred and callused.

His eyes rolled like those of a locoed horse as Bo approached. "Take it easy, old-timer," Bo said, speaking in a calm, quiet tone as he would have if he'd been trying to settle down such a horse. "Nobody's going to hurt you. I don't know what happened here, but my friend and I will help you."

Still on his knees, the man stared up at Bo and said, "Are you real?"

"Real as can be," Bo assured him.

"You're not . . . not like them?"

"Like who?" Bo didn't think anybody else was around here, but it wouldn't hurt to ask.

The man placed his hands over his face, the bony fingers with their knobby knuckles splayed out across his gaunt features. "Them," he said with a shudder. "The ones who torment me."

"Who?" Bo asked again, as it suddenly occurred to him that the old man might be talking about some of those renegade Apaches who snuck across the border now and then. Apaches were known for being the most skillful torturers on the face of the earth.

But they weren't who the old man had in mind. As he lowered his hands he gazed up with the most fear-haunted eyes Bo had ever seen. "Them," the old man croaked. *"The children!"*

Then he pitched forward on his face, either in a dead faint—or just plain dead.

With all the debris around, Scratch didn't have any trouble finding enough scraps of dry wood to start a fire. He built a small one in the shade of a building that was still upright, a two-story structure with a sagging balcony along the front that had probably been a hotel or a saloon. Bo lifted the old man and carefully carried him into that same shade. The old-timer didn't weigh much at all; his body was like a bundle of twigs inside his leathery hide.

Scratch got some coffee brewing, using water from their canteens. Bo made sure the old man was still alive. He found a threadlike but fairly steady pulse in the hombre's neck. He checked the man's body but didn't find any wounds.

"Looks like he's about starved to death," Scratch observed.

"Starved to death . . . and scared to death on top of it," Bo said. "We'll have to get him awake again so he can tell us what happened here."

"Whatever happened, it's too late for us to do anything about it. And it ain't really any of our business, either."

Bo just looked over at Scratch, who sighed and went on, "Yeah, I should've knowed better than to say that, shouldn't I? You'd reckon after all this time I'd know you can't abide a mystery, Bo Crecl."

"Let's just get a little food and coffee in him and see if it helps."

The old man roused enough to gulp at the coffee

when Bo held a tin cup to his lips. He had let the strong black brew cool off some first so the old-timer wouldn't scald himself. When the man had swallowed some of the coffee, Bo spooned beans into his mouth. The old-timer swallowed without even chewing.

"Whoa there, mister," Bo said. "Take it easy. I know you're hungry, but you're liable to make yourself sick if you keep that up."

The old man's rheumy eyes flickered open. "Who . . . who are you?" he choked out. His voice was hoarse from the screaming he had done earlier.

"My name's Bo Creel. This is my partner, Scratch Morton."

Scratch tugged on the brim of his Stetson. "Howdy."

The old-timer looked back and forth between them. He was still a little wall-eyed. "Wh-what are you doing here?"

"Just passing through," Bo explained. "This is Duster, isn't it?"

The man's head jerked in a nod, bobbing a little on the skinny neck.

"We figured on buying some supplies here," Bo went on. "We didn't know that something had happened to the town."

"A deluge," the old man muttered. "The rainbow was a promise from God that never again would the world be destroyed in a flood, but that night . . . that terrible night . . . I began to doubt the word of the Lord."

"Came a gully-washer and a toad-strangler, did it?" Scratch asked.

The old-timer shuddered. "The heavens opened,

and a torrent came upon the earth. When the ridge gave way, it was like a wall of water came roaring down on the town. An avalanche, only of liquid rather than stone. I saw it coming." He lifted his hands and covered his face again. They muffled his voice as he went on, "I tried to get the children out of the orphanage, but it was too late. They fled to the upper floor, thinking it would be safer there, but then . . . then . . ."

Frowning, Bo and Scratch glanced at each other. Bo leaned closer to the distraught old man and said, "That big brick building on the edge of town . . . it was an orphanage?"

The man lowered his hands and nodded. "Yes. There were more than thirty children living there." His voice was hollow with agonizing memories. "I . . . I was the director. George Ledbetter is my name. The Reverend George Ledbetter, although God has turned His back on me now, and rightfully so."

"You shouldn't ought to feel like that," Scratch said. "Ain't no way one man can stop a flood."

"No, but I should have died in there with them," Ledbetter rasped. "The older children hustled the little ones upstairs, trying to save them, but then . . . the flood washed out the foundation. The men who built it must not have used the proper materials . . . oh, dear Lord, the sound as the timbers began to creak and then snap, the rumble as the walls began to collapse . . . but even over those sounds, even over the terrible noise of wind and water, I could hear the screams from inside."

The old man began to shake and sob.

Bo let him get some of it out, then said, "You

must not have been in the building when the flood hit."

Ledbetter managed to nod. "I went out to make sure no one had been left outside and then couldn't get back in. I thought the children would be safe on the second floor, that the water wouldn't reach that high. I actually thought that I was in more danger than they were, and I did come near to drowning as the water swept me away. I . . . I had no idea that the building would fall. . . ."

"You couldn't have known that it would," Bo told him. "What happened to the rest of the people in town?"

Ledbetter passed a trembling hand over his face. "Many of them were killed. When the waters receded I performed funeral services for what seemed like days on end. The few who survived didn't want to stay here any longer, and no one could blame them. They left. But I couldn't. I had to stay."

"How long ago was that?" Bo asked.

"Six months? Eight?" Ledbetter shook his head. "I don't really know."

"And you been here ever since by yourself?" Scratch asked.

"Yes . . . but I'm not really alone. The children are here too."

Bo and Scratch looked at each other again, then Bo said, "I thought you said all the children were killed when the orphanage collapsed?"

Ledbetter nodded. "They were. But they are still here nonetheless. They come to me and torment me with their sad eyes and their drowned faces. I see them, pale and lifeless, accusing me with their pathetic gazes. Their spirits will never leave me alone, because I deserted them in their hour of need. They will never know rest, and neither will I."

"You're talkin' about ghosts," Scratch said.

Ledbetter waved a shaking, bony hand at their devastated surroundings. "What better place for them?" he asked, unknowingly echoing what Bo had said earlier.

Neither of the drifters had an answer for the old man's question. Bo said, "Drink some more coffee, Reverend, and then have some more of these beans. You need to get your strength back."

"Thank you, Mr. Creel. This is more than I've talked for quite some time. My throat is rather dry."

Ledbetter slurped down more coffee, and Bo helped him put away a good serving of beans. By then Scratch had fried up the last of their bacon, and the reverend ate some of it ravenously too. Then he leaned his head against the wall of the building and moaned. He closed his eyes and seemed to fall asleep almost immediately.

Bo and Scratch moved off far enough so that their low-voiced conversation wouldn't be overheard in case Ledbetter was really still awake. "What in tarnation are we gonna do with the old pelican?" Scratch asked.

"We can't leave him here," Bo declared. "He'll starve to death if we do."

"But he don't want to go. He could've left with the other folks who lived through the flood, if there was anywhere else he wanted to go."

"That's only because he feels guilty about what happened to the children in the orphanage."

"You can sling him on a horse and tote him away

from here," Scratch said, "but that won't make him feel any less guilty."

"I know," Bo admitted. "But I can't just ride away and leave him here to die, either." He glanced at the sky. "It's too late in the day to decide anything. We'll camp here tonight and try to figure it out in the morning."

Scratch nodded. "Bueno."

Ledbetter was still asleep, snoring softly. Bo and Scratch tended to their horses, unsaddling the animals and giving them a good rubdown. The settlement's public well, at the far end of the street, had water in it and the crank that lowered and raised a bucket still worked, so Scratch filled a trough that hadn't washed away in the flood and Bo gave the horses a little of the grain they had left.

Taking Ledbetter along with them meant that they would have to stretch their meager provisions even further, but as Scratch had pointed out, jackrabbits were abundant in this part of the country. Surely they would come to a settlement sooner or later.

Dusk didn't amount to much around here. Once the sun dipped below the western horizon, full darkness came quickly, along with a wind that whipped around the ruined buildings. But during that brief half-light, something stirred inside Bo, a warning prickle that maybe something wasn't quite right.

He and Scratch hunkered beside the fire, sipping coffee and eating the last of the beans and bacon that Ledbetter had left. Bo set his plate aside and came to his feet. "I think I'm going to take a look around town," he said.

Scratch glanced up at him. "Something wrong?"

"Probably not," Bo said with a shake of his head. "I just want to make sure we're really alone here."

"Don't tell me *you're* worried about ghosts."

"Of course not. But we're close enough to the border that there could be a few Apaches skulking around."

"Yeah, you're right." Scratch reached for his Winchester, which lay on the ground beside him. "Want me to come with you?"

"No, stay here and keep an eye on the horses and the old man," Bo said. "I'll be back in a few minutes."

Taking his rifle with him, he walked along the street. Thick shadows had begun to gather around the wrecked buildings. Movement seen from the corner of his eye caught his attention. He swung his rifle in that direction, then relaxed as he spotted a coyote slinking off into the dusk. Bo chuckled at this uncharacteristic display of nerves on his part. He started walking again and looked in front of him.

Two children stood there.

Bo stopped like he'd been punched in the chest. The kids, a boy and a girl around ten or twelve years old, were about forty feet away from him, standing in front of a building that leaned over at a severe angle. Bo couldn't see them that well because of the uncertain light. He started toward them and said, "Hey. Hey, you kids—"

They disappeared.

With the thickening shadows it was hard to tell, but it seemed to Bo that the children were there one second and gone the next. But that was impossible, of course. He was too hardheaded to believe in ghosts. He loped forward, looking on both sides of the street for them.

But they were gone.

Bo wasn't the sort of hombre who cussed very often. If he had been, he would have let out a few choice words right then. Instead he tucked the Winchester under his arm, fished a lucifer out of his pocket, and snapped it into life with his thumbnail. The glare from the match lit up the dirt as Bo lowered the flame toward the street. He was looking for footprints, proof that the two children he'd seen had really been there.

He didn't find any.

Duster lived up to its name; the dust in the street was thick, and Bo didn't see how anybody could have walked through it without leaving some sign. He grimaced as the flame reached his fingers. He dropped the match and ground it out with his boot heel.

"You kids come out," he called softly. "Nobody's going to hurt you, I promise."

There was no sound except the soft whistling of the wind that had sprung up.

That was the explanation, he thought. The wind had wiped out any tracks the kids left. Sure, that had to be it. The children were small and wouldn't leave deep prints in the dust. It wouldn't take long for a stiff breeze like the one blowing now to blur them beyond recognition.

Bo wasn't sure if he believed that or not, but it made a lot more sense than thinking those two youngsters were ghosts from the collapsed orphanage.

And yét, Reverend Ledbetter had insisted that the spirits of dead children came to him and tormented him. He seemed to believe it wholeheartedly. Bo had chalked that up to the guilt the old man felt, but what if—

No, he told himself. No what if. There were ghost towns scattered across the West, and Duster certainly qualified. But that didn't mean they were populated by real ghosts, because there weren't any such things.

Bo finished looking around the town, and by the time he got back to where he'd left Scratch and Ledbetter, night had settled down completely. "Find anything?" Scratch asked.

"Not a blessed thing," Bo replied. He didn't like lying to his partner, but he didn't want Scratch to think he was losing his mind.

Ledbetter still slept. Bo and Scratch sat beside the fire and talked quietly for a while. The night was quiet except for the wind, which made the flames flicker and dance. Then a rumble sounded in the distance. Bo and Scratch both looked up, and Scratch said, "Thunder?"

"Sounded like it. Might come a little shower up in the mountains. But that doesn't mean it's going to flood down here again."

Scratch looked around as the horses shifted nervously where they were tied with picket ropes to an old hitch rack about twenty feet away. "Somethin's spooked those cayuses," he said as he got to his feet with his Winchester. "I'll take a look."

"I saw a coyote earlier," Bo said. "That's probably what's got them nervous. They must smell him."

"Yeah." Scratch walked toward the animals.

Before he got there he let out a startled yell and flung the rifle to his shoulder. He didn't fire, though. Bo uncoiled from where he sat on the ground, drawing his Colt as he did so. "What is it?" he asked.

"I . . . I thought I saw somethin'," Scratch said. "Over by the horses."

"That coyote?"

"No." Scratch hesitated. "It looked like . . . a couple of kids."

Scratch's shout had roused Ledbetter from sleep. The old man heard what Scratch said, and he shrieked, "They're back! Oh, dear Lord, the children are back!"

There was no point in keeping anything from Scratch now. Bo told him what he'd seen earlier. "Yeah, a boy and a gal," Scratch agreed. "No more'n twelve years old, either of 'em."

Ledbetter moaned. "Those are the spirits that always appear to me. The girl's name is Ruthie. The boy is Caleb. They died when the orphanage collapsed."

"That don't hardly seem possible," Scratch insisted. "Folks don't just get up and walk around when they're dead. It ain't natural."

"Nothing is natural about this accursed town, my friend." Ledbetter shuddered. "Nothing."

A distant flicker of lightning to the north made Bo glance in that direction. Ledbetter noticed it too and whimpered, probably at the memories that sight must arouse. No doubt those were the first warning signs the inhabitants of Duster had had on that night months earlier: the rumble of thunder like the sound of distant drums, and fingers of light clawing their way across the ebony skies.

"God is about to visit His final judgment on Duster," Ledbetter went on. His voice rose on a note of hysteria. "You should leave, my friends. Leave while you can still save your immortal souls!"

The ragged old preacher leaped to his feet and began dashing back and forth, howling like a madman. Scratch said, "Dadgummit!" and tried to grab him, but Ledbetter was too fast. Scratch missed. Bo moved to get in the old man's way, but Ledbetter darted past him too—then tried to stop as a dark shape loomed around the corner of the building, blocking his path. Ledbetter bounced off of whatever it was, stumbled, shrieked, and fell to his knees.

This was no apparition, Bo knew. Ledbetter had run into something—or someone—solid. Bo reached for his gun, but the metallic ratcheting of a revolver being cocked made him freeze.

"Hold it, both of you hombres," a deep, gravelly voice rasped. "Keep your hands away from them hoglegs."

Several more men came around the building. Starlight glinted on the barrels of the guns they held. Bo couldn't make out many details about them, but he felt the menacing undercurrent in the air.

"No need to go waving guns around," Bo said in a calm, level voice. "We're not looking for any trouble."

Ledbetter lay huddled on the ground, whimpering. The first gunman jerked his Colt toward the preacher and asked, "What the hell's wrong with this old coot?"

"He's just scared," Scratch said. "There ain't no need to hurt him."

"Scared o' what?"

Ledbetter looked up and sobbed, "The Lord's vengeance! Save yourselves! Flee while you can!"

One of the other armed men said, "He's loco, Tarver. You'd be doin' him a favor if you put a bullet in his head."

The leader turned sharply toward the man who had just spoken. "You're the one who's loco, you damn fool! You know better'n to go spoutin' my name all over the place."

"Sorry," the man muttered.

But the damage was done, and they all knew it— all except Ledbetter, who didn't seem to know anything except his fear. Sam Tarver was the leader of a gang of outlaws that had been plaguing West Texas for months. Posses hadn't been able to run him and his men to ground, so now the army was giving it a try. Bo had seen a newspaper article about Tarver in El Paso, before he and Scratch left in a hurry.

Tarver turned toward Bo and Scratch again and came close enough for them to see that he was a big man with a craggy face and several days' worth of beard. "You fellas got horses," the boss owlhoot said. "We want 'em."

"We only have two horses," Bo pointed out, "and there are . . ." He made a quick head count. "Five of you."

"Yeah, well, that'll still let us rest two of our

mounts," Tarver said. "Anything that helps us move a little faster and stay ahead o' that cavalry patrol."

So the army was catching up to the gang, Bo thought. In fact, he seemed to recall reading that Tarver's gang was larger than five men. He wondered if the outlaws had already fought a skirmish or two and lost some of their members.

"We'll want any supplies you got too," Tarver went on. "And hell, you might as well go ahead and hand over any dinero in your pockets. We'll make it a clean sweep."

Lightning flashed as he spoke, and a crash of thunder followed his words like punctuation. Reverend Ledbetter howled like a kicked dog and curled up on the ground again.

"Maybe you're right, Harry," Tarver added. "Puttin' a bullet in this crazy varmint's head would be a blessin'."

"I thought you said we wasn't supposed to use each other's names."

Tarver shrugged. "Well . . . it don't hardly matter now, does it?"

Bo and Scratch both knew what that meant. The outlaws didn't intend to leave anyone alive in Duster. They didn't want anybody telling the cavalry patrol which way they had gone. Five to two odds were pretty heavy, especially when the five already had their guns drawn, but the drifters had faced worse in their adventuresome career. And since they still had their guns, they'd be damned if they would die without a fight.

But before Bo and Scratch could hook and draw, one of the outlaws who hadn't spoken before suddenly said, "Look yonder, Tarver! It's a couple o' kids!"

"What?" Tarver exclaimed. "Where?"

"Right over there," the owlhoot said, pointing. "I . . . I . . . Where the hell'd they go?"

"Spirits!" Ledbetter screeched. "Spirits of the dead!"

"Shut up!" Tarver roared. "I'm gettin' mighty tired o' you, old man—"

"Hey, mister. . . ."

The childish voice floated through the air and seemed to come from everywhere and nowhere. It caused all of the men except Ledbetter to jump a little and look around, even the usually iron-nerved Bo and Scratch. They had already encountered the mysterious youngsters, and now they heard the boy's voice.

The girl chimed in a second later, saying, *"Over here, mister . . ."* The voices were so wispy they didn't seem real.

But what else would you expect ghosts to sound like, Bo thought?

"No, over here, over here!" the boy called.

"There!" one of the outlaws cried. He triggered wildly, Colt flame blooming in the darkness as the shots gouted from his gun. He emptied the weapon, and as he lowered it, he said, "Where the hell'd they go? I hit the little bastard, I know I did!"

"Stop shootin', you idiot!" Tarver said. "That's a little kid you're blastin' away at!"

"No, it's not," Bo said, figuring that any distraction would work in his and Scratch's favor. "That little boy and girl were orphans who were killed in a flood here months ago. The water made the orphanage collapse. More than thirty children died that night, and their spirits are here in Duster." Bo paused as more lightning glared across the sky. "They've come back tonight."

"Over here . . . over here . . . over here . . ."

The outlaws twisted and turned frantically, looking for something that wasn't really there. Scratch leaned close to Bo and said, "That one hombre never reloaded his gun."

"I know," Bo replied. "That makes it four to two. Good enough odds for you?"

"Damn good enough," Scratch snapped, and slapped leather.

"Look out!" Tarver yelped. "Get those two saddle tramps!"

The outlaws' panic had given Bo and Scratch a chance to draw their guns. Both Colts blasted as the two drifters split up, Bo going right and Scratch going left. Bo hoped that Ledbetter would have sense enough to keep his head down.

One of the outlaws spun around with a harsh cry as a bullet from Bo's gun drilled through his body. Another doubled over as one of Scratch's slugs punched into his belly.

But then Tarver and the desperado called Harry began to return fire, forcing Scratch to dive behind the old water trough. Bo dashed for the far side of the street, but it was too far away. He would never make it.

Sure enough, a bullet traced a trail of fire across the outside of his left thigh. The wound was minor, but the impact was enough to knock his leg out from under him and send him tumbling to the ground. He knew he would be ventilated good and proper before he could get to his feet again.

But he had landed so that he was turned toward the old hotel or saloon or whatever it was, and in the light of the campfire Bo saw Reverend Ledbetter rise from the ground and throw himself at Sam Tarver. "No!" the preacher screamed. "Vengeance belongs to the Lord—and to the children!"

A pair of shots erupted from Tarver's gun. Ledbetter crumpled as the bullets smashed into him. His action gave Bo time to draw a bead on Tarver, though, and before the boss outlaw could fire again, the walnut-handled Colt leaped in Bo's hand. Three shots rolled out, all of them hammering into Tarver's chest and driving him backward so that he fell heavily on the old boardwalk. The planks were rotten. Tarver busted right through them.

At the same time, Scratch fired from behind the water trough at Harry. One of the slugs smashed the outlaw's elbow; the second tore his throat out. He went down with blood fountaining from the wound. It looked more black than red in the firelight.

That accounted for four of the five outlaws, but the one who had emptied his gun at a ghost was still on his feet. His gun wasn't empty anymore, either. He had been desperately thumbing fresh cartridges into the cylinder as the battle went on around him, and now he snapped the weapon closed and lifted it, grinning as he aimed it at Bo.

It was Bo's gun that was empty now. He couldn't do anything as the outlaw shouted to Scratch,

"Drop your guns, mister, or I'll blow holes in your pard, I swear I will!"

Bo heard the curses coming from Scratch and called, "Kill the varmint!" He wasn't surprised, though, when Scratch stood up a moment later and tossed his Remingtons to the ground in front of the water trough.

"All right," Scratch said. "Now what?"

The outlaw chuckled. "Now I get a fresh horse, and an extra one too. No way those troopers'll catch me."

Bo knew the man was about to pull the trigger, but before that could happen, something large and dark plummeted from the old balcony. The outlaw never saw it coming as it crashed into his head, shattering as it knocked him to his knees.

Scratch left his feet in a dive, snatched one of the Remingtons from the ground as he rolled over, and came up firing. He had two shots left in the ivory-handled gun and put both of them into the fifth and final outlaw. The man went over backward, twitched a couple of times, and then lay still as a dark bloodstain spread over the front of his shirt.

Around him were scattered the remains of the old rain barrel that had fallen on him.

Bo lifted his eyes to the balcony, saw the gap in the railing where the barrel had been pushed through it. He saw the two children standing there as well, looking down at the street. He halfway expected them to disappear again, but they didn't. Instead the boy called, "Reverend Ledbetter! Reverend Ledbetter, get up!"

The preacher wasn't moving, though. Scratch

hurried to Bo's side, helped him to his feet, and whispered, "Them ghosts are back."

"They're not ghosts," Bo said with a shake of his head. "They're real, and they just saved our bacon." He called up to the children, "Ruthie, Caleb, you kids come on down. We won't hurt you. That's a promise."

Another rumble sounded close by. Scratch said, "That ain't thunder. That's—"

"Hoofbeats," Bo said.

Followed a moment later by the sound of a bugle.

The cavalry patrol's grizzled Irish sergeant took charge of the children while Bo and Scratch explained to Lieutenant Stilwell what had happened here in Duster, both tonight and months earlier, when the flood washed away most of the town.

"I got a chance to talk to those kids a little before you rode in," Bo said. "They made it out of the orphanage that night before it collapsed, because Ruthie got too scared to stay there and ran out, and Caleb went after her. He's her brother."

"Then they were never ghosts?" the lieutenant asked. Scratch grunted like that struck him as sort of a dumb question.

Bo shook his head. "No. They didn't leave when everybody else did after the flood, because this was the closest thing to a home that they had. And Reverend Ledbetter stayed, so they wanted to be where he was. They tried to take care of him, but his mind was already twisted around. He didn't believe they were alive. He was convinced they were ghosts."

"What about the way they disappeared?"

Scratch said, "They been livin' in this ghost town for months, scroungin' for food and shelter and tryin' to take care o' the reverend whether he wanted 'em to or not, so they know every hidey-hole and shortcut around here. They didn't know whether to trust Bo and me when we first rode in, so they didn't come all the way out, just spied on us and eavesdropped until they figured out we wouldn't hurt 'em. Then Tarver and the rest o' them owlhoots showed up."

"And thanks to Ruthie and Caleb taking a hand, we survived that little ruckus," Bo added. "That's the story, Lieutenant. It'll be up to you now to take care of those kids."

Stilwell nodded. "We'll take them back to Fort Stockton with us. I'm sure we can find people to care for them."

The cavalry surgeon who was riding with the patrol had been working on Ledbetter. He looked up from his task and called, "Lieutenant, maybe you'd better get those kids and bring them over here."

Stilwell nodded, his face grim. "All right, Corporal." He and Bo and Scratch went over to where Ruthie and Caleb were talking with the massive Sergeant O'Hallihan. Stilwell led the children to the boardwalk where Ledbetter had been placed on a blanket while the surgeon examined his wounds.

Ledbetter's head was propped up on a folded blanket. He lifted a trembling hand, managed to smile, and said, "Children . . . Ruthie, Caleb . . . you're real?" Although the old man's eyes were filled with pain, they were clearer now.

"We been tryin' to tell you that for months, Reverend," Caleb said. "We just wanted to help you."

"And in my grief and guilt, I . . . I would not allow it." Ledbetter's lined face contorted. "I'm sorry, so sorry . . ."

"Don't worry, Reverend," Ruthie said. "We know you were just too sad to be thinkin' straight. We were sad too. All of our friends died. You were all we had left."

Tears trickled down Ledbetter's leathery cheeks. The children each took one of his hands and clutched it. "You'll have new homes now," he whispered. "Real homes. Thanks to these men . . ." He looked at Bo and Scratch. "God bless you. My deliverers."

A long sigh came from him as life faded from his eyes. Ruthie and Caleb started to sob, still holding his hands.

Scratch looked over at Bo and said, "I can't figure it. We didn't deliver him nothin' but a mess o' trouble."

"Not to his way of thinking." Bo looked up at the mountains. The thunder was faint now, and the lightning only a fading glow. "Looks like the storm is moving on."

St. Elmo in Winter

Margaret Coel

"St. Elmo oughtta be up ahead somewhere," Liam shouted over one shoulder. His voice was muffled in the canyon, almost lost in the wind whispering in the pine trees and the swoosh of snow falling from the branches. He hunched forward over his cross-country skis, knees slightly bent, and stared at the GPS cushioned in the palms of his black ski mitts. He'd planted his skis across the trail. "Another half mile," he said. Then he looked back. "Think you can make it?"

Charlie dug both ski poles into the snow and pushed another few feet up the steep incline. Half a mile? They might as well be going to the moon. She flashed Liam the most reassuring smile she could muster. The temperature must have dropped fifteen degrees in the last ten minutes. Her fingers felt like icicles inside her gloves. The cold was seeping past her scarf and crawling around inside her jacket. It was starting to snow. They hadn't seen any other skiers on the trail in more than an hour. Probably the other skiers had already turned back. But she and Liam had set out this morning for the old ghost town of St. Elmo, and she didn't want to admit that the steep trail, the falling temperatures, and a little snow were more than she could handle.

"You have to see St. Elmo in winter," Liam had told her—what, a thousand times? "It's just like it was in the 1880s. All the shops and houses up and down Main Street are the same. The wooden sidewalks are still there, and the log railings where they used to hitch the horses."

"And how would you know St. Elmo looks the same?" She could never resist teasing Liam about his ongoing love affair with Colorado history. It rivaled his affair with her, she sometimes thought, and she wondered which he would choose, if he had to choose between them. A graduate student in physics, in love with history! "You're in the wrong field," she'd told him, but had he taken up history, she never would have met him. He'd been her instructor in physics lab class. She guessed she probably wasn't the first student who had fallen in love with Liam Hollings, with his black curly hair and green eyes, and when he wore his cowboy hat and boots, he looked as if he'd stepped out of the Old West. There were times—when he was lost in a novel about the Old West or one of those grainy cowboy and Indian films—that, she thought, he wished he had lived back then.

"We could drive to St. Elmo next summer," she'd suggested. But Liam had gone on about how St. Elmo in the summer just wasn't the same. It was perfect in the winter, so isolated and still in the snow, like one of those miniature towns in a snow globe or a little town under a Christmas tree. He'd gone to St. Elmo many times, summer and winter. Winter was best.

Liam smiled at her now as Charlie dug her poles in hard and pulled alongside him. There was a light dusting of snow across his backpack and shoulders, and snow flakes were popping out like ice crystals on the sleeves of her own jacket. She edged her skis to keep from slipping backward and tried to catch her breath. She could hear her heart pounding. The freezing air stung her lungs. The world had been blue and white and golden when they'd started out, the sun blazing in a clear blue sky, the snow on the ground glistening so white it had stung her eyes. The sun had disappeared some time ago, and now the sky looked like a sheet of lead pressing down. The snow on the trail had turned gray.

"Looks like a few flurries, that's all." Liam shrugged the snow off his shoulders. "The storm isn't forecast until tonight." He threw a glance up the trail. "See the fork ahead?" he said, but even as he spoke, the gray sky seemed to drop down and envelop the fork. "St. Elmo's just a short distance on the right. We have plenty of time to see the place before we have to ski back down."

They were staying at a cabin at Mount Princeton at the foot of Chalk Creek Canyon, and the thought of the fireplace and the way the warmth of the fire last night had spread into the small living room and the red firelight had licked at the log walls sent a shiver down Charlie's spine. Even if they were to start back now, it would take the rest of the afternoon to reach the cabin. Her legs and arms felt numb with the cold.

"Ready?" Liam said, but he was already skiing up the trail, poles pounding the snow.

Charlie started after him. It felt better to move, loosen her muscles, get the blood flowing. She could see her breath floating ahead in gray puffs. Liam was right, she told herself. He was always right. He knew Chalk Creek Canyon, all the old gold mines and mining camps, all the ghost towns. He'd hiked and skied the trails with his grandfather when he was a kid, filling up on stories that his grandfather told about the way things used to be. And Liam had been hiking and skiing to ghost towns ever since.

"We'll follow the old railroad bed up the canyon," he'd told her this morning, a map of the area spread on the table in front of them, their coffee mugs holding down two corners. "The Denver South Park and Pacific ran up Chalk Creek Canyon to the gold mines. Four or five trains a day, imagine, and every one of them stopped at St. Elmo. Passengers coming and going, all kinds of freight being loaded and unloaded. The depot was like Grand Central Station. St. Elmo was the biggest town in the area in the boom days of the 1880s and 1890s. Miners and railroaders lived there. Ranchers came into town on the weekends. There were boardinghouses, all kinds of stores—merchandise and hardware—a livery and fire station, the town hall where dances were held every Saturday night. Saloons and gambling parlors and whore houses. Then the mines played out. The trains kept running for a while, but pretty soon there wasn't much reason to go up Chalk Creek Canyon. The tracks were finally pulled up in 1926. The few folks still living in St. Elmo just walked out the front doors and left everything the way it was."

"I get the picture," she'd told him, and she'd even admitted that St. Elmo would be something to see, a town that had stayed on in the canyon when everything else had left. Mines shut down, tracks pulled up, people gone away.

"We'll have to watch ourselves on the trail," Liam had said. "It's not very wide. The old narrow gauge trains didn't need much room."

Now Charlie planted her poles as hard as she could and tried to ski faster. Still Liam seemed farther and farther ahead, a gray splotch moving up the trail carved into the mountainside. The dark shadows of pine trees, boulders, and gray snow covered the slope that loomed over the south side of the narrow railroad bed. On the north side was the sheer drop off into the canyon several hundred feet below. Charlie tried to stay close to the slope, but the snow was getting heavier, blowing across the trail and stinging her face. She had to keep her head down, her chin tucked inside the folds of her scarf. Her face felt like ice. Her goggles were fogging. It was hard to make out where she was on the trail. She concentrated on staying close to the line of trees. If she swerved too far to the right, tipped her skis over the edge, she could tumble into the canyon before she knew what had happened. No one would ever find her. She could taste the panic beginning to rise inside her, like the burning aftermath of a spicy dinner.

She couldn't see Liam! The realization took her breath away. "Liam!" she shouted, but it was only the sound of her own voice that echoed in the silence of the falling snow. She made herself ski faster, digging the poles in hard to pull herself along. The snow cracked like ice beneath her skis, and the driving snow crusted on the front of her jacket and ski pants. She shouted again: "Liam, wait up!"

She'd reached the fork in the trail, she realized. It had to be the fork because directly ahead were the dark shapes of trees looming out of the snow. She was in a whiteout, nearly blinded by the whiteness everywhere: air, sky, ground. She felt disoriented, slightly dizzy, and she had to lean forward on her poles a moment to regain her equilibrium. The storm predicted for tonight, when she and Liam had planned to be back at the cabin cooking steaks on the little grill in the kitchen and roasting potatoes in the fireplace and sipping hot wine— that storm was here now. Weather forecasts seldom got it right about the mountains: sunny and beautiful one moment, a blizzard the next. She could barely make out the branches of the fork. St. Elmo on the right, Liam had said.

She headed to the right, still trying to stay with the line of trees, using their dark shadows as a guide. St. Elmo had to be close by. Houses and other buildings were still there, Liam had said. He was probably already in town looking for someplace where they could get in out of the storm. He'd come back for her. He wouldn't leave her alone out here. "Liam!" she shouted again, hearing the panic rippling through the echo that came back to her.

The trail was getting steeper, and that was almost funny, because she couldn't see that she was climbing higher. But she felt the tightness in her chest, the strain in her calf muscles. Only the grooves in the base of her skis kept her from slipping backward. Exhaustion pulled at her, as if iron weights had attached themselves to her legs and arms. Her backpack felt like a hundred pounds. The cold had worked its way into her bones. She tried to flex her fingers, but they were numb. You could die in a storm like this, that was a fact, just lie down in the snow and go to sleep. She had to keep moving. Every few minutes, she heard someone shouting for Liam, and she realized that she was shouting and that she had settled into a weird rhythm: Ski, ski, shout. Ski, ski, shout.

And then she was skiing downhill. She started telemarking to slow herself. Gradually the dark shadows of the trees gave way to another shadow coming toward her. She blinked hard to bring the shadow into focus: a rectangular building of some kind, snow clinging to the sloped roof and bunching beneath the windows. A house! She'd skied down into St. Elmo, but where were the other houses? The main street with vacant shops? The town hall and the saloons? She called out again. "Liam, Liam! Where are you?"

Nothing but the hush of the falling snow and the shush of her skis as she turned left off the trail and headed for the shadow. A log cabin, she could see now, slanted to one side, as if it had followed the slope of the mountain, with a little porch at the front almost buried in the snow. She got to the porch before she stepped out of her skis. Then she picked them up so they wouldn't get lost in the snow and, struggling with the skis and poles, stomped across the porch. Her boots made a soft, thudding noise in the snow. She tried the door-knob, but when it didn't turn, she threw herself against the door. It creaked open, and she stumbled into the darkness inside, dragging the skis and poles with her, knocking her backpack against the frame.

The house was as cold as the outdoors, but it was a different kind of cold, like the cold in a freezer, compacted and still. She was shaking with the cold. She managed to swing her backpack off her shoulders, then she removed her gloves and began rummaging in the backpack for the emergency kit that she always carried on a cross-country ski outing. Her fingers were frozen claws, her hands refusing to work. Finally she managed to drag out the kit. She let the backpack drop to the floor and concentrated all of her energies on the kit. It was a moment before she found the flashlight. Still shaking, she shone the dim light around the little room. The light beam flitted over the plank floor, jumped across the clumps of paper wallboard peeling off the log walls.

This was it then, a one-room cabin, and yet, what more did miners need? They had never planned to stay in the West, Liam had said. A place where they could eat and sleep and stay warm in a storm was all they needed until they hit the big lode of gold. Then they planned to go back East and live like kings.

But here was something: a fireplace built out of stone, no wider than a column set into the far corner. And she could see she wasn't the first to seek shelter in the cabin. Someone had been here in the last few days, judging by the trace of ashes in the fireplace and the two small logs stacked next to the hearth.

She set the flashlight on the floor and started digging in the kit for matches. She always carried matches; where were the matches? The beam from the flashlight made a starry pattern of light on the plank floor. Then her fingers closed on the narrow matchbook. Five matches inside, but that would be enough, if she were careful. She realized that the possibility of getting warm—the fireplace and logs and now the matches—had rolled over her, obliterated every other thought, even that of Liam. But if she could get warm she told herself—if she could just not be so cold—she would go back onto the trail and look for him.

She began ripping off pieces of the paper wallboard, tearing at it with raw, frozen hands. The wallboard came off in chunks, brittle and hard. She built a pile in the fireplace and went back for more, moving through the dim beam of light patterning the floor, trying to ignore the tiredness that dragged at her. Then she lay the logs on top of the wallboard, just the way Liam had stacked logs on top of crumpled newspaper to build the fire at the cabin last night. She crouched next to the fireplace and struck a match. It flickered a second, but before she could get it to the wallboard, it went out. She leaned in closer and held the matchbook next to the wallboard. Her hands were still shaking. She tried to steady them before she lit the second match. This time the wallboard caught on fire. Another moment and the logs started burning.

Charlie crawled over to the flashlight and turned it off. The little house shimmered in the firelight, and the air was filled with the crackling sound of fire. Inside her backpack, she found the folded plastic cloth that she and Liam had spread in the snow about halfway to St. Elmo, when the sun was still shining. They'd sat on the cloth and eaten nuts and dried fruit and shared a bottle of water and turned their faces to the sun. She crawled back to the fireplace, smoothed the cloth on the floor in front of the hearth, and lay down, hugging herself. The warmth leapt out and caressed her tingling face and hands. A few minutes was all she needed. Then she would find Liam and bring him back to the house. Liam would know how to get more logs, and they could wait out the storm and stay warm.

Liam, Liam, where are you?

Charlie awoke in the freezing cold. Coming through the darkness was the faint sound of laughter and music. It took a moment to get her bearings. At first she thought she was in the cabin at Mount Princeton, but why was it so cold? Liam must have let the fire die down. Then it came to her, like an arctic blast of wind, that she was in an abandoned house in a ghost town, and the fire had burned out, and she was alone. Except that she wasn't alone. Outside somewhere, somebody was having a party!

She managed to get to her feet; her legs and arms as numb and heavy as logs. She struggled into her backpack and gathered up the skis and poles. She hadn't meant to fall asleep. Liam was out there somewhere looking for her, but now there were other people around. Someone could have seen him. She could get other skiers to help her find him.

Charlie stepped out onto the porch and stopped. It was night, and the sky was light and clear. The blizzard had worn itself out, leaving little flurries of snow swirling in the air. The main street of St. Elmo stretched ahead in the moonlight that flooded the snowy ground. Wooden sidewalks ran up and down the street in front of the buildings—houses and stores shouldering one another, painted blue, red, and yellow. She could see the black lettering painted on the front windows. There were boot tracks in the snow on the sidewalks. Snow drifted over the roofs and piled behind the second-story false fronts.

Amber lights glowed in the windows, and in a nearby house, she could see a woman seated at a dressing table brushing her hair. Outside a horse was hitched to a small sleigh. The music and laughter was coming from the building about halfway down the street, lights shining in the front window. The saloon, Charlie thought. Everything was just as Liam had described it, a little town in a snow globe, a little town beneath a Christmas tree.

Two men came out of a shop and hurried along the sidewalk. One called out to someone on the other side of the street. Charlie hadn't noticed anyone else, but now she realized there were a lot of people walking along the sidewalks. Most were men, but there were a few women, and the women wore long dresses that swept over the snow.

Charlie swallowed hard. Her mouth had gone dry, and she could feel the cold working its way back inside her. There was a party going on, all

right, a party that she and Liam had known nothing about when they had set off for St. Elmo.
Some historical society must have scheduled a get
together in the old ghost town and people had
brought clothes from the 1880s. Somebody had
even driven a horse and sleigh up the trail. There
were societies like that, Liam had said, people who
dressed up like mountain men and went to rendezvous, just like the mountain men in the 1800s,
and people who dressed up like cavalry and Indians
and staged mock battles on old battlegrounds.
Liam would be furious, she thought, when he saw
all the people here. He had wanted St. Elmo in
winter just for the two of them.

Charlie stepped into her skis and started down
Main Street. There were tracks everywhere made by
hooves and wheels and sleigh runners. The gathering, whatever it was, had been going on for some
time. She expected the tracks to be frozen, but the
snow was soft, glinting like diamonds in the moonlight, and her skis glided through them. "Hello!"
she called to several men wearing long black coats
and brimmed hats. They stood in a little circle in
front of a shop with a false front and black letters
that spelled TOBACCO painted on the window. "Can
you help me?" But they ignored her and kept on
talking, one of them puffing on a cigar, another
throwing back his head and laughing into the night
sky, as if no one saw her, as if she didn't exist.

"Hello! Hello there!" Charlie called out to a
couple walking arm in arm along the sidewalk, but
they kept walking. "Hello!" she called to two men
heading into the shop with letters that spelled
HARDWARE on the window. The door shut behind

them, and she skied toward two other men farther down the street, standing on the sidewalk, heads dipped in conversation. Still no response, as if she weren't there. It was as if the people attending the gathering had decided to ignore anything—or anyone—from the present.

The music was louder. A tinny sounding piano pounded out a ragtime piece that burst out of the saloon and floated down Main Street every time someone opened the door. Above the door, St. Elmo Saloon was painted in red letters across the false, second-story front. Charlie took a diagonal route across the street. She left her skis propped against the hitching log at the edge of the sidewalk. Farther up the street a black horse was tied to another log. She walked over to the front window of the saloon. It was crowded inside, women in brightly colored, shiny dresses that sloped off their shoulders, with ruffles at their ankles that showed off their high-heeled shoes; men in dark suits with white shirts and black string ties, some with cowboy hats pushed back on their heads.

Across the room, a line of men stood shoulder to shoulder in front of the bar, but Charlie watched the line break up and the men turn around as a tall woman in a blue dress, with blond hair stacked on top of her head, walked over. There were a half dozen round tables set about where men were laying down cards on the green baize tabletops. A shiny-dressed woman perched on the lap of one of the card players.

It was then that she spotted Liam. The black-haired man with the mustache—he'd always wanted to grow a mustache—and the red-headed woman in a green dress leaning over his shoulder, brushing her face against his. Several cards lay face down in front of him. Deftly he lifted the corner of one card, then tossed some gold coins toward the coins stacked in the middle of the table. The dealer dealt out a round of cards, and then it seemed to be over. Liam reached out both hands, circled the stacks of coins, and pulled them toward him. He handed some coins to the woman. Grasping his chin with one hand, she turned his face toward her. She kissed him on the lips.

Charlie pressed her face against the freezing window and tried to blink back the tears that had made the saloon seem watery and unreal. At first the tears felt warm on her cheeks, but then they turned to ice. Still she couldn't take her eyes away from the black-haired man with the mustache, staring at the new round of cards that had been dealt, pushing a small stack of coins into the center of the table. It was Liam, and yet it was not Liam. The truth hit her like a sledge hammer: the Liam that she knew and loved was dead.

The saloon door opened and two men spilled outside and walked past. Charlie made herself move away from the window. She walked over to the edge of the sidewalk where the men stood looking up and down Main Street, as if they were expecting someone. She reached out and tried to take hold of one of the men's arm's, but the sleeve of his jacket dissolved in her grasp. There was nothing but air. She could hear the rumble of a train, the shrill sound of the whistle, and the swooshing noise of steam coming closer. They had pulled up the tracks in 1926, Liam had said.

Later, Charlie barely remembered stepping into her skis and heading back down Main Street, past the lights in the windows and the people walking about. Barely remembered the freezing cold and the blizzard starting up again and the snow driving against her face as she skied up the incline past the little cabin and started downhill toward the fork in the trail. She remembered only skiing as fast as she could, the music and laughter receding into the night behind her and the words pounding in her head: *Get away from here. Get away from here.*

"Can you hear me?"

A man's voice cut through the blackness, and Charlie tried to fight her way upward into consciousness. She blinked into the bright spotlight shining somewhere above her. The face of a man with a knitted ski cap pulled low on his head was coming closer, and she struggled to bring him into focus. Snow was everywhere: snow on her jacket and gloves, snow piled over her legs. She was buried in snow. She tried to sit up, aware of the strength in the hands pressing on her shoulders.

"Better lie still until we make sure you don't have any broken bones," the man said. Then he shouted: "Over here! We found the woman off the trail."

Other men were stomping through the snow, and a woman too, and then all of them were hovering over her, brushing the snow from her jacket and pants. She could barely feel the hands moving over her arms and legs. It was as if they were moving over stone.

"Can you tell us what happened?" The man's voice again. "Did you fall?"

"I don't know," she said. "It was snowing. I was so cold."

"Maybe she just lay down," the woman said.

"What about your friend, Liam Hollings?" The man's face came into focus now: a prominent nose and flushed cheeks. Light eyes peering at her from beneath the cliff of his forehead.

"Liam," Charlie said, feeling the softness of his name on her lips.

"Any idea where he might be? When did you last see him? Did he fall off the trail?"

Charlie closed her eyes. She and Liam were skiing up the trail together, the old railroad bed. *We'll have to watch ourselves. The old narrow gauge trains didn't need much room.* She could feel the tears starting again as she looked at the man. "He got ahead of me. Somewhere around the fork. I couldn't see him."

"Trail gets real narrow in that area," the man said. "Not much room for mistakes." He dropped his head into the hush that moved over them. Charlie could hear the soft thud of snow falling off a branch and the quiet sound of her own weeping. Then the man said, "We're going to move you onto the snowmobile. An ambulance is waiting in Mount Princeton to take you to the hospital in Salida."

Already the strong hands were sliding her out of the snow.

"You're lucky you didn't get any farther off the trail." The woman's voice came from somewhere behind. "Another foot and you would have rolled into the canyon. We never would have found you."

The Salida Journal:

The search for missing skier Liam Hollings has been called off after two weeks, according to a spokesman at the Chaffee County Sheriff's Department. Hollings, 29, and Charlie Lambert, 26, graduate students in physics at the University of Colorado, had set out the morning of January 6 on a cross-country skiing trip along the abandoned railroad bed in Chalk Creek Canyon. When they didn't return that evening to Mount Princeton, where they had rented a cabin, the manager notified the sheriff. The county search and rescue team located Lambert around 10 P.M. about a mile from the abandoned town of St. Elmo, but the team has been unable to find any sign of Hollings.

"The extreme winter weather, with deep snows and freezing temperatures, makes it highly unlikely that Hollings can be found alive," the spokesman said. "The skiers were on a very steep and narrow expert trail. The rescue team believes that Hollings became disoriented in a blizzard and may have skied off the trail into the canyon."

Lambert was evacuated to Salida Community Hospital where she was treated for hypothermia, frostbite, and exhaustion before being released last week. She could not be located for comment.

Mr. Kennedy's Bones

Johnny D. Boggs

Get your filthy hands off me, you damned greasers. I ain't done nothin'. Let go of me. What the hell—don't any of you ignorant bastards speak English! English! *Sabe* English? Get off me. Listen . . . what . . . what is this? Robbery? You bunch of . . . the rope's tight. Sons-of-bitches, ever' damned one of you. Stop. You're makin' a mistake.

Hey . . . hey, you! Get away from him, you bean-eatin' bastard. Get away, I tell you. Leave Mr. Kennedy alone. Leave him alone, I say. He ain't no concern of yours. Don't touch him. Don't you greasers look at me like that.

What the hell are you doin'? Listen. Get that damned rope off my neck. Good God, y'all ain't hangin' me. For what? What are you sons-of-bitches doin'? I ain't done nothin'! I ain't no grave robber. I'm buryin' Mr. Kennedy is all. And you don't hang grave robbers! I'm not diggin' him up. I'm plantin' him. Bringin' him home after thirty years.

Get that rope—

Fools! Wait a minute. Wait a damned minute! You're makin' a mistake. Well . . . God! For the love

of Christ, at least give me a minute. Let me pray.
Confession. Oh, hell, what's the word? Confession.
Priest. *Padre.*

That's right. *Confesión.* Bless me Father for I've
sinned. That kind of shit.

That's right, you ignorant sons-of-bitches. Take
your hats off. *Padre?* You a priest? You speak English? No. Hell, of course you don't. You understand a thing I say? Well, ain't this a joke. You hear
that, Mr. Kennedy? Yeah. It's a hell of a joke. Stop
laughin', Mr. Kennedy. It ain't that funny.

Maybe it is. Ha! I'm makin' my confession to
some dirt-poor peon who ain't even a priest. Don't
speak no Mex to me, you bastard. I don't speak it
none, can't you tell? All these years in New Mexico
Territory, and I never learned nothin' but a handful of words. Just shut up and listen. Maybe you can
tell your *padre* somethin' 'bout Moses Q. Logan.
Yeah, you tell your *padre* to pray for old Moses
Logan's soul. And Mr. Kennedy. Pray for him too.
Me and him's been partners for years.

Hell, dyin' ain't that bad, I guess. Ain't that right,
Mr. Kennedy? You should know. Ha. At least I'll be
able to sleep. Ain't had a decent night's sleep in
thirty years. Not bad dreams, nothin' like that. No
hobgoblins. No haints. Just a bunch of treetops,
blowin' in the wind. I see 'em all the time. Pon-
derosa pines. Swayin'. Can you figure that one out,
peon? You're just some miner, I warrant. Found any
color? No, that ain't likely. Not the way you're
dressed. No, these here mountains played out years
ago. Like this town. Like Mr. Kennedy. Hell's fire,
like me.

Wasn't that way back in '68 and '69. This was

Elizabethtown. E-Town, we called her, for short. The first incorporated town in New Mexico Territory. Colfax County seat. All 'round Baldy Mountain, folks found gold. Before long, E-Town had two hotels, three dance halls and seven saloons. That's when I come up. Struck up a bargain with my pard yonder, Mr. Kennedy. Charles Kennedy's his name.

Charles Kennedy. You recognize that name, huh? Yeah, I reckon Mr. Kennedy's a name remembered well in these parts. He should be. And Clay Allison? Heard tell of him? No? That's a surprise. Clay was a good hand with a gun. He's dead now. Been dead. And was gone from these parts long before his demise. But I'll get to that directly.

Back then, I was what you might call a trader, like my pa and his pa, who was runnin' trains from Missouri 'long the Santa Fe Trail before your pappy was born. But my interest was in medicine. Wanted to be a doctor. Wanted that real bad. And tradin' was what I done to get me close to that dream of mine. Costs a passel of money to learn to be a sawbones.

So I partnered up with Mr. Kennedy. He had him an inn on the pike betwixt E-Town and Taos. In that meadow over that way. The inn's long gone. Clay and the boys burned 'er down. It's all gone now, ain't it? Nothin' left but rottin' cabins and some old stone buildings.

You was right, Mr. Kennedy! You cursed E-Town good. Cursed all of us mighty fine, ol' pard.

Sorry, Mr. Mex. Let me get back to my story. My confession. Yep, ain't much left to E-Town but this here graveyard. I knowed this boneyard well. Over yonder, that's where folks say Charles Kennedy is buried, but you know that ain't true as Mr. Kennedy's been travelin' with me. But there's where we planted Pony O'Neil. Vigilantes rubbed him out in '68. He ain't there, neither. Nor is Wall Henderson over by that dead tree.

I dug 'em up.

Both Pony and Wall made mighty fine corpses, and any doctor'll tell you that a good cadaver is hard to come by in medical school. So that was my trade. I dug 'em up and packed 'em in a barrel full of charcoal and such. Freighted 'em to Cheyenne durin' the early years, till the Denver Pacific reached Denver City in 1870. And from there, just ride the rails all the way to Ann Arbor, Michigan, and the University of Michigan's medical school.

Then, after sellin' my prime specimens, I'd buy wares and come back to Cheyenne, Denver, and down to E-Town. Bring somethin' here that folks wanted, and haul somethin' in need at Ann Arbor. That's the way you run a freightin' enterprise.

"Your cadavers are superb," Professor Sawyer told me. "Young, healthy men."

Which they was before they got kilt. You wouldn't find many old-timers and younguns in a minin' camp like E-Town. Just young men, full of vim and vigor. And, later, full of lead. Which is when I visited 'em.

Yep, Professor Sawyer sure liked me fetchin' him top-rate cadavers. And ever' once in a while, he'd let me watch his young students go to work.

But then folks started suspicionin' certain unwanted activities at the cemetery here. E-Town was boomin'. We had us a newspaper, mercantiles, billiard halls, and whores. A man could buy the best old Kentucky whiskey in the territory, or try his hand buckin' the tiger at a faro layout. There was a Chinaman who had a laundry, and folks was buildin' this big ditch to bring in water from the high country. The Moreno Water and Minin' Company, they called it. Didn't pan out. But they sure tried to make 'er work. E-Town was buckin' to become more than just a county seat. Folks saw 'er on 'er way to become the best by-grab minin' burg in the Southern Rockies.

'Bout that time was when I discovered that Mr. Kennedy and I was good pards. You see, I was what you might call a silent partner in his inn. Mr. Kennedy was greedy, though—most folks who come to E-Town was greedy. Hell, it was greed that brought us all to this high country. Anyhow, Mr. Kennedy had this here side business. Some miner would have a poke full of dust on his way to Taos, maybe Santa Fe, and they'd never be seen or heard from again. Maybe Mr. Kennedy would slit a throat. Maybe he'd just brain the poor bastard with the blunt end of an ax. Then he'd burn the body and bury what was left, if anything was left.

But I changed the burnin' part once I learnt what he was doin'. It was luck. Fate. Somethin' like that. I just happened to walk in on him one evenin' when he was draggin' Jim Witherspoon from the supper table. He seen me, dropped the body, and reached for his ax, but I always carried a Navy .36 in those years, and before he could take a step toward me, he was starin' into that cold barrel.

"What you gonna do with him?" I gestured at the late Mr. Witherspoon with the Colt.

He didn't answer. Never was much of a talker, Mr. Kennedy. So I took a chance and lowered the hammer on the Colt, slid it into my holster, and made a bit of a proposition. After a few long, cold, silent minutes, Mr. Kennedy set that ax aside, and me and him stuffed Witherspoon into a barrel of mine.

Professor Sawyer praised Jim Witherspoon's corpse too. And when I brung him the prime bodies of some sharper and his concubine, well, that's when the professor told me that he just might be able to help me get into the university there so I could study to be a doctor. Study proper. In a few years, I'd be hangin' a shingle with my name on it. Finally, I'd be Moses Q. Logan, M.D. Professor Sawyer told me to look him up next time I was in Ann Arbor, which I always done when I had a new cadaver or two for him and his students.

Things could have been goin' no finer. I loaded up on apples, calico, and whiskey, which I hauled to Cheyenne, Denver City, and down into E-Town, New Mexico Territory.

Only . . . ain't that the way of the world. Here I was, two jumps from seein' my dream come true, drinkin' a whiskey with Clay Allison and the boys in the Senate Saloon, when Mr. Kennedy's wife come pushin' through the batwing doors, hands and face covered with blood.

She wasn't his real wife. Not in the eyes of God. Hell, I didn't even know what name those injuns had given her. Nope, she was nothin' but a Navajo bitch he'd bartered for some years back, and she didn't speak English no better than you did, but she was a woman, injun or not, her eyes ablaze with terror, and Clay and the boys was in their cups. All she yelled was some words in Spanish, but that got the boys' blood boilin', and mine icy with fear.

Asesinato. Asesinato. Asesinato.

You *sabe* that, huh? Yeah, me too. I knew exactly what she was sayin' at the Senate Saloon that cool autumn day.

Murder.

Murder.

Murder.

Don't know what all had happened, but, well, I suspect Mr. Kennedy had gotten contrary with her, and her with him. She didn't hold with his killin', told him so, so he had tried to kill her. Put a nasty cut atop her head, must have thought she was dead, but she come to while he was pullin' a cork on a jug of forty-rod, and she run and fetched Clay Allison.

"Sumbitch," Clay said. He run over and helped Mrs. Kennedy to a chair, then drawed his Colt, and yelled, "Let's go, boys! There's trouble at Kennedy's inn!"

That saloon emptied real quick, except for Russ the barkeep, and his swamper, a little old greaser named Pedro. And me. My legs wouldn't work. I just kept starin' at that Navajo, wonderin' if she planned on informin' Clay and the boys what I had been doin'. I wasn't even sure she knowed what I was doin'. Pedro, after he doctored that head of hers, he started conversin' with her real soft in that Mex lingo, while Russ and me just stared, mutterin' some flapdoodle, mainly waitin' on the boys to return.

I spied a good bay mare at the hitchin' rail and figured I could fork that saddle and light a shuck for parts unknown if Clay and the boys come back suspicionin' me.

That fat Navajo knowed aplenty. She told Pedro that Mr. Kennedy had been murderin' guests in their sleep, which he done sometimes, but other times, he'd kill 'em whilst they et supper. She said he had buried a few after he had burned the bodies. She never looked at me, just at Pedro and Russ. And 'bout ten minutes later I heard the boys. Shoutin'. Madder'n hornets. Yes, sir, that bay mare was lookin' mighty temptin' to me 'long 'bout then.

My legs workin' once more, I stepped onto the boardwalk and saw 'em, draggin' Mr. Kennedy down the street, a rope 'round his neck, Clay proddin' him with his .44.

"Fiend!" one of the boys called him.

Mr. Kennedy, he just stared at me when they reined up in front of the Senate.

"Found a poke under his bed," Clay informed us. He held out a leather bag that had the initials E.W. burned into it.

"That'd be Eugene Willis," Russ said, and he walked up and spit in Mr. Kennedy's face.

"I ain't seen hide nor hair of Gene since he lit out for Taos," another gent said.

Then Zeke McMasters held out a box he was carryin', and as Pedro informed 'em all what Mrs. Kennedy said, Zeke dumped some bones into the dust.

Well, you never heard nothin' like the roar that shot out of Mr. Kennedy's mouth. Pretty good yell, it was, 'specially considerin' that rope pullin' tight on his neck. He was howlin' like the devil hisself, and starin' right at me. Starin' through me. Then he started talkin'.

He cussed us all. Cursed us, rather. Cursed me and Clay Allison and his Navajo woman. Cursed us to the deepest depths of Hell's fires. Cursed Zeke McMasters and Russ the barkeep. And cursed E-Town.

So I drawed my Navy and shot him.

Had to. You see that, don't you?

What you gotta *sabe* is this, *amigo.* I ain't never kilt nobody before in my life. Not till then. I dug up bodies, sure. But you need to see it this way. I was doin' the work of science, helpin' teach young doctors what they needed to know. I was the cadaver man. Mr. Kennedy, he was the killer. Ask him if you don't believe me. He never lied to nobody. Not once in more'n thirty years I've knowed him. He was the one murderin' all 'em travelers. It was him that kilt Jim Witherspoon and Gene Willis and all those others. Sure, we split what money we found in their poke, but I never laid no hand on 'em . . . till after they was dead.

But the boys might not have seen it that way.

So I kilt Mr. Kennedy.

Clay Allison, he allowed that mine was a scratch shot, but it wasn't no such thing. I knowed where I was aimin', learned a thing or two at Ann Arbor, by grab. That bullet severed the subclavian artery, and Mr. Kennedy bled out real quick. Never said nothin' else. Didn't have no chance to after I shot him. He just fell and was dead by the time Clay and McMasters rolled him over.

"We was gonna hang him!" Zeke McMasters yelled at me, angry that I had spoilt all his fun.

"A fiend like that," I said, "don't deserve a rope. He just deserves killin'!"

Then Clay yelled out that we rid E-Town of that blight in the meadow, so they all run back down to the Mr. Kennedy's inn, and burned it to the ground.

You might have heard stories, *amigo,* that Clay and the boys chopped off Mr. Kennedy's head, that we rode down to Cimarron after killin' Mr. Kennedy and put his head on the post in front of Lambert's place, just to let folks be warned that E-Town didn't tolerate no mischief of the most fiendish kind. Falsehoods. Them's shameless falsehoods. And some folks say Mr. Kennedy was hanged from the tree. That tree yonder. The dead one. Others say that Clay and the boys dragged him to death. Nope. Didn't happen that way, did it, Mr. Kennedy?

And there have been some that say that the bones that got found at the inn wasn't even human bones, but dog bones. The bones was human, I guaran-damn-tee you, but they wasn't Gene Willis's remains, although they got buried as such on the far side of this boneyard. Nope, Gene Willis was in one of my apple barrels, ready for the trip to Ann Arbor.

I looked over at my wagon, started to sweat, and then I seen that Navajo wife of his'n just eyein' me.

So I kilt her that night after Clay and the boys had gone down to Cimarron, and I said I'd bury Mr. Kennedy myself, since I had kilt him. They agreed to that, but it wasn't Mr. Kennedy's body that I buried in that pit I dug. It was his wife whose throat I cut that night whilst she slept. The next morn, when Zeke McMasters asked 'bout her, I told him and the boys that I figured she'd gone back to her own kind, and they accepted that.

Yeah, I thought about takin' her 'long with me to Ann Arbor, but I wasn't sure they wanted no bodies of no dirty injun. I mean doctors didn't practice medicine on injuns, just white folks like Mr. Kennedy.

And he would be a prime specimen. So would Gene Willis.

So I loaded Mr. Kennedy up in another barrel, freighted 'em to Denver City, and from there I rode the rails to Ann Arbor, Michigan, where I sent word to Professor Sawyer that I had two new specimens for him. We met that night, as we always done, at that dark old building. I backed the wagon in, unloaded the barrels, and waited for the professor to pry off the lids.

The gas lamp flared gently, and Professor Sawyer marveled at Gene Willis as we laid him on the doctorin' table, brushed off the charcoal dust, and I told him Gene wasn't nothing, wait till he laid eyes on my other cadaver, told him that I was ready to start my studyin'. He didn't say nothin', busy as he was openin' that other lid, and then he looked down, and tumbled away, retchin', his face turnin' ashen quicker than I'd kilt Mr. Kennedy.

"You bastard!" The professor pulled hisself to his feet, wipin' his mouth with his sleeve, jerkin' away from me when I reached out to help him. "You bloody damned fool!"

I didn't understand none of it. "But . . ." was all that come out of my throat, and then I looked at that barrel, inside it, and that gas lamp didn't need to be no brighter, because I seen it. Seen it fine. Seen the worms and the maggots and Mr. Kennedy's eyes, just glarin' at me. Laughin' at me.

"I . . ." I turned back to Professor Sawyer. "I packed him in charcoal . . . like . . ." I looked back. Couldn't believe it. Nor explain it. He couldn't decompose like that. Not that quick. Not with all the precautions I taken. "Like I always done."

"Get out of here!" He was stumblin' away, runnin', gaggin' more.

"But . . ."

"And take that . . ." He stopped just long enough to point at the barrel. "Take . . . that . . . with you!"

"It won't never happen again!" I told him, but the professor just yelled that he never wanted to see my face again. That if I ever showed up, he'd sic the constable after me.

I looked down at that horrible sight, and slowly put the lid back on that barrel, tamped it down with the mallet, heaved Mr. Kennedy back on the wagon, leavin' Gene Willis on the table for all those lucky young doctors. When I closed that lid, I knowed I was closin' the door to my dreams, knowed I'd never become no doctor.

It was charcoal. I hadn't done nothin' wrong. Wasn't hot or nothin', A body like that should keep, like Gene Willis done, but Mr. Kennedy didn't. So I took him back to New Mexico, to the cabin I'd built next to that little pond that's fed by the creek. The worms and the maggots was gone, just disappeared, when I reached the territory again, but it hadn't been no dream. No, they had done their work on him, foul critters, manglin' that corpse somethin' fierce.

That's when 'em dreams started. The ones where all I can see is 'em treetops swayin' in the breeze. I'd go to sleep, and then wake up, and that was most peculiar because I wasn't dreamin' of Mr. Kennedy and the maggots eatin' his face. Just pine trees.

Well, I told Mr. Kennedy, "What am I to do with you?" And struck me, it did, that Mr. Kennedy would make a mighty fine skeleton. Maybe I'd teach myself to be a doctor, so I got him out of that barrel and drug him to the table, sharpened my knives, and went to work. Yes, sir, the coyotes et real good that night outside my cabin. I got Mr. Kennedy dissected.

Best way to get a skeleton cured proper, I'd learned from one of 'em young students in Michigan, is to bleach the bones underwater. Carefully, I loaded Mr. Kennedy into some shoe boxes, which I sunk with rocks and let Mr. Kennedy sit there and think 'bout the pain he'd done caused me, crushin' my doctorin' dreams, and let him rest there for the winter.

My plan to be a M.D. wasn't the only thing that went bust that year. E-Town started to die up too. It was like Mr. Kennedy had cursed this town after all. Must have been two thousand folks there the year before, but by the followin' spring, there was only a couple of hundred. Clay pulled out. So did Russ and Zeke McMasters and the rest of the boys. The fools that stayed didn't stay long, saw there wasn't no future in E-Town. Gold's fickle. Like dreams, I reckon.

Oh, I stayed. Probably would have stayed the rest of my days if 'em kids hadn't come by. It was April, and the lake was still frozed, but one of 'em boxes of Mr. Kennedy's bones had floated up somehow. Rocks hadn't held it or somethin'. Maybe it was just Mr. Kennedy, tryin' to reach the surface. Mr. Kennedy, he never told me why or how he done it, but it got done. Some boys from Cimarron had come over to do some ice-fishin'. But they seen that shoe box, and they picked it out usin' the ax, opened it up, and went off screamin'. Screamin' 'bout murder and bones.

I barely got out of here with my life. I found the bones the boys had dropped, packed 'em up in my war bag, and that's when I heard the posse ridin' down. Ridin' for me. They must have figured that I'd kilt some fellow just the way Mr. Kennedy done all 'em boys, and that one strumpet. Wasn't right sure they'd believe my story, 'bout me becomin' a doctor, and if they learnt who I was, they might recollect 'bout Mr. Kennedy, might start thinkin' that I had somethin' to do with those murders, might recall that it had been me that had shot Mr. Kennedy dead. Might have strung me up like you greasers plan on doin'.

Rode off to Fort Union, and stayed there till the melt, but I couldn't leave the rest of Mr. Kennedy in that pond yonder. I mean, we was pards. So I rode back, got the rest of those shoe boxes up from the depths, and the bones had bleached mighty good. But I couldn't stay in these mountains. Nothin' left 'round E-Town no how.

Went south I did. Oh, I tried doctorin' some, after I got Mr. Kennedy's bones assembled proper. He made a right pretty skeleton, but nobody would let me doctor on 'em. Not in Santa Fe. Not Cerrillos. Not Golden.

I drifted down to Socorro for a spell, and that's where I joined up with this fellow named Sherman.

I partnered with him in the Doc Sherman's Nostrum Remedium Elixir & Magical Medicine Show. Mr. Kennedy was a big part of that show, his bones so white and perfect, and that skull . . . well, I had done a mighty good job with my dissection. I think it was Mr. Kennedy that kept us in business more than Doc Sherman's Hadacol, which wouldn't cure much of nothin' but would sure give you a headache and was one mean preservative. As Doc Sherman found out.

It was down in La Mesilla when he drunk two bottles of his liniment, and his belly got to hurtin' so much it must have burst. Me and Mr. Kennedy buried him on the banks of the Rio Grande—he wouldn't have made no top cadaver, old as he was, and, well, my days of providin' specimens had ended. Mr. Kennedy, he seen to that. So me and Mr. Kennedy rode out the next morn.

Durin' the years I kept with that medicine show, I never bothered changin' the name. Folks started callin' me Doc Sherman, and I let 'em. Hell, it felt mighty good to be called a doctor. But always, Mr. Kennedy and me was even partners. Never forgot that. Like that time in Hillsboro. 'Em miners got riled up that our Nostrum Remedium Elixir was just snake oil and had got some washerwoman real sick. So they covered me with tar and feathers and sent me down the mountain, after they'd burned my wagon and put Mr. Kennedy in Black Range Saloon.

But I come back to fetch my pard.

They was pourin' him a drink, just tossin' good whiskey, or as good as a body could get in a bucket of blood like the Black Range, down Mr. Kennedy's throat. Laughin'. Laughin' at Mr. Kennedy. And laughin' at what they had done to me.

Down in Hillsboro, I bet they still talk about that fight. I picked up two pick handles, and I must have busted a dozen or more skulls. Knowed I broke the bartender's neck when I slammed him, but it was only after I'd kilt him that Mr. Kennedy told me to look at him real good, and I did. It was Russ, the old Senate Saloon barkeep from E-Town.

Well, my killin' Russ had put the fear of the Lord in the rest of 'em Hillsboro miners, and I told 'em that they wasn't to bother Mr. Kennedy, that he only drunk with his pards, and if they ever laid a hand on him again, I'd kill 'em all.

Stole a buckboard, I did, and me and Mr. Kennedy left that town.

Hard times come after that. I didn't have no Hadacol to sell, no wagon after I traded the buckboard in Chloride for a couple of mules. Which is what me and Mr. Kennedy rode when we left New Mexico Territory. Went down to Texas. That's where Mr. Kennedy said he wanted to go.

Me and Mr. Kennedy was enjoyin' a rye at this little store in Pope's Wells. And who should walk in but Clay Allison hisself.

"My God," he says when he recognized me. "Moses? Moses Logan?"

"In the flesh," I said, and held out my hand. Clay just stared. He wasn't a man to lose his speech, but he couldn't say nothin' to me. Wasn't even lookin' at me now, just starin' at Mr. Kennedy. That had to be '87, and Clay Allison wasn't the wild gunman he had been all 'em years earlier up in E-Town. Clay had gotten hisself hitched to a gal named Dora, and now he was runnin' a ranch and raisin' a little girl, with another child on the way.

"You remember Mr. Kennedy, Clay," I tells him. "Charles Kennedy. Used to run a inn in E-Town on the road to Taos."

"I . . ."

It was Clay, sober I reckon, who started talkin' to me, tellin' me that, well, maybe I should bury Mr. Kennedy. He was the first one to say maybe Mr. Kennedy wanted to be buried.

"But we's partners," I told him. "Me and Mr. Kennedy are pards. You ought to know that."

So Clay done somethin' he shouldn't have done. Gnawed at him, it did, seein' Mr. Kennedy like that. Clay said he was goin' to fetch us a bottle, but instead he buffaloed me from behind with his Colt, and he took Mr. Kennedy, just loaded him on the back of his buckboard, and rode off for Pecos. The barkeep said Clay told him he would see that Mr. Kennedy got buried.

Turned out it was the other way 'round.

They found Clay's body a few miles from Pecos. He had fallen off a wagon, and the wheel had run over him, breakin' his neck. Fallen, they say, but I reckon I knowed what really happened. It was Mr. Kennedy. He pushed him.

Mr. Kennedy told me, you see. Durin' the funeral. We both attended, 'long with Dora, Clay's widow, and the little girl of theirs, and some of Clay's brothers and a bunch of ranch hands. You should have seen how 'em mourners looked at me and Mr. Kennedy.

That's when it struck me that Mr. Kennedy had cursed his Navajo wife, and I'd kilt her. And he'd cursed E-Town, and she was dead too. So was Russ, his neck broken over in Hillsboro. Now Clay Allison was dead. So I shot Mr. Kennedy a stare and asked him, "You don't plan on murderin' me, do you, pard?"

He just grinned.

All this time, I'm still havin' that dream. The dream of trees. After Clay's death, Mr. Kennedy and I rode back to New Mexico, and that's where we run into Zeke McMasters. Wasn't lookin' for him. Fact was, by then, I was a mite ready to dissolve my partnership with Mr. Kennedy. Didn't trust him no more. Thought maybe he was plannin' to do me in like he'd kilt all those wayfarers. And Clay Allison.

He kilt Zeke too.

Zeke was tryin' to find paydirt up 'round Grafton, but all he found was his tombstone. I'd heard he had a claim, and Mr. Kennedy told me he wanted to see ol' Zeke, so we rode out. Yeah, I knowed what he planned to do. Knowed he was gonna kill ol' Zeke. But I didn't know how.

When Zeke seen Mr. Kennedy, he run into that hole in the ground. Timbers wasn't sturdy, I guess. And his screamin' didn't help none. The dust come pourin' out of that cave like smoke. Mr. Kennedy laughed, and we just rode out of those hills.

A few nights later, me and Mr. Kennedy got to talkin', and it was then that I figured maybe Clay Allison was right. Maybe it was time to bury Mr. Kennedy proper. Mr. Kennedy, he said, yep, it was time. He'd done just about all he had to do. So we come up here, back to E-Town after all those years.

This is the damnedest thing, though. All these

years I spent diggin' up bodies for Professor Sawyer, and you damn-fool sons of bitches plan to hang me for buryin' a body. Buryin' Mr. Kennedy. My pard.

That's my story. What's it a man's supposed to say? Amen.

Well—

Get your filthy hands off me! I ain't done talkin'. Get that rope off. You stupid Mexican sons of bitches! Stop laughin' at me. Why . . .

Oh, hell, it ain't you greasers laughin'. It's Mr. Kennedy. Shut up. I tell you, shut up. I thought we was pards! You're dead, like this damned town. You ain't nothin' but a bunch of bones.

You . . .

God. I can't believe it. All these years, all those dreams, all that time seein' those pine trees swayin' in the wind and wonderin' where they could be and what it all meant. And now I see 'em.

See 'em I do. See 'em clear. And hear Mr. Kennedy, my double-crossin' pard, hear him laughin'.

Gunfight at Los Muretos

Bill Brooks

Ten years in prison breaks a man.

It broke him.

Youthful indiscretions had landed him with the wrong bunch. Now he was a free man again—had a new wife and three kids. Had found the Lord and Jesus and preached off a stump for a full year, winter, summer, wind, rain, and snow. Folks started coming round listening to him preach. Fire and brimstone, the wages of sin, Glory Hallelujah.

She was a good woman, Anne Pryce. Her kids were good too. Treated them like his own and he loved them greatly.

The community got together and built him a small church. Put up the frame in one day. Started on a Wednesday and the whole thing was up and ready for a full-out sermon by that Sunday.

He could smell the fresh pine sap warmed by the sun. Looked out at the faces upturned and thought: *What'd I do to deserve all this?*

He worked hard trying to raise enough vegetables to feed them all—a hog to be butchered in the early winter. Between these and scant donations they got by. Preaching wasn't fast money, it wasn't even slow money. You didn't have to take money from people—whatever came, they readily gave. And if they didn't give money, sometimes they gave a chicken or vegetables and once a shoat hog. It was a different life than the one he'd led and he liked it better this way than the old way. Getting by on little and have around you those who loved you, those you could trust was a sight better than having a lot and not being able to trust anybody, worried about getting shot in the back by a man who called himself "friend."

That's all he needed, was to stand it, figuring it would sooner or later come to better times financially if he could just hang on long enough, get through enough winters. Anne took in laundry, the kids helped best they could. Three years as a free man came and went. He thought sure he'd die old in his bed now he got beyond the early years of wildness and settled down. Thought maybe he'd die in the rocking chair reading the Good Book, Anne there by his side, the kids, singing him to his heavenly home with sweet hymns.

He thanked God for his good fortune of finding her and them, for finding the path of the straight and narrow life. This new life helped him forget about those long lonely days looking through iron bars at freedom.

They'd broke him good.

Then the third winter came and brought sickness with it. The littlest girl was the first taken. Little Alice they all called her; little and sweet she was too.

He led the prayer over her grave, felt soul's grief sliding down his cheeks. Her little face like a doll's wearing a tatted bonnet. In less than a month the same sickness took the two boys—Ike and Jack—and it seemed like to him he'd suddenly and somehow been handed the life of Job.

"Please, no more," he prayed aloud, down on his knees in that small church they'd built him. Folks stopped coming around, afraid the sickness was still there in the walls, the floor, and all around. Feared God had for some reason saw fit to curse the place, the man, his family, even though they couldn't name a reason why He should. He couldn't blame them for not coming, for being afraid. They were folks who believed in unseen powers, and left all reasoning to God. He was having trouble holding on to his own belief, for what God would ring down such hardship? He told himself and her, they'd be no different if the shoe was on the other foot.

"You're wrong," she said.

It came down to just him and her, and still she believed in him, but he knew she was all wrung out with sorrow. Every day he had to look into those sad, hollow eyes and try and lift up her spirits when he could barely lift up his own.

"I ain't strong as you might think," he said to God.

She got so she wouldn't eat and went about calling the names of her dead children as she stalked the night, the empty rooms. Word got around she'd lost her mind and it scared folks even more. They stopped coming to the house, as well as the church. They stopped bringing by pies and chickens and a little something from the garden. Superstition is a powerful thing that spreads like its own sort of disease and sickness and infects everyone.

"All those years I was locked up," he said to the

God he could neither see, nor who spoke back to him, "it's as if that wasn't enough punishment for the wrong things I done. Why this? Why them kids, those innocents? And why her, now, after all she's already suffered? Better me than them. Kill me, crush me, break me upon your wheel and let her be. Have them put me back in prison. Anything but doing it this a way."

But the God he sought remained silent in the silent heavens. The winter bore on long and harsh as he'd ever seen a winter. Its weight of snow was like a white mountain. Its sharp winds were like knives. Its cold was like iron you couldn't break.

He found her on just such a brittle cold morning. She had tied the bucket rope they used to lower into the well around her neck. She must have tied it sitting on the rock edge then slid off into the black hole. He went out looking for her and the taut rope drew his eye first—a pair of small shoes empty in the snow beside the well.

Prison had broken him but this broke him worse than prison ever could.

He did not know if he could survive after finding her like he did. He hauled her small, frail body up from the well. He carried her into the house blinded by his own tears. He no longer had any purpose he could see. And, as if all that weren't enough, someone came in the night and burned the church to the ground after word got out Anne had killed herself in that terrible way. He figured rightly enough that those who had built it felt it their rightful duty to destroy it, and thereby destroy whatever curse had befallen the place and the man who stood in its pulpit—the man who had now lost his entire family through unexplainable tragedy. Surely there must be some reason behind all the terribleness!

He'd awakened in the night to a dream of flames that seemed like hell had surrounded him, saw the fiery yellow tongues licking at the black night. He heard the window glass shatter, heard the crack of timber, its sap popping. He saw first the roof cave in, then frame walls collapse in on themselves as the church came tumbling down. He did not bother to get out of bed.

In the morning, he walked among the charred and blackened dreck poking through a fresh snow. Strangely enough he found his Bible, the pages curled and brittle so that when he picked it up the words of God sifted through his fingers like tiny dead black birds.

"That's it," he said to no one. "It's finished." And immediately felt crucified but not redeemed.

Took a trip to town and bought all the whiskey he could afford and drove back again to the small clapboard house, wondering if they'd take it in their head to burn it down too, maybe with him in it. The cold wind reddened his face and chafed his hands while the whiskey fortified his innards and stole his senses. He wandered drunkenly among the unmarked graves of his wife and children—the sunken places sagging with snow—and sat cross-legged and talked to them.

He figured just to lie there next to them and drink himself to death. He had heard that death by freezing wasn't such a bad way to go. Heard it was just like going to sleep.

U.S. Marshal Tolvert found him before he had a

chance to fully expire and put him into the back of his spring wagon, then wrapped heavy wool blankets around him and took him into town thinking he could well have hauled in a corpse by the time he got there. He had hauled in plenty of other corpses and this would just be one more.

The town's physician did not believe in such things as spirits or vengeful gods or curses, but believed in science and medicine and with these revived Wes Bell to working order by means of hot compresses, rubbing his limbs with pure wood alcohol and submerging him in a copper tub of brutal hot water and Epsom salts.

"It's a wonder you didn't lose your parts," the marshal said afterward. "I've seen men with their fingers and toes froze off. Even saw one feller had his nose froze off and another with both ears turned black."

"You've wasted your time saving me," he said. "I don't appreciate your interference."

"Duly noted," the marshal said. "But you wouldn't be the first I hauled in half dead, nor the first I hauled in fully so. As an official of the law it is my duty to save those I can and kill those that need killing."

The next day the marshal came again, dressed in his big bear coat and sugarloaf hat and said, "Well, since you ain't going to die this time around, how'd you like to do a decent deed and make some money doing it?"

"I don't give a damn about money or doing any more decent deeds," he said.

The marshal winced at such talk.

"I thought you was a preacher."

"I was a lot of things I ain't no more."

The marshal had eyes as colorless as creek water that danced under shaggy red brows that matched his shaggy red moustaches. "From what I understand you are a man who has fallen on hard times. Now tell me this, what does a man who has fallen on such hard times and without a pot to piss in or a window to throw it out of plan on doing next?"

"I'll tell you what such a man plans: he plans to join his wife and children."

"Well, sooner or later you will get your wish—that is a natural fact. But for now, maybe you'd be interested in a little job I'm offering."

"You must spend all your time in opium dens."

This brought a chuckle from the marshal.

"I'm an excellent reader of a man's character," he said. "I've had to deal with woebegone folks and fools and killers all my professional life—I'd judge you to be somewhere in the middle of that bunch.

"I don't believe you want to die while still an able-bodied man with plenty of good years ahead of you yet. Why, you can't be more than forty. Look here, I'm proposing to offer you a fresh start. Who can say what awaits us, or why God intends us to be here on this earth—what our purpose is?"

"Believe what you want, lawman. But me personal, I'm done believing. I'm quitting the game."

The marshal slipped a fine Colt Peacemaker with stag horn grips from his holster and handed it over butt first.

"She's loaded," he said. "If you aim to finish yourself, might as well do it right this time. But before you pull the trigger let me stand back out of the way because I don't feature having your blood and brains splattered all over this nice coat of mine."

And the marshal stood away from the sickbed there in the physician's fine old house with its gingerbread scroll work and tall windows and fancy shake roof and flocked wallpaper.

Wes took the revolver and remembered in an instant when such a thing in his hand was as familiar to him as breathing. But it wasn't nothing he wanted to be reminded of now, nothing he wanted to take up again.

He thumbed back the hammer.

"Before you pull that trigger," the marshal said, "I understand your people rest in unmarked graves."

Such talk pinched his nerves.

"Wind and time will rub out any trace of those poor folks—your wife and children. Is that what you want, for them to be forgotten—yourself along with them?"

He turned the cocked gun instead at the man who had offered it to him.

"It don't matter about me," he said.

"Shooting me won't solve any of your problems," the marshal said. "It'll just make them worse. Let me tell you, hanging is about the worst way a man can die. Bullet's much easier and quicker and a lot more honorable, case you place any stock in honor."

He lowered the hammer on the pistol and set it on the bed.

"I'd pay you good money," the marshal said. "Enough to buy your family some nice headstones. There is a fellow in St. Louis—an Italian—who carves the best headstones you ever laid eyes on.

Carves them out of marble comes all the way from
Italy, and gets a handsome price, but you could
easily afford it on what I'd pay you. Think how nice
that'd be—headstones for your wife and children.
Why a hundred years from now people would be
able to see who they were and where they rest,
maybe put flowers on their graves out of sheer kind-
ness 'cause that's the way some people are. They
aren't all like you and me, Wes."

"You've got a hell of a gift of gab," Wes said.

"Don't I, though?"

"How much money?"

"Let's say two hundred dollars, cash."

"What do I have to do for this cash money?"

"Kill a no good son of a bitch who needs killing."

"What makes you think . . . ?"

The marshal lit a cigar he'd taken from the
pocket of his waistcoat, blew a stream of blue smoke
toward the plaster ceiling, noted the fine wood furniture that adorned the room. *French,* he thought.

"I know all about you, Wes Bell. I know more
about you than your Ma."

"You don't know nothing about me."

"No sir, you're wrong. It's my job to know about
people—and what I don't know, I find out and I
found out everything about you. I know before you
took up preaching you was in Leavenworth prison.
I know how bad you was. And that is why I've come
now, to ask you this thing, because I know you got
the grit to get it done."

"Killing for money ain't part of me."

"You've killed plenty for free before the law
caught you and put you in the jug. Now tell me if
I'm wrong."

"That was a long time ago and I never killed nobody who didn't deserve it or wasn't trying to kill me first."

"Hell, me too. But you haven't forgot how to pull a trigger on a man have you? It's like riding a bicycle."

"No, I haven't forgot how."

"Let me just go ahead and tell you about this fellow," the marshal said, retaking his seat by the bed and taking up his hogleg again and putting it back in his holster. "He's a scourge, worse'n the plague. Everywhere he goes he leaves a bloody trail behind: dead folks, raped folks, hurt folks. He ain't never done a good thing in his life. At least you seen the light, Wes. You got broke down and turned your life around 'cause that's what a normal human would do at some point when he saw the errors of his ways. But not this fellow. This fellow is as bad a seed as ever was planted in the devil's garden and he needs weeding out."

"It makes no sense you asking me to do it. You're the law, why don't you do it, if he's so bad?"

"Oh, believe me, I'd do it in heartbeat, wouldn't think twice about doing it. Hell, I'd hang him and then shoot him and then burn his body just to make sure no man woman or child ever had to cross his path again. But I can't do it, Wes."

"Why can't you?"

"'Cause I'm a dead man myself. Got cancer of the ass. Eating me up bad and there's no way of knowing I'd find him before the grim reaper finds me."

The marshal smoked casual as though waiting for his steak to come.

"There is one other thing about this fellow, Wes,

one more reason I come to find you and no other for this job."

He waited to hear what the marshal's reason was.

"He's your brother, Wes. This no good son of a bitch is your kid brother, James, and if there's anybody knows his ways and where he'd go to ground when he's being chased it would be you, Wes."

"James?"

"None other."

James was only nine years old when Wes got sent to the pen. And while behind those bars, his ma took James to somewhere in New Mexico, he'd heard, and married a miner and all contact between them was lost.

"I haven't seen him since he was a kid," he said to the marshal.

"Yes, that's probably true, but kin is kin and blood is blood and I do believe of all the men in this world you are the one who could find this little murderer and put him down. Do you want to know what all crimes he's committed? Should I tell you about the raping of women and young girls, how he slashed their throats afterward? Should I tell you about how he murdered an old man and his grandson who weren't doing anything but fishing and he shot them in the back of their heads merely for what was in their lunch pails? Shall I tell you how he burned down a house with a man and his family still in it because they were colored? Shall I tell you such tales, Wes, or will the money be enough?"

"Oh, you give a long and windy speech, marshal . . ."

"Yes, I do, Wes. Yes, I, by God, do."

"Even if I agreed to do it I wouldn't know where

to begin and would not know if and when the time came I could do it—not my own blood, my own flesh. Could you do it?"

"Yes, by God, I could and I would."

"Still . . ."

"I know all about blood being thicker than water—but its blood he's spilling more than water and the blood stains you as it does all your people who ever carried or will carry the Bell name and only blood kin can make it right in the eyes of the innocent. Only *you* can set things right with James, Wes Bell."

The marshal blew a ring of smoke toward the ceiling and watched as it became shapeless before dissolving altogether. Then he leveled his gaze at Wes.

"You see, I have studied you like a schoolboy studies his books and I know everything about you and everything about that little killing son of a bitch brother of yours, James. Ironic ain't it, in a way, you're preaching the gospel and him named James, which was Jesus' brother's name. You ain't Jesus, are you, Wes? You ain't the second coming, are you?"

"To hell with you."

"To hell with us all if that boy keeps up his killing and rampaging. To hell with every last man, woman, and child he comes across in this old world unless you stop him."

Then the marshal reached into the side pocket of his bear coat and pulled out a triple-framed tintype of a woman holding an infant and two other children—a boy in each of the attached frames.

Anne and her youngsters—and pressed it into Wes's hand.

"To hell with them too," he said, "for the sickness that took them is no less than the sickness that sets in that wild boy's mind, Wes. No different. Dead is dead no matter how you come to be that way. But what is different is whether or not you just drew a bad hand in life's game or some no good son of a bitch come along and took life without the right to do so. How'd you feel if it was James killed your wife and those kids instead of them dying of sickness?"

Then the marshal stood and adjusted the weight of his heavy coat and settled the sugarloaf on his head.

"I'll come round tomorrow for your answer, Wes. And the two-hundred dollars if you so decide."

"Five-hundred," Wes said. "Gold double-eagles, no script, and the name and address of that stone carver in St. Louis."

"Well now, Wes, you sure you wouldn't like to make it thirty pieces of silver . . ."

And so it was that the very next morning the marshal came again and stacked five gold double eagles on the bedside table and a piece of paper with the St. Louis stone carver's name and address written on it.

"Down payment," the marshal said. "The rest is waiting for you at the bank upon your return and proof the deed is done. Now raise your right hand so I can swear you in official with Doc Kinney here as eyewitness."

Doc Kinney looked on at the abbreviated ceremony.

Then the marshal placed a small badge stamped out of brass next to the double eagles and said, "Get her done, son. Sooner rather than later. I'd like to still be breathing when I read the good news."

"What makes you think I won't just take the money and run?"

"Because," the marshal said, with an air of confidence, "you know what the inside of that state prison looks like and I venture to guess it ain't worth no two hundred dollars to go back. I hired you and I can hire others to track you down and for a lot less money. Sweet dreams, bucko."

Fifteen days had passed since he struck his bargain with the marshal.

He began the trail where the marshal said the last crime had been committed—a place called Pilgrim's Crossing, a small Mormon community in the high country of Utah. Saw the woman's grave and asked her husband to describe the man who had raped and killed her. The man described had a mark on his cheek like a red star. James had been born with it—the one single thing he could recall about the kid before they hauled him off to prison: the red star birthmark.

The man had pointed to some distant mountains when asked which way the killer went.

"I just come in from working in the silver mines when I saw a man on a paint horse riding fast away toward them mountains then found Lottie tore up and dead."

The man was dressed in dark clothing, looked

like a crow, soft gray eyes that spoke of nothing at all.

"What lays that way?" he asked the man.

"Los Muretos is all I know," the man said.

"How come you didn't follow?"

The man gave a slight shrug.

"I have other wives to care for," the man said. There were four small houses on the land each with a bonneted woman staring from the doorways.

"Well then, I suppose you are one lucky son of a bitch you got spare wives to concern yourself with. Most men just have one and some don't have any." He felt disgust and turned his horse toward the north road.

Another day's ride and he met a man pulling a handcart.

"How far to Los Muretos?" he said.

The man was large as an ox himself and needed to be. The cart was burdened with a full load of watermelons.

"Five or ten miles," the man said, thumbing back over his shoulder.

"You come from there?" he asked.

The man nodded. A blue scarf kept his straw hat tied down against the cold air.

"Three days ago."

"Any chance you come across a man with a red star on the side of his face?"

The man shook his head.

He rode on and the man took up his load again—each man seeing to his duty.

Two more days of riding brought him to the top of a rocky backbone of a ridge where he looked down upon the town. In the long distance, a line of saw-toothed snow-covered mountains shimmered under a cold dying sun.

A song of wind sang along the ridge and fluttered through his clothes and ruffled the mane of his horse. It chilled his blood, or something did.

He glassed the town below him with a pair of brass Army field glasses. Then he swept them along the brown slash of road that ran uneven west and east. He saw nary a solitary thing moving along the road.

Nothing moved in the town either, but it was still some distance off and maybe too far to see human activity. He was sure from the campfire he'd found that morning he had closed the gap between him and his kid brother—embers still sighed in the ashes.

"We'll wait," he said to the horse. There was nothing for the horse to graze on among the rocks. "When the sun is down good and proper, we'll ride down there and find James."

He squatted on his heels and waited for the sun to sink below the mountains, thinking of his lost family as he did, the real reason he was doing this thing, and when the sky turned dark as gunmetal and night came on like a cautious wolf, he tightened the saddle cinch and mounted the horse and began his descent into the town he figured had to be Los Muretos.

With darkness he saw the town's lights wink on. A hunter's moon rose off to the east casting the landscape in a vaporous light. He and the horse traversed the slope and came to the very edge of the town's first buildings.

He went on.

The street was empty but he could see shadows moving behind the lighted windows. And farther up the street he heard the sound of a piano being played roughly. He followed the sound to its source—a solitary saloon, false-fronted, in the center of town.

He tied off and stepped cautiously through the doors.

Rough-looking men were bellied up to the long oak bar, the soles of their worn boots resting on the tarnished brass rail. They drank and laughed and swore. A cloud of blue smoke hung over their sweat-stained Stetsons, the smoke so thick it turned the men into shadows of men.

The interior of the saloon was narrow and dim—like the inside of a cave—and there was a feeling about the place that did not set well with him: a feeling of trouble and danger and worse.

The saloon girls were dressed in dark crimson gowns and looked like wilted roses lost in their seeking the sun as they moved wraithlike among the men.

Along the wall opposite the long bar men played cards at tables, their backs to him, their faces shaded by the brims of their hats.

He stepped inside quick, shutting the door keeping out the wind. Nobody bothered to look up. His right hand rested inside his mackinaw on the butt of his revolver.

He'd had plenty of time to think about what it would be like to shoot his own brother. Told himself he wouldn't feel anything because he never knew the boy that well, and if he was as snake mean as the marshal had claimed, well, then it was simply an act that if he didn't do, someone else would. Blood and kin had nothing to do with it he told himself. Justice had nothing to do with it. Italian marble headstones is what it had to do with.

His gaze took in the men along the bar and he did not see anyone he recognized as being James, a man with a red star birthmark on his face. Even without the red star birthmark he figured he would know James in spite of the long passage of time. Like a mother cow knows its calf, a brother knows his brother.

Then his gaze shifted to the card players and not one of them felt familiar to him either.

He moved farther into the saloon, pushing his way through the crowd, fingers curled around the gun-butt riding his left hip.

He wanted to see who was there in the back.

A sloe-eyed woman neither young nor pretty pressed suddenly against him. She had the cloying scent of dead flowers, and awful teeth when she opened her mouth. He tried not to look at her directly for fear of what he might see.

"How's about buying a gal a drink, cowboy?" she said, and before he could stop her, her hand snaked between his legs. "A drink will get a free toss with me."

He looked down then, but her own eyes were averted to where her hand now rested. "Well, how about it?" she said through the din.

He'd consorted with many such women in his younger days and taken pleasure from them. He had drank with them and fornicated with them. He was as wild and wooly and reckless as a Texas cowboy. This woman's presence reminded him of every such woman he had sinned with and he didn't have any favor for her, or any other woman since Anne.

He took two bits and set it on the wood and said, "There's your drink, Miss, but the rest don't interest me." He pushed on through the crowd toward the back where he saw a wheel of chance and a faro table with men bucking the tiger. But none of them at either station had a red star birthmark on his face.

There was a low flat stage against the back wall and to the left of it a set of stairs leading up to the upper level where several private boxes ran the length of the saloon. These were the places the saloon gals took men and fleeced them like sheep—fleeced them of their money and their pride and still left them wanting more.

His every sense told him James was in this place, in one of those boxes.

He took the stairs and looked down upon the crowd below, the miasma of writhing human desperation it seemed to him, and was just as glad to have left it down there. To see them from this vantage point caused his belly to clench, his flesh to sweat, his muscles to knot. He could not imagine himself like those below ever again.

An odd thing happened just then as he was looking down: a face of one of the men at the bar looked up, and it could have been his twin. Then the man looked away again, down at his drink there on the hardwood. Wes was sure it was all his imagination.

He eased down the narrow hall to the first private box and drew back the curtain enough to peer inside. A pudgy man stood with his trousers down around his ankles facing a woman sitting on the side of a narrow cot doing what such women do.

Wes let the curtain fall back and he moved on to the next box. This time he saw a young soldier sitting talking to his gal, both of them facing away—just sitting there on the small bed holding hands the way lonely people do.

He eased down to the next box and the next, finding three in a row empty.

Then there was just one curtain left to draw and he moved to it, the pistol in his hand, cocked and ready. Oddly, he felt calm. His heart rhythm was slow and steady as an old Regulator wall clock. He nearly always felt the same way as a young buck when trouble presented itself. He didn't know what it was or why the calm had descended on him, it just had.

And when he eased the curtain back with the barrel of his pistol, he saw the man he'd been looking for. James with the red star birthmark sat in the bed, his eyes shut. A slattern with black hair lay against his chest, his hand stroking her head as one might a cat.

It would be easy enough just to push his way into the room and empty every round and be done with it. But he'd have to kill the woman to do it. He didn't ride all this way to kill a woman.

Looking upon that rosette-marked face he saw a single scene from their past, when James was just a small kid running around in a hardscrabble yard chasing chickens, flinging rocks at them. Even then the boy had a cruel streak in him. The old man whipped James with his strap, trying to beat the meanness out of him, but it could be he'd just beaten more meanness into the boy than out. And maybe the old man knew the family secret, that James wasn't of his own seed, but the seed of another man and that's why he beat him so terrible.

There on the bed's post hung a gun rig within easy reach. A holster with a fine ivory-handled Colt. It was the sort of gun a man used to gunfighting might own. Not your typical twelve-dollar single action bought in some hardware store to let rust on your hip.

And in spite of everything, he suddenly felt a strange connection to the boy, but not one that could be described exactly as brotherly love—more a simple indebtedness of same bloodlines.

James suddenly shifted his weight and the woman fell away from him, exposing the stain of blood on James's hairless white chest. Wes could see now the gaping wound of her exposed neck, the straight razor lying open and bloody on the floor next to the bed.

He drew back the curtain fully now and stepped quickly into the room aiming the revolver right where the woman's head had rested. James's eyes fluttered open.

"Wes," he said as casually as if they'd just seen each other yesterday, that there'd never been any separation between them. "I figured you'd be along some day, and now here you are."

"And now I'm here," he said.

"They sent you, didn't they? Them who want me dead?" James looked at the still form of the woman beside him.

"Her name is Chloe," he said. "She was real nice

to me for a time. Then she got like the others—like Ma used to get. You don't remember none of that, I bet. You was up in the prison doing your time whilst I was at home doing mine with Ma once the old man passed and she went in search of another. Gambling man he was . . . and a pimp to boot. Made sure we earned our keep, Ma and me." A smile drew the boy's lips up at the edges. "He was the first son of a bitch I ever killed."

So there it was, some of the reason at least, if James could be believed, and maybe he could and maybe he couldn't.

"Call me sinner, Wes, call you the saint. Heard you went to preaching and married yourself a fine woman. How's that working out for you, Wes?"

"Never said I was nothing but what I am, but I never killed a woman or anyone else that was innocent."

"Innocent! Ha, ain't none of us innocent, Wes. You think *she* was? You think any son of a bitch in this place is?"

"I only came just for you, James."

"Then you're a fool, Wes."

"Maybe so. I guess time will tell."

"I guess maybe it will."

"I'll give you a chance to defend yourself," Wes said. "We're kin of some sort according to the heavens, otherwise I'd already have shot you."

"Jesus Christ, Wes, but that's awfully white of you."

"You can defend yourself or not, either way, I'm going to pull this trigger."

"Hell, Wes, you're wasting your sweet time, boy. We're already dead, men like you and me, been dead since we first drew breath. Same God that made you, made me. Go on and pull your trigger, Wes. I'm ready to go. Question is, are you?"

"I wouldn't be here if I wasn't," Wes said.

James was snake quick, just like Wes thought he would be.

Both men fired at once. Witnesses said it sound like a single gunshot, but they were wrong.

At last he felt a great peace, for the first time since he'd fallen in love with Anne and his days of winter became days of summer. He saw James buck on the bed, then his hand empty of the smoking gun, and close his eyes as if falling asleep, a bright ribbon of blood flowing from his heart.

Good-bye, James.

Wes found himself ankle deep in new snow play-ing with Anne and the kids, throwing snowballs, laughing. Her smiling face made him happy. Then she faded into mist—all of them.

He opened his eyes and found himself standing on a rocky windswept ridge glassing the town below and the road that cut through it and saw not a soli-tary thing moving. Somewhere down there in that place they named Los Muretos was the man he was looking for—his kid brother.

He waited until dark, then rode his horse down the slope in the moonlight and entered the town from the east and and went on up the street to the only establishment open—a saloon with the words LAST STOP—painted on a hanging sign out front that the wind blew back and forth, the two small chains holding it creaking with rust.

He tied off and went in and worked his way through the smoky crowd until he saw the stairs, the private boxes on the upper level. A woman in a bloodred dress cut him off and asked if he wanted to buy her. He swept her aside with a hard look and went up the wood steps leading to the upper boxes.

He tried each chamber until he came to the last and found James marked by the red star cheek and a dead woman. And for a moment it was uncertain as to what he would do and what James would do, but now that they had faced the storm, there was nothing to be done. James's pistol was in his hand just that quick, a wicked grin like the devil's own followed in a split second by a resounding blast of gunfire.

And in the white storm that followed he opened his eyes and found himself again standing on the same windswept spine of rock overlooking the ramshackle town below, the shimmering mountains beyond, the dying sun in a glazed sky off to the west.

He had a deep and abiding sense he had been here before, that he had ridden in the moonlight down the slope of loose rock and entered the town and found James, but how was that even possible?

He thought he heard Anne's voice calling him and looked around but no one was there. And when he looked back down toward the town again, he saw a lone man riding a white horse ascending the ridge.

The rider came on steady, the hooves of his mount clattering on the stones until at last the rider and his horse topped the ridge and rode along it to where Wes stood. The rider dismounted. He had a red star cheek.

"You might as well give in to it, Wes," James said.

"Give in to what?"

"To the fact you're dead."

"I'm not dead."

"Yes, you are dead and so am I. We killed each other that night in the Last Stop—don't you remember?"

"No, I don't remember nothing except I shot you."

"And I shot you," James said rolling himself a shuck and lighting it with a match pulled from his waistcoat pocket, the wind snuffing out the flame almost as quickly, carrying away the first exhalation of smoke.

"I was goddamn fast, but you weren't too slow."

He saw it then, James, quick as a snake strike, jerking his pistol free of the hanging holster, felt faintly the bullet's punch even as James bucked back on the bed, eyes rolled up white in his head.

"It ain't as bad as you'd a thought," James said "Is it?"

Wes turned round and round looking in all directions at the world spread out—the sky, the mountains, the town. He felt like if he'd had wings he could fly.

"We're still down there," James said pointing to Los Muretos. "We're down there with all the others who died there in those glory years when the mines were still giving up their silver. We're still down there with the whores and the gamblers, the merchants and the pimps who came for the easy money. Some were lucky and left when the silver ran out, but you and me and some of the others weren't so lucky, Wes. We came and never left."

The wind sang over the ridge like angel voices.

"Come on, Wes, let's go back down—they are waiting for us—Chloe, the one you found me with that night, and that whore who wanted you to buy her a drink and you wouldn't—she killed herself that same night, Wes. When a whore can't sell herself for the price of a drink, she's got nothing left.

"Me, it was my time to go. Sooner or later, some law dog or bounty hunter would have run me to ground if you hadn't. In that way, I'm glad it was you, Wes, and not some stranger. I'm sorry I killed you. You were always the better of us two. You didn't give me no choice. I guess it was meant to be like everything is—like brother slaying brother, Cain and Abel. It's in us to kill when we feel we have to. We're a lonesome bunch to be sure . . ."

"No," Wes said. "I was hoping you would. I let you do it because I didn't have nothing more to go home to. I just wanted to go home to them is all."

"There's nothing for any of us to go home to, Wes. Yonder is your home. Down there in Los Muretos. It's home, not some other. No heaven and no hell—just the place we died in—where our corpses rot and our bones turn to dust again, and our spirits are once more free. That's what going home is, Wes."

Along the road something raised up the dust.

"What is that?" Wes said.

"Automobile, Wes—it's what they ride these days, the curiosity seekers, the historians, the tourists.

They want to see how we once lived, to see a town that is as dead as us. A ghost town. What better place than Los Muretos where we got ghosts aplenty? They come because they read about the gunfight, about how two brothers killed each other in a whorehouse—over a woman or over gold—the story keeps changing with time and every telling. They tell how one was a good Christian man and the other was an outlaw. And they like to believe we're still there, in the town, raising a little hell, scaring the kids, the hucksters selling us like boiled peanuts and ice cream, putting our photographs on picture postcards.

"They even stage the gunfight—paid actors— men with bellies hanging over their belts—only they do it out in the street and not inside in that little whorebox where it happened. They bring folks in on buses just to see you and me kill each other again—three shows a day except on holidays.

"They must have written a hundred stories about that night and that town. And we'll be here always—as long as the sun rises and sets over the mountains. We'll be here long as it rains and the snows fall and the oceans curl against the shore.

"We are legend, Wes. They'll never let us die or rest in peace. We'll live forever as punishment for our sin.

"You and me.

"Come on down, Wes. Ride with me for a little while."

Iron Mountain

Candy Moulton

The darn fool boy never should have been on his Pa's bay that morning, nor wearing his slicker, even though misty rain dripped from a slate sky. I told LeFors it was the best shot I ever made and the dirtiest trick I ever done. But that wasn't the way of it. Not at all.

I sat my own bay in the rocks above the rough-hewn homestead, saw the boy's peach-fuzz face although he kept it dipped low so the rain flowed off his hat to puddle at his feet instead of down his neck. It was clear the work I had to do wouldn't get done this day, and so I'd reined around and leaned into a ground-eating trot headed north.

Didn't take long for word to get around about the killing. It would have spread quickly no matter who lay in the dirt. But this tale burst forth like a wildfire because Willie had been the one found faceup, stone-cold by the gate. Most everybody at Iron Mountain knew immediately the bullet that got the boy had been intended for his Pa. Kels was burly and mean, had a sharp temper, and fast hands with a knife or his fists. His Irish wife handled their pack of kids as effortlessly as he landed an uppercut to the chin of a rival. I never paid much mind to the younger children, but that Katie, now she had caught my attention months before, and since I'm a truthful man, I'll tell you she was an eyeful and the reason I liked to hunker down in the rocks and brush above their cabin.

She'd come out in the morning carrying a milk pail, making her way to the four-stall barn. Sometimes I'd creep close enough that I could hear the squirt of warm milk against the tin pail, hear her hum to the old cow and talk to the cats. Certain days, Mondays I'm sure because I pay attention to such details, she'd roll up the sleeves of her blue dress—she only seemed to have one dress—and do the wash. The brown ringlets she'd piled up on her head would look ever so tidy when she started, but after scrubbing shirts and wool pants, socks and undergarments, they'd start tumbling and flying like spiderwebs, sticking to the back of her damp neck, lying across her honey-colored cheek. After scrubbing and scouring, rinsing and wringing, she'd put the wet garments in a heavy wicker basket, then haul it over to a rope line strung between two trees that shaded the west side of the house. One by one, she shook out the dripping clothes, draped them over the line, forcing wooden pins in place to hold them in the wind that always seemed to flow through the canyon.

Katie's sister, Ida, and her mother seldom helped with the washing, never with the milking. But I saw them gathering the eggs, butchering chickens, working in the garden, wrangling the youngsters. And staying out of Kels's way. He had built a solid house of stout logs, showing some real craftsmanship by notching the corners into a double dove. And he'd added the barn, some corrals, a privy far enough from the house to be private, and, more important, downwind. There was a root cellar and a shed where I'd heard him and Willie pounding iron and seen the black smoke pour out when the forge got hot.

I knew right off when I saw the place they were at Iron Mountain to stay and to be truthful again, that was fine with me, especially if Katie might somehow come into my personal picture.

Course I was quite a bit older than she and I'd been around some. Had scouted with and packed mules for General Crook down Arizona way, helped rout old Geronimo out of the hills and sent him off to the swamps in Florida. I darned well knew how to tie a good knot, and it always irritated me to see Kels take a load in to Cheyenne City. He'd pitch a butchered hog or some sacks of potatoes into his wagon not caring whether they stacked neatly or not. Then he'd bark at Willie to cover it with some osnaburg before pitching ropes over the top and tying them down in a set of knots that weren't no better than what I tied when I was barely six.

The first chance I had to see Miss Katie up real close was at Iron Mountain School. It was near Christmas and as always happened, the townsfolk at Iron Mountain gathered for a pageant put on by the children. In fact, that was the first time I saw Glendolene Kimmell too. She'd moved up to Iron Mountain in the fall and began instructing the children in reading and writing and arithmetic. She had pinned her black hair back into a neat bun at the base of her neck, and that pulled her face tight over her high cheekbones and accented her dark, almond-shaped eyes, making her look exotic. She intrigued me right off because I could tell she was no homesteader's daughter. She wore a dress that stretched tightly across her bodice and drew in at the waist. Now I suppose a man shouldn't notice things like that, but let me tell you, she wore it in such a way that it was obvious she wanted a man to notice things like that.

After putting the students through their drills, she had us push back the desks, Otto got out his fiddle, and the fun began as we all danced until dawn. When I think back on it, I realize that was the only time I ever saw the Nickells and the Millers in the same room, hell, the first time I saw them in the same town, where they was getting along and not fighting. Course now that I think on it, I realize that's because at Christmas Kels was raising kids and pigs, cattle and horses.

Iron Mountain life started going haywire in the spring. Kels trailed some of his horses to Cheyenne City and came home with range maggots. He was just too belligerent, and I'd have to say ignorant, to realize that bringing sheep into cattle country was going to cost him more than the value of some horses.

Jim Miller struck the first blow, killing several of the sheep when they strayed onto his range. Kels hammered back, taking down more than a mile of fence between the two places. Then the Miller and Nickell boys got into it, throwing insults and taunts in the schoolroom, and following with their fists during lunch break. Miss Glendolene Kimmell had more than attracted my attention at the Christmas event, and so I rode over by the school pretty regular to check on her, make sure the boys weren't causing too many problems, occasionally stealing a kiss when we thought nobody was looking, especially Katie. For I sure didn't want her to think I had any regular gal.

I wasn't the only man around those parts visiting the schoolteacher. More than once I'd meet someone else leaving the schoolroom as I arrived, making me wonder how she kept her beaus apart. Even though I wasn't interested in any long term alliance with Miss Kimmell, I do think I led her affections. Most of the others were cowboys who'd never been far from Iron Mountain. Having been to other places in the West, I could talk geography with her. I could tell her about the big saguaro of Arizona Territory and the rocky crags of Colorado. I could talk with her about the Apaches and scouting for a military expedition.

As I turned my horse away from Iron Mountain one spring day, I knew I'd have some more geography to discuss before long. I'd been asked by my employers to ride down to Brown's Park and deal with a couple fellas who'd been throwing long loops and using a running iron.

In my line of work, you can't move too quickly, or too carefully, so I was away from Iron Mountain several weeks. It took me that long to locate Matt Rash and Isom Dart, monitor their cow work, finally get a bead, and take care of the problem. This was a particularly difficult situation because Rash and Dart were seldom alone. They worked the cattle with other riders and had people in and out of their two-room log cabin like they were hosting a party. I'd never risk taking a shot if someone might see or hear me do so and that delayed my work, but of course, I'm a patient man so eventually my preparation met opportunity and I caught them alone. Not wanting to draw attention to myself, but knowing my employers would not pay me if I did not mark the end of the job, I carefully placed a rock beneath each of their heads as they stared with lifeless eyes at a cloud-filled sky. Then I rode north along the Little Snake and spent some time at the Dixon Club where the whiskey was smooth and the girls pretty. I did a little day work to establish myself as a fitting hand should I ever need to return to this country for a job before crossing the Sierra Madre and the Laramie Range on my return to Iron Mountain.

I considered this little community to be my home now and I certainly didn't want to do anything that would hinder my ability to move freely hereabouts. I spent the early summer riding for the Two Bar and my good friend John Coble who had backed me in more than one tight spot and paid the best wages to boot. I'd always been good with a rope and had an easy way with cattle so I helped with branding, watched Jimmy Danks try to tame a black outlaw horse he had started calling Steamboat, and rode by the Nickell homestead on occasion for a glimpse of Miss Katie. You see, I was just biding my time. I knew in another year or so, she'd be of marrying age, and I intended to be the one to set her up in her own home.

I hadn't thought of that for many years, a home; a place where a man and a woman broke bread, and broke night silence. But the more I watched Miss Katie, well, the more I was ready to settle in to a permanent situation at Iron Mountain. But a man has to ease the pressure sometimes, so I found myself more than once over at the schoolhouse where Glendolene Kimmell was always eager to share my embrace.

The tension at Iron Mountain that started with schoolboy fisticuffs had escalated while I was away in Brown's Park and then working on the Two Bar. By the Fourth of July, Jim, Victor, and Gus Miller were taking potshots at Kels and his sheep, warning him to get the maggots out of the country or else they would drive the blatting animals over a cliff and Kels with them. He didn't back down, not one inch, so the anger just continued to fester.

Like I said earlier, it was raining the morning of July 18. I'd seen Willie saddling his father's horse just after dawn, and then I kicked my own bay into a trot, his hoofbeats muffled by the drizzle. A couple hours later, the sun was driving water dogs from the timber as I lay in the rocks watching for my quarry. He moved into position and I squeezed the trigger of my thirty-thirty, hearing the ricocheting echo from a rifle fired several miles away before I felt the explosion from my own weapon. Satisfied that my shot had hit the heart, I eased up from the rocks, whistled for my horse, went to my target to finish the job.

Sometimes it's hard to know what's real and what's story. Now it is real that I headed down to Denver where I had a few drinks. I shared some stories there about the killing of fourteen-year-old Willie Nickell. When the boys didn't believe me, I trumped the cards, "Boys, it was the best shot that I ever made and the dirtiest trick I ever done." They was so impressed by my stories of chasing Geronimo, I figured one more wouldn't do no harm.

But U.S. Marshal Joe LeFors heard about my stories, found me at Harry Hynds' Saloon in Cheyenne City a few days later, and joined me for a few drinks. Soon we were upstairs in the marshal's office, a small room with a tall grimy window that allowed light in just barely. He had me sit in a chair facing the back wall of the room, angling it away from him even though he said he needed to be sure he could hear my answers clearly, and then he grilled me over and over about how I killed Willie. I just kept on a-telling him the same story about it being my best shot and dirtiest trick.

What I didn't realize is that he was taking his best shot and playing his dirtiest trick. Before I knew it, I'd been pinched for the crime because he had Deputy Les Snow and Charles Ohnhaus in the room beside his office. Their door had been rigged so they could hear and see me, though I did not know it at the time. While LeFors and I talked, Ohnhaus scratched my words onto a pad, and before I knew it, I was locked up in the city jail and told to prepare a defense.

By then I knew that there'd been further bloodshed on Iron Mountain. Kels took a bullet in the leg, another in the arm, but got help and lived. Already he was planning to leave the country, go over to the Grand Encampment, and claim new land there. He'd take Katie with him, I knew. And even if he didn't, I recognized that my chances with her had fluttered into the wind along with my stories of killing her younger brother.

I spent my days behind the iron bars braiding horsehair into a rope and planning an escape with "Driftwood" Jim McCloud. I had some accomplices on the outside—I won't name them even now after all these years—and McCloud could pick a lock slicker than a cat could slide down a greased pole. We forced our way out of our cell, tied up the jailer, grabbed a couple of thirty-thirty Winchesters, and raced out the west door of the cell block, just as deputy Snow realized there was a break. The crack of Snow's rifle quickly alerted the sheriff and the town so McCloud and I barely made it to the horses that had been left in the livery for our use by friends of mine, when we heard the mob and split. I raced into the alley and ran headlong into a posse on bicycles and an irate circus man who fired his revolver twice before cracking me over the head with it. Imagine that, I'd made my living on a horse and now here I was captured by men on two-wheelers.

At my trial two people stepped up that could have gotten me out of my predicament. Two Bar cowboy Otto Plaga had seen me the morning Willie died. At the time I was miles north of the Nickell homestead and had a freshly killed deer draped over the back of my horse. Fiddle-playing Otto told the judge all that, saying it was impossible for me to have fired the fatal shot at Willie because I could not have made such a ride between the two places in the time that had been known to elapse from when Willie left the homestead on his Pa's horse to when he was found facedown in the mud at the gate. I watched Otto's sincerity, knew he was telling the truth, as he always did, stood up, and shouted across the courtroom, "Of course I could make such a ride, I'm Tom Horn after all. Plaga is wrong about the time and wrong about my location." That was one nail in my coffin. And I put it there.

Glendolene Kimmell also came to my aid, or tried to. She wrote letters to the governor, she pleaded with the prosecutor, she took the stand, and would have said I was with her at the time Willie was killed, but looked into my eyes before such a perjury and instead admitted we weren't together, but she just *knew* I did not kill Willie. I might have stood up then and shouted to the courtroom, "Well, if not me, then who?" But chivalry kept me in my chair, my mouth closed.

You see, she and I are the only two people who know about the killing of Willie Nickell. I realized as I sat in that musty courtroom that if I told what I knew, I would not gain my freedom, but instead would be forever burdened with it. And with Miss Katie now almost certainly out of my life, I realized there would be no happy home for me, that my breed was a relic. Truthfully, I just didn't care any more.

My fate was inevitable. The rock under Willie's head was the final straw that pitched the jury to guilty. I didn't place it there, but I put it there by telling the wrong person how I marked my jobs so my employers could pay me. It didn't much matter to me. Katie was gone with her family to the copper boomtown at Grand Encampment. Glendolene left Iron Mountain, moved to California. The Millers stuck around for years, finally starved out. I swung from a new rope in Cheyenne City as C.B. and Frank Irwin sang "Life's a Railway to Heaven" and they took my bones to Boulder.

But I came home to Iron Mountain. Been here ever since. It was the best home I ever had, the place I was happiest. Now I keep an eye on the site where Willie died, occasionally roam through the rotting structure that was the Iron Mountain School and the crumbling remnants of the Nickell and Miller homesteads.

I saw the law dogs come that day a century after Willie died. They intended to solve the murder once and for all. They had heat-sensing sonar, Geiger counters, crime tape, cameras. They pulled out the transcript of my trial, forensic microscopes, and some beers. It was going to be hard, hot work solving this Wyoming crime. For days they poked and prodded in the rocks, along the road, around the gate, theorizing and speculating, accepting and rejecting details.

This is the way they set it up. Willie, riding his Pa's horse and wearing his Pa's slicker and hat, left the house to go find a hired hand who was with the sheep a couple miles from the homestead. He rode up to the gate, dismounted, started to open the gate, and from a distance of two hundred yards, I shot him with my thirty-thirty, firing three rounds, two of which struck him. Then I walked to the body, placed a rock under his head, got on my horse, and left the scene. Later I went to Denver, bragged about the killing, did the same in Cheyenne, had a fair trial, and was hanged for a deed I did commit.

Or so they said. They never took into account that it only ever took me one bullet to get my man.

Having solved the case once again, these lawmen built a big fire, threw some potatoes, carrots, cabbage, sausage, and water into a milk can they had on the fire, and started cooking as they drank more beer, slapped each other on the back, and congratulated themselves for their crime-solving abilities.

And then the reporter arrived. She drove up in a rusty gray pickup, climbed out, and pulled on a ball cap. Wearing scuffed brown boots, faded Wranglers, and a chambray shirt, she took out her notebook, stuffed in into her hip pocket, poked a pen above her ear, and took a firm grip on a blue bag that she slung over her right shoulder. Walking purposefully she approached the law dogs, their fire and their cooler, but she looked at the land. Her brown eyes moved intently over the ridgeline to the east, swung across the road toward the west, took in the fence and the gate.

"You find anything interesting?" she asked the lead investigator.

"You bet. Some thirty-thirty casings over in those rocks," he pointed toward the west. "Measurements coincide with the trial transcript. It's clear Willie rode up, got off his horse, and Horn shot him. Fired three bullets. Two struck the boy who made it sixty-five feet toward home before collapsing."

The reporter didn't respond, walked to the gate, looked around, and headed for the rock outcrop and cedar trees where the law dog said I'd been. She moved slowly and even before she got to the place, I knew she sensed something they hadn't. She pulled her camera out of the blue bag, put on a long lens, pointed it toward the rocks. And looked right at me.

The shutter never snapped, so I know she didn't take the photo. But she saw me all right. And in that instant the story came clear for her as it had for me.

"You've got it wrong," she told the law dog as she pulled a Coke from her bag.

"How so?"

"Well, for one thing, Willie would not have been off his horse to open the gate."

"Oh?"

"No fourteen-year-old boy who'd been riding horses since he was two would ever dismount to open a gate," she said. "He'd ride up to the fence, angle his horse against the gate, reach over, and open it. Then, with the gate in one hand, he'd swing the horse through and shut it."

"Oh, ya?"

"Of course, the shot that killed Willie came before he could shut it," she added. "Who are your suspects?"

"You know them: Tom Horn and Jim Miller mainly."

"And it wasn't either of them."

"Who then?"

"Obviously the one who tried so valiantly to save Tom Horn, who swore at his trial he had not fired the fatal shot," the reporter said smugly.

"Don't tell me you think the schoolteacher did it?"

"Don't tell me you've never heard of passion and jealousy as a motive for murder?"

She turned and strode toward her truck, pausing

as she reached the rusty vehicle, "And boys, mind your backs, he's watching you even now."

AUTHOR'S NOTE: *Most of this story actually occurred on Iron Mountain. All of the names are real, although I have compressed some events to fit my story line. The killing of Willie Nickell is one of those Wyoming legends where the truth is so deeply buried it is difficult to discern, but the answers are there somewhere in the rocks above the crumbling Nickell Homestead. I know. I was there with the law dogs. And I had my camera.*

The Defense of Sentinel

Louis L'Amour

When the morning came, Finn McGraw awakened into a silent world. His eyes opened to the wide and wondering sky where a solitary cloud wandered reluctantly across the endless blue.

At first he did not notice the silence. He had awakened, his mouth tasted like a rain-soaked cat hide, he wanted a drink, and he needed a shave. This was not an unusual situation.

He heaved himself to a sitting position, yawned widely, scratching his ribs—and became aware of the silence.

No sound. . . . No movement. No rattling of well buckets, no cackling of hens, no slamming of doors. Sentinel was a town of silence.

Slowly, his mind filling with wonder, Finn McGraw climbed to his feet. With fifty wasted years behind him, he had believed the world held no more surprises. But Sentinel was empty.

Sentinel, where for six months Finn McGraw had held the unenvied position of official town drunk. He had been the tramp, the vagabond, the useless, the dirty, dusty, unshaven, whiskey-sodden drunk.

He slept in alleys. He slept in barns—wherever he happened to be when he passed out.

Finn McGraw was a man without a home. Without a job. Without a dime. And now he was a man without a town.

What can be more pitiful than a townless town drunk?

Carefully, McGraw got to his feet. The world tipped edgewise and he balanced delicately and managed to maintain his equilibrium. Negotiating the placing of his feet with extreme caution, he succeeded in crossing the wash and stumbling up the bank on the town side. Again, more apprehensively, he listened.

Silence.

No smoke rising from chimneys, no barking dogs, no horses. The street lay empty before him, like a street in a town of ghosts.

Finn McGraw paused and stared at the phenomenon. Had he, like Rip van Winkle, slept for twenty years?

Yet he hesitated, for well he knew the extreme lengths that Western men would go for a good practical joke. The thought came as a relief. That was it, of course, this was a joke. They had all gotten together to play a joke on him.

His footsteps echoed hollowly on the boardwalk. Tentatively, he tried the door of the saloon. It gave inward, and he pushed by the inner batwing doors and looked around. The odor of stale whiskey mingled with cigar smoke lingered, lonesomely, in the air. Poker chips and cards were scattered on the table, but there was nobody. . . . Nobody at all!

The back bar was lined with bottles. His face

brightened. Whiskey! Good whiskey, and his for the taking! At least, if they had deserted him they had left the whiskey behind.

Caution intervened. He walked to the back office and pushed open the door. It creaked on a rusty hinge and gave inward, to emptiness.

"Hey?" His voice found only an echo for company. "Where is everybody?"

No answer. He walked to the door and looked out upon the street. Suddenly the desire for human companionship blossomed into a vast yearning.

He rushed outside. He shouted. His voice rang empty in the street against the false-fronted buildings. Wildly, he rushed from door to door. The blacksmith shop, the livery stable, the saddle shop, the boot maker, the general store, the jail—all were empty, deserted.

He was alone.

Alone! What had *happened!* Where *was* everybody? Saloons full of whiskey, stores filled with food, blankets, clothing. All these things had been left unguarded.

Half-frightened, Finn McGraw made his way to the restaurant. Everything there was as it had been left. A meal half-eaten on the table, dishes unwashed. But the stove was cold.

Aware suddenly of a need for strength that whiskey could not provide, Finn McGraw kindled a fire in the stove. From a huge ham he cut several thick slices. He went out back and rummaged through the nests and found a few scattered eggs. He carried these inside and prepared a meal.

With a good breakfast under his belt, he refilled his coffee cup and rummaged around until he found a box of cigars. He struck a match and lighted a good Havana, pocketing several more. Then he leaned back and began to consider the situation.

Despite the excellent meal and the cigar, he was uneasy. The heavy silence worried him, and he got up and went cautiously to the door. Suppose there was something here, something malign and evil? Suppose— Angrily, he pushed the door open. He was going to stop supposing. For the first time in his life he had a town full of everything, and he was going to make the most of it.

Sauntering carelessly down the empty street to the Elite General Store, he entered and coolly began examining the clothing. He found a hand-me-down gray suit and changed his clothes. He selected new boots and donned them as well as a white cambric shirt, a black string tie, and a new black hat. He pocketed a fine linen handkerchief. Next he lighted another cigar, spat into the brass spittoon, and looked upon life with favor.

On his right as he turned to leave the store was a long rack of rifles, shotguns, and pistols. Thoughtfully, he studied them. In his day—that was thirty years or so ago—he had been a sharpshooter in the Army.

He got down a Winchester '73, an excellent weapon, and loaded it with seventeen bullets. He appropriated a fine pair of Colts, loaded them, and belted them on, filling the loops with cartridges. Taking down a shotgun, he loaded both barrels with buckshot, then he sauntered down to the saloon, rummaged under the bar until he came up with Dennis Magoon's excellent Irish whiskey, and poured three fingers into a glass.

Admiring the brown, beautiful color, the somber amber, as he liked to call it, he studied the sunlight through the glass, then tasted it.

Ah! Now that was something like it! There was a taste of bog in that! He tossed off his drink, then re-filled his glass.

The town was his—the whole town—full of whis-key, food, clothing—almost everything a man could want.

But *why?* Where *was* everybody?

Thoughtfully, he walked outside. The silence held sway. A lonely dust devil danced on the prairie outside of town, and the sun was warm.

At the edge of town he looked out over the prairie toward the mountains. Nothing met his eyes save a vast, unbelievable stretch of grassy plain. His eyes dropped to the dust and with a kind of shock he remembered that he could read sign. Here were the tracks of a half-dozen rigs, buckboards, wagons, and carts. From the horse tracks all were headed the same direction—east.

He scowled and, turning thoughtfully, he walked back to the livery barn.

Not a horse remained. Bits of harness were dropped on the ground—a spare saddle. Every-thing showed evidence of a sudden and hasty de-parture.

An hour later, having made the rounds, Finn McGraw returned to the saloon. He poured another glass of the Irish, lighted another Havana, but now he had a problem.

The people of the town had not vanished into thin air, they had made a sudden, frightened, panic-stricken rush to get away from the place.

That implied there was, in the town itself, some evil.

Finn McGraw tasted the whiskey and looked over his shoulder uncomfortably. He tiptoed to the door, looked one way, then suddenly the other way.

Nothing unusual met his gaze.

He tasted his whiskey again and then, crawling from the dusty and cobwebbed convolutions of his brain, long befuddled by alcohol, came realization. *Indians!*

He remembered some talk the night before while he was trying to bum a drink. The Ladder Five Ranch had been raided and the hands had been murdered. Victorio was on the warpath, burning, killing, maiming. *Apaches!*

The Fort was east of here! Some message must have come, some word, and the inhabitants had fled like sheep and left him behind.

Like a breath of icy air he realized that he was alone in the town, there was no means of escape, no place to hide. And the Apaches were coming!

Thrusting the bottle of Irish into his pocket, Finn McGraw made a break for the door. Outside, he rushed down to the Elite General Store. This building was of stone, low and squat, and built for defense, as it had been a trading post and stage station before the town grew up around it. Hastily, he took stock.

Moving flour barrels, he rolled them to the door to block it. Atop the barrels he placed sacks, bales, and boxes. He barred the heavy back door, then blocked the windows. In the center of the floor he built a circular parapet of more sacks and barrels for a last defense. He got down an armful of shotguns and proceeded to load ten of them. These he scattered around at various loopholes, with a stack of shells by each.

Then he loaded several rifles. Three Spencer .56s, a Sharps .50, and seven Winchester '73s.

He loaded a dozen of the Colts and opened boxes of ammunition. Then he lighted another Havana and settled down to wait.

The morning was well nigh gone. There was food enough in the store, and the position was a commanding one. The store was thrust out from the line of buildings in such a way that it commanded the approaches of the street in both directions, yet it was long enough so that he could command the rear of the buildings as well, by running to the back.

The more he studied his position the more he wondered why Sentinel inhabitants had left the town undefended. Only blind, unreasoning panic could have caused such a flight.

At noon he prepared himself a meal from what he found in the store, and waited. It was shortly after high sun when the Indians came.

The Apaches might have been scouting the place for hours; Finn had not seen them. Now they came cautiously down the street, creeping hesitantly along.

From a window that commanded the street, old Finn McGraw waited. On the windowsill he had four shotguns, each with two barrels loaded with buckshot. And he waited . . .

The Apaches, suspecting a trap, approached cautiously. They peered into empty buildings, flattened their faces against windows, then came on. The looting would follow later. Now the Indians were suspicious, anxious to know if the town was deserted. They crept forward.

Six of them bunched to talk some forty yards away. Beyond them a half dozen more Apaches were scattered in the next twenty yards. Sighting two of his shotguns, Finn McGraw rested a hand on each. The guns were carefully held in place by sacks weighting them down, and he was ready. He squeezed all four triggers at once!

The concussion was terrific! With a frightful roar, the four barrels blasted death into the little groups of Indians, and instantly, McGraw sprang to the next two guns, swung one of them slightly, and fired again.

Then he grabbed up a heavy Spencer and began firing as fast as he could aim, getting off four shots before the street was empty. Empty, but for the dead.

Five Apaches lay stretched in the street. Another, dragging himself with his hands, was attempting to escape.

McGraw lunged to his feet and raced to the back of the building. He caught a glimpse of an Indian and snapped a quick shot. The Apache dropped, stumbled to his feet, then fell again and lay still.

That was the beginning. All through the long, hot afternoon the battle waged. Finn McGraw drank whiskey and swore. He loaded and reloaded his battery of guns. The air in the store was stifling. The heat increased, the store smells thickened, and over it all hung the acrid smell of gunpowder.

Apaches came to recover their dead and died beside them. Two naked warriors tried to cross the rooftops to his building, and he dropped them both. One lay on the blistering roof, the other rolled off and fell heavily.

Sweat trickled into McGraw's eyes, and his face became swollen from the kick of the guns. From the front of the store he could watch three ways, and a glance down the length of the store allowed him to see a very limited range outside. Occasionally he took a shot from the back window, hoping to keep them guessing.

Night came at last, bringing a blessed coolness, and old Finn McGraw relaxed and put aside his guns.

Who can say that he knows the soul of the Indian? Who can say what dark superstitions churn inside his skull? For no Apache will fight at night, since he believes the souls of men killed in darkness must forever wander, homeless and alone. Was it fear that prevented an attack now? Or was it some fear of this strange, many-weaponed man—if man he was—who occupied the dark stone building?

And who can say with what strange expressions they stared at each other as they heard from their fires outside the town the weird thunder of the old piano in the saloon, and the old man's whiskey-bass rolling out the words of "The Wearing of the Green"; "Drill, Ye Tarriers, Drill"; "Come Where My Love Lies Dreaming"; and "Shenandoah."

Day came and found Finn McGraw in the store, ready for battle. The old lust for battle that is the birthright of the Irish had risen within him. Never, from the moment he realized that he was alone in a town about to be raided by Apaches, had he given himself a chance for survival. Yet it was the way of the Irish to fight, and the way even of old, whiskey-soaked Finn.

An hour after dawn, a bullet struck him in the side. He spun half-around, fell against the flour barrels, and slid to the floor. Blood flowed from the slash, and he caught up a handful of flour and slapped it against the wound. Promptly he fired a shot from the door, an aimless shot, to let them know he was still there. Then he bandaged his wound.

It was a flesh wound, and would have bled badly but for the flour. Sweat trickled into his eyes, grime and powder smoke streaked his face. But he moved and moved again, and his shotguns and rifles stopped every attempt to approach the building. Even looting was at a minimum, for he controlled most of the entrances, and the Apaches soon found they must dispose of their enemy before they could profit from the town.

Sometime in the afternoon, a bullet knocked him out, cutting a furrow in his scalp, and it was nearing dusk when his eyes opened. His head throbbed with enormous pain, his mouth was dry. He rolled to a sitting position and took a long pull at the Irish, feeling for a shotgun. An Apache was even then fumbling at the door.

He steadied the gun against the corner of a box. His eyes blinked. He squeezed off both barrels and, hit in the belly, the Apache staggered back.

* * *

At high noon on the fourth day, Major Magruder, with a troop of cavalry, rode into the streets of Sentinel. Behind him were sixty men of the town, all armed with rifles.

At the edge of town, Major Magruder lifted a hand. Jake Carter and Dennis Magoon moved up beside him. "I thought you said the town was deserted?"

His extended finger indicated a dead Apache.

Their horses walked slowly forward. Another Apache sprawled there dead . . . and then they found another.

Before the store four Apaches lay in a tight cluster; another savage was stretched at the side of the walk. Windows of the store were shattered and broken, a great hole had been blasted in the door. At the major's order, the troops scattered to search the town. Magruder swung down before the store.

"I'd take an oath nobody was left behind," Carter said.

Magruder shoved open the store. The floor inside was littered with blackened cartridge cases and strewn with empty bottles. "No one man could fire that many shells or drink that much whiskey," Magruder said positively.

He stooped, looking at the floor and some flour on the floor. "Blood," he said.

In the saloon they found another empty bottle and an empty box of cigars.

Magoon stared dismally at the empty bottle. He had been keeping count, and all but three of the bottles of his best Irish glory were gone. "Whoever it was," he said sorrowfully, "drank up some of the best whiskey ever brewed."

Carter looked at the piano. Suddenly he grabbed Magoon's arm. "McGraw!" he yelled. "'Twas Finn McGraw!"

They looked at each other. It couldn't be! And yet—who had seen him? Where was he now?

"Who," Magruder asked, "is McGraw?"

They explained, and the search continued. Bullets had clipped the corners of buildings, bullets had smashed water barrels along the street. Windows were broken, and there were nineteen dead Indians—but no sign of McGraw.

Then a soldier yelled from outside of town, and they went that way and gathered around. Under the edge of a mesquite bush, a shotgun beside him, his new suit torn and bloodstained, they found Finn McGraw.

Beside him lay two empty bottles of the Irish. Another, partly gone, lay near his hand. A rifle was propped in the forks of the bush, and a pistol had fallen from his holster.

There was blood on his side and blood on his head and face.

"Dead!" Carter said. "But what a battle!"

Magruder bent over the old man, then he looked up, a faint twinkle breaking the gravity of his face. "Dead, all right," he said. "Dead *drunk!*"

Paradise Springs

Sandy Whiting

The field appeared as though the earth had given up its dead. Bodies baked under the lingering autumn sun. Only these remains had never rested in the earth, safe in a pine box for all eternity. No satin pillow to ease the soul's journey into the twilight of time.

Time. What was time? Where was its keeper? How could yesterday exist? And what of tomorrow? Time was now, the heartbeats between breaths divided by the count of stars in the night sky.

Although he couldn't think past now, Private Joseph Scriven craved time, another day, another moment. Instead, he clutched at his side, blood oozing through his fingers. A sickly stain spread across the fibers of his blue woolen shirt.

All around him, cannon fire rippled waves of deafening thunder. Pockets of gunfire erupted, accenting the terror in his head. Screams of the wounded were obliterated by unending artillery. Quantrill had shown no mercy, firing at all who dared stand.

Joseph had sworn to himself no retreat. Fight for

Mr. Lincoln, for the Union. Yet when a bullet had torn his squirrel rifle from his hands, piercing his side, he had run. Each breath burned his throat—blazing a fiery path to his lungs.

Battling through the woody brush, each step a new lesson in agony, he knew his survival depended on finding the creek they'd crossed. Go north, away from the battle. Hide from Quantrill's men.

Stumbling through a thicket, Joseph plunged into the knee-deep October water. Shivers raced along flesh like waves. Gasping, he wedged himself under a pile of brown and gold leafy branches, ears continuously alert.

"He come this a-way! He cain't of gone far, not with that lead in his belly. You look yonder. I'll look here. Give 'im no quarter!"

Joseph clenched his jaw, stifling chattering teeth and squelching errant moans. Footsteps. Too close. Icicles chased up his spine then terror locked his teeth on his lip when the chill of a gun prodded his cheek.

"Well, looky what we got here."

Staring through the brush, Joseph squinted up though the dying leaves, gaze locking on a wrinkled face. Venomous pale eyes glared back, and a hand grabbed his chin, turning it this way and that.

"Hey, Yankee boy, you barely got whiskers on yer face. How old are ya anyway?"

Joseph's fate was sealed. A little lie wouldn't change that. "N-nineteen, sir."

The fire of hell burning in his eyes, the man yanked Joseph's soggy shirt and pulled him up through the fiery fall leaves. "You lying Yankee! I oughta take you to Quantrill myself. He'd enjoy puttin' it to ya. Tell me the truth, and I might spare ya . . . for a while." His laugh echoed like a banshee at midnight.

The lie had bought Joseph nothing but dust. What did his age matter anyway? "I'll be seventeen," he corrected, ". . . was going to be seventeen next month." He thought about his family and where he'd been on his sixteenth birthday. Was it only a year?

The man turned loose, allowing Joseph to slide neck deep into the water. "I'm gonna be real nice on account ya told me truth. Ya go on and look 'tother way, and ya won't feel a thing."

Joseph scrutinized the man's soulless, faded orbs. Perhaps that's what happened to men who had seen too much of war. And, strangely, the pain of the ripped flesh in his gut had dulled. His legs felt warm. Maybe that's what it felt like to know his master clock had spun down, death ready to claim him.

The bent nail. He must find the nail his father had forged into a circle, a last grasp of home. With his left hand still clutching his side, Joseph let his right drift under the water. Instead of the nail, his hand came to rest on his skinning knife, a gift when he'd turned sixteen. Death had seemed so distant . . . then.

Looking toward the opposite shore, Joseph spotted a girl, arms outstretched. He'd once sneaked a kiss with a neighbor girl. If he died now, he'd never taste such sweetness again. A burst of energy surged. He wasn't yet seventeen and still had his life before him.

New strength coursed through his veins. Joseph yanked the knife from its strap, snatched his would-be slayer around the neck, and thrust it under the man's ribs.

A brief struggle, and the soldier quieted. Joseph plunged the grizzled man under the water and held him, his own pulse pounding in his head. What had he done? War meant death, and to die, someone had to kill, rob a soul of heartbeats.

Minutes passed. Twilight settled. Joseph yanked the blade from the man's chest, his own fingers dripping watery blood. Nausea rising in his throat, he scoured his arm and the knife. But no amount of scrubbing could wash the gruesome memory from his head.

Where would he go? Left? Right?

The current jostled the rebel's body, rolling it faceup just below the surface. As if trying to speak, air bubbled between bluish lips. The dead reawakened? No! Pain ripping through his own side, Joseph stabbed blindly, snagging the knife on a root. It flipped into the murky depths.

"Forgive me!" Joseph fled toward the other shore lest the mortal remains of the deceased wrap lifeless arms around his neck and drag him under, down to the depths of Lucifer's lair, to be trapped for all eternity. The sand sucking at his feet, he lurched toward the sanctuary of the rocks just past the water.

Soon absolute night nipped the last vestiges of twilight. The cold and blood loss clouded his eyes. Blood still oozing from his body, the young Yankee grasped trees to guide him through the night's woods. Perhaps the girl he'd seen earlier lived nearby. Yet she hadn't come to his aid. Perhaps he'd imagined her. But if he hadn't seen her, it would've been his lifeless body floating in the river.

Gasping, Joseph fell to his knees. Rifle, knife. Lost. Glancing down, he realized somewhere he'd lost a shoe. "Oh, Lord! Master! You called me to this fight. I beg, do not abandon me! This price for freedom, it is so high!"

A distant rumble penetrated the night's stillness. Joseph willed himself to stand. He knew that if he stayed, he'd become one of the many soldiers buried in a nameless grave. Or like Quantrill's man, destined to float away, never to return to the earth. Joseph shook his head, willing the fatal image to cease.

The rumble intensified, shaking the very earth upon whence he stood. Slowly, Joseph recognized the sound of horses and wagon. He staggered forward and found himself in the middle of a rut-gouged road.

He squinted into the ink dark of night. In the distance, a light rocked to and fro. Summoning new-found strength, he propelled himself toward the light, hand outstretched. Blue, gray, it didn't matter. "Help me!" His voice echoed against the night's walls.

Suddenly, the wagon bore down on him. The driver had no head!

Fear paralyzed his legs. It wasn't the companionship he sought but the Grim Reaper himself.

"No!" Panic and bile rose in his throat. For an instant, fear froze his feet. Another instant and terror thawed his frozen limbs.

He sprang toward a dark sanctuary of trees. His foot snagged in a merciless rut. Bone twisted and snapped. Nerves in his left leg screamed. Agony raced from his heel, ending its flaming journey in the back of his head.

The reaper left the wagon and stood over him. No face, only a halo of darkness.

"Oh, Lord, please, no!" Joseph pleaded, desperately trying to crawl away.

As the headless creature thrust forth a hand, lightning shot through Joseph's spine. He glanced up in time to see an arm so thin it could only be the bony remains of a skeleton. Pain shoved his mind into oblivion.

The "Grim Reaper" threw off her hood as she studied the fallen soldier. A smaller version appeared at her side.

"He looks like he's seen a ghost, Sarah. Sure you wanna help him?"

Sarah turned to her younger brother. "I do, Skeeter. Get the blanket, and let's get him to Paradise Springs."

Fighting against the cords binding his wrists, Joseph drifted in and out of the nether world of fear. It felt like he lay on a bed. But who would tie a man to a bed unless they planned harm? Perhaps it wasn't a bed at all but a way to torment the living while they served an eternal sentence in Hell.

The pallid eyes of the old man he'd knifed came into focus. "Get away from me!" Joseph rasped. The eyes stared on, into and through his soul, empty, yet familiar. "I'm sorry! You left me no choice." The words spewed from Joseph's mouth as the spear in his side ripped through mutilated flesh. "Please, Lord, don't let it end this way!" Again, oblivion claimed him.

The spent musket ball fragment plinked into a tin pan.

Slowly, the world began to lighten. In the distance, voices whispered. Joseph used them as a guide back from the trial of ceaseless night. The fragrance of fresh baked bread filled the air. His stomach grumbled, mouth drier than August in Kansas. Perhaps if he could find his own voice, the other voices would hear.

"Water," he whispered. "Water . . . please." He heard footsteps. Although it seemed cobwebs covered his eyes, he couldn't mistake the outline of a woman's face.

"He's awake."

Joseph turned toward the voice and saw a boy about twelve.

"Shush, Skeeter. I can't hear him."

Joseph refocused on the woman. "Water, please." As soon as he said it, a white china cup rimmed in gold was pressed to his lips, and soft arms held him up to drink.

"Thought you were a goner. What's your name, mister?"

"Skeeter, let him rest."

Joseph struggled to form the words to his name. "Joseph Scriven."

"I'm sorry we have to keep you tied up, Mister Scriven, but you wouldn't stop fighting and trying to get up."

It took a moment before Joseph realized she was

calling him Mr. Scriven. No one addressed him as mister. His commanding officer had always said Private Scriven. "It's Joseph. Who are you? Where am I?"

"I'm Sarah Blessing. And this is my brother Skeeter. You're in Paradise Springs, in our home."

"I'm grateful, Miss Blessing."

She smiled. "Sarah, if you please. I'll untie you, but you have to be absolutely still, or you'll bust open the stitches and unset your leg."

"I promise."

The young woman reached to free his hands, her brown curls brushing his arm. The fragrance of lilacs filled the air. Her hands felt silky soft against the roughness of his arms. Dressed in pink satin with white lace trim, he thought her close to his own age.

Perhaps time still held a little more life after all. He settled under the blankets, the rich sleep of the living overtaking his mind. His leg and body would mend in this tranquil refuge. Given time, maybe his soul would also find peace.

Christmas and New Year's arrived and departed without fanfare. The days seemed only a faded memory. Had time really passed? Reason told him it had.

Before he knew it, Sarah had turned the calendar to February. In March he managed to walk without assistance, though he hadn't yet been allowed out of this single room. Whenever his caretakers had brought him a meal, they relocked the door. Mostly mended, the endless trek of the clock's hands stirred within him a new restlessness.

Behind him, the key clicked in the lock. Sarah appeared, a biscuit and fruit laden tray in her hands. Since his rescue, he'd grown almost two inches. His shirt struggled to properly clothe him. At this rate, his head would brush the ceiling by fall, though inside a skinny boy with stilts for legs still lurked.

A warm smile crossed his benefactress's face. "Good morning, Joseph. I trust you slept well."

He sniffed at the offered feast. "Fine, thank you. Do you think I might be allowed outside today? There's barely a wind, and the sun is bright." Though she tried to hide it, Joseph saw a cloud in his guardian angel's eyes.

A quick smile chased away the flicker of darkness. "If you promise to do exactly as I say, and when I say it's time to come in, you'll do so without question. And you'll not leave the veranda."

After this lengthy convalescence, he'd have consented to climb a tree feet first. "Agreed, Miss Sarah." He watched her cheeks redden when he squeezed her hand. He'd grown fond of her. She was, so he'd discovered from Skeeter, only a year his junior. No doubt the war prevented suitable gentlemen callers. Perhaps her parents didn't think her old enough. Maybe he'd ask permission himself, if he ever met them.

"I'll fetch Skeeter." She left, the door ajar behind her.

Something itched in the back of his mind at the thought of the whereabouts of the elusive Mr. and Mrs. Blessing. Why hadn't they come to see what kept their children occupied? Sarah had mentioned it was to keep any visitors from discovering the room harbored a Yankee. Perhaps they worked clandestinely for the North, or ran an underground railroad.

Sarah's voice jarred him from his thoughts. "Are you ready?" She handed him an overcoat, which smelled of old wood smoke.

With Skeeter in front and Sarah at his side, he took the stairs down one at a time then stepped outside. Fresh, new air assailed his nose. Full of questions, he eased onto the wooden porch swing. "How come you haven't been burned out, or this home seized? How do you get those lilacs to bloom so early? Do you mind that I'm a Yankee?"

Sarah's laughter resonated from deep within. "The lilacs bloom because it's their time. And as to why we haven't been burned out, well, I suppose it's because the road through Paradise Springs travels a different path. As to your being a Yankee, it's what lives in a man's heart that defines his life."

Joseph rested his arm on the back of the swing and gazed at the ripening fields and summer garden. Behind the north cornfield, he spotted a white picket fence. "What's there?"

Biting her lip, Sarah turned away. "It's time to go inside."

"But we just got here," he protested. Then recalling his promise, he stood, offering his hand. "Maybe again tomorrow."

They entered through the library doors, Sarah leading. "You'll stay in here now. Father will be away for another month, and he hoped Dickens and perhaps the works of Shakespeare would keep your mind occupied."

After several weeks, even *David Copperfield* couldn't ease the insatiable itch to roam past the railed veranda. The war needed able-bodied men, even if they were all of seventeen and an Army private. He should see about rejoining his unit.

Today, though, he ventured to the fully tasseled field of corn, plucked a single ear, shucked, and sunk his teeth into juicy yellow kernels. Still following his feet, he wandered toward the white picket fence.

One foot through the whitewashed gate, he heard a storm rumble in the distance. A glance at blue skies told him it was not rain. He raced back to the house.

"Sarah, Skeeter! The war! I hear it! Get in the root cellar!" Once inside, he pounded on the library doors and twisted the knob. As usual, they were locked.

"What's the matter, Joseph?" asked Sarah who suddenly appeared behind him, Skeeter skidding to a stop on her heels.

Spinning, he gripped her arms. "I heard it! The war! Quantrill! You have to hide."

"And what will you do?"

What had he planned to do? Hold off the entire South by himself? A boy who'd only recently found a reason to use a razor on his face?

Taking his hand, Sarah led him onto the veranda. "I don't hear anything."

Cocking his head to the side, Joseph listened to

the silence. "I know I heard large artillery, three pounders."

Outside, Joseph saw the ear of corn that he'd dropped. Shame of betrayal of her trust blazed on his face.

Without the expected scolding, she pointed him back to the library. "I think supper is ready. War's an ugly thing to listen to anyway."

Sarah served up a pile of mashed potatoes with butter, fried chicken enough to feed a dozen hungry soldiers, and pie. Instead of leaving him to eat by himself, she joined him in the library.

"That was excellent, my regards to the cook. If we had a little music we could dance." Joseph laid his fork where the cherry pie had been.

A dimple appeared in his companion's left cheek. She thrust the key in the door's lock. "Skeeter! Get your strings! There's dancing to be done."

As if he'd been waiting the call, her brother appeared, fiddle in hand.

"A waltz, please, young man," Joseph said, offering Sarah his arm.

The fiddling wasn't quite a symphony, but it matched the dancers perfectly as they stepped and stumbled over each other's feet.

Giving up the dance before he broke his other leg, the two of them flopped onto the settee. Joseph glanced at Skeeter. "Thank you."

The boy blushed. His freckles accented the carrot color of his hair. "Thank you, sir."

"Sir?" Joseph asked. "I'm only five years older than you."

"It fits." Skeeter gestured toward a mirror then ducked through the library doors.

Joseph studied his reflection. Well, there were quite a few more hairs on his chin, and he'd put on a few pounds, grown a couple of inches, but those were on the outside. Inside he didn't feel like a man. At the moment, he felt like his family nickname Pup-jup.

The glow of the dance still burning, Joseph took Sarah's hands in his and pulled her to her feet. "This has been the most wonderful day of my life. Thank you." He kissed her on the cheek. "I'd like to come back after the war. I mean if your father would allow. I mean, would you wait for me?" The words tumbled from his mouth.

A smile trembled on the young woman's lips. "I'll never leave Paradise Springs. But now it's time to rest, and the hour is late." She brushed his face with her fingertips then scurried through the doors, locking them behind her.

Curious answer, he thought while stretching arms and legs over the settee. Maybe that was a southern way of saying yes. A content smile on his face, he slumbered.

He'd been asleep for what seemed like only a minute when an explosion rocked the house, throwing him to the floor. Arms flailing, he struggled to stand. He couldn't breath. Smoke choked his throat, burning his eyes.

Suddenly, a dozen hands pulled on him. "Sir, you gotta get out of here! The fire!"

Joseph swung his fists and kicked his feet. "No! Sarah! Save Sarah!" Smoke robbing him of his last breath, he fell into the arms of the rescuers.

* * *

A single pair of hands shook his arm. "Sir, please wake up. You're scaring the whole camp."

Joseph's eyes popped open, and he found a boy, younger than Skeeter, peering down at him. Joseph bolted off the cot and grabbed the child's arms. "Did you save them? Sarah and Skeeter. Did they get out?"

The boy winced as Joseph's fingers dug into his flesh. "I don't know no Sarah or Skeeter, sir. Maybe Colonel Siegel does." No sooner had Joseph turned loose, the boy lit out of there as though he'd seen the devil.

Determined to find answers, Joseph followed and burst into another tent. The man at the table glanced up.

"Glad to have you back, Lieutenant Scriven. Thought that fever was going to be the last of you."

Lieutenant? Only then did Joseph notice his clothes, discovering he wore an officer's uniform with a single bar on the shoulder strap. This was *not* right!

Joseph opened his hands. "Lieutenant? Sir? I'm where? How? The fire?" He stood there; face as blank as new paper.

The colonel motioned toward a crate. "Sit down, son, before you fall over and hurt yourself. Can't have you snap your neck now that your fever's finally broke."

Remembering the bullet he'd taken, Joseph reached for his side. "I had a fever, and my leg was broken, but . . . ?"

"Well, don't know about the leg but it was one

haystack of a fever. Felt like a fire, doc said. Never saw a rabid dog fight as hard as you did last night. Got the whole camp riled. Who's Sarah?"

The colonel didn't wait for an answer. "None of my nevermind. You can write her later. Right now, I want you to get yourself put together and meet me at the west edge of camp. Dismissed."

Still mystified and uncertain he was awake, Joseph returned to the other tent. There, he found a small basin of water.

Face scrubbed and coat buttoned, Joseph gazed long and hard at himself in the mirror. Holding it closely, he recognized his eyes but when he pulled it farther away, it seemed as though he'd been slipped into the skin of his father. And when had he grown a beard?

The officer's uniform. It fit as though it'd been made for his now six-foot frame. Certain the word "private" had been written on his enlistment papers, he squeezed closed his eyes, trying to visualize the word. His mind saw only illegible squiggles of ink.

With memories dashing madly through his head feeling as though they belonged to someone else, he wandered to the edge of camp. Enlisted men saluted him. Uneasily, he returned each gesture.

A half hour later, the colonel met him in front of a couple dozen ragtag men bunched on the ground. "Lieutenant Scriven, these are prisoners of the United States of America. You're to see that they are properly treated and not allowed to escape until such time as we can figure out what to do with them. Sergeants Linn and Tiswell are at your command. Any questions?" Again, the colonel didn't wait for any.

"Understood, sir." Though he had questions and didn't know where to begin, Joseph saluted. How had he gotten here? Wherever here was.

"I think he's plumb crazy," whispered one of the prisoners. "Did you hear all that screaming last night? Heard it was him."

"We won't last a week," said an anonymous voice.

"Be lucky to get a day."

Surveying his new command, Joseph counted forty-nine men, give or take. Hogs wouldn't wallow with them they were so filthy. Sergeant Tiswell waved him over.

"Them two yonder is sick. Want me to get rid of 'em?"

Joseph focused on the two. True, they both had a cough but it had been raining. Raining? No, the day had been sunny when he walked through the field. And what'd happened to all the leaves on the trees? Sarah had just yesterday turned the calendar to April . . . ?

"No. Feed them," Joseph said.

Tiswell raised both eyebrows. "Sir?"

"You heard me. Have the cook bring them food."

Tiswell brushed a half salute to his head. "Yeah, suhr. Anything else, suhr? Cup of hot coffee?"

Joseph refused to return the disrespectful salute or acknowledge the sergeant's ugly remark. Instead, he walked away. He needed time . . . to think . . . to remember.

Nothing made sense. Not the uniform, nor the smoke, nor this colonel and most of all, Sarah. He continued to walk, searching for answers that wouldn't come.

Full darkness descended, and the answers were more elusive than ever. His own men echoed the hushed whispers of the prisoners. Nothing seemed right yet nothing seemed unduly wrong except . . .

He heard a cry, like the howl of a wild creature found only in nightmares. Had the company been attacked by wolves? He hurried to the yowl.

Back at the prisoners, Joseph saw Sergeant Tiswell snap a horsewhip, raising another red welt across the back of one of the Confederates. Another, smaller, young lad, was being restrained by other Rebels, a boy who couldn't be more than twelve at most—Skeeter's age. Was the South so desperate that Lee allowed children to take up arms?

Tiswell laid another blow. "That'll teach you to steal food! That bread belonged to Mr. Lincoln, you slime dog reb."

The lad raised his arms toward Joseph. "Please, Lieutenant, make them stop! I took the bread. Don't let it end this way!"

Memories flooded Joseph as he recognized the boy's words. Hadn't he himself said the same thing when he'd stood at death's door? He'd spent all night wandering in this new wilderness of war. Just as the sun cast its first warming rays over the horizon, he knew the answer to one of the millions of questions roaming in his head.

Walking as though he'd been born to the rank, Lieutenant Scriven snatched the whip. "Enough," he said, his voice resonant with the authority of command.

Tiswell rounded on the lieutenant spraying spittle. "Says who?"

Joseph went toe to toe with Tiswell and found that he towered over the little man. "Tiswell, are you refusing an order?"

"You ain't no officer. There's somethin' not right about you."

"Sergeant!" Joseph barked, gripping the attention of both friend and foe. "You will never mistreat a prisoner."

"Yes, sir!" The man growled the words, his eyes blazing the fires of hell.

Just then, a cook arrived with food for the two sergeants, along with a half dozen soldiers who came to witness the ruckus.

Tiswell reached for his breakfast. Joseph blocked the way. "The good Sergeant has decided to give his food to the prisoners. And you, Linn, will see that he does or join him in his fast. The rest of you lollygaggers," Joseph glared, "will also surrender your breakfast if you aren't out of here in five seconds." He turned to the prisoners of war. "And you. I promise that as long as I'm in charge, you will not be abused or mistreated. But, if you try to escape, you will be hanged. Is that clear?"

Heads nodded. "Yes, sirs" sounded through the captive ranks.

"Maybe he's not touched," whispered a voice.

Later, with the rebs sequestered in a Union prisoner of war camp, Joseph remained with Siegel's regiment. Standing before the colonel one year later, the new Captain fingered the double bars on his shoulder strap.

"Congratulations, Captain Scriven. Fine job. Terrible fine job."

"Captain? My papers said private, and I'm digging privies. Next thing I know I'm an officer."

"Rapid field advancements happen in these times of war."

A wry smile crossed Joseph's face. "I don't think anyone has ever been promoted as fast as I was, sir."

The colonel cocked his head to one side. "You are what you were needed to be, Scriven. Never forget that."

"Sir, may I ask a question?"

The older man tweaked the ends of his moustache. "You may."

"Do you believe in God?"

"As sure as the sun comes up in the morning."

Joseph bit at his lip. "Do you believe it's okay to fight and kill people? I don't mean like murder them without reason. What I mean is . . ." What did he mean?

Leaning against his desk, the well-seasoned man continued to tweak his moustache. "Scriven, since you came under my command, something's been fretting your mind. Time and place opened the door to opportunity. As to religious matters, I believe in God and know what's right and wrong, but the battle details? I leave them to an officer of a higher authority." While pointing heavenward, Siegel popped open his pocket watch.

On the inside of the watch, Joseph noticed the word MASTER emblazoned in gold.

Siegel closed the timepiece and returned it to his

pocket. "Soon, and I pray to God it's soon, we'll all have fought the last battle."

As wars always do in time and after the spilling of an ocean of blood, it ended. From back home in Kansas, Joseph posted letters to Miss Sarah Blessing, Old Cross Road, Paradise Springs, Missouri. Eventually the postmaster at nearby Chance Springs took pity and returned a stack of unopened envelopes along with a note indicating that the town of Paradise Springs had long been abandoned.

Heart aching, Joseph traveled east then south, arriving at the bottom edge of the burnt district of Missouri. At each settlement, discouragement plagued him. Unwilling to admit defeat, he rode his horse through a section of river he knew had to be where he'd hidden. But it had been fall then and now it was late spring. Trees in full leaf disguised that October's death.

Giving his horse its own mind, aimlessly, Joseph ambled through the remains of a town. No name was posted, but it had to be Paradise Springs. The Blessing home should be just to the east. He traveled on. Occasionally, he felt as though someone trailed. At each look behind, only leaves fluttered in the faint breeze.

Presently, a knee-high field of untended wild corn reached sunward. Opposite, the blackened ruins of a home's fireplace stood, a solitary sentinel.

After tossing the horse's reins over a sprawling lilac bush, he meandered toward the stone foundation.

Gone. Everyone. War had claimed this house and his heart.

His eyes roamed, leading his feet across the corn field, through the broken cemetery gate and to the stones that stood within. Drawn by a force he could not resist, he knelt and pulled the weeds from the words that were etched in white marble. Sarah Blessing 1837–1853, Beloved Daughter. He pulled the grass from the stone's twin. Jonathan "Skeeter" Blessing 1841–1853, Beloved Son.

Joseph's brain stopped, stuttered, and came to a halt.

"It's a shame, damn shame to die so young, especially like they did. She was a pretty one too with all those brown curls."

Joseph leapt to his feet, heart pounding, pulse racing through his veins. "Please, sir! I have only one life. Don't scare it out of me." Commanding his breath to slow, Joseph dropped to the ground and leaned against the paint-scrapped pickets. "Did you know the Blessings? The ones I knew couldn't have died in 1853."

"Them two died when that house yonder burned. The girl ran back to save her brother. He had the cutest freckles too and red hair. Neither 'un made it out. Whole town up and left soon after. The Indians call this the place where spirits never sleep. Been abandoned nigh onto a dozen years now."

On his knees again, Joseph fingered the grooves in the headstones. "But . . . Sarah saved my life. I'm sure this was the place. This cannot be right."

The stranger, as washed out as the paint on the worn fence, knelt beside the stones. "Some folks have so much to give, their spirits walk the earth

searching for those in need. Others of us filch and
plunder until we've stolen so much time won't take
us until we've given back seven fold."

Joseph yanked the weeds from the earth, leaving
a hole as deep as the empty one in his heart. His
dreams . . . "She said she'd wait for me, that she'd
be here forever." Joseph stopped his furious prun-
ing. "I guess she is here, forever. But the year? This
can't be my Sarah." He blinked back a tear that
threatened to run down his face for a love that
could never be.

The wisp of a man grasped the younger man's
shoulder. "I believe this might be yours." In a frail,
ghostly white hand rested the knife Joseph had lost
to the river.

Joseph gazed into the eyes of the stranger. The
faded blue orbs held a weariness that emanated
from the soul. They reminded him of the eyes of
the man who'd died because of that knife.

The stranger stood. "You got a rattler on your tail.
Yonder in that line of trees, past the old spring."

"A what?" Joseph spun, scrutinizing the woods.
"Where?"

Silence. Joseph turned back to the pale man. No
one, not even a footprint remained of the stranger.
Joseph hadn't heard him approach, and he hadn't
heard him leave. But there in his hand was the
knife.

What had the stranger said? About making
amends, righting wrongs, returning that which had
been stolen? Time refusing their souls?

Leaving the cemetery, Joseph kept to the trees
that grew alongside the corn. With a jerk from

behind, he snared the rattler by the collar. "Who are you, and why are you following me?"

"Ow! Lieutenant Scriven. You're hurting me."

Joseph turned loose of his game as a cascade of brown hair fell over his hand. He studied the girl. "It's Captain Scriven. Who are you?"

The girl tamed her brown locks with a bright pink ribbon. "You once saved my brother's life the day that big fever let loose of you. I never got to thank you."

Remembering that terrible day, Joseph said, "There were no girls with those soldiers." Joseph pursed his lips and eyed her. "What's your brother's name?"

"Jonathan, Reverend Jonathan Atherton. Local preacher and farmer over by Chance Springs. His back still aches when it turns cold, but he's alive."

The only person who fit Joseph's memory was the man Sergeant Tiswell had whipped. "You were that 'boy' who stole the bread? How'd you get with the prisoners?"

Shrugging, she took his arm. "Long story. Let's go to my brother's home and have some lemonade. I know he'd like to thank you."

He led her toward his horse. "You still haven't told me who you are."

"Sarah."

Joseph started, caught his toe on a blackened brick, and stumbled. A deep ache twisted, reminding him of his broken leg. Glancing toward the charred remains of the house, he saw the hazy outline of a young redheaded boy and a girl, a girl with brown curls who would never grow old. Joseph could have sworn she smiled.

"You scared me almost to death screaming my name that day." She knelt in front of him. "Are you all right, Captain?"

"Call me Joseph. War's over." On his feet again, he glanced back at the house but the only thing visible was the chimney, ever standing the lonely sentinel toward the heavens.

He boosted Sarah onto his horse then swung up. She pinched his arm.

He batted at her hand. "Ow! What was that for?"

"I just wanted to see if you were real . . . This time. I've often dreamed of seeing you after the war, but never thought I would. Then I saw you ride into Paradise Springs. Nobody goes there anymore. Except me . . . sometimes."

Riding double, they passed a well-tended field of corn that reminded him of the ear he'd sampled the day he and Sarah had danced. It'd been, March? April? Impossible! Corn didn't ripen until late July early August, and he distinctly remembered the ear sugar sweet.

The rest of the date on the tombstone suddenly popped into his mind's eye, August 1. Sarah and Skeeter had both perished when the corn would have been ripe. Or had they? Perhaps the impossible was as possible as morning itself. He and Reverend Atherton had much to discuss.

And time continued its endless journey.

Silent Hill

Larry D. Sweazy

I followed the trail, and the wind, into the town. My throat was raw, my nose filled with dust and dirt, and my chest heaved like my lungs were soaked in kerosene. Oddly, as winded as I was, I could not feel my heart beating in my chest.

I had no map, and after wandering for days, I was certain that I was lost. The town, no name posted on its perimeter, offered hope, a reprieve, a place to rest.

As is my custom when arriving in a new town, I headed straight for the saloon.

The barkeep waited for my two bits to appear out of my pocket before he offered to pour my whiskey. I obliged, though reluctantly. Lady Luck left my side a hundred miles ago, leaving my coffer, as well as my body, in a meager, unhealthy state.

"You look like you need more than a dose of whiskey." A half-full glass slid toward me after the last of my coins disappeared in the barkeep's massive hand. "If you're lookin' for a game, the players that matter won't be in until the sun sets."

The pomade had long since washed out of my

hair, and my linen vest was covered with the same dust that filled my nose, but I imagine a barkeep knows a down-on-his-luck gambler when he sees one.

"Could be," I said. "But I was hoping you could help me find a woman."

I coughed, then fought it back so I would not alarm the few patrons in the back of the bar. My malady had yet to fully show itself, but I could feel it growing, eating away at my insides like a maggot gnawing on the flesh of a winterkill elk.

The barkeep's eyes narrowed. His stomach was as big as a side of beef, his arms looked like hammers, and his apron was worn and tattered at the hems. Just like the saloon, the barkeep looked like he had seen better days.

"This ain't a cat house, stranger." He grabbed a broom.

"No, no. You misunderstand." I reached into my pocket, not breaking eye contact with the barkeep. "My name's Eddie. Edward, really. Edward Blackstone. Most folks call me Blackjack Eddie."

Before I could pull out the neatly folded placard from my breast pocket, the barkeep took a hard swing at my head with the broom, and sent me sprawling to the floor.

The placard flew from my hand and skittered across the floor.

I have only two items in my possession that remain of the life I once lived, the placard and a small locket I wear around my neck. They both are more valuable to me than a bag full of gold.

The locket and placard are dear to me, for they are the only love I have known since my boyhood and the long, two-thousand mile train ride west.

Without them, a long ago promise will remain unfulfilled, and I will be truly alone in this world . . . and, perhaps, the next.

My father arrived home, every day, promptly at 4:30 in the afternoon. He would usually have a fresh cut of meat in hand for our dinner, and the day's newspaper for stories to regale afterward. He always had time for a warm and generous hug for my younger sister, Gillian, and me. Father did not play favorites, his affection was measured just like everything else in his life.

He worked as an accountant in a financial firm, Slade, Crothers, & Leiberman, a block from the new Chemical Bank. Everything was a bustle in New York City then, new construction, new people arriving every day. The city throbbed with vibrations of every sort—language, food, and music.

It was enough to overwhelm the senses, but as a child my environs just fed my taste buds and my ability to appreciate the most delicious aromas. All are just a memory now, evoked only in dreams and nightmares.

My mother taught piano to those who could afford it. Her reputation had followed her from her home country, England, and her wares floated out of our third-story apartment window like sweet cooing doves.

Every afternoon, our parlor was filled with the comings and goings of well-heeled girls, prim and proper, and a few reticent boys, as our mother took them through the paces of Bach, Beethoven, and Chopin.

Music was the heart of our home, but to me it was mostly the unstructured noise of tiresome beginners.

We were by no means wealthy, but we did not have to look far to know how lucky we were. My parents had prospered once they arrived in America, unlike so many others, left to the dingy streets of New York to fend for themselves, with little skills and no family.

I have seen coyotes show more manners than some people fresh off the boat.

I loved the city, loved the warmth of our apartment with the heavy mahogany furniture and thick wool carpets shipped across the ocean, and the wondrous taste of biscuits and cucumber sandwiches set upon silver plates with our afternoon tea.

But Gillian loved the city, and our life, even more than I. She was a prodigy on the piano. My mother's best student. She could play "Chopsticks" and make us all cry—but she was beyond that, even at five.

Each note of Chopin's Piano Concerto no. 2 in F Minor was so full of exuberance and emotion that you thought your eardrums were going to shatter and your heart was going to break.

People would gather on the street below to listen to the sweeping arpeggios and themes from various nocturnes.

Gillian was unaware of her gift, of the attention it brought to her. Her talent was not a surprise to anyone in our household, no more so than my growing skill of calculating large numbers off the top of my head—a game my father and I used to play as we walked the streets on an errand for my mother.

Our life was a dream come true.
Until the fire took it all away.

The barkeep's foot rested heavily on my wrist.
"I've seen way too many derringers appear out of
nowhere, from the likes of you, to risk my life over
a shot of whiskey."

"I assure you, sir, I have no intention of drawing
a weapon." I struggled to pull my hand out from
under the man's buffalo-sized boot. My chest
burned like it was on fire. Spittle seeped out of the
corner of my mouth.

He pressed his boot down harder, eliciting a
sharp groan from the depths of my gut. I feared my
wrist was going to break, an injury that would surely
be my last—for my body has chosen to rebel against
itself.

"Liars are a dime a dozen. I have the scars to
prove it," the barkeep said.

"Let him go, Moses."

It was a woman's voice, strong and demanding,
coming from behind me. The pressure on my wrist
immediately ceased as the heavy man stepped away.

I sat up, my eyes scanning the floor for the placard and the physical presence of my rescuer.

My bones were intact, but what pride or hope I
had left had almost escaped me entirely.

The woman was two heads shorter than the barkeep, Moses, I presumed, but her bulky frame was
similar to his, as were her eyes, narrow and dark
as a moonless night, void of pupil or emotion. She
was no dancing queen, but she was attractive, in
an odd sort of way, with flaming red hair, and

dressed in a green satin dress that was perfectly fitted. Her frilly hat was made for Sundays and sashaying down the street of a finer city than the one I had found myself in. The brilliance of her colorful appearance was calming, like a rainbow after a fierce storm. She looked oddly out of place, and for a moment, I wasn't sure she was real.

The woman unfolded the placard as I sat up, and was staring at me curiously. "Gillian?" she whispered softly.

I nodded. "Yes. You know of her?" I coughed again, deeper this time. I had found the placard posted outside a saloon five years before, my first clue that Gillian was still alive, playing piano professionally like I always knew she would.

She returned the gesture. "Pour the man a drink, Moses. A friend has joined us."

The blow had weakened me, but the woman's acknowledgment of Gillian's presence gave me a boost of energy that I thought was long gone.

I was on my feet without any effort at all.

Moses scurried behind the bar, his head down.

"You'll have to forgive my brother, Mr. Blackstone."

"Edward. Eddie if you prefer."

"Moses and I try to run a clean establishment, Edward. To many we are sinners, but that does not mean we cannot offer entertainment services to those who seek them. Though we do not profit off of the sale of feminine pleasures, we do profit off a fair bottle, an honest game of faro, and the best music to be found anywhere near or far. What remains of our clientele appreciates our efforts, but I fear our days here are numbered. This town is on its last breath, as is our establishment. The Devil has decided to claim our property and dreams. We are all on edge. Leery of strangers."

"I didn't intend to offend anyone," I said.

"Moses is quick to react since his heart was broken by a woman of, how shall I say it? Nightly manners?"

"Gillian?" My own heart sank.

The woman laughed suddenly like I had said something funny. "Oh, no. I'm sorry to imply such a thing." She extended her hand. "My name is Ruth Hathaway, or Miss Ruth, as your sister insisted on calling me on our first meeting. Please sit down, Edward. We have a lot to talk about."

I led Gillian out of the blazing apartment building in the wee hours of the night, smoke roiling around our feet, wet shirts thrown over our heads. We both thought our mother and father were right behind us, for it was they who had roused us out of bed when the fire broke through to our apartment. But we got separated in the trample, in the chorus of screams, in the disorienting pleas for help from the floors above.

They died when a flaming beam fell on them. Their bodies were crushed and burned beyond recognition.

I would like to believe they had left us only to offer someone of less strength and courage aid and rescue. The only identifying remnants of their earthly existence were their wedding rings and the two small gold lockets my mother wore around her neck.

The lockets held pictures of Gillian and me. The picture of Gillian was taken when she was just a girl of five, golden curls flowing over her shoulder onto a fragile lace collar—an expensive portrait that serves as another reminder that our lives were once full, and rich. Gillian's angelic beauty was evident, even then.

I have worn the locket around my neck ever since. And Gillian wears the locket that holds the picture of me, a miniature version of my father in physical appearance and like mind.

Void of any relatives, we were whisked off to The Children's Aid Society shortly after our parents' bones and ashes were ceremonially laid to rest in a pauper's grave.

The fire destroyed everything that they owned, and though my father worked at a financial firm, there was no record of any investments—we had no money. At least that is what we were told, by a man with thinning hair and tobacco breath who stood in representation of Slade, Crothers, & Leiberman, at the end of the funeral.

The Children's Aid Society offered few comforts, and more terror than one child, much less two, should be left to imagine.

The only thing that Gillian and I had to hang on to was each other. We vowed early on, after our shock and grief began to subside, to remain together no matter the cost.

And so we did.

Until that solemn day when we both boarded the Orphan Train, and were shepherded out of our wonderful city on the harbor, full of tall ships, teems of people, wonderful smells of food, and the memories of our parents.

We began our journey west, nervous and afraid, to a land that seemed barren, dry, and populated with people who eyed us with only opportunity and greed.

Moses set a full glass of whiskey on the table in front of me. Miss Ruth sat across from me, her mass so large the chair all but disappeared in a sea of green.

"Tell me of Gillian, please. You are the first person in my travels who has known of her. Is she still here, in this town?" I asked.

Miss Ruth shook her head no. "I'm sorry, Edward, she has been gone from here for nearly two years. Ages, it seems, since someone has touched the piano with such fineness. She was a sweet nectar, her talents were far above the stature of our lowly establishment. Her presence was a blessing, and I was sad to see her go. My pockets have not been as full since, and I don't expect they ever will be again now that we teeter on the edge of loss."

I smiled, ignoring the soulful moan of Miss Ruth's mention of her current calamity. How could I not? "I always knew Gillian would be great, perhaps even famous. She would have traveled the world if our parents hadn't died when we were children," I said.

"Instead of playing for kings and queens," Miss Ruth said, "she played for the likes of Moses and me. All the while, watching out of the corner of her eye, hoping that you would walk through the door."

"She searched for me, as well?"

"Still does, as far as I know."

I took a drink of the whiskey. My chest had began to boil, and the last thing I wanted to do was break into a coughing fit.

The news of Gillian was an elixir, a salve that soothed any thought of my illness. I wanted to touch the keys on the piano that she touched and feel close to her, feel the warmth of her touch, share the sameness of our blood and memories that have been missing from my life for so long, but I could not move. I was weak, and afraid I would miss a word of Miss Ruth's tale of my long-lost sister.

"She knew of your reputation," Miss Ruth continued. "Knew that you gained a certain amount of fame yourself. But you moved around too frequently for her to catch up with you. She missed you by two days in Dodge City. She searched all sixteen saloons until, finally, someone at the Long Branch told her of your victory in a card game there."

"Blackjack Eddie? She knew of me as a gambler?"

"You look surprised."

"My father would be ashamed that I have used my skills for a deviant cause."

"Surviving is not deviant."

"Ah, but cheating is."

"Gillian told me of your skills, so please be aware that you won't be counting any cards here. My till is thin enough."

"My gaming days are nearly at an end," I said. "My pockets are empty, and I have lost the will to maintain my fame. I promised Gillian that I would come for her, and I hope to fulfill that promise. Do you know where she went?"

"Yes," Miss Ruth said. "I do."

We did not know we were leaving until the day before. It was a Monday bath that warned us. Of course, by then, we had seen many children leave the confines of The Children's Aid Society before us. They vanished like they had never existed, nary a trace of them left behind. Our fear, Gillian's and mine, was that we would be separated; only one of us sent west, while the other remained behind in New York.

Fate spared us the blow of separation, if only temporarily, when we both found a new set of clothes on our beds and our hair tended to like we were to be department store models after our "special" bath.

The next day, we were herded to the train station and pushed on board the Orphan Train under the watchful eye of the placing agent who was to accompany us. The man's name escapes me, but he was flustered and mean, overwhelmed by the forty or so waifs and street urchins put in his charge.

The novelty of the train ride soon fell away. It was miserably hot inside because of the unrelenting summer heat. The seats were thin and uncomfortable, and worse than anything else, the passenger car was filled with the smell of bile from children suffering from the constant sway of the railcar. Gillian was afflicted far worse than I.

We held hands continually.

"Promise me we'll always be together," Gillian said just after we crossed the Mississippi River.

Our parents had been dead for nearly three years. Gillian was ten years old, and just as I was a mirror image of my father, Gillian favored my mother. I could not look into her eyes without wanting to cry.

"I promise."

We had both been cheated, stolen from, and lied to since the day of the fire. I wasn't sure I could keep my promise to her any longer, but I could not bear to see her afraid.

She rested her head against my shoulder, the golden curls straight now and lacking any hint of luster. Even then Gillian looked frail, haunted by fire and the misery of loneliness.

I could only hope the home we were going to would be gentle, our new parents understanding and kind. Anything had to better than the institutional life two thousand miles behind us—at least, that is what I thought at the time.

Sleep came intermittently, and our nerves were on end at every stop. No one knew how long it would take us to arrive in Kansas. Each time the brakes squealed, Gillian clutched my hand with all of the energy she had, afraid that we had arrived at our final destination.

I can still feel the pain of her touch when I squeeze my hands together.

"Gillian told me to tell you that she would go to Silent Hill and wait for you there. If the wait became too long, she would leave word of her whereabouts at the saloon, just like she has done here," Miss Ruth said.

"Silent Hill," I uttered, barely able to speak the name of the town aloud.

"Gillian felt the same way, I'm afraid. But she thought you might look for her there."

"I vowed never to return."

"I tried to persuade her to stay. But she is willful."

"She was good for your business."

"It was more than that," Miss Ruth said, clenching her teeth after the words had left her mouth, forcing the fullness of her face to draw so tightly her lifeless eyes bulged.

"I'm sorry, I didn't mean to offend you, Miss Ruth. My sister and I have been on the stiff for so long cynicism has become a code."

"I cared for your sister. She was like a canary with a broken wing. I have never had any children of my own so love does not come easy for me. Moses has always been my protector, my closest confidant. I felt her emptiness immediately."

I sat back in my chair and studied Miss Ruth. Her emotion was forced, her eyes averted to the door, away from me. For the first time since our conversation began, I felt like she was not telling me everything, that she was hiding something. My gambler's instinct warned me something was wrong—that it was time to stand up from the table before I lost everything I had.

I was uncertain of my location, how far I had wandered before stumbling on Miss Ruth's saloon. "How far is Silent Hill from here?" I asked, as I pushed my chair away to stand up.

"A day's ride, more or less, true north," Miss Ruth

said. "Why don't you rest up for the night before leaving? There's a bunk in the storeroom, and a good meal wouldn't hurt you none."

The thought of climbing back in the saddle did not appeal to me, at least not physically. I wasn't sure I had the strength to make the trip. But knowing Gillian was close, that I had caught a whiff of her trail, gladdened my heart, even if I had trepidation about Miss Ruth's intentions.

I relaxed back into the chair, wooed by the thought of food. "In the morning, then."

"Good," Miss Ruth said. "But I have a favor to ask of you before you leave."

"A favor?" I was as far down on my luck as I could go, and I was short of favors—but Miss Ruth had given me something that I had longed for, a thin piece of hope that Gillian still walked this earth. Still, even with the gift, I was distrustful.

The door of the saloon pushed open and a sudden burst of wind snaked around my ankles. A cold chill, that had no association with fever, ran up the back of my neck. I followed Miss Ruth's gaze to the door.

Upon seeing the fellow striding into the saloon, dressed impeccably, fresh pomade eliciting a confident shine that extended all of the way down to his highly polished boots, I knew the favor Miss Ruth asked of.

She aimed to profit off my skills, just as she had Gillian's. I knew the gentleman, and the gentleman knew me.

Mysterious John Harvey and I had a long history. If my instinct was still intact, something told me there was far more at stake for me than a set of clean sheets and a piece of well-cooked meat.

Rain had just stopped falling when the train came to its final stop.

There were twelve of us boys and only one girl, Gillian, remaining on the train. The rest of our group of orphans from The Children's Aid Society had already set upon their new lives at various stops across the state of Kansas. I could only hope that their journey, like ours, would lead to a happy end.

A creaking sign, waving in the persistent, cold wind informed us that we had arrived in Silent Hill, Kansas.

The placing agent led us single file down the main street of town.

Silent Hill looked nothing like New York City or anything Gillian and I were accustomed to. Muddy streets. Single-level wood frame buildings that were sparse and weathered. The sky was larger than I could have ever imagined it truly was—gray and moody, full of rolling, bubbling rain clouds that seemed to go on forever.

Even in the middle of the day, there was an eerie quiet, a lack of human activity in the town. The only consistent sound was the whine of the wind. It felt strong enough to topple us over, or go in one ear and all of the way out the other.

"I don't like this place," Gillian said.

I could hardly feel my fingers, she was squeezing my hand so hard.

"It's not so bad," I lied.

A crowd was hovering outside the opera house. They parted silently as we approached.

As we passed, I searched the crowd, hoping to find a kind face, a nod, an acknowledgment, from someone that seemed recognizable. I realize now that I was looking for love, a hint of it anyway. Why would someone agree to adopt an unknown child from two thousand miles away if there was not love in their heart?

I saw only fear and judgment in the eyes of those we passed. Love was a lost memory, never to be truly found again.

I was to be a workhorse, a laborer, a body to tend to as if it were nothing more than an animal that could easily be put down and replaced.

My boyish desire for comfort and understanding was dying as I made the walk up to the stage in that opera house—but I didn't know it, couldn't imagine it, then. I still believed in the goodness of people . . . and myself.

We stood there like cattle, facing a crowd of strangers whose presence promised to change our lives forever.

The placing agent, who looked even angrier and more exhausted than he did when we first left New York City, joined three men and one woman. They spoke in soft tones, and pointed to the crowd. The three men and woman were obviously members of the committee in Silent Hill that had lined up potential families to adopt those of us from hopeless circumstances.

One of the men, dressed in black and no bigger around than a twig, announced that, "The children are now available for inspection."

The placing agent nodded in agreement.

Slowly, the crowd broke apart, and people approached us curiously. Some checked our ears to see if they were clean. One man grabbed my arm and squeezed as hard as he could, trying to determine the size of my muscles.

I jerked my arm away, and though I was tempted to spit at the man, I restrained the urge. I didn't want to make a bad show of myself. I knew my manners, and I hoped my discomfort at being prodded and poked would not overcome them.

The man eventually moved on, though he eyed me like he might have found what he was looking for.

Gillian stood behind me, shivering.

Fear has a metallic taste to it—and the air was filled with gunmetal, iron, and hidden tears. Each time someone touched me, I nearly let go of my bladder.

A woman dressed in widow weeds stopped in front of me. The placing agent was two steps behind her.

"Well," the woman said. "Aren't you a fine looking little fellow."

I could hardly believe my ears.

The woman sounded just like my mother, her accent proper English. Not only did the woman look formal, fully in mourning, but there was a softness in her eyes that made my heart melt. I could almost taste a cucumber sandwich.

Gillian peered out from behind me.

"And you must be the girl I've heard so much of," the woman said, a smile appearing on her face like a ray of sunshine peeking from behind a dark cloud. "I understand you play the piano beautifully. Is that true?"

"Yes, ma'am," Gillian whispered.

"Oh, that is lovely. Just lovely. I have a piano in my parlor. Would you like to come and see it?" The woman extended her hand, a gold band still on her finger.

"Yes." Gillian had not touched a piano since the night before our parents died. She took the widow's hand and looked over her shoulder at me. "What about Edward?"

It was then that I noticed the man who squeezed my arm, standing behind the placing agent. The taste of cucumber sandwiches washed out of my mouth, replaced by iron and gunmetal.

"I'm sorry. I only have room for one."

Gillian's screams sounded like the wind on the worst Kansas day. Her eyes were filled with terror and tears as she disappeared from my view for the last time, fighting to escape the widow's grasp.

The placing agent, and the man who would become my adopted father and tormenter, restrained me as I fought futilely to reach Gillian. It was the end of everything I knew—and the start of an even more miserable existence.

"I'll come for you, I promise!" I screamed after Gillian. "I'll come for you."

But I couldn't. I was a prisoner on a farm in Silent Hill, fed gruel and beat with a belt when I didn't do what I supposed to do, or sassed back at Wilmer Beatty, the meanest man in the world. Even though I quit believing in God, I prayed every night that Gillian's life was better than mine.

I escaped when I was seventeen, and not being

privileged to the location of the widow's home, I've been searching for Gillian ever since.

Mysterious John Harvey sat down at the table, opposite me. "I heard you were dead," he said.

"Funny. I heard the same thing about you."

Harvey motioned for Moses to come over to the table. Miss Ruth was now standing at the bar, watching us both with trepidation, the exact details of her favor interrupted by Mysterious John Harvey's entrance.

"A whiskey for me and my friend."

"I've had enough," I said.

"A game then? If I remember right, the last time we met you walked away from the table before I had the chance to empty your pockets."

"My pockets are empty now." Our last meeting was a hundred miles ago, when Lady Luck and my body turned on me the final time, and I was too weak to keep count of the cards. I wandered for days, in and out of consciousness, in and out of towns, where I heard Mysterious John Harvey was shot, just outside of Dodge City when he was caught cheating, an ace up his sleeve.

Moses set a whiskey in front of Harvey. "No," he said to me, "they're not. He's playing for the house, Mr. Harvey."

A laugh escaped Mysterious John Harvey's tight mouth. "You have very little left to lose, Ruth. I will own this place if Blackjack Eddie's luck is as miserable as it looks. Are you sure you're willing to risk everything on a stranger?"

"He's no stranger," Miss Ruth said.

"Very well. Eddie?"

I stared at Harvey, knowing full well he would do anything to win. I had to wonder if I was up to the challenge, even if it was prideful. I turned my attention to Miss Ruth. "So if Mysterious John wins, your establishment is his? What is my prize?"

Before Miss Ruth could answer, Moses plopped down a deck of cards between Harvey and me. "Your freedom," he said, digging a handful of chips out of his apron.

I must have had an astonished look on my face, because Harvey burst out laughing. "Looks like a high stakes game. Stud poker?"

"I'm sorry, Edward. I should have told you. Gillian took the last of our prospects with her. You're our only hope. You have to stay to repay her debt."

I took a deep breath, not fully comprehending the situation, other than I knew I had to play. And I had to win to repay whatever my sister's debt was. "Stud poker it is," I said.

Time seemed to stand still. The light outside did not change, and I would not have noticed if it did. A man in the back walked to the piano and began to play "That Old Gang of Mine." I had not noticed him before; he seemed to appear out of nowhere.

Our stacks stayed even for several hands, until the luck shifted and Mysterious John Harvey hit a winning streak. I suspected he was cheating. He knew I was counting, but my marks weren't holding, my mind foggy, so I quit the effort.

"Take off your vest, Harvey. I want to see your sleeves."

Miss Ruth and Moses hovered behind me like I

was giving birth to a baby. My whiskey glass was never empty.

Harvey did not do as I asked; instead, he glared at me and dealt. "This is a fair game, Eddie."

My first card up was an eight of clubs. The hole card was a queen of hearts. I had no choice but to bet. I was growing weaker by the moment. The next card, dealt up, was an ace of spades. I bet half of my stack. Harvey did the same. He was showing a pair of kings. My chances of winning were slim, and we both knew it.

The next card Harvey dealt me face up was an eight of diamonds. I bet half again, leading Harvey to do the same in kind, raising three times until I had one chip left.

My chest heaved and my vision was beginning to blur.

The last card dealt was an ace of hearts. Harvey was showing a pair of kings, an ace of clubs, and a two of diamonds. I did not take my eyes off him. The piano player quit playing. Silence engulfed the room when I threw in my last chip, called and flipped over my cards. Aces and eights.

"The dead man's hand," Harvey whispered.

"Take off your vest, Harvey," I repeated, as I slid my hand under the table and grappled for the derringer in my boot.

This time Mysterious John Harvey obliged. An ace of spades spilled onto the table out of his sleeve. I smelled a familiar aroma, iron—fear, I thought, until I saw the bullet hole and bloodstain on Harvey's shirt, just underneath his heart. He smiled at me and nodded, acknowledging what I had feared since I had began to play. My weapon would do me no good against a dead man.

I realized then that tuberculosis had somehow captured me, soaked my lungs one last time. I just couldn't place when—somewhere in my wandering, along the dusty trail, before I stumbled into Miss Ruth's saloon. Dead, even though I didn't know it.

Harvey turned his card over, all in all he had a pair of kings, an ace of clubs, a two of diamonds, and a two of spades. My guess was he was going to slip in the ace of spades until he saw mine. He'd done it before.

"What is the name of this town?" I asked, trying to stand.

"Purgatory," Miss Ruth said. "You're in Purgatory."

There was piano music in the wind as I entered Silent Hill. The opera house looked like it had received a new coat of paint, the streets were clean, free of mud, and the sky was crystal clear. Sapphire blue. The color of Gillian's eyes. I never imagined Silent Hill would look like Heaven, if there was such a thing.

I felt revived, free of pain, once I left Miss Ruth and Moses in Purgatory. Mysterious John Harvey was left to pay off his debt—I'm not sure what his penance was. Mine had been playing a fair game, winning, without cheating.

I could not contain myself when I walked into the saloon. Gillian was sitting at the piano, playing Chopin. She turned and looked at me, blond curls falling over her shoulder, a glow about her I could only remember seeing when she was a child, and rushed to me, her embrace warm and happy. Tears flowed down her cheeks.

"I've been waiting for you," she said happily.

"I know. I'm sorry it took me so long."

We stood looking at each other for what seemed eternity. Death had taken her too, somehow, somewhere. She obviously had a debt to repay—it was the only way to explain her presence in Purgatory. I was burgeoning with questions about her life.

After a moment, Gillian grabbed my hand. "Come, we must go."

It was then that I heard the train whistle, felt the thunder of the locomotive pulling into town.

"Where are we going?" I asked.

"Home," Gillian said with a smile. "Back to our city. Together. Forever."

End of the Line

Lori Van Pelt

On the last Tuesday of the town's existence, Monty Long rode into Benton. As he reined his bay to a stop, a swirling cloud of alkali dust turned crimson by the fading rays of the setting sun framed the man sitting straight in the saddle, Stetson shading his face. The horse, nostrils twitching, shook his black mane, wreathing his rider in yet another powdery veil.

The men nearby merely glanced at the stranger and then continued with their tasks. The singsong clang of hammers against spikes had not yet ceased for the day. The horseman dismounted and tied the gelding to a post at the corral. Wiping the pale grit from his sweaty face with a worn blue bandanna, he caught the elbow of a passerby.

"I'm looking for Emil Long. Could you tell me where to find him?"

The man shrugged but pointed toward a rail car. "Ask over there."

Monty pocketed his bandanna, doffed his hat, and stepped into the car.

A small, fine-featured man sat at a plain pine

table. Raising his eyes from his paperwork, he glimpsed at Monty. "We don't have work today, but we'll be packing up and moving out tomorrow, near as I can figure."

Monty nodded, rubbing the brim of his hat with his thumbs. "I'd be glad to help you, but I didn't come for a job."

The man laid down his pencil and took stock of the tall, muscular man standing before him. "Oh?"

"I'm looking for Emil Long. Do you know him?"

The man shook his head. "I can't say as I do. Why are you looking for him?"

"I'm his brother."

The man's eyes narrowed, and then he turned his attention back to the stack of papers on the table.

Monty realized that his sudden presence in a notorious end-of-the-tracks town might seem odd, and his reasons for searching for Emil, straightforward though they were, could easily be misconstrued under the circumstances. He shifted his stance. "Do you know anyone else I could ask?"

The little fellow shook his head and tapped his pencil against his papers as if eager to return to his task.

"Thank you, then. I'll be on my way." Monty donned his hat and turned to go.

Something in his courteous manner made the railroad man pause. "Wait," he said, and stood. As he rose the chair legs scraped the floor. Monty winced at the rasping noise. The other man retrieved a metal box from a shelf. "I can check the payroll for you."

He lifted a hefty ledger from the box, opened it, and ran a finger along one of the columns. "Yes.

Emil Long. Works as a hostler." He gazed at Monty.
"He collected his pay last week. That's all I can
tell you."

"I hitched my horse at the corral but no one was
around."

The man gave this remark some thought, and
then said, "Probably took fresh horses up to the
front. Everything's a little off-kilter today. We're
moving out tomorrow."

"Thank you, sir." Monty offered his hand, and
they shook.

"The Big Tent's over there." He pointed to a
huge tent standing among a group of smaller, similar structures. "Some of the men gather there.
They might know. Otherwise, he'll likely be back
afore long."

As the twilight deepened, Emil sat with Harry
O'Malley, the harmonica player. Having returned
early from taking fresh stock to the front of the
line, he stopped in the makeshift restaurant that
Harry ran. He often came and helped his friend
with the cooking. Slicing potatoes and kneading
bread, even churning butter, were restful tasks for
him. Something about the homey chores gave him
a settled feeling. In appreciation for this volunteer
service, Harry played his harmonica, something
they both enjoyed.

"They promoted me, Harry," Emil confided.
"The last fellow just up and left, and since I'm a
good hand with the horses, they put me in his
place." He tossed a potato peel into a bucket.

"Aye now. Good for you. More pay, then?" He

saw the wistful expression as his friend nodded. "But not enough to forget about her, eh?"

Emil shook his head. "I should have never let her come between Monty and me." He gestured with the paring knife like a schoolmarm emphasizing an important topic. "Our grandfather always told us that family was the most important thing in life. He lived that rule. I haven't."

"We all make mistakes," Harry said. "A man who hasn't made a mistake ain't tryin' very hard. But I do agree with your granddad. Me, I'm itching to get back to my Miriam and young Tad. Meantime, she sends me letters." He stopped and tapped his friend's shoulder. "Say, have you tried sending your brother a letter? That might help."

Before Emil could respond, a group of men entered the restaurant, ready for their supper. Harry gave a plate of bread to another helper, who offered it to the workers.

"I'll play a last one for you," he said to Emil, who had finished the task, "and then I'd best be seeing to this. Will you be stayin' now or eatin' later?"

"I'll come back," Emil said. He liked Harry's idea and had decided to return to his tent and compose a letter that expressed his feelings of remorse.

Harry played "Woodman, Spare That Tree," causing the men who were munching on their snack to break into raucous laughter. There were no trees for miles around, just vacant land stretching beyond them toward the mountains, and the yawning star-speckled sky above.

* * *

The poker game began earlier than usual. Nate Hollander pulled up a chair and tossed a silver dollar—one of his last—onto the table with as much nonchalance as he could muster. This time, he was determined to beat Philippe DeVrees. His luck had run strong last night until DeVrees caught a mighty winning streak. Nate knew he should have been seeing to his job tending the stock, but the lure of the late afternoon game and the chance to defeat the haughty gambler proved a more enticing pursuit. Besides, Emil had already taken the fresh horses to the front. By the time he returned, Nate's game would be completed. No one need be the wiser for his absence from work.

As the afternoon waned, he found many reasons to regret his decision. The more he played, the more he lost. As evening fell, he found himself indebted to the card sharp holding a mark against his wages.

Philippe DeVrees eyed him from across the table. "Well?" He drew the word out in an almost musical way.

"Two," Nate answered. The word felt like dust in his mouth. He held three queens and discarded the deuce of spades and eight of diamonds.

DeVrees smiled and passed him two cards. He continued until each of the players had received their allotted cards.

Nate studied his hand. Three queens. He had drawn a four of clubs and a jack of hearts.

DeVrees laid down a flush. He straightened his shirt cuffs.

"We'll play again, Hollander, after we've eaten," he said, gathering the money and chips. "You can

square your marker and play again and try to
redeem yourself. If not—" He shrugged, leaving
the rest of the sentence unspoken.

Monty nursed a whiskey at the saloon, watching
people parade inside and out as they stopped for
refreshments or went about their work. The stench
of sweat, bitter cigars, and strong whiskey perme-
ated the saloon tent. Two men sat on a platform in
the corner, playing something classical sounding
on a guitar and a mandolin. Below the musicians, a
trio of scantily clad women twirled a haggard group
of men in a rugged rendition of a waltz. A huge
mirror reflected their movements.

In the short time he had been sitting there,
Monty witnessed two fistfights and narrowly missed
becoming involved in one himself. The bartender
had no information about Emil. Monty swallowed
the last of his drink. He did not doubt the bartender's word. This was not at all the type of place
that his brother would frequent.

As he turned to leave, someone shoved him
aside. Surprised, he lost his balance and landed
hard on a barstool. "Hey," he said.

Nate Hollander looked back and offered a short,
"Sorry, mister," before pressing forward through
the rest of the crowd and heading outside.

Monty rose to follow but felt a hand on his arm.
"Hey, aren't you the fellow rode in this afternoon
on that fine bay? I've been lookin' to buy a better
horse. Yours for sale?"

"No." He glanced after Hollander, and then
asked the man about Emil.

That produced no information about his brother but resulted in a lengthy discourse on the nags the man had ridden during his time with the railroad. By the time Monty disengaged himself from the conversation, Hollander was long gone, and the darkness had deepened outside.

After his discussion with Harry, Emil returned to his tent. He had intended to write the letter to Monty but the right words escaped him. After several frustrating minutes, he put aside paper and pencil and decided to take a walk. The cool air felt refreshing after the long, hot day.

He stopped at the corral. The horses had been watered and had plenty of hay. As he walked south toward the ridge, he heard the hum of conversations and laughter and the general din of the townspeople going about their evening activities.

Emil stayed quiet, the sounds of his footfalls lost in the background noise but the motion stirring puffs of dust behind him. He shoved his hands in his pockets, caressing the smooth case of Grandpa Long's pocket watch. If his grandfather were here, Emil felt sure he would be proud to learn of his grandson's promotion. He reached the top of the ridge. Proud, yes. But disappointed too that the boys he had raised as sons had fallen out over a woman.

Emil turned and looked down at the town of Benton. A variety of canvas tents, some large and some small, spotted the flat landscape. From this perspective, the town laid in a line along the edge of the railroad tracks as if some thundering locomotive had scattered its freight while speeding west. The flickering of lamps inside the tents cast a golden hue against the pale canvas, creating eerie shadows and strange spectral patterns.

The place was named for a United States Senator, Thomas Hart Benton, a man who was a passionate supporter of the westward movement. But the town's hell-on-wheels reputation surely did not suit a lawmaker. Scarcely any laws existed down in that mass of tents and degenerate humanity.

The forlorn yips and howls of a pack of coyotes increased Emil's feeling of melancholy. He longed for a place he could call home. He realized that he must overcome his anger at having lost Celinda to Monty. He was the one who should make the first move toward reconciliation. He pinched off a piece of minty-smelling sage and rolled the leaves in his palms, breathing deeply of the stringent scent. With renewed resolve, he headed back to town.

Nate stood alone in the middle of the small tent he shared with Emil Long. He had nothing of value to present to DeVrees as payment for the sizable debt he had incurred. He fingered the worn wool blanket covering his cot. That, plus the clothes he wore, were the only things he had left. The more he thought about his situation, the harder his heart pounded in his chest. Outside, the clamorous noises of people partying grew louder. He dropped to his cot and covered his face with his hands. Staring at his worn brogans, he watched a tiny black spider crawling through the alkali soil of the tent's floor. The spider reached the leg of the small table that held a single coal-oil lamp and Emil's books.

In an effort to distract himself, Nate picked up the top one, Plutarch's *Lives,* disinterestedly thumbing through the well-worn pages. Emil still had things. This book, his Bible. What might they be worth, he wondered, replacing the book on the table. As he did so, he realized that Emil, who still had books, likely still also had money. Emil had everything, and the more he thought about it, the angrier he got. He had introduced Emil to the hostler in Laramie City and that's how Emil had gotten this job. Even so, Emil refused to lend Nate money when he came up short before payday. In a way, then, Emil owed him. If Nate could find Emil's money, he could take some of it with a clear conscience.

He stood and rifled the blanket on Emil's cot. He threw his pillow in the air and clapped his hands against it. Feathers fluttered about the small room. Perplexed, he stood in the deepening twilight. Perhaps Emil was clever like some of the other men he had known who had kept their money in their shoes. One couldn't be too careful in a place like Benton.

A displaced feather lit on the black cover of the Bible. Nate had almost grown to hate that book, so often did Emil insist on reading it late into the night when he should have been asleep instead. Whenever Nate complained, Emil said, "Some folks value sleep, but I treasure reading."

As Nate recalled his words, a wicked grin spread across his face. He grabbed the Bible. Holding the book by the spine, he spread the covers and let the pages splay out like the wings of a clumsy bird in flight. Out fell money—mostly National Bank notes—but a few wildcat notes and three coins. Nate shook the book some more and then tossed it onto the bed. He picked up the half-eagles before kissing them and stuffing them in his shirt pockets. He jammed the papers into his trouser pockets.

"What are you doing?"

Nate whirled to see Emil standing inside the tent's flaps. Despite the dimness of the tent's interior, his gaze traveled easily to the disheveled Bible lying on the bed.

"Nothing that should concern you," Nate retorted.

Emil started forward to retrieve the Bible. With a quick movement, Nate drew the derringer he kept on his belt for emergencies and shoved the gun at Emil's waist. The noise outside, growing ever louder as the evening progressed, masked the smart pop of the gunshot.

Emil's face registered disbelief as he clasped his abdomen. He lifted his blood-soaked hands and looked at them, incredulous, before collapsing in a heap on the floor.

Working quickly, Nate wiped the blood from his own hands on the wool blanket on his bed. He searched Emil's pockets. He found a couple of dollars, a pocket watch, and a knife in a leather case, and he kept them all.

He pulled the blanket from Emil's cot. The Bible dropped onto the dirt. Blood that seeped from Emil's wound stained a corner of the book. Nate swore and tossed the soiled book on top of the dead man. He wrapped the body in the wool blanket, wiped his hands again on his own blanket, and rolled that around Emil as well. The blankets soaked up some of the blood still staining the pale floor. Nate covered up the rest by kicking dust on it.

He peeked from the tent. The night was fairly dark with only a slight sliver of a moon shining in the sky. Nate let his eyes adjust to the darkness. Knots of men crowded around the Big Tent and the nearest restaurant. There were still a few gathered at the flat cars loading them with tent canvasses and poles. Some of them packed as much as they could now so they could carouse longer tonight and sleep later in the morning.

He hurried to take down his own tent and kicked the bundle of blankets onto the canvas. He rolled the canvas around the disgusting bundle and secured the ends with rope. With some difficulty, he dragged the heavy roll toward the flat car.

"Here, I'll help." A man grabbed the opposite end and together, they lifted the roll onto the flat car among several other similar packs. "That must have been a big one."

Nate shifted a hip and sat on the flatcar, his back against the canvasses.

"What?"

The man jerked a thumb toward the canvas heap. "The tent."

"Oh. Yeah." He fingered his shirt pocket, felt the coins there, and found the makings for his cigarette. With slow and deliberate actions, he licked the paper, sprinkled tobacco on it, rolled it together, and twisted the ends. He struck a Lucifer against the rough boards of the flat car. The quick flare of the match cast a garish light on his angular face, sweaty from exertion.

He saw the other man's scowl before shaking out the match and dropping it. "Want one?"

"No, thanks." Monty Long recognized the man who had shoved past him in the saloon. He hesitated for a moment and then stated his case. He had repeated the story so many times that afternoon that his words sounded to his own ears like a memorized school day recitation instead of a sincere plea for help.

When he finished, Monty thrust his hand through the long dark hair at his forehead. The strands stood straight up for a moment before falling back into place, giving him a boyish appearance. "I'll never give up," he said. "I have a hunch I'm awful close to finding him," he said. "It's only a matter of time."

Nate Hollander sat almost motionless as Monty had spoken of the lost brother he hoped to make amends with, shifting position only to rest an arm on one of the pale bundles behind him.

When Monty finished speaking, Nate puffed on his cigarette and held the smoke in his lungs for a long moment. He exhaled slowly. "Time's runnin' out in this place." He took another puff. "You might try Harry's," he said finally. "I've seen Emil there sometimes in the evenings."

Monty nodded. "Thanks for your help." He strode toward the tent containing the restaurant, and midway, he realized he had not asked the man his name. He turned but the man was already gone.

Harry O'Malley welcomed Monty into his restaurant tent as he ushered a group of others outside. "We're closing up. Moving out tomorrow," he said, as he untied one of the ropes that held the tent to its poles.

"I'm looking for Emil Long," Monty said. "I'm his brother."

The heavyset man shook his head. "You don't say." He thrust a hand the size of a small shovel toward Monty. "Emil's a great friend. Pleasure."

Monty shook and asked if Harry knew where to find him. A frown crossed the man's face and he rubbed his peppery beard. "Come to think of it, Emil's not been back yet. He said he'd come back to eat. Not like him to miss a meal."

Monty laughed. "You do know my brother."

Harry's expression had changed to one of concern. "Sometimes he walks about at night. Probably nothing to worry about." He offered Monty bacon and bread. "He knows we're packing up. Maybe he'll be back by the time you've eaten."

Philippe DeVrees cocked an eyebrow when Nate came back to the game. He produced fifty-five dollars, falling thirty dollars short of what he owed.

The cardsharp, his voice smooth and even, said, "That doesn't cut it, Hollander." He raised his smooth hands. Unlike those of most of the men Nate knew, they were clean and free from calluses and blisters. "But you will work off the rest. A dollar a day. Or should I say night? You'd have to keep your daytime employment as well I suppose."

"No," Nate said. He produced the pocket watch and tossed it onto the center of the table. "This'll do and more. I'll win the rest back."

DeVrees tapped his slender fingers against the polished pine. After a moment, he made a welcoming gesture. "All right. Thirty dollars. But if you lose, you'll work off what you owe."

Distraught and exhausted, Monty Long entered the saloon. Emil had not returned to Harry's. He had suggested that Monty take another look at the corrals and then, as a last resort, try the Big Tent. "I've never known him to bet his wages," Harry had said. "But sometimes men behave differently when we're closing a town. Philippe DeVrees has gained many a coin that way."

The bartender directed him to a table in the back, motioning toward a slender man wearing a dark frock coat who stood talking to two others. When Monty approached, he greeted him cautiously.

"Our game has ended this evening," he said. "Follow along with us tomorrow and we'll take another turn in another town."

Uninvited, Monty pulled out a chair and sat down.

The surprised DeVrees dismissed the men he had been talking with and sat opposite Monty. As he did so, Monty's eyes came to rest on the loot piled in the center of the table. He reached out and retrieved the pocket watch.

"Pardon," the gambler said, miffed by the man's effrontery.

Monty held the watch by its leather strap. "This watch was my grandfather's."

"I think not," returned DeVrees. "I won that just this evening in a game." He watched as Monty twirled the watch on its strap, and then cradled it as delicately as if he were holding an injured sparrow. With a slight smile and a light chuckle, DeVrees said, "The young man who presented it could not possibly have been your grandfather."

He earned a wan smile for his poor attempt at humor. "Could it have been my brother?" Monty's eyes locked on the darker ones of the cardsharp. The gamester analyzed the dusty man seated before him. Deep creases fanned his dull eyes and framed his tight lips.

DeVrees leaned forward. "Possibly. What makes you so certain that watch belonged to your grandfather?"

Monty tugged on the slim leather strap. "He lost his hands in an augur accident working with wheat when he was a youngster," he said. The lines around his lips deepened as he demonstrated the way his grandfather had retrieved the watch from his pocket.

"Ah," DeVrees said. "Clever indeed. But many men carry similar timepieces. This one is not of great value, and it has no engravings to indicate ownership. Anyone might have attached a strap."

"Yes," Monty admitted. After a moment, he returned the watch to its place on the pile of coins and paper money. He rose to go.

DeVrees, intrigued by the man's behavior, plucked the pocket watch from the table and handed it to him. He described Nate Hollander.

Monty shook his head. "That's not my brother," he said.

A brief silence ensued. DeVrees said, "I'm feeling generous this evening. Clearly, this piece means a great deal to you."

Monty shook his head. "I don't want to be beholden to anyone."

"And your brother?"

"I don't know where he is," Monty explained. "I came here hoping to find him, but I've missed him again."

"Perhaps I could be of help to you." DeVrees clapped his hands, and one of the men who had been near him when Monty entered came to his side. "Bring us some whiskey," he said. To Monty he said, "Tell me about your brother."

The servant brought a decanter and two cut-glass goblets. In silence, he poured with care and departed.

Once again, Monty related the story. "I came to make amends," he said. "I should have never let Celinda come between us." He sighed and took a sip. "Turned out she played us against each other. When she found out she had me, she up and left. Set her sights on some other poor bastard."

"Women." DeVrees smiled. "I've had my share of troubles with them myself."

"I've searched Benton all evening," Monty said. "This"—he held up the pocket watch again, watching it as the lamplight gleamed on its plain polished silver case—"is the closest I have come to finding him."

"I've never had the pleasure of meeting your brother, Mr. Long," DeVrees said. "At least, as far as I know. Some players don't tell me their names. But I have ways of knowing who they are."

"Emil's not a gambler. But this watch . . ." Monty swallowed the last of the whiskey, savoring the burning sensation as the liquid slid down his throat. He stood up. "How much did you take it for?"

"Thirty dollars."

Monty let out a slow whistle. He searched his pockets. "I don't have thirty," he admitted. "Would you take twenty and a thank you for the whiskey?"

DeVrees said, "Sir, if that watch truly belonged to your grandfather, I cannot accept any payment from you for it."

Monty laid the money on the table. "And because it belonged to my grandfather, I cannot take it from you without paying. It's a matter of family honor."

DeVrees stayed silent for a long moment. And then he stood and extended his hand. "Thank you," he said. "It is my fondest wish that you find your brother, and when you do, I hope you will introduce us. You are a rare man indeed."

Nate clicked his teeth against his tongue. The bay, standing near the pole fence, ignored him, but a sorry-looking sorrel with a gimpy hind leg tottered closer. Nate moved away from the sorrel and tried again. The bay's ears pricked but he did not move. Nate kicked a toe in the dirt, sending a spray of white dust into the corral. The bay eyed him and moved away. Nate swore. The sorrel nickered, and other horses in the pen responded with sympathetic whinnies.

Nate decided to change tactics. This time, he stepped on the bottom rung of the fence. He climbed and was ready to swing a leg over when he heard the mournful notes of a harmonica. He swore again and leapt to the ground. The music grew louder. Nate hid in the shadows behind some spike barrels.

The horses in the corral shifted their positions and neighed as the harmonica player approached. Nate recognized the tune, "Tenting on the Old Campground." He stifled a groan, listening as the footsteps came closer. He drew his knees tighter against his chest, leaning forward just enough to see Harry O'Malley approaching the corral.

The stout Irishman rested an arm on the fence. After a few moments, he turned to leave. Nate relaxed and changed his position, ready to spring to action. He wanted to catch the bay and ride south, away from lingering gambling debts, from railroad work, from everything. He could sell the bay for a good price and start over somewhere else. He began to stand but heard Harry call out to someone. Nate pulled Emil's knife from its sheath.

"Any word?"

"No," Monty said. "He isn't here, is he." He spoke the words as a statement rather than a question.

"Not with the horses," Harry answered.

"I think I'll stay awhile anyway."

"Try to rest. We'll look again in the morning."

Nate crouched lower as Monty approached his hiding place. He came so near that the toes of his boots stirred the chalky dust between the spike barrels. Nate tried to calm his breathing so that he would not sneeze. His heart pounded with such force in his chest that his whole body seemed to pulse with each beat.

Monty reached above the barrels, snatching a soogan from the top of a wagon filled with supplies. He turned and took a couple of steps, and then began unrolling the bedroll on the other side of the wagon.

Nate knew he had to move fast or be discovered. Raising himself from the crouch, he bent forward, ready to run. At that moment, the harmonica played again. "The Blue Tail Fly," the annoying tune that Emil used to whistle or hum ceaselessly. Startled, he lost his balance, and struggling to regain his stance, reached for the spike barrel. The force of the blow toppled the half-empty cask. Spikes clattered into the dirt. Nate fell forward across the keg, his weight splintering the sides. The harmonica notes broke off in the middle of the tune.

"Who's there?" Monty called. He drew his pistol.

Nate raised himself from the dust. His clothes, already grimy with wear, were now cloaked with a layer of the gritty white alkali. His face, powdered with the pale dirt, took on a ghoulish appearance.

Monty recognized Nate, even though he did not know his name. "Hey. You the one who stole my brother's watch? Where is he?"

Nate raised the knife. "Gone to join the angels. Just like you will."

The revelation stunned Monty. "Why?"

Nate took advantage of his astonishment by rushing forward. Using his free hand in a swift motion, he knocked the pistol from Monty's hand. The knife was inches from Monty's waist.

Monty staggered backward. He sidestepped as Nate, shrouded in white dust, slashed at him. He reached to grab Nate's wrist but missed. The knife blade nicked his hand and drew blood.

Nate chuckled. The two men skirted the corral.

Intent on their menacing dance, neither one noticed Harry's return.

"Stop!" He grabbed Monty's pistol and aimed at Nate.

The pistol's pop frightened the horses. They trotted to the other side of the corral. The pounding of their hooves raised a wicked cloud of snowy powder, obscuring the fighting men from Harry's view.

Harry's shot missed. Nate lunged forward with the knife. Monty jumped back.

Nate stumbled on the pile of spikes, landing hard on his chest.

Harry and Monty closed in, but Nate did not move.

Puzzled, they stood quiet as the dust settled, revealing the splintered barrel and scattered spikes.

Nate lay spread-eagled in the dust, one arm raised above him. Harry toed the man's hip, rolling him over. The knife handle protruded from his blood-soaked chest.

"Be damned," Harry said. He grabbed the weapon and tugged it free. He wiped it on the dead man's shirtsleeve and turned it over in his hand, squinting at the sinister object in the darkness.

Winded from the fight, Monty sagged against the poles of the corral. "Too late now to make things right with Emil. I don't even know where his body is. Can't even give him a proper burial."

"No." Harry peered at the knife, certain he had seen it before. "Ah," he said.

Monty continued on as if he had not heard. "If only I had come sooner. I might have saved him. I've gone and ruined everything." He ran a hand through his hair and then covered his face with his hands. Blood dripped from his knuckle where the sharp blade had scratched the skin.

"No," Harry said. "This is rough country. You might have been right here when it happened and been unable to stop it. Don't be so hard on yourself."

After a few moments, Monty regained his composure. "He didn't even know that I came here. Didn't even know that Celinda left." He stood up and whisked the soil from his trousers. "It was all for nothing."

"No," Harry said. "Not for nothing. Emil wanted to make amends with you, too. Told me so himself." He clapped a hand on Monty's shoulder. "Didn't know how to go 'bout it, I reckon. Here." He handed him the knife. "Looks to me like he patched things up in his own way after all."

Monty examined the knife. Even in the dim light, he saw the initials "EL" carved on the handle. "Emil's," he said softly.

"Yes." Harry scowled at the dead man. "Let the gandy dancers deal with him. Come along, let's get a whiskey afore this place gits stirring again."

They walked toward the place that used to be Benton, past disassembled tent frames and stacks of lumber and through the immense dusty space that had only yesterday housed the gambler's den. As they came to Harry's wagon near the tracks, the first feeble rays of dawn cast a sallow glow on the jumbled heap of ragged canvasses stacked on the railroad flat cars waiting to travel west.

The Town That Wouldn't Quit

Deborah Morgan

Anybody with a lick of horse sense could tell you by evidence of its very name that the town had troubles. Boulder Creek River. That alone implied there had been an argument between one settler and another (or, one group of settlers and another group) over whether the creek was a creek, or the river was a river, or the creek was a river, or . . . well, you get the idea.

It doesn't matter that the body of water seldom appears, which leads me to call the thing a creek. Of course, it's been raining like Noah's nightmare for over a month, with no end in sight. That sort of fact used to give *me* nightmares, but those days were long before the turn of the century and for very different reasons.

A week's ride west and you'll fall into the Pacific. No, wait, that was back when the settlement was founded. Now, I hear tell a cowboy what can't find work can drive one of them there automobiles out to Hollywood in a few days, and upon arrival lasso a paying part in an oater before sundown.

Me, I'm faring well. But then, I'm a bartender.

Whether a town's flush or fold, a man needing a drink will spend his last two bits for it. Back in the day, I was considered the best in the territory. Like any good tapster, I was paid as much for listening as I was for pouring drinks. Nowadays, I'm a right chatty fella—no longer just a bottle opener with ears. My clientele seems weary of its own threadbare tales. But the old souls that hang out down here are more than just regulars. They're loyal.

You see, the town moved to higher ground longer ago than most care to remember, or can. Sad, though, none of those folks had the foresight to know how far they should've moved the place, and the new highway system bypassed the little municipality by two miles. Allowing that everybody taking to the open road is in such an all-fired hurry to get somewhere, that two miles might as well be two hundred.

The little town was floatin' on the fumes of post–World War Two promise, but it didn't have much to show for 'em. It wasn't fortunate enough to claim gold (the few veins below the streets had bled dry about the same time Custer did) and all them fancy Victorian houses people love to visit had washed away in a flood.

Their Chinatown was a short-lived affair during the equally short-lived run of the gold mines. Once crowded with busy workers at steaming pots of soapy water by day and opium den attendants by night, it now consisted of one family that ran the town's only dry cleaner. The bodies of a brother-sister pair said to have run the long-defunct opium den in the darkest regions of—well, everyone in Boulder Creek River had to admit that they weren't sure *where* the opium den had been located—were buried in the town cemetery.

The unsavory had settled the area, and it had taken five generations to water down the liquor, knock the plugs from the opium pipes, and build a community of people who were at least trying to earn a stamp of approval from their peers.

Ah, if only it were that easy, or even could be done in so brief a stint of history. Valiant, though, was the attempt.

The sad fact is this: Boulder Creek River suffers from threat of a chronic disease called extinction.

Oh, you wouldn't think it to look around. The state and county governments hold out their hands to collect taxes, telephone lines stretch overhead like circus wires, and living, breathing people move along its streets (though barely enough of them to keep the grass beat down that sprouts up from between cracks in the pavement).

Sure, the town has more than its share of abandoned businesses. What struggling town doesn't? The latest list of casualties includes the sawmill, the blacksmith, a couple of land offices, and one of the newspapers. The mom and pop café shut down after mom's heart wore out, and Hillis and Martin Attorneys-at-Large—excuse me, Attorneys-at-Law—lit out like singed cats, leaving behind everything from a fine-looking leather-bound set of the state statutes to a partner's desk the size of a boxing ring.

Modern additions to the garden variety establishments (general and hardware stores, barber and beauty shops, three churches, and a gas station with a white-capped attendant) are a new Dairy Queen over on the west side, and a theater that can usually manage to get a feature within three months of its premiere. Next to The Bijou is Woolworth's five-and-ten, so the whole block smells like fresh-popped corn. To the east, a place offering something they call "fast food" just went in across from the two automobile dealerships.

The town meeting is held the second Tuesday of every month, and on the second Tuesday of every month the residents face the pressing task of trying yet again to fabricate a means by which to generate tourism. But, before they get down to that Old Business, the meeting always turns into a heated discussion over the name of the town. Over whose ancestors *settled* the place. Over whose ancestors *named* the place. And, over who residing here now should be granted no small amount of respect, having proved their lineage to those first settlers.

There was just one problem with their thinking: they wouldn't follow those thoughts through to their logical conclusion. If they weren't so dead set on erasing the unsavory pasts of those business-savvy prostitutes and closed-mouthed charlatans that are their ancestors, they might recognize the grit and gumption of those raw and bawdy folks who defined the Wild West. For a fact, those founders had raised hell and reached underneath for an extra handful. But, they'd also offered up somethin' that intrigued enough upstanding citizens, which in turn got 'em to move in and kept the boomtown from going totally bust. Believe me, I know. I was there.

Anyway. Every month along this path to self-righteousness someone brings up the abandoned clapboard hotel on the south side of town, and many in attendance catch the emphasis on the word "hotel," and in that emphasis know that the speaker really means "brothel." That starts the same old argument all over again about the hotel's sordid past, and the subject is tabled until the next meeting.

Tonight's meeting'll be no different, and once Phase One is past, they'll dutifully move on to the next piece of Old Business.

Why, looka here. I've jawed on till I didn't realize we'd arrived. The meetin's in the big room upstairs, and it sounds like they've already started. . . .

The janitor had cranked up the heat against what promised to be a chilly soaker, and the radiators all but steam-dried the meeting's attendees. This made the town hall smell like a combination of wet hound, boiled mothballs, and Burma Shave.

Cy Harkreader, who had changed from his field-plowin' overalls into his Sunday-go-to-meetin' overalls, pointed out (yet again) the possibility that the apparent wishy-washiness indicated by the town's name made people steer clear for fear of confronting a bunch of bumbleheads.

"But, our name is part of our charm," countered Marybelle Monroe Adams Young Brown Evans. She'd been widowed four times—one for each decade of her life—and collected the names all together like teacups on a shelf. Folks who had tired of trotting out the monikers—and usually in the wrong order, only to be corrected by the widow—began calling her by the acronym Mrs.

Maybe (or Maybe Not, as the riffraff liked to add).
She didn't object to Maybe, and had seemingly
never heard the "Not."

Harkreader said, "Well, maybe—"

"Yes, Cy?" Marybelle touched a white-gloved
hand to her throat.

The man scowled. "May*haps*," he said, thwarting
any notion of adding his surname to the chain and
thinking how it would sour the spelling and his
stomach in one turn anyway, "we should get back
down to business. Those hogs won't get theirselves
over to the county fair come mornin'."

"You won't get no argument from me," said Billy
Young, who was a cousin-once-removed to Marybelle's second late husband. "I got two horses to
saddle-break at first light, and"—he paused to
brush thumb and forefinger along the edges of his
handlebarred cookie duster as if he were parting
the Red Sea—"these meetings are gettin' harder to
sit through than a picture show in The Bijou's
cheap seats."

A rumble of laughter came from the crowd.

"You're right about that," piped Luke Whitney
before the rumble faded. It was Mayor Whitney's
feeble attempt to take control of the meeting. He
seemed but a lad, what with his freckled face and
short-cropped red hair. In fact, he was thirty-six,
and lately made it a point to add "almost thirty-
seven," obviously believing that the double-syllable
number added maturity. Luke Whitney's day job
was rolling coins over at the First State Bank
and Loan.

I don't know which is more painful, watching
him try to corral coins or people. Between you

and me, I can't figure out how he got appointed mayor in the first place. Whitney's grandfather was a cowboy, but somewhere along the line that seed got strained through pillow ticking, and out came Luke.

The town's latest scheme was just as weak, if you'll pardon me for sayin' so; though, I admit it intrigued me more than the first two because it was located darn close to my saloon. Truth of the matter, not even I could've predicted the sorry outcome.

But, I'm gettin' ahead of myself.

First, of course, there was Scheme No. 1, and I will give them credit for effort. The enterprising citizens of Boulder Creek River threw one wingding of a rodeo. They somehow managed to book this singer by the name of Hank Williams who was getting a lot of air time on the radio. They hired Hatch Show Print out of Nashville, Tennessee, to make the posters, and the boys they paid to put 'em up didn't miss a shop window or a telephone pole between Dallas and Denver.

Mr. Williams's automobile broke down the night before he was to arrive for Friday's festivities, but his driver called ahead and assured the town they'd arrive Saturday.

Well, Saturday never came, because on Friday night the rodeo clown was killed by a bull named Lucifer's Ghost.

As with most rodeos, that night's grand finale was the bull riding event. I'll swear, those bulls were shipped here straight from hell, that's how mean they were. Now, a rodeo clown ain't just there to tickle folks. He's also got the job of protectin' the contestants from hoof and horn.

Before Lucifer's Ghost came outta the chute, a rider from up in Missoula got hisself in a pickle with an old Brahma called The Devil's Assistant, and this same rodeo clown seized up and left that cowboy to fend for hisself. Lucky the rider was seasoned, and thus able to save his own bacon—no thanks to the low-belly with the big red nose who was hiding in the barrel.

Most of the folks who saw what happened after that fiasco were heard saying that they didn't even like clowns, and that this particular example hadn't been a good clown to begin with. The AP had gotten wind of the dead clown, so I'm sure it appeared in newspapers all across the country. The town got ribbed some, but it seemed to boil down to this: The real tragedy was in the public nature of the whole thing and what it did to tourism.

For Scheme No. 2, the fair citizens created a full-fledged pony express stop. Mind you, they did not unearth, they did not dust off, they did not discover: they *created*. A traveling salesman whose home base was here in town had bought up memorabilia from a real stop in a Kansas town that was going belly-up. They used one of the abandoned land office buildings, and in no time they had the place looking dang near authentic. All they had to do was sit back and wait for the pigeons to flock in.

There was just one thing that the enterprising citizens hadn't taken into account. The mobilizin' of America had fueled more than its economy, it had fueled knowledge. America was doing its homework before striking out for points unknown.

And the first batch of tourists who ventured off the beaten path to check out Boulder Creek River's Authentic Pony Express Stop started asking questions practically before their kids had time to climb up on the plow horse tethered at the side of the building.

The tour guides (really no more than shills) stuttered and stammered those folks right back into their automobiles, which they in turn drove to the next town. There, those lost prospects used their refunded tour money to buy lunch, fuel up, shop for souvenirs, and help put that place on the map.

Strike two for Boulder Creek River.

Things had never looked worse for our little town. I had to hand it to them, though, because they looked the third pitch right in the face, and came up with their next swing for tourism: the Lucky Lady Gold Mine Tours, *complete with a real nugget of fools' gold at the end of every tour!*

So intent were they upon cashing in on the upcoming summer vacation season (as well as on erasing any memories of the previous failed attempts at tourism) that they shifted their efforts into high gear.

They unboarded one of the old shafts, hung lanterns on the original timbers, and opened for business. That's all they figured they needed: Bring 'em in, usher 'em out, easy as pie, quick money. They cut corners six ways from Sunday so they could be up and running by Memorial Day. They blocked off a second shaft without giving it a second thought—no need to tempt curious little spelunkers into getting lost—and, in so doing, blocked a treasure the likes of which they could not have dreamed up.

Now, it seemed that one more misstep and they might as well drive a stake through the town's heart (which, if anybody could pinpoint that faint-beating thing, the community might actually have a fighting chance).

Tsk, tsk. Makes me sigh, don't it you? However, we must bear in mind: This is the town that won't quit, no matter how misdiagnosed, no matter how anemic its veins, no matter how broken its back, the capillaries that are its citizens course blindly on.

Watch.

Mayor Whitney said, "I went over to the hospital in Hallston City earlier today. The Chastains are showing much improvement."

The crowd responded to this piece of good news with a round of applause.

"Furthermore, I am happy to report they have agreed not to sue Boulder Creek River."

More applause, louder this time and with whistles.

"We dodged a bullet there," Whitney added. "And, we were lucky to have Jupiter Briggs as our tour guide. He's done enough mining in his life to have learned some rescue procedures, and emerged with only a few bumps and scrapes besides."

A couple of men slapped Old Man Briggs on the back, and he waved off the attention.

"We need to learn from this experience," Whitney continued, his tone serious. "Why, if the Lucky Lady cave-in had killed anyone. . . ."

Aurora Graham cringed. Talk of death always made her cringe.

The old woman knew more of Boulder Creek River's history than anyone currently living there. She'd watched as the last of the Indians were subdued and herded onto reservations, she'd witnessed the first motor car jostle through, she'd seen presidents perched on platforms of steam-belching locomotives, and she'd seen presidents glance out windows of escorted limousines, giving the little town an indifferent glance.

Indifference. That was what she felt she received from the youngsters currently running town politics.

Despite this feeling, she was about to attempt once again to raise the attention of the city council when the mayor interrupted his speech and peered toward the back. "Ladies, would you care to share?"

A hush swept over the room. Gladys Roberts glanced about, and found all eyes watching her and Dottie Winters.

Dottie blushed, and focused her attention upon a spec of lint clinging to her sweater.

Gladys sat up, a position that seemed to help her put on even more airs than she'd shown up with. The effect, of course, was heightened by a new dress and matching hat. "I was just telling Dottie that it takes too long to get products way off out here, and I had to go all the way to Hallston City for the latest Roy Rogers line for Little Roy's bedroom. I originally ordered from Carson's General Store—as you know, I always advocate supporting local business, particularly since my husband, Big

Roy, owns the Chevrolet dealership—but, it was back-ordered—*twice*. The Roy Rogers bedding, that is." She spent a smile that said *nothing* from the dealership ever had to be back ordered, then continued. "At that rate, I was afraid Little Roy would outgrow the notion before he had a chance to sleep one night on those sheets." She shrugged. "I had no choice.

"Besides," she went on, "who can resist those new department stores with seven floors, attendants in the elevators, and restaurants overlooking the capital."

Oohs and aahs echoed throughout the room, mostly of feminine voice.

Cy Harkreader said, "You're either loyal to Boulder Creek River, or you ain't, Gladys. You can't paint both sides of that fence." This was followed with hey-hou's and guffaws from all the men.

"Cy Harkreader," Gladys said, "you've got a lot of room to talk. Isn't the real reason you want to wrap things up early tonight is so you can drive your harvest to Hallston City tomorrow in your *Ford?*"

"If you want to complain about something, talk to your sister over at the café. Her coffee gets any weaker, and she'll have to rename it Lorena's Tea Room."

The mayor slammed gavel against oak.

(Everyone knows that Cy and Gladys have a history going all the way back to high school.)

Byron Knox (known as Mr. Lorena's Tea Room among the riffraff) said, "Trying to talk to that woman is like catching smoke. You'll just stir things up, and come out empty handed every time."

Gender wasn't particular over this one, and everybody laughed.

Everybody, save Aurora. The old woman sighed and dropped chin to chest. It had happened again. The townsfolk were so caught up in their own selves that they had once again failed to hear the cracking, old voice of the ragged woman leaning for support against the back wall. She chewed over ways to get them to notice her, to give her the floor, to make them listen. It seemed to her that the more frustrated she became, the more they ignored her. She wanted to cry out, *"You were so close! The other shaft, the big one, will never cave in!"*

Not only that, she thought, *it leads to a tourist draw to beat all tourist draws. But, first, you have to quit treating me as if I'm invisible.*

She glanced out the window. The rain was picking up. She remembered a time when the citizens of Boulder Creek River worried something fierce over the rainy season.

The dam had changed all that. Flooding was no longer a concern. As a matter of fact, water was no longer their enemy. Just about the time farmers like Cy Harkreader were nigh on to giving up, God would smile down upon the land, provide just the right amount of rain, and the crops would prosper. In turn, those farm families would win blue ribbons at the county fair, the wives entering jars of jelly, canned tomatoes, bread and butter pickles, and doodads with stitches so straight they'd gone near blind sewing them. The men would choose the biggest and best from vine and stalk: pumpkin, ears of corn, cukes, watermelon. They'd crate chickens, load hogs—anything that fit a judged category made the trip to the fair. Prize and pride usually helped homestead them through another long winter.

But, this time around, they'd held on almost too long.

"Still, that doesn't put gravy on the biscuit," said Widow Parsons, but I'd missed what she was referring to. Lucy Parsons ran a little poultry business on the west side of town. "Sure, we're scraping along. But you know as well as I do that bringing more people into town helps all of us—that is, as long as Lyle Vincent over at the IGA and the town's three restaurant owners keep buying my eggs and the Harkreaders' produce and pork."

"There's the rub, Mrs. P," responded Vincent. "You know we're trying to keep things local. But, the tin can distributors are offering some pretty sweet deals if we'll buy in bulk."

"The *rub,* Mr. Vincent, is that there aren't enough people in Boulder Creek River to justify buying in bulk." The Widow Parsons nodded her head once for emphasis.

"There will be if we get more people to move in."

Harkreader said, "You'll drive out us farmers with that kind of thinkin'."

"I see where you're coming from," said Vincent. After a brief pause, he went on. "Now, here's an idea. You ranchers and farmers could put on a chuckwagon show! When I was back east last week for the Independent Grocers Convention, a store owner from New York City talked about taking his family to one. He said they had a whale of time.

"It's like this." He stood and faced the group, then continued. "You give city folk the opportunity to ride on a hay wagon, eat chuckwagon beans, let their children ride ponies, and listen to some lively music. Harkreader, you and some of the other fellas play music, don't you?" He didn't wait for an answer. "Your wives could do the cooking, you could do the entertaining, and you'll make a profit off them watching what you do every day anyway."

"Sounds *swell*." Harkreader didn't even try to sift the sarcasm from his voice. "Get up at five in the morning, work our fingers to the bone all day, then stand on our feet all night pickin' and grinnin' while city folk look at us like we're monkeys in a cage. No, sir."

Someone near the front said, "Well, nothing against the farmers, but what if we move the town closer to the highway?"

"Won't work," said Vincent. "The folks in West Packersville tried that and the place was dead and gone before your boots hit the floor that night."

Things quieted down as that sunk in.

After a moment, a young woman broke the silence. "We *can't* let this town die."

Her quiet plea was more like a cry, and Mayor Whitney's response had a kind tone to it the like of which no one knew he had in him. "Go on, Mary."

"I . . . I didn't want to bring this up before, but—" Mary's husband put his arm around her shoulders and gave her a squeeze. She gulped air, then blurted, "My baby is buried out at the cemetery, and I simply cannot leave him here alone in that tiny grave."

The place was so quiet, you could hear the clock ticking from across the hall.

Aurora stared at the young woman, realizing for

the first time that she wasn't the only mother who'd lost a child. Out of habit, she reached in the pocket of her threadbare sweater and rubbed her fingers over the little case that held the photograph.

"Mary's right," said the husband. "We've got to think of something to save the town. I don't care what it is."

"How does it work when a town dies?" This came from a young woman standing in the back with a toddler propped on her hip. "I mean, do we just up jump the devil and drive? I don't know about the rest of you, but I don't have any place else to go."

It had been a long time since any of the community's young people had showed an interest in saving the town, and the town took it like a booster shot. The gathering livened up a bit.

"We'll come up with something," said John Larkin, proprietor of the Gold Nugget Hotel. "I'm sure of it." He'd been doodling in a notebook, ready to come up with new business names to consider as soon as the town settled on its next scheme. Larkin had been first in line at Tinley's Signs to commission the change of his shingle for the throngs of rodeo folks expected. That's when Larkin Inn became Lariat Inn. Then, for the pony express stop, he had it repainted to read The Mail Bag Hotel. For the Lucky Lady Mine? The Gold Nugget Hotel. (After the cave in, Larkin tacked a length of tent canvas over the words "Gold Nugget" and everyone knew he was itching to have another crack at that sign.)

Mrs. Isaiah Carson, who didn't keep secret her belief that the practice of renaming one's business was a waste of time and good sense, said, "Carson's

General holds steadfast to the notion that a good product, backed by solid business sense, will speak for itself."

Larkin scoffed. "It's thinking like yours that put Tinley out of business."

What had happened regarding the Tinley family was no secret. After all the sign painting for Scheme No. 1, Ike Tinley put back enough money to buy his sixteen-year-old daughter a new Mustang (the automobile, not the horse).

Scheme No. 2 found people a bit more skittish, and put Tinley up against a passel of haggling over price quotes for repainting.

Third time around, the handful who changed the names of their businesses tried their own hand with a brush (exceptin' Larkin). Tinley gave up and moved his family to California.

"Speaking of signs," said Mrs. Carson, "I must again point out that our highway sign, 'EAT GAS' is *not* an appealing invitation to prospective tourists."

Mayor Whitney shrugged. "It was all we could afford, after paying out so much to Tinley."

Folks apparently had run out of steam, because no one countered.

At length, the mayor called for a motion to table the issue of tourism, and to hold a special meeting the next Tuesday to field new ideas.

"I'll make that motion," said Harkreader.

"Second," said Larkin.

"Those in favor, say 'aye.'"

A halfhearted "aye" came from an unquestionable two-thirds majority.

Mayor Whitney stood. "Tuesday at seven, then.

Meanwhile, put your thinking caps on." He dropped the gavel.

The meeting broke up the way most meetings do. Several attendees milled about and made small talk, a handful kept controversies going, and the few who wouldn't speak up during the meeting buttonholed others in order to give their two-cents' worth. Aurora took one more look around, then slipped unnoticed out the door, and into the night.

It was raining harder, and she drew her shawl tighter around her shoulders. Head bowed against the pelting rain, she made her way several blocks toward the portal to Downtown.

She entered the alley between the abandoned blacksmith building and the dilapidated clapboard hotel, and shuffled carefully along the cobblestones toward the dead end. When Aurora reached the weathered and worn fence that covered the portal, she counted over to the sixth board, then began maneuvering the maze of sliding planks. It wasn't necessary; simply a ritual she'd performed upon every return to the underground town for a hundred years. Or, was it a hundred ten? She was beginning to lose track.

Board after board, she worked the puzzle, sidestepping through slender openings, closing—without conscious thought—each piece behind her, until at last she was on the other side. She slowly made her way down the dark stairway, steadying herself with her hand against the dank stone wall.

* * *

The street lanterns flickered, reaching for scarce oxygen in the confines of the underground town.

All seven saloons were packed. Aurora knew the crowds: gunfighters looking for a moment's reprieve, thirsty cowboys fresh off the trail, cardsharps facing wary marks, hard-hearted madams looking to make a buck, and scant-clad soiled doves looking to make a nickel.

Jesse James walked her direction from across the muddy street, toting a Bible and wearing a sign that read "justice." Two prostitutes trailed him, offering their wares. He ignored them.

Aurora detoured, preferring the quiet of the alley that would lead her over to the next street and beyond to her destination.

Here, in the darkest regions of the underground town, the old woman stepped inside the opium den. Kim Wong looked up lazily from the divan upon which he reclined and nodded solemnly to her before passing the pipe to his sister. Aurora returned the gesture—exactly as she had every night for sixty years—then went out through the back door.

Morgan Earp was on the boardwalk up ahead, checking that the lock was secure on the mercantile's door. He tipped his hat in greeting.

"Wyatt have a game going tonight?" She asked.

"Down at your boy's place, same as always."

"Doc there, too?"

"Nobody's seen him. Must have got the go-ahead to move on."

This gave her pause. Presently, she nodded, resumed her pace.

Upon entering the saloon, she glanced around

to determine whether anyone else besides Doc Holliday was missing. In the far corner sat Hickok, playing poker with his back against the wall. Jack McCall stood on tiptoe nearby, twirling aimlessly in circles and tripping occasionally on the frayed length of cut rope dangling from the noose around his neck.

"Aces and eights *again?*" bellowed Wyatt Earp. "When did you get so damned lucky?"

Hickok smiled and raked in the winnings.

"Aurora," I called, motioning her over to the bar where I'd poured her favorite.

She hoisted herself onto a barstool, sipped the brandy. "The dry creek bed will be a creek by morning, and if those rains continue like they did back in 1846, it'll be a river by end of week."

"Won't make no never mind to us." I pulled the tap and drew a beer for myself. "You been up there again, ain't you?" I knew she had, of course, but she didn't know I'd been there too.

"Don't matter if I have. They never listen anyhow."

I smiled. Most of the beings here in Downtown accept the fact that they are between worlds. Once every sixty or seventy years, though, a soul like Aurora comes along—one who can't let go in order to move on.

"This place would save them." She sipped more brandy. "People would come from all over the country to see it. It's perfectly preserved, exactly like it was before the big flood pushed them to re-grade and build a new town on top of the original. This one recovered, like it had always done before, but they'd had enough. They buried it once and for all."

I said, "I'll admit that after the dam was built, it changed everything. We don't have to worry about flooding down here anymore."

"Downtown's twice the size of Uptown. Their solution is right under their feet."

"Maybe so," I said, "but there's no way of lettin' them know that."

"I'm going to keep trying. I can get them out of their fix."

Poor Aurora. She won't accept the plain fact that the folks Uptown can't see or hear her. Her rantings reach them as gusts of wind that rattle the windows or slam the doors. When it happens, those who are scared by it tell themselves, *there's no such thing as ghosts, there's no such thing as ghosts, there's no such thing as ghosts.* Believe me, I know. I've heard them.

Edward Knowles, a banker whose claim to fame is delivering telegrams as a boy in Deadwood to Teddy Roosevelt and Seth Bullock, slammed back a rye whiskey and said, "Don't you see, Aurora? They don't *want* a solution. They think they do, but if they had a bona fide solution to this problem, they'd have to come up with another problem." Knowles tapped the bar twice—his signal for more rye—and continued. "If it weren't for those town meetings, Harkreader would have the dreary task of sitting at home and watching his wife cut up potatoes for planting. In turn, she would have to watch him do something or other that she'd once found endearing only now to find that it irritates her to distraction. Will they say anything to remedy their domestic plight? No. They've all stopped listening to one another at home, and yet there's still enough regard in public to maintain a semblance of listening at those meetings."

"Ha," said Aurora. "They don't listen to me."

Knowles waved her off, his expression clearly showing that he was giving up on her. He rose, drank the rye I'd poured, and started toward the batwings. "If you'll excuse me, I'm going to look again for Misters Roosevelt and Bullock."

I shook my head. He wasn't going to find those two in Downtown. I had watched this replay every night since the banker arrived after driving his new Cadillac off a bridge. He claims it was an accident, but I happen to know he'd just got news of the stock market crash in twenty-nine.

Aurora finished her drink, then fished in the pocket of her tattered sweater and retrieved the tintype. The red velvet that covered the case was worn to a sheen, the rounded corners rubbed through to the metal frame. She untied a silk ribbon as pale and worn as she was, and the case fell open. No one in the crowded bar heard the faint jingle of the broken clasp, but Aurora had heard it enough times to know its sound, like the tinkle of a little bell for her little angel.

She stared at the image inside, and searched the depths of her audio memory for the girl's voice. It too had grown fainter with time.

I leaned over and gazed at the photograph. "Happy birthday, little sister."

Aurora looked up, wide-eyed. "It *is* today, isn't it?"

I nodded. "Fair Emily was born on the eighth of September, 1842."

I watched her as she studied the image, and thought about our history together. I was ten when

Aurora, my mother, took her own life. I always felt she blamed me for my little sister's passing, and I forgave her for the blamin' because I somehow knew it was her way of handling the grief. There's no explaining how the mind works after such a loss, when the hole in your heart is too big.

At thirty, I lost my life to a stray bullet during a fight while bartending in this very spot. But Aurora knew me instantly when I arrived here, and that eased some of the childhood pain.

Aurora said, "I'm fading, Josh. I can feel it."

I didn't want to tell her I knew that, or how. "Bringing the living down here won't keep it from happening, though. What's worse, it'll push us out, force us to some unknown place."

Irony is a fascinating thing, and I've seen more than my share of it as a fixture down here. Aurora took her own life in order to join her little girl, and has been suspended for what seems to her like forever in this transitory world. Is it because she left me as a child to fend for myself? Is it because she performed an unacceptable act? Is that why all of them are stuck here, waiting for approval to move on?

I've witnessed more times than I care to count the range of emotions: fury to the brink of insanity, followed by aggravation when they realize they're powerless in the face of a force they can't fight—or even see, for that matter—then withdrawal to examine their inner hell and, finally, surrender to their fate.

I polished a glass, then turned and lined it up on the shelf with the others. When I glanced in the mirror at Aurora, the reflection was so faint I could barely see her.

"Let go of the past, Aurora, so you can go on up and see Emily."

"But what about you?"

Her reflection flared, as if some fire inside her had been fanned. I said, "What do you mean?"

"I left you behind once. I don't want to again. What's holding *you* here?"

My mouth dropped. After a time, I clamped it shut.

She smirked, raised a brow. "We all have our demons, don't we, son?"

What's she talking about? I wondered. I wanted to say, *I'm here to help you, don't you know that?* But, I didn't. I looked around. I'm here to help all of them.

I shook my head to clear it. She was leaving soon, that was obvious. This nonsense must be her way of trying to hold on.

"No skeletons in my closet, Aurora." Then I distracted her with the obvious. "What demons do you have, other than those folk Uptown who ignore you? Admit it, I'm the only one who doesn't ignore you."

"You have to give people credit, though, Josh. The town just won't quit."

I smiled. "Which one?"

Now We Are Seven

Loren D. Estleman

"Well, Syke, it appears to me you can't stay away from bars of any kind."

It was the first friendly voice I'd heard since before the bottles broke. I sprang up from my cot—hang the hoofbeats pounding in my skull—and leaned against the door of my cage. "Roper, you're a beautiful sight. Come to bust me out?"

"Why do it the hard way? Gold's cheap." He grinned at me in the light leaking from a lamp outside the door to the cells. Same old Roper, gaunter than the last time we rode together and kind of pale, but maybe he'd been locked up too. There was lather on his range clothes and his old hat and worn boots looked as if they'd take skin with them when he pulled them off. He'd been riding hard.

"If gold was cheap, I wouldn't be in this tight," I said. "I got into a disagreement with a local punk shell a couple hours ago, and now I'm in here till I pay for smashing up a saloon. I drunk up all the cash I had. I should of just went on riding through."

He sent a look over his shoulder, then pushed

his smudgy-whiskered face close to the bars and lowered his voice. His breath was foul with something worse than whiskey, like the way a buzzard stinks when it's hot. "I'll stake you, if you'll come in with me on a thing. There's money in it and some risk."

"Stagecoach or bank? I quit trains. They're getting faster all the time and horses ain't."

"Bank, and a fat one. Look." He glanced around again, then drew a leather poke from a pocket and spilled gold coins into his other palm. They caught the light like a gambler's front teeth just before he pushed them back out of sight.

"Damn, you hit it already."

"I scooped 'em out of a sack they was using for a doorstop. They've got careless. It's been years since anyone tried to stick up the place."

"Bull. What stopped you from picking up the sack?"

"I didn't want to put them on their guard. I intend to go back with help and clean the place out. A sack of coins only goes so far, but what's in the safe could shore up the likes of you and me for life."

"If it's as easy as that, how come it ain't been stuck up in so long?"

"The local law's got a reputation. Fellow name of Red pinned on the marshal's star a good while back and shot five good men as they come out the door with the gold. Another man wanted in Texas and Louisiana tried to beat him to leather when Red braced him. He had the edge on everyone in New Orleans and San Antonio, including two Rangers, but Red put him in the ground with one shot. Things kind've fell off after that."

"Red who? A man with that behind him ought to have his last name plastered over six territories."

"Well, it's a sleepy little town name of Sangre, most of a day's ride from this jerkwater. Three hundred years back it was a mission. Some tin-hats from Spain used it to coin the gold they stole from the injuns down in Mexico and store it till they got back, only they never did. The folks that still live there each claim an equal part."

"No job's that good," I said. "Dry-gulch this Red and just ride out rich as J. P. Morgan? You're drunk."

"Ain't had a drop. I rode all night hoping to find a man experienced enough to help me get the bulge on that lawman. When they told me at the saloon you was in here I figured God must want me to be rich."

I drummed my fingers on the bars. "Well, I got a heap of doubts, but anywhere's better than here. First thing in the morning—"

"What's wrong with right now?"

"Court ain't open at night. You can't just settle up my bill with the deputy."

He was still holding the poke. He bounced it up and down on his palm, making the coins inside shift around with a merry little noise. "I didn't hear him squawk when I slipped him one of these to let me in past visiting hours."

"I'd as lief not risk it. If he gets a sudden fit of honesty, I'll have a cell mate."

"I'll just go feel him out. I'm a fair horse trader, don't forget." He left before I could stop him, closing the door behind him and leaving me in darkness.

In a few minutes a crack of light showed and he

came back in, rattling the key on its big brass ring in his hand. "Told you he was reasonable," he said, inserting it in the lock.

The office was dim, lit only by the lamp on the desk with its blackened chimney. The deputy sat on the edge of the light resting his head on his arms folded on the blotter. A bottle of busthead whiskey stood nearly empty at his elbow. He'd stunk of it when he locked me up. You just can't get good help in public service out on the frontier.

He was a sound sleeper. He didn't stir when Roper hung the key back on its peg and took down another to get my pistol rig out of a drawer in the gun rack. My hat was on the hall tree, my bedroll leaned up in a corner, and I got those. We let ourselves out of the quietest room I'd ever been in with a drunk passed out in it. He didn't snore so much as a sister of mercy.

My tough little piebald was saddled and tethered next to a big gray with Roper's outfit on it at a rail behind the jail.

"I got your horse and gear out of the livery after I left the saloon," he explained. "I was pretty sure you'd take me up on my proposition."

I strapped my roll behind the cantle and stepped into leather. "I hope to hell you're right about that gold. I'm already in to you for more than I'm worth."

He grinned at me in the moonlight, gathering his reins. His eyes looked as bright as if he'd had a stiff snort. I figured he'd helped himself from the deputy's bottle. "We'll work out something."

* * *

It was desert country. The sun came up red as a boil and made its way clear across the sky and we didn't meet anyone on the road. By daylight Roper looked even paler and more gaunt than he had at night; at times I could swear I could see right through him, but that was the heat. It looked to be taking more out of him than it did me, though I never once saw him drink from his canteen, even when he poured some in his hands to water his horse. I was sure he had and I'd just happened to be looking at all that fine scenery—mesquite, cactus, and the odd darting lizard—but when I drank my last drop and he offered me his, it was almost full.

"This trooper I talked to one time said he'd been a camel wrangler, some kind of cavalry experiment that didn't pan out," I said, corking it up and handing it back. "He said the critters can go a week without water. I didn't put any store in it then, but I reckon now you must be part camel."

He grinned, teeth long and yellow in his fleshless face, and slung the canteen back onto his saddle horn. "I don't seem to need as much as I used to."

Shadows were getting long when we topped a low rise and there was this little mud pueblo at our feet. It looked like some you see out in that waste, a cluster of rounded buildings, some caved in, around a well that didn't look as if it would give up anything but a bucket of dust. When Roper picked up his pace I figured we were stopping there to rest our horses in the shade, but then we passed a board from an old wagon nailed to a post with SANGRE painted on it in dusty brown letters that must have

been bright red when they were new. My heart
dropped straight into my boots at the sight of it.

"Hell, it's a ghost town. Why'd you want to pull
my leg with all that gold talk?"

"Keep your spurs on, cowboy. How long you think
it'd stay put if the place looked prosperous?"

I didn't say anything. I was biting mad. I was
grateful to him for getting me out of a hole, but this
dried-up pimple of a place didn't look like much of
an improvement. If there was any water at all in that
well I'd fill up my canteen and ride on to a town
with life in it. That's how far my hopes had shrunk
in eighteen hours, from a new horse and outfit and
a spread of my own to a wet whistle.

Sangre didn't look any more promising from the
middle of it than it had from on top of the hill. The
saloon was still standing with the roof posts sticking
out in a row and no door, but the livery and general
store had fallen in and I only knew the purpose of
these establishments from their signs, painted right
on the crumbling adobe in the same faded brown
as the name of the town. I considered it an indication of ill fortune that the one building that looked
sturdy enough to stand on its own happened to be
the jail.

"I hope that marshal you told me about is one of
your stretchers," I said, drawing rein. "If he ain't,
he's the only other thing breathing in this bump in
the desert."

"Oh, Red's real enough. The breathing part's up
to you and me to fix."

I stepped down and tied up in front of the saloon
without a word. I knew for sure then he was full of
sheep dip, talking about bushwhacking right out

there in the open where anyone could hear. That sickly look made sense now; he'd eaten a mess of crazy grass or drunk from a bottle of Dr. Sloan's thinking it was Old Pepper and it had cooked what little brains he'd had. I unslung my canteen and strode over to the well, ringed with rocks in the center of what had been the town square.

I couldn't see to the bottom, but it didn't even smell like water. The length of stiff rawhide that hung over the edge and down inside wasn't encouraging either; it looked brittle as hell and if there was a bucket on the end of it the bucket wouldn't hold so much as its breath. I started hauling anyway. I didn't expect to draw anything out.

There was weight on the end. That gave me hope, but not much. Sand's as heavy as water. I pulled up twenty feet of rope if I pulled up an inch, took hold of a wooden-stave bucket by its bail, stood it up on the edge of the well, and looked inside. When I saw what it contained I yelled and let go. The bucket fell to the ground and split open, spilling out a pile of bones.

It wasn't as bad as I'd thought at first. At second look they weren't human. I recognized a cannon bone and pieces of rib too big around even for Goliath and there were some thin hollow shards like pipestems that would belong to roadrunners or those little lizards that raced around on their hind legs like they had somewhere to go. I used the toe of my boot to separate a piece of oblong skull I figured belonged to a gila.

Roper came over to see what I was kicking around.

"Huh. Critters hereabouts must be as clumsy as fat acrobats."

"They couldn't've all fell in. Them horse bones wouldn't fit with the horse still attached. Somebody put 'em there."

"Kind of funny when you think about it."

"Kind of crawly. Who collects carcasses and dumps them in a well?"

"Injuns, most like. They do all that heathen stuff to keep their gods happy. Thirsty?"

"I'm dry as a deacon. You think I came here first thing to suck on some old bones? Where's your canteen?"

"I didn't mean water. Let's go in the saloon."

I stopped being grateful to him then. The jail back in town was starting to look good. "You fixing to stand me to three fingers of dirt? Who stocks a bar with nobody to sell whiskey to but horseflies and rattlers? Where's that bank stuffed full of double eagles? There ain't even a bank!"

"There's a bank, but there ain't no double eagles in it."

"I knew it, you—"

"I told you they're Spanish coins. They stamped them right here in town out of bullion they shipped up from Mexico." He took out his poke, plucked one from inside, and laid it on my palm.

It was about the size of a cartwheel dollar but heavier, with a foreign-looking jasper gaping off the edge and on the other side a ship. Even with the sun going down it glowed there in the desert like a small sun its ownself. The side with the head had Spanish writing stamped on it in a half-circle: MONTON DE HISPANIOLA NUEVA—CIUDAD DE SANGRE.

"I'll be damned."

"Look at the date."

1540. "I'll be double-damned."

Roper was grinning that horse grin. "Now you want to take me up on them three fingers of dirt?"

"I'm buying." I flipped the coin high, caught it, and stuck it in my pocket. He shrugged and took the lead.

Inside, the saloon was as dark and cool as a cave. It didn't have any windows. It didn't have any bartender either, and only two customers. When my eyes caught up to the dim I saw the bar was a thick cedar plank laid across two barrels that might have been as old as that coin, and cedar shelves behind it holding up rows of squat bottles black as ink, with dust on them.

"Stock's limited." Roper stepped behind the bar as if he owned it. "What'll it be, wine or rum?"

"Wine, I reckon. I never had rum."

"When'd you ever have wine?"

"Rum, then. Where the hell is everybody?" I'd never seen a ghost town where a man could get drunk without bringing his own. Drifters would've cleaned the place out years and years ago.

"Siesta'd be my guess. Mex habits die hard in these here mission towns."

"I didn't see no mission. Anyway, siesta's always at noon."

"We passed it on the way in. Cross probably fell off the roof back when George Washington was a pup." Roper uncorked a bottle, sniffed at it, and thunked it down on the bar in front of me. Dust jumped up from the plank and settled back. "It was just like this when I rode in yesterday about this time. Place gets right lively come sundown. Everybody in town shows up."

"How many's that?"

"About five." He struck a match and lifted the chimney of a green brass lantern on a nail. What little light there had been was almost gone.

"Regular mee-tropolis, ain't it?"

"They're the five richest folks in the territory, don't forget. A fifth part of what's in the bank'd stake old man Vanderbilt to a bushel of railroads." He finished lighting the lantern and leaned his elbows on the bar. He hadn't gotten a bottle for himself. I asked him if he was keeping temperance.

"Ain't thirsty."

I didn't rise to that a second time. If he wanted to dry up and blow away it was his business. I took a careful pull from the bottle. The place didn't seem to have glasses. The stuff inside tasted musty, but it had a nice little kick. I helped myself to a swig and started feeling better right away.

"What makes a rich man stick around a pile of buffalo chips like this?" I wanted to know. "I'd take my cut and light a shuck for San Francisco."

Just then a new voice joined the conversation. "San Francisco's full of thieves. Red can't protect 'em there."

I'd gotten so accustomed to just Roper for company I nearly choked on rum. I spun around, scooping out my heavy Colt.

The woman I drew down on was pretty as day break, and about as scared of getting shot as a ouff of warm air. She was delicate-boned, with a mass of yellow hair that fell in waves to bare white shoulders that looked polished. She had on a white dress with black spots and nothing holding it up but a pair of bosoms I could see nearly all of. Her feet were bare and she wore gold hoops in her ears like the women you sometimes saw dancing on tables down in Mexico, only she wasn't Mexican. She had blue eyes and red lips and little sharp teeth that showed when she smiled, as she was doing then. She stood in the doorway with one hand resting on the frame and the other on her hip.

"That there's Cora," Roper said. "Cora, meet Syke. He's skittish in the heat."

Sheepish was the word. I holstered the Colt and muttered a howdedoo.

She took me in without moving her eyes. They were the coolest things in that burnpatch, but they set me on fire worse than the rum. "Your friend looks healthier'n you. Roper. Been up to something you shouldn't?"

Now it was his turn to look sheepish. "Back off a dally, Cora. I'm a greenhorn."

"Green don't last out here. You best listen to good advice when Red's giving it."

I couldn't follow the conversation any more than a trail across rock, but I was starting to smell something bad and it wasn't the bones in the well. I turned on Roper. "You both sound tight with this here Red. I thought he was the lawman we're trying to avoid."

"It's a mite more complicated than that." He was looking at the ground now. That floor was made of dirt packed harder than iron.

Cora said, "Cork that jug, stranger. We got a business meeting to attend."

She stepped away from the door then. The pool

of light from the lantern was lopsided and when she passed through shadow them blue eyes glowed like red sparks. I corked the jug. A little stimulant seemed to go a long way in Sangre. Anyway when she came back into the light her eyes looked normal, though not ordinary.

After that the place started to fill up, and nothing was ever normal again.

They slunk in without so much as a rustle of cloth or the clink of a spur—going out of their way, I thought, to avoid the shine of that lantern, like wolves circling a campfire. Three there was, ragged saddle tramps in greasy hats, shirts missing buttons, and Levi's faded white, with holes enough to embarrass a scarecrow. These clothes and their bandannas hung off skin and bone, and the shanks of their broken-down boots wobbled on their ankles so loose they could step right out of them if they lifted their feet high enough. As it was they shuffled, raising clouds of dust, and their eyes glowed red to a man, all but the one that was covered by a leather patch the man had cut right out of his vest, where it matched the hole. In a few seconds they and Cora and Roper had me surrounded in a half-circle like the writing on the coin in my pocket, with the bar at my back.

Roper was with them, I saw now. He'd stepped away and turned to face me with the rest. His eyes were alight too, but not as fierce, just a glimmer like the first weak spark from flint and steel. I hadn't noticed it last night, and we'd ridden miles in the dark.

I was shaking, but the weight of the Colt was back in my hand and settled it. None of them was packing that I could see.

"This the best you could rustle up, Roper?" It was the man with the patch talking. I could smell his breath six feet off. It was worse than Roper's. It belonged down there in the well back when the meat was putrefying. "He don't bring much to the pot."

"I did the best I could with the time you gave me." I turned my gun on Patch. "I got six slugs and there's five of you. Stand aside or I'll blow down the lot."

Roper said, "Put it up, Syke. It's a dogfall."

I swung the muzzle his way. "You just moved to the head of the line, you snake. All I got's my horse and outfit. You could've bought them fair and square for what you paid the deputy to bail me out instead of hauling me clear out here just to dry-gulch me."

"I didn't give him a cent. You didn't look at him too close."

"What'd you do, buffalo him? I didn't hear a shot."

Cora gave me a pitying look and turned on Roper. "That was taking a chance. You heard what Red said."

"I made it back, didn't I?"

The air changed, as if the saloon still had a door and someone had kicked it open, creating a current. The half-circle broke in the middle and someone tromped in to fill the space, raising more ruckus than the rest of them out together. He wore heavy silver spurs, the kind vaqueros wear below the border, and they jingled and clanked like irons on a condemned man. The boots they were strapped to were cavalry, the stovepipe kind with flaps that cover the knees, and they fit, but they were in as poor shape as the rest, run down and cracked. He had on a rusty black frock coat, cavalry trousers with stripes up the sides, with darns and patches, and a star on his lapel that looked as if it had been hammered out of brass by someone who didn't know much about smithing. A forage cap with a square visor sat atop a nest of hair that bushed out and tangled with a beard that covered him from cheek to brisket. It was the color of copper.

"I'll ante up and reckon you're the one they call Red." My voice was shaky but I reined it tight. I shifted my target to him. He had six inches on the next tallest man there and more gristle than the rest combined and was the easiest to hit.

His eyes barely lit on me before shifting to Roper. They were coal black with no red in them, at least not there in the light. "You fed." His voice was rain barrel deep and hard.

"I had to." Now, *there* was a quaver for you. "It was a long ride into town."

"And a long ride back. For you, almost an eternity. I told you what happens after the first time. The sun won't hurt you until then. The effect may be delayed but not avoided. An hour this way or that can make a difference, and you wouldn't have survived a second dawn. You put us all at risk."

"He came through, Red." Cora sounded timid. I hadn't known her three minutes, but it seemed out of character.

"Don't take his part unless you want to have horse instead."

That silenced her. Red didn't yell, but his words

rang like a hammer on an anvil. He seemed to have some kind of accent—Mexican, maybe, despite hair color and pallor—but it might just have been his careful way with the language I noticed, as if he was borrowing it and wanted to give it back all in one piece.

I cracked back the hammer. The Colt was a double-action, but I wanted his attention. "I come here for gold, but I'll just take my horse and go. Nobody's eating it tonight or any other."

The big man looked at me full on for the first time. "It wasn't your horse I was talking about. Roper's has served its purpose. Do you want to see the gold?"

"I seen it. I figure what I seen is all of it. If I wasn't hung over I never would've fell for no bank out in the middle of nowhere begging to be robbed."

"Hernando."

He barked the name without taking his eyes off me. A man with two little triangles of black moustache at the corners of his wide mouth turned and shuffled out. He was back in a couple of minutes dragging an army footlocker. At Red's direction he scraped it into the middle of the room and lifted the lid. It was filled to the top with yellow fire. The coins matched the one Roper had given me. The sight pretty near disarmed me, but I tightened my grip on the pistol.

"Go ahead, fill your pockets," Red said. "You'll need an explanation for how they came into your possession, but I've found gold evaporates suspicion. It makes partners out of strangers and friends out of enemies."

"Talk sensible. Roper said your job was to protect it from road agents."

"Admirable. Inspired, no doubt, by this star I made from a coin. It quiets newcomers long enough to hear my proposition."

"I knew you wasn't no law."

"Oh, but I am. Hundreds of men and women were slaughtered on my word alone, many years ago. Pardon my ill manners. Out in this waste one comes to neglect the proprieties. I an General Alejandro Rojas, late in the service of Charles, King of Spain and Emperor of the Holy Roman Empire. That's his likeness." He gestured toward the coins.

I laughed high and harsh. "You fried your brains in the heat. Them coins are three hundred years old."

"Three hundred thirty-three. I had the pressing equipment shipped from Gibraltar in 1537 and supervised the first run. Of course, that was before the curse."

I let him jabber. I couldn't get my mind off that footlocker. I'd raised my goal to include survival *and* making away with all it contained. I'd bluffed folks less simple.

"We drafted native labor to transport the gold from Tenochtitlan. We weren't gentle about it, and many of our prospects resented the whip and thumbscrew. One was a priest, who when we dragged him from the temple said something in his savage tongue and spat in my face. Naturally I had him dismembered. I didn't know the significance of his action until the Hunger."

That distracted me from the gold. I remembered I hadn't had a bite in twenty-four hours. That run on an empty stomach had commenced to make me hear things he couldn't be saying.

"Chupador de sangre." He enjoyed the taste of the foreign words. "Bloodsucker, a fresh title for my string. I was voracious, but the sight of solid food sickened me. Upon impulse I preyed on an Aztec slave. I was fortunate in that our expedition was only hours from home. I felt the weakness in the sun that Roper knows so well. I slept, satiated, but when the orb rose the following morning the first shaft burned me on my pallet. I fled for the darkness of the mission, where I avoided immolation, but the burn would not heal. Later I had all the religious iconography stripped away and buried. Once the building was desanctified I recovered. I am, as I said, cursed."

I kept my mouth shut. He was loco sure enough. I hoped he wasn't so far gone he'd try to jump an armed man. I'd drop him, but if the others joined in I'd have a fight on my hands.

He seemed to know what I was thinking. "Gentlemen. Lady."

The men wore bandannas around their necks, all except Red, whose throat was bare. Now they drew them down and advanced into the light. Each had two tiny craters three or four inches below the left ear, as if they'd tangled with barbed wire. Cora's showed when she swept back the mass of hair tumbling to her shoulders. Roper's looked redder and rawer than the rest.

"I alone am unmarked," confirmed Red. "My condition was caused by black magic, not by having been fed upon. I am like Adam, who alone among men has no navel.

"We subsist on blood. When humans are unavailable—a chronic condition here—we make do with stray horses and other creatures that are barely sensate and so have no souls to animate them when they perish. Their remains go into the well, as the spectacle of a pile of bones might frighten away intelligent bipeds. "Do you know now why you've been summoned?"

I was feeling as pale as the rest, but I kept my fist tight on the grip. "You got particular bedbugs is all. They prefer necks. Now go fetch some sacks and get to work emptying that there box. I'm fixing to ride out of this crazy house a rich man."

Roper said, "You always was slow, Syke. When you ride out, it'll be to fetch someone back to take the taste of horse and gila out of our mouths. All the towns close enough to ride to and back are too far away for them that's fed to make it home before we burn up like ants in a skillet. I took my turn, now it's yours."

"Don't forget them coins for bait." This was the man with the patch on one eye. "See can you interest more than one in our little old bank. We'll be hungry an hour after you're sucked dry, scrawny fella like you. Roper's horse won't hold us nor yours neither, once you got your use out of it."

I laughed again, making out like I was enjoying myself. Truth was they had me jumpy as beans in Chihuahua, and half believing what they said there in the night. Come sunup I'd be laughing for real, by which time I'd be well on my way back to civilization, rich as Pharaoh. In another minute Red would be claiming him as a personal acquaintance.

"So you're all desperadoes," I said, "stuck in a

trap set with money. What's that make Cora, one of them bandit queens you read about in dime novels?"

"She came with Perkins there, fleecing their way across the West with cards and the old badger game." Red indicated the last member of the party, with big ears and what must've been a honey of a pair of handlebars before the wax run out. "She was a windfall, although keeping her in clothes is a challenge. Some of our citizens came with changes in their bedrolls, but she's our only woman. Fortunately she's handy with a needle and thread. What she's wearing used to be a nightshirt."

"You like it?" She spun around on a bare foot, letting the dress billow. "I made the spots with dye from a deck of cards. I'm partial to patterns."

Red said, "Look for yard goods while you're about it. Cora let out these rag-bag items Patch brought back, but they want mending again. Think of it as a trip to town for supplies—and provisions."

"That's a right smart ghost story, but it's smoke. What keeps 'em from just riding on?"

The big man smiled, teeth as long as Roper's and as sharp as Cora's in the red beard. "We'd be more than six if that didn't occur from time to time. Not much news reaches us, but I assume some got caught in the sun after they fed and then returned to the earth as dust. I can't imagine even a few others surviving long once townspeople started dying and coming back as one of us. There's always a wise padre or an immigrant from a European village versed in the old methods of destruction.

"It's not as tragic as you think," he continued. "You'll exist without fear of age, illness, or death, and we're an entertaining crowd. I can tell you stories of the conquest, and Hernando knows all the gossip from the old Spanish court. He was a viceroy as well as a colonel under my command. He was also my first companion in this condition, after the Aztec slave I fed on passed the seed to him, then fled into the desert, roasting himself to a crisp. All the other soldiers deserted, which was a pity. What a mighty band of immortals they'd have made."

"Don't forget you're rolling in gold." Patch's sneer climbed one side of his face to his ruined eye.

"Quite right. You'll have an equal share, and you can amuse yourself betting at cards or throwing coins at Cora's feet when she performs. She knows all the songs that were popular in St. Louis when she came to us thirty years ago."

"Red, you charmer," she said.

I'd had my fill of his charm. I shot him point blank.

When the smoke cleared he was still grinning. "That takes me back. You can have no concept of the relief I felt when a frightened corporal fired his matchlock in my face. Spanish armor wasn't designed for this climate. I let him run away with the others and took off the breastplate for good."

I fired again, with the same result, and tried my luck with the rest. Roper was the only one rattled, but when he checked for holes and come up dry he blew a stinking blast of air my way and uncovered his horse choppers, which had grown pointy since the last time.

I stumbled back against the bar, knocking over the bottle of rum and fumbling at my belt for fresh cartridges.

Red seemed to lose patience. He pointed his

shaggy chin at the one called Hernando, who lunged and seized my gun arm with cast-iron fingers. It went numb and the pistol thumped the ground. Roper got me on the other side, and although his grip wasn't nothing next to the foreigner's it was stronger than I remembered from arm wrestling him. Patch and Perkins squatted and grabbed my ankles. I was pinned like a bug.

"Ladies first." Cora's face blurred as it came close, leaving only eyes red now in the light and those teeth.

I woke up in dead dog darkness and knew it was the mission where we all slept, though there were no sounds of breathing or of any of the little stirrings that people make in their beds. They'd fed and were resting contentedly. I lay on straw scattered on hard earth.

They built those adobes to last in the old days— Red's time—with walls two feet thick and not a window or even a chink to let in light and heat, but I knew it was daytime just the same; I could track the sun across the sky by the throbbing in the holes in my neck. In a little while it would let up and I'd have the strength to sit a saddle. I hoped I could hold out longer than Roper without feeding, but I hadn't had anything but rum in so long I knew what it was like to be a gaunt wolf when game was scarce. I didn't want to make a mistake and burn up, and I didn't want to let anybody down. It was my turn.

Contention City, 1951

Jeff Mariotte

My first mistake was buying that last whiskey at the Sundown Saloon. No, I take that back. My first mistake was following Donna Lambert into that roadside honky-tonk. My second through fifth mistakes involved the whiskey.

The Sundown was five or six miles from Fry, a town that had grown up around Fort Huachuca. My military career had taken me far from southern Arizona, which was how I liked it. But soldiers from the fort drank at the Sundown, and apparently during my time away, Donna had decided that soldiers—those currently in uniform, not those who had disgraced it and spent time in the stockade— were more deserving than me of having those long, dark eyelashes batted at them.

Donna had always been generous with her attention and affection, even in high school. She had grown up since I left for the war; there were now fine, faint lines at the corners of her mouth and around her green eyes, but still, all she had to do was shake that sandy hair down or cock a hip at me and I'd have gone anywhere for her.

The fact that the place I went for her was the Sundown was, as already mentioned, the beginning of a string of bad ideas.

The place was jumping. Ranch hands and cowboys, which I had been, filled the booths on one end of the room. Soldiers, which I had also been, stood at the bar and gathered near the juke, hogging the tables around the sawdust-covered dance floor.

She spotted me as soon as I passed underneath the neon sign and through the front door. She had already made her way to the military side of the room. Since men outnumbered women by about five to one, she was surrounded. She threw a scowl my way and whispered something to the gathered soldier boys. My cheeks burned when they laughed and shot me angry glances.

Not that I blamed them. I'd have done the same, a few years before.

Hank Williams wailed on the jukebox as I crossed the room, crunching peanut shells and sawdust under my boots. I wore a snap-button shirt and dungarees, and the crewcut under my straw hat was still army short.

The soldiers' glares warned me that if I approached Donna, they'd toss me out on my ass. Instead, I squeezed close to the bar and ordered that first shot of courage.

The smoke and the chatter of conversation and the loud music and the clinking of glasses wore on me. So did the booze. The joint was hot and sweat pooled under my arms, running down my ribs. When I downed my fourth and turned to look for

Donna, the floor tilted up under me and I almost lost my balance.

I decided I needed another drink, to steady myself.

The fifth one did the job. Either I was steady or the room spun at the same speed I did. I needed to talk to Donna, and I meant to do it now.

She was dancing close with one of the soldier boys. I tapped him on the shoulder.

"Marshall," Donna said. She sounded weary, but I suspected she was just tired of me. "This isn't a good time."

The soldier hadn't let her go, so I shoved him out of the way. "There hasn't been a good time since I got back," I said. "Y'know, what with my mom being dead it hasn't been that great a time for me either, but I've at least tried to talk to you."

"Maybe she's avoiding you for a reason," the soldier said.

"Are you still here? Me and the lady are talking."

He put a hand against my chest. "Look, Mac—"

"Marsh," I interrupted. "Marsh Sinclair. You don't want to mix it up with me, but if you're fixing to, at least use my right name."

Donna said something quiet. It sounded like an insult, but I wanted to be sure. On the jukebox Kitty Wells was crying about something, for about the fifth time since I had entered the Sundown, and I couldn't take any more of her. I staggered to the juke and yanked the plug, then turned back to Donna. The joint had gone dead quiet.

"I can hear now, if you want to repeat that," I said.

I started toward her, but one of the biggest, ugliest GIs in the place cut me off. "That was my song," he said, putting a big cold hand against my chest.

I reached in my pocket. "I think I got a nickel, so keep your pants on. You can play Kitty again when I'm done talking to my girl."

"Don't sound like she's your girl," the gorilla said. "Not to hear her tell it."

"I haven't been your girl for years, Marsh," Donna said.

"You wrote me, in France."

"Twice. Once to tell you we were through."

"I figured on account of I was at war, you didn't really mean that." I was taking a chance, depending on what she had told her new friends about my service record.

As it happened, she had told them plenty.

"I'm surprised you brought that up," the big man said.

Somebody else spoke too, but by then the juke had been plugged back in and the big man had thrown a fist into my gut and another soldier had grabbed my arms and pinned them behind me, and whatever was said got lost in the confusion.

When my eyes opened again, I was flat on my back in the parking lot. Deputy Brian Wallis looked down at me. The sky behind his head was littered with stars.

"That's a lot of stars," I said. "In New York you can't see that many."

"This what you came back for, Marsh? To get the crap kicked out of you in some dive?"

"Not specifically."

"Can you move? You need a doctor?"

"Is my head still attached to my body?"

"Looks like it."

"Then I'm probably okay. Longer I lay here, the more everything's starting to hurt."

Brian hooked an arm under me to help me up. Even that much activity made pain lance through me. "Easy," I said. I took a couple of quick breaths. "Guess they did a job on me."

"They did. Said it was self-defense. That you pushed one of them. That true?"

I wiped blood out of my eyes. I could taste it too, and my tongue fit into a slot where a tooth used to be. My hat was on the gravel next to me, crushed almost beyond recognition. The knuckles on my right hand were skinned and sore, so I must have gotten some licks in. "How many of them said it?"

"All of 'em. Including Donna." Brian had gone to high school with us and knew our history. Like seemingly everyone else in the state, he knew my more recent history as well.

"Then it won't matter much what I say, will it?"

"Not if it goes to court," he agreed. "I'm gonna have to take you in, Marsh. Let's get going."

He helped me to my feet. My right knee buckled and he caught me before I fell, but it made everything hurt all over again. "For fighting?" I asked.

"For drunk and disorderly, to start with."

I tried to gauge my mental state. "I *was* drunk," I said. "But if I was still drunk I wouldn't feel this much pain, would I?"

"You smell like the inside of a bottle," Brian said. "They tell me you were knocking 'em back pretty hard in there."

"Guess I was, then." I shook free of his grip and walked to his patrol car under my own power. "Your place got pillows?" The army's guardhouse had been short on such luxuries.

"You can wad your shirt up and sleep on that," Brian suggested.

On the way over, I made Brian stop once and let me out so I wouldn't vomit all over his backseat. I didn't last more than about twenty minutes in the cell before I was asleep. I hadn't taken my shirt off, since I was sure that process—not to mention bruises I didn't want to see—would make me puke again.

From the cell, I thought I heard a telephone ringing, but couldn't tell if it was in a dream. A little later, Brian unlocked the door and shook me awake. "Get up, Marsh!"

Remembering where I was took a few seconds, and remembering how I got there longer than that. "Why?"

"We got an emergency call," he said. "You know George Moffat?"

I pictured an old man, hands always shaking a little, fingers starting to hook inward like claws. He had a ready smile, a few teeth short of a full set, and eyes that had almost disappeared behind folds of skin while I was still in grade school. "He still around?"

"He was. His sister called in and said he's wandered off by himself."

"Is that a problem?"

"He's not right in the head, Marsh. Senile, I reckon. She takes care of him. It's just them two on their ranch and they don't really work that anymore. She doesn't know where he's gone or when he left."

The fog in my mind began to lift. I had always liked George Moffat. Hell, everybody liked George. He was a character, a long-time rancher with roots in the area stretching back further than just about anybody's. He always had a penny and a wink for kids he met in town, and a grin for their parents.

He had been forgetful for years, it seemed. But I hadn't heard that he'd gone so far downhill. It was a cool night, and if he was stumbling around in the dark, he could do himself some serious damage. Over a few days, he could die of exposure.

"Sheriff says you can join the search party," Brian said. "We need every able-bodied man we can get looking for him."

"My head is still pretty—"

"I'm sorry for not being clear, Marsh. Sheriff says you'll join the search party or he'll make sure the county prosecutor throws the book at you. You'll be charged with drunk and disorderly, assault and battery, property damage, and whatever else they can think of."

"Isn't blackmail still against the law?" I asked. "Or did they change that while I was away?"

Brian didn't think I was funny. "Your call," he said. "You coming, or am I locking you in here by yourself?"

"You got a jacket I can use?" I asked. "And water and maybe a gun? My stuff is all in my truck."

"We'll swing by and pick it up," he said. "It's on the way to the Moffat ranch."

* * *

As Brian promised, we drove back to the Sundown Saloon. I got my denim jacket off the truck seat, my Winchester rifle from the rack, and what was left of my hat off the ground. I punched it a couple of times and made it look more like a hat, but it'd never keep my head dry again.

About thirty people had gathered at the Moffat ranch. The women would stay with Shirley, old George's sister, who had to be at least seventy. The men had come to search. I had the feeling most of them had not just been arrested or beaten up.

Brian took a backseat to Herman Fairhope, who was fifteen years older than us and acted as if he'd been with the sheriff's office since the days of Wyatt Earp and the unpleasantness in Tombstone. Herman handed down search rules like they were commandments from on high and he was slightly more important than God. Stay with your team, don't get out of sight, carry water and a firearm for protection and to signal with.

I recognized a few of the men. The local faces got older but otherwise didn't change much. Kids grew up and left the area, and like me, sometimes came back. It was hard for ranch families to keep them around, and getting harder all the time. Then the war had disrupted families everywhere.

These were hard-bitten men with leathery, raw-boned faces chapped by wind and weather. They wore denim jackets like mine or canvas barn coats, work boots, and hats that they toiled in every day. Most had arrived in trucks, some towing horse trailers. The horses were turned out into a corral; we would be searching on foot, the way Shirley believed George had gone.

By the time we got underway, the sun skinning over the Dragoon Mountains was spreading pink undertones across cloud bottoms. It hadn't rained since mid-September and Halloween had passed, so the ground was dry and hard. Old George hadn't left much in the way of tracks, just a few scuff marks that might have indicated he had gone east. The search party broke into groups of five and set out toward the various points of the compass. My group, which included Brian Wallis— presumably so I wouldn't escape—headed into the rising sun.

We worked our way across grassy pastures that hadn't been recently grazed. Pigweed grew as tall as a man, as did sunflowers, their blooms long gone. Yucca stalks erupted from spiky balls and probed the sky. Thorny mesquites dotted the landscape, their leaves darker green than the creosote bushes trooping around them. Dried-out Russian thistle had stacked up against fences and more grew wild, along with yellow-tipped rabbitbrush. The scant tracks that might or might not have been George's had long since vanished; no path showed through the overgrown fields.

Besides Brian and me, our group consisted of Lester Crain, a beefy guy who had been a friend of my brother Dayton Jr., an older rancher named Pat Griffin, and a slender, gray-haired man who looked familiar but who I couldn't place. We had been on the trail a couple of hours when a search plane flew over, wagging its wings at us. We watched it go by, and then Brian called a rest break. I glanced at the man I didn't know, who sipped from one of the blanket-sided canteens the sheriff's officers had loaned us. The sun had been beating down on us, warming the day considerably.

He caught my eye as I unscrewed the cap off my own canteen. "You're Maude Sinclair's boy?" he asked.

I swallowed, drew the canteen away from my lips. "Yes, sir. Marsh Sinclair."

He covered the distance between us with his hand outstretched. "Isaac Schultheis," he said, and instantly I knew who he was. "I'm sorry for your loss, and sorry I never got to know your mother better. She seemed like a fine woman."

Easy for him to think so, since he didn't know her. Isaac Schultheis owned a grocery store in Fry that she wouldn't patronize because he was Jewish. I had met plenty of Jews in the army, and Italians, Irishmen, and Negroes too, and more in New York afterward. As long as they weren't phonies or too full of themselves, they were all okay with me.

Truth was, my mother had a mean streak, and as she got older she stopped trying to control it. She seemed to think age gave her license to make any nasty, hurtful comment she wanted, and rarely offered anything but complaint and criticism. I didn't come home after getting out of the stockade partly because I was embarrassed to see my friends, but mostly because I didn't want to see her. Phone calls were bad enough. You'd think once she had told me a hundred times how disappointed my father would have been in me, that would be plenty, but she wouldn't let up.

"Were you in the war?" Schultheis asked.

"Yes, sir." When I didn't elaborate, he searched my face for a minute. I could tell when he remembered what he'd heard about me, although he tried unsuccessfully to hide it. I didn't look away until he did, opening his canteen and taking another drink.

"Guess we'd best get on with it, then," he said.

"Right."

My mother was right about me, was what it came down to. My father, Dayton Sinclair, had served in the first war. He never talked much about what had happened there, but it was assumed because of the kind of man he was that he had been a hero. He had been dead for nine years by the time the Japs bombed Pearl Harbor.

The next day my brother Dayton—we all called him Day, and that suited my mother, who had believed that the sun rose and set for him since the instant of his birth—enlisted. Day was killed at Normandy, cut in half by Nazi machine-gun fire while storming the beach. The soldier who told us that also told us that his friends blew up the machine-gun nest, as if that made it somehow less horrible.

I supposed I could have stayed out of it, since my father and brother were both dead and my mother needed someone to help run the ranch. But she didn't protest when I told her I was enlisting. She found some Mexican workers through the *bracero* program and they did a good job on the ranch, and she probably liked them better than she ever had me. Anyway, I had Nazis to kill, an older brother I idolized to avenge.

Only it didn't turn out that way.

The army was full of fakes and creeps, guys who had never ridden a horse or milked a cow, much less pulled a stubborn calf out of its mother at four in the morning in ten-degree weather. Some thought

I was a dumb farm kid, which maybe I was. I thought they were too slick for their own good.

But I got through basic at Fort Hood and made it to France a few months before the end. That was where I learned that real combat, as opposed to the idea of it, scared the hell out of me. I didn't want to be on the front shooting Germans, but behind thick, solid walls someplace.

What ended my military career was a long night in a little French town called St. Fromond-Eglise. We moved in on the town, which had been occupied by the Nazis, through fog so thick I couldn't see three feet past the end of my rifle. We had spread out too far, and at some point I realized I had no idea where the rest of my patrol was. I couldn't call to them, because I didn't know where the Krauts were. I was walking blind, feeling like my ears had been stuffed with cotton, and so scared of walking into a nest of Nazis that I could hardly swallow.

I almost bumped into the wall of an old stone farmhouse before I saw it. Feeling my way to a window, I peered inside. There didn't seem to be anyone home. Figuring I could hide out until the fog lifted, I broke the lock on the door and went in.

It was cowardly, but I had been coming to accept the fact that I was not courageous. At least not without a few drinks inside me. In the kitchen I found a couple dozen bottles of wine. I thought maybe I could pour myself some bravery, get back out there, and find the rest of the guys.

I cracked open the first bottle.

And then the second. I didn't stop drinking. I finished that bottle, most of another, and fell asleep at the kitchen table. When I woke up, it was almost noon.

Twelve of our men had died in a firefight during the night. A battle I had missed, sleeping right through in a drunken stupor.

Still half-drunk, I stumbled outside reeking of wine. The fact that our guys had won the fight didn't make things any easier on me when I found them. I had been AWOL, drunk on duty, and exhibited extreme cowardice under fire. The battle I had slept through would be my last. Until my dishonorable discharge came through, I spent the rest of my enlistment in the guardhouse. My military career at an undistinguished end, I bummed around the East Coast for a few years. Three weeks after my mother's death, the sheriff managed to track me down and I came home to figure out what to do with the ranch and all her things.

Then, of course, booze got me in trouble again, and here I was, hung over and aching from the fight, tramping through the brush looking for a lost old man. So far all I had seen was a coyote, a few field mice, and about a dozen jackrabbits. Vultures circled overhead, and every time they swooped low, someone gave a shout and ran over to see if they had found George. So far, they hadn't.

Mid-afternoon, a sheriff's deputy in a Jeep found us, bringing bologna sandwiches and refilling our canteens. None of the other search teams, he reported, had turned up anything. The plane had flown over the whole region, farther than even a healthy man could walk, much less one as old as George, without success. We took twenty minutes to eat the sandwiches, then continued our search.

We had almost reached the San Pedro River when the sun went down. The cottonwoods lining the riverbanks had lost most of their leaves, but a few stragglers still clung, yellow and faded. We approached with the sunset at our backs, passing north of the ruins of the old Spanish fort called *Presidio Santa Cruz de Terranate*. It had only been occupied for five years before the Apaches drove them away, a century before the little town on the river's far side, Contention City, had been established.

"We're going to camp at Contention," Brian Wallis informed us. "Supplies should already have been dropped off there, and we'll continue the search come daylight."

"Aw, Brian," Les Crain grouched. "I got stuff to do."

"We all do," Brian said. "That's why we asked everybody to agree before starting out that they'd be in on this until the end."

"I didn't think it'd go overnight. How could that old man cover so much territory?"

"Sheriff's called for more searchers and airplanes," Brian said. "Tomorrow I'm sure we'll find him, but for tonight, unless you want to walk back by yourself, you're stuck with us."

Les's gaze bore into me. "Stuck is right," he said.

It wasn't hard to figure out what he meant. He had been one of Day's best friends. The fact that I had come home instead of Day had upset my mother tremendously, and she wasn't alone in that regard.

In the half-light of dusk, we scrambled down the west bank and forded the river, which was only

about eighteen inches deep here. Contention City
rose on the east bank—what was left of it, anyway.

The town had been built as a mill site for Tombstone. Tombstone had miners and money but no
wood or water, and Contention City had both, as
did Fairbank and Charleston to the south. All were
empty now, mostly forgotten. Ghost towns.

Contention City had been constructed mostly of
local stone and adobe, with some wooden walls and
floors and ceiling timbers. Little remained except a
few walls, most half-obscured by mesquite. A former
mill, where ore from Tombstone's mines had been
crushed, was the tallest remnant. Contention City
also had the nearest train depot to Tombstone,
and part of that was still standing as well.

Sure enough, someone had dropped off bedrolls
and tarps, cooking gear, and some grub for dinner.
Brian and Pat Griffin set to clearing a fire ring and
starting a fire with downed branches. It turned out
that Pat had brought a couple bottles of tequila in
a knapsack he'd been toting all day, and before
dinner was even cooked, people started in on one
of those. Every inch of me ached, so I lowered
myself gently onto a carpet of cottonwood leaves
and waited for the bottle.

When I reached for it, Brian Wallis shot me a
look that could have frozen the flames. I passed the
bottle to Isaac, who took a swallow and handed it
off. "His family lived in Contention, didn't they?"
he asked. "George Moffat's?"

That sounded right, and I said so. I must have
looked surprised that he would know.

"I've made kind of a hobby of local history," he

said. "It's a fascinating region, and I like to know about the place that I live in."

"I think there was some old story about the Moffats in those days," I said, but the details were lost to me.

"There was an altercation of some kind," Isaac said. "One of the participants was a Moffat, I'm sure of it. Just give me a few moments." The bottle made it back around to me. I skipped it. Once again, Isaac took just enough to wet his throat. After his every swallow, Lester Crain stared daggers at me, folding thick arms across his chest.

"It involved a big cat," Isaac said. His eyes were closed, like he was visualizing a page of a book he had read. "A jaguar. A white jaguar! That's what it was."

"Never heard of such a thing," Pat Griffin said.

"Of course not," Isaac replied. "This is a story, and stories have to include things that aren't commonplace. That's the whole point. Anyway, as I remember it, this Moffat fellow was hunting outside of town. He said the white jaguar had been attacking local livestock, and he shot it. When he returned with the carcass, townsfolk worried. To the Apaches, they said, the white jaguar was sacred, and they worried about what might happen when word spread that one of their own had killed it. The Apaches were still a real threat, given that Geronimo didn't finally surrender until 1886. The incident in Contention City would have been a couple of years before that, maybe eighty-two or eighty-three."

"What happened? Was there an Apache attack?" I asked.

"As I understand it, the town suffered a rash of

bad luck. Fires, accidents, a mill building collapsed. Finally, something especially tragic happened . . . I think the drowning of a young boy in the river. That was the spark that set things off. Guns came into play. Someone took a shot at one of the Moffats. Apparently a Moffat fired back, and the battle was on." He offered a wan smile. "The mechanics of gunfights are, I'm afraid, outside my area of expertise. Let's just say bullets flew and a fire started, some say coming down the hill from the old *presidio*. When it was all over, dozens were dead and much of Contention City was destroyed. It was the beginning of the end for this place."

The sun had gone down, the only light now coming from the fire pit. Brian passed out bottles of Coke and plates of cold *carne asada* and warmed beans, and conversation died while we wolfed down our dinners. When we were done, Brian poured some camp coffee he had brewed and Pat opened his second bottle.

They had barely touched it—I was sticking with coffee—when Lester Crain started in on me.

"You said the search party would be all men, Brian," he said, staring straight at me. "Ain't how it looks from here."

"What are you . . . oh, let it go, Les," Brian said.

"Let it go? His brother was the only one in that family worth a damn, and yet *he's* the one sittin' here. How'm I supposed to let that go?"

"Lester," I said. "I miss Day too, you know. If I could bring him back—"

He glared at me, his jaw thrust aggressively in my direction. "Funny, I thought this was how you wanted it. You inheriting the whole ranch, not having to share anything."

"Guess you don't know me that well, do you?"

"Know as much as I want to. I know you're a coward, a worthless—"

"That's enough, Les!" Brian snapped.

From my seat I could see up the slope of the opposite riverbank, toward the old Spanish fort. A three-quarter moon didn't do much more than paint the leaves of the mesquite and other plants with a silvery brush, but I thought I saw light flickering near the ruins. "Look!" I said.

"What is it?" Isaac asked.

"A light, up on the hill."

Everybody watched, but it didn't recur. After a minute, people began grumbling and hitting the bottle again.

"I'm going to take a look," I said. Before anyone could protest, I stormed away from the campsite, across the cool, muddy river, and started up the far side. I was sure I had seen something. And I wanted to get away from Les before he started a fight. I hadn't volunteered to investigate the mystery light because I was some kind of hero, I just didn't want another beating.

Away from the fire and with my legs soaked, the night's chill took on a bite. I drew leather gloves from my jacket pockets and pulled them on. Thorns snagged my clothes as I climbed the slope, but I ignored them and kept going.

The crumbled adobe walls of the *presidio,* most less than four feet tall, made a flat pattern among acres of mesquite, spectral in the moonlight. I paused at the edge of the ruins, listening.

There came another flicker of yellow light, like distant lightning through thick clouds. In that instant of illumination I saw a lean figure. "Hello!" I called, trying to keep my voice strong. "Who's there?"

"You best get outta here!" a male voice responded. It was thin, barely carrying across the short distance. An old man's voice. "Might already be too late."

Goose bumps raised the hair on my neck. "Mr. Moffat? Is that you? It's Marsh Sinclair."

"Young Marsh. Seems like just last week I was pullin' pennies outta your ears."

I started weaving my way through the brush and adobe walls. "That's right. You okay, Mr. Moffat? You're not hurt?"

"I'm fine."

"There's a search party out looking for you. They've gone every which way. Flying airplanes over and everything. There's a few of us across the river, in Contention City."

"Never meant for anything like that," he said. I could see him now, headed toward me. He walked with his usual lanky stride, his steps shorter than they had once been, but his head held high. One sleeve of his shirt was torn almost completely off and his pants legs hung in ribbons around his boots. He gripped a flashlight that glowed weakly, then blinked out, no doubt the source of the flickering light.

"What did you mean, too late?" I asked, half afraid of the answer.

"Let's get your friends out of there," he said. It

didn't tell me much, but the urgency he said it with was convincing.

On the way down the steep slope from the plateau, me holding his arm much of the time to help his balance, he started telling me what he had come for. "You know my people helped found Contention, right?"

"I've heard that," I said.

"Well, it's so. Only there's been a story goin' around . . . a lie, I believe, and I wanted to put it straight while I still could. My mind ain't what it once was, maybe you heard."

"I heard you were having some trouble remembering."

"That's the nice way to say it. I'm gettin' old and forgetful, and reckon the time I got left is short. I wanted to find a way to prove the lie before I'm gone, even if it's only to myself. To witnesses would've been better, but I couldn't figure out how to do that." He allowed himself a dry chuckle. "Course, we don't get you and your friends away from here, I might have more witnesses 'n I counted on."

"What do you think's going to happen?" I asked him. We had just started across the river. My legs were still cold and damp from crossing it the last time.

Before he could answer, a gunshot sounded from the direction of the camp and a bullet whipped through branches above us. I swore and pushed George down in the river. I had left my rifle back at the camp.

"It's begun," he said in a hoarse whisper.

"What has?" I asked. But when I raised my head and looked toward the town, I knew what he meant.

The crumbled buildings still stood where they had been, faintly limned by moonlight. But around them, towering above them in some cases, were the ghostly images of those buildings as they had been in the town's prime. Tall and proud, their doors and windows and roofs intact. People—not real ones, but apparitions—darted about. Through the people and the buildings, the trees and tangled brush remained visible.

I could hear—faintly, as if from far away—a steady pounding noise. I realized it had to be the town's stamp mills, each with twelve to fifteen stamps driving down a hundred times a minute, crushing ore. Over that were alarmed voices and gunfire. The smells of wood smoke and gunpowder tinged the air.

"I have to get in there," George said. He lurched up and started toward the bank. I grabbed him but caught his bare arm, slick with river water, and it slid from my grasp. He splashed through the last few feet of water, then through the reeds at river's edge and into Contention City.

"Mr. Moffat!" I called. "I don't think—"

He was barely aware of me. The specters of Contention City's populace were shooting at each other from behind cover. Bullets whizzed past us—ghost bullets, I hoped, that couldn't do any real damage. But I could also see my fellow searchers, and they had responded by drawing their own weapons, which could kill.

"I gave almost ever cent I had to this ancient *bruja*

down Sonora way for this spell," he said. He knew I was there after all.

"*Bruja?*" I repeated. "Spell?"

He tried to look in every direction at once, like a kid at his first carnival. "A witch. She said it'd only work one time, and then only because we come from here." He held my gaze for a second. "Something like that. Her English was about as bad as my Spanish, so I missed a lot of it."

Three men hurtled down the street, right toward us, wearing old West garb and carrying rifles. They could have stepped off a movie screen. I grabbed Moffat's arm, tried to yank him out of the way, but I was too late. One of them passed right through Moffat, firing on the run.

"What's going on, Mr. Moffat?" I demanded. Another shot from the camp came our way—maybe someone responding to what he thought was a threat. Or maybe not—Les Crain stood behind the fire with his rifle near his shoulder. I tried to steer George that way, figuring Les wouldn't shoot him. "Look!" I shouted. "I found him!"

But even though the noise of old Contention City was muffled, there was enough of it that those at our campsite couldn't hear me. I didn't know for sure if any had even seen us.

George twisted out of my hands again. "I gotta see," he said. He walked fast for an old man who'd been exposed to the elements for almost twenty-four hours, as if the success of his "spell" had given him renewed energy.

"See what?"

George ducked behind a stone wall without

answering. I followed, figuring it would offer cover from the search party's guns.

He strode up the hill, past that wall and the house that it had once been a part of. Excited voices, no louder than if they came over telephone lines, sounded behind us, and when I glanced back I could see through two men. From farther up the hill, a cowboy drew a bead on one of them with a revolver. He fired. I didn't bother dodging his shot. The ghostly bullet slammed into me with the force of a thrown rock, passing through my arm and out the other side, spinning me around and bouncing me off the wall.

"Ahhh!" I cried. "That hurt!"

Down the hill, the round had struck one of the men behind us, and he fell to the ground with blood fountaining up from his throat. "I thought these were just ghosts or something."

"Something like that, I think," George said. He looked as clear-eyed and sharp as he ever had. "Come on, we have to hurry."

The bullet had torn my sleeve and skin, but it hadn't pierced all the way through—that had been part of the whole surreal illusion. I was bleeding just the same. I figured that since sights and sounds were only partly there, a little of their physical presence was as well.

Which might mean that a close range shot could be fatal.

"I don't know where you're going, Mr. Moffat," I said. "But be careful!"

George nodded offhandedly, like he'd barely heard me, and continued up the hill past the cowboy. Gripping my wounded arm, I trailed behind him.

George stopped at an intersection, looking at another house, stone below but with wooden walls above the first three or four feet. There was a man in the doorway, hopping on one foot while he tugged on a boot. Behind him, watching through fearful eyes, were a woman and a boy of seven or eight.

"I *knew* it," George said, watching as the man grabbed a rifle from behind the door. "It's just like he always said, he was inside when the shootin' started. It weren't him."

"Who's that?"

"My pa. That youngster's me." He said it as casually as if he'd been identifying cattle. *That one's a Red Brangus. Over there, that's a Hereford.* But then, it was something he had expected to see, maybe for a long time.

"What are we looking at here, Mr. Moffat?" I asked him. "What's going on?"

"This is the gunfight that got my ma and pa just about rode out of town on a rail. Everybody blamed him for startin' it, but you can see for yourself it was already goin' on by the time he got out the house."

"That's the way it looks, all right. But what—"

George turned away from the spectacle of his own father—less than half the age the son was right now—striding down the road to get involved in the shooting, and met my gaze. "What's it prove? Maybe nothin' to anyone but me. As long as my folks lived, they told me this was how it was. But to everyone else in Contention City, and most of the people in this part of the country, the whole deal—

the fight, the fire, all of it, was on my pa's head. Sixty-four people died that day, couple dozen houses burned, and everybody says Contention City never recovered from it."

"So you wanted to see the truth for yourself."

Gunshots punctuated our conversation—some of them echoes from the past, others loud and close, the search party reacting to an assault they couldn't understand. "Now that you've seen, is there some way to end it?" I asked him. "Someone's like to get hurt."

George blinked a couple of times, as if it had never occurred to him. "I don't rightly know."

Another level of sound joined the racket that already echoed between the hills hemming in the river. More gunshots, but from farther away, accompanied by something else.

"Apache," George said, at the same time that I realized what it had to be.

"But they never attacked Contention, did they?"

"Nope. Did *Santa Cruz,* though."

He was right. The Spanish force there had been driven away by persistent Apache raids. Isaac Schultheis had claimed that the night of the big battle in Contention City, flames had swept down on the town from the *presidio,* abandoned for more than a hundred years by then.

None of it made sense, but it all connected in a nightmarish way that carried its own logic. Something had started in the *presidio,* then spread to Contention City when that became the next white settlement in the immediate area.

"If it's gonna be stopped," George said, "it'll be there."

We were relatively protected at our corner, with walls, real and half-real, beside us. The last thing I wanted was to leave that safety and go back up the hill, through a ghostly Apache raid and into a Spanish fort where the denizens were shooting at everything that moved.

But if we didn't stop it, would it just keep going? Would the fire start again, racing through the dry brush and trees, maybe spreading to surrounding ranches and homes?

No way to know. But I hadn't started it, and I was safe right where I was.

"You comin'?" George didn't wait for an answer. He started back down the hill, toward the river. Toward where the ghostly bullets flew with greater frequency.

Shy of any better options, I followed.

My nightmare was complete. Another couple of slugs stung me, and I saw some hit George, staggering him. Acrid gray smoke swirled around us, thick as fog, blotting out most of the spectral buildings. George kept going so I did too, walking unarmed on unsteady legs into the thick of war. All around us people were dead or dying, and still the lead flew. I could differentiate the solid crack of real guns from the muffled thuds of ghostly ones and the booming of muskets on the hill.

We reached the river and splashed across. George walked with a determined stride, blood trickling from a gash on his temple. I trailed behind him like he was some sort of good luck charm and could keep me from being killed. As we climbed the hill, Apache warriors ran through us, some on horseback. I could feel the impacts, like someone bumping into me, hard but not too painful. The bullets hurt worse, stinging like sharp stones.

Higher up, musket balls crashed through the brush around us. One hit my leg, almost knocking me down. George pressed on. I stayed with him.

Flames began spreading down the hill toward us, warm as the desert in summer but not scorchingly hot. But as we hiked through them, I noticed fire igniting the scrub—the *real* scrub—in spots. If there was a way to end this, we had to find it soon.

It was harder than ever to know what was real and what was the result of George's spell. Smoke and noise and pain and fear mingled in my head until each step was harder to take than the last. Somehow we made it to the fort's walls (full height now, not the few inches or couple of feet they usually were, but we could step through the higher part). Spanish soldiers ran about, firing muskets over the walls. Apaches rained bullets and arrows down on them.

As if drawn toward it, George led me to an open plaza. The soldiers were at the walls; here there were only a few women and some frightened children. They didn't seem to see us. Horribly, in the center of the plaza was what looked like an ancient Apache man lashed to an upright pole, white stringy hair covering his face. He was naked, his bare chest crisscrossed with the marks of a whip.

Worse, his hands and bare feet weren't those of a man, but of a big, pale-furred cat. My gut lurched.

A young Spanish girl looked at us, her hair dark, her eyes wide and liquid. "Help him," she said, her English as clear as mine. "Free him."

George nodded once, as if he'd been expecting her command, and went to work. I joined him, trying to untie the man's bonds. They were surprisingly solid in my trembling hands, although his form was as ghostly as any of the others. The girl helped us loosen the ropes from his ankles. As we worked, the old man *changed,* sleek white fur growing thick on his arms and back, then vanishing, then flickering between flesh and fur as fast as I could blink. He let out a long, low growl.

Finally, we had him untied. One of the women saw us then and started to scream. As the old Apache fell forward, he changed again, transforming into the white jaguar that I'd somehow known he must be. He looked at us each in turn, then bounded away. Soldiers came running, summoned by the screams of the women.

The little girl smiled at us as if we had done her a favor.

This was the end, I knew. When those soldiers came into close range and fired those big musket balls at us, one after another, they would kill us. We were in the middle of their fort, and they had turned their attention from the Apache attack to us.

The first soldiers into the plaza aimed their weapons, pulled the triggers—

—but even as they did, they became less material, more ghostlike. Musket balls flying toward us seemed to slow and stall in midair.

Then they were gone: soldiers, structures, muskets, and all. The ruins were as I remembered them, low mud walls worn almost to nothing. The last thing to vanish was the girl, her wide smile beaming at us until she too had faded away.

Elated whoops from Contention City split the sudden silence. "Come on, Mr. Moffat," I said. "They'll want to see you."

"That girl back there," George said on the way down. "The Spanish one?"

"The one who spoke English?"

"Sounded like Spanish to me," he said, "but I knew what she meant. Anyhow, the strangest thing—you remember I told you about that *bruja,* in Sonora, about as old as Moses."

"Yeah."

"I'd swear, that girl had her eyes. And more teeth, but the same dang smile."

"You think she was an ancestor of the *bruja's*? That had to have happened in the 1770s, right?"

"We've seen a lot of crazy things tonight, Marsh. Crazier'n I'll ever see again, for sure. But I'd swear that was the same person."

Descending toward the river, the sharp tang of burnt brush in my nose, aching from a dozen ghost-bullets, I didn't doubt him a bit. I didn't know what it all meant, and he probably didn't either.

But I knew that jaguar had given us each a blessing. For the girl, a long life and incredible powers. For George, answers to questions that had plagued him all his life, and the chance to put right his father's mistake. And for me, a realization. I could wait around forever hoping to feel brave, but courage wasn't some separate sensation that would well up inside me like fear or hope. It was simply understanding what had to be done, and doing it.

We had survived the night and we had borne witness. As if thinking the same thing, George offered me a weary smile. If I lived long enough, maybe I could become half the man he was.

It was a goal to work toward, anyway.

The Ghost
of Two Forks
Elmer Kelton

A railroad was often a blessing to early Texas towns, but it could as easily be a curse. Many new towns sprang up and thrived along the rights-of-way as track layers moved into new territory eager for improved transportation. But other towns, once prosperous, withered and died because the Eastern money counters and the surveyors favored a route that bypassed them.

Such a town was Two Forks, for years a county seat. Its voters had approved a bond issue that built a fine new stone courthouse with a tall cupola that sported a clock face on each of its four sides. From the day its doors first opened for business, it had been Sandy Fuller's job to sweep its floors and keep its brass doorknobs bright and shiny. In winter he kept wood boxes full for the several pot-bellied heaters. All these were tasks he enjoyed, for he had hand-carried many of the stones that went into its building, and he felt he owned a share of it.

Most people would say Sandy was not among the brightest members of the community, that his limited skills restricted him to the most menial of tasks. At fifty his back was beginning to bend. Toting all those heavy stones had not been good for his arthritis, either. But whatever his own short-comings might have been, his two Jersey cows gave more milk than any in town, and his three dozen laying hens kept much of the community well fixed for eggs. He also kept a dandy little garden, selling much of its produce to his neigh-bors, giving it to those who could not pay.

Those assets, along with his housekeeping job at the courthouse, yielded everything Sandy needed for the good though simple life. He told his cowboy friend Cap Anderson that he hoped it would last all of his days and that Heaven would be just like Two Forks. He and Cap had ridden broncs together in their younger years, until too many falls forced Sandy to find less strenuous work. Cap still held a steady ranch job, though now he rode gentler horses.

Everybody in town knew Sandy, but a thousand miles away, in a cloud of cigar smoke at the railroad directors' conference table, decisions were made by men who had never heard of him. All they knew of Two Forks was that it was in the wrong place. The surveyors had marked a route that would miss the town by at least six miles. They were about to strike a death blow to the prosperous little community, but that was Two Forks' misfortune and none of their own.

Sandy had every reason to remain where he was, among friends, working in a courthouse he had helped to build. Among other things, he visited the cemetery almost every day, carrying a bucket of water to sprinkle on wildflowers that grew over two graves. One tombstone marked the resting

place of Ardella Fuller, loving wife and mother.
Beneath the shadow of the other, topped by the
carved figure of a lamb, lay the infant daughter of
Sandy and Ardella. The date of death was the same
on both stones.

For months Sandy had heard rumors that the
railroad was coming. He shared his neighbors'
early enthusiasm, because the shining rails could
bring fresh enterprise to the town he loved. Sandy's
thin wage might not increase, but it pleased him to
think it would be a boon to his friends and neighbors. Meanwhile, he kept the courthouse spotless
and clean. It was the town's crowning glory, and
his own.

He paid little attention to whispered rumors that
surveyors were placing stakes across the Bar M
ranch far south of town. It seemed unreasonable
that the railroad's builders would not want to make
the fullest use of a promising community like Two
Forks. It was already a landmark of sorts, its courthouse clock tower standing proudly three stories
high, visible for miles across the open prairie. The
striking of the clock was music to Sandy's ears.

Not until he heard the county judge talking
to two of the commissioners did he begin feeling uneasy. He stopped pushing his broom to
eavesdrop.

The judge said, "I met with the railroad people.
They tell me we've got no chance to change their
minds. The Bar M offered them the right-of-way
cheap because Old Man Mathers figures to sell
town lots. The graders are already at work."

A commissioner asked, "What kind of a county
seat will this be then, six miles from the railroad?"

"Old Man Mathers figures sooner or later we'll have no choice but to move it to his town."

"We can't move a stone courthouse, and this one ain't half paid for."

"No, but you can be sure Mathers will try to convince the voters to build a new one over on the railroad."

The commissioner declared, "He'll play hell doin' it. Most of the county's voters live right here in Two Forks."

That sounded reasonable to Sandy. He went back to his sweeping and put the worry behind him.

That night as he watered the wildflowers on Ardella's grave, he talked to her just as he had talked to her when she was alive. "Don't you be frettin' none, honey. The folks ain't goin' to go off and leave a good town like this, especially one with such a pretty courthouse, and it not paid for yet."

But it played out like the judge had said. The graders followed the surveyors, and the rails followed the graders. Old Man Mathers had a crew staking out town lots along the right-of-way. He donated a large town square for the building of a new courthouse. He put up a big new general store and guaranteed that his prices would be lower than those in Two Forks because he could obtain his goods directly from the railroad without the extra cost of freighting them in by wagon.

Sandy refused to acknowledge the writing on the wall, even when he stood with Cap Anderson and watched skids being placed beneath the Jones family's frame house. He watched a six-mule team slide the structure across the prairie toward the new town of Mathers.

"They'll wish they hadn't moved," he told Cap. "They'll get awful lonesome over there without their old neighbors."

But one by one, the old neighbors moved too. House after house made the six mile drag to a new site on the railroad or rode over there on wagonbeds extended in tandem. In time, Two Forks began to look as if a tornado had skipped through, taking out structures at random, leaving behind only cedar-post foundations and falling-down sections of yard fence. Weeds grew where flowerbeds and gardens had been.

"Town's not the same anymore," he told Ardella. "But the courthouse ain't changed." He swept every day, for dust from the abandoned lots made it more difficult to keep its floors clean. He polished the doorknobs and, as he could get to them, washed the windows.

Cap Anderson sympathized. "You can't blame folks for leavin'. They've got families, most of them. They've got to go where they can make a livin'." Cap lived north of Two Forks. The new town was a hardship for him because it meant he had to travel six miles farther than when he could do all his business here.

Time came when almost the only people still living in Two Forks were those who worked in the courthouse: the judge and his wife, the county clerk, the sheriff, a deputy, the jail keeper, and Sandy. The operator of the last general store loaded his goods on wagons and hauled them to a new building in Mathers. His old place stood vacant. It made Sandy think of a dogie calf. One night some young vandals from the new town sneaked in under the cover of darkness to break out the store's windows, and those of what had been the blacksmith shop.

The judge was the first of the courthouse crowd to surrender. He had his big house sawed in two and hauled over to Mathers. Sandy heard that one section was sprung a little during the trip so that the two never fit back together just right. After some loud cussing, the judge grudgingly accepted the patching job, though his wife was never again satisfied with the house. The county clerk was not long in following the judge to Mathers.

The sheriff and his crew had to stay because the jail was still in Two Forks, though the lawman spent most of his time enforcing the ordinances in the new town. The few residents remaining in Two Forks were not given to crimes and misdemeanors.

The judge became increasingly vocal about the nuisance of living in one town and working in another. Sandy heard his voice ringing down the hall. "There is no longer any question about it. We've got to move the county seat to Mathers."

Sandy almost dropped his broom.

The sheriff agreed with the judge's opinion but pointed out that such a move would require a vote of the county's citizens.

The judge said, "Most of them are in Mathers now. Who is left to vote for staying in Two Forks?"

As it turned out, the only dissenting votes were Sandy's and those of some farmers and ranch people like Cap, afraid of higher taxes. Sandy listened disconsolately as the ballots were counted in the clerk's office. He quickly saw that his vote was being crushed beneath the weight of all those others.

He heard the judge say, "Now we've got to have a bond vote so we can build a new courthouse."

The sheriff was skeptical. "The county still owes ten years' payments on this one. Do you think the landowners are goin' to vote another tax burden on themselves?"

"The people in town outnumber the country voters," the judge argued. "They're tired of having to come all the way over here to do business with the county government."

And so it was. The new citizens of Mathers were overwhelmingly in favor of a new courthouse, especially after the judge pointed out that most of the added tax burden would be levied upon landowners and not themselves. Old Man Mathers was especially pleased. His son-in-law was a builder and a cinch to get the construction contract from the commissioners' court. The stone would be quarried from the south end of the Mathers ranch. It was a foregone conclusion that the price of building stone was going to run high.

Watering the flowers, Sandy told Ardella, "It's goin' to take them a while to get that new courthouse built. I'll bet it won't be nothin' like as pretty as this one here."

He was right. He sneaked over to Mathers one Sunday afternoon to steal a peek at the construction work. The side walls were up, and the roof was half built. He took a measure of satisfaction in the fact that this courthouse was going to be butt-ugly. It offered no imagination in its architecture, no adornments, just four plain square walls and a row of deep-set windows that reminded him of the eye sockets in a skull.

What was more, he had been told that this courthouse was costing twice as much as the older one. There would be hell to pay for the judge and some others when the next election rolled around. But that was still more than a year off.

From people who came to the old Two Forks courthouse to do business with the county, Sandy heard rumblings of discontent. Cap led a petition drive, demanding that the county refuse to accept the new structure on the basis that it was badly designed, shoddily built, and uglier than a mud fence. But the judge ruled that the petitions did not represent a large enough percentage of the voters and thus was invalid.

Construction was completed, and the new courthouse was approved by the commissioners' court. The next step was to move the records from the older building. Sandy's hopes soared when a dozen ranchers and their cowboys, including Cap, surrounded the Two Forks courthouse and vowed to stop, at gunpoint if necessary, any transfer of documents.

The judge and the sheriff foiled that attempt by bringing in two Texas Rangers to enforce the court order. The ranchers and their cowboys might have gone up against the United States Army, but they knew better than to oppose the Texas Rangers. Sandy and Cap watched crestfallen as the county records were placed in a line of wagons and hauled away.

That night he told Ardella, "I don't know what I'm goin' to do now, except for one thing. I ain't leavin' you and the baby, and I ain't leavin' my courthouse."

The judge came to him the next day with a

proposition. "You'd just as well give it up, Sandy, and come on over to Mathers. We need a janitor to take care of the new courthouse like you've taken care of this one."

Sandy knew one reason they wanted him was that they could not find anyone else willing to do the job for the same low pay.

"No sir," he said. "I'm satisfied where I'm at."

"But there's nothing for you to do here."

"This courthouse is still here, and it needs somebody to care for it."

The judge began to show impatience. "Don't you understand? This courthouse is vacant. Retired. We don't need anybody to take care of it."

"But it still belongs to the county, don't it? We're all still payin' for it, ain't we?"

"That is beside the point. We can't pay you to sweep out an abandoned building. We *will* pay you to take care of the new one."

"One way and another, I reckon I'll get by. If anything ever happens to that new courthouse, you'll be glad you've got this one sittin' here waitin' for you."

The judge shook his head in disgust. "A man who would argue with a fool is a fool himself." He turned away but stopped to say, "Your paycheck ends today."

Money had never been an important issue with Sandy. He could get by on very little. Between his garden, his chickens, and his milk cows, he would not go hungry.

He told the judge, "If you ever need me, you'll know where to look."

"Damn it, man, don't you realize that Two Forks is a dead town?"

"It ain't dead as long as somebody lives in it. That'll be me."

Sandy cooked his meals and slept in a plain frame shack. It would be a stretch of the language to say he actually lived there. He *lived* in the courthouse. He was accustomed to going there before daylight and making sure it was ready for business. In winter he built fires in all the stoves to take the chill off before the first of the staff arrived. Now, though, it was summer. He opened windows so a cooling breeze could freshen the air. Everything continued the same as before with one important difference: no one was in the courthouse except him.

With all the desks and chairs removed, the sweeping chore was easier because he did not have to work around the obstacles. The empty rooms looked larger than before. In the county clerk's office the shelves were bare where once they had been full of records of land transactions, court decisions, marriages and births and deaths. Sandy did not need the records to help him remember, however. He had been a witness to almost everything that had happened here.

Having more time on his hands, he spent longer at the cemetery, talking to Ardella. He wiped dust from the carved lamb atop the baby's tombstone. "It's awful quiet here now," he said, "but in a way I kind of like it. Sometimes I got tired of all that noise. And I don't have a lot of people throwin' their trash around. You ought to see how clean the courthouse is."

He almost never went to Mathers. The sight of that squatty new courthouse made his eyes hurt. He still bartered enough butter and eggs to trade for the few groceries he needed, mainly coffee and bacon and such. Every two or three days, Cap or some other rancher or cowboy took his produce to town for him and brought back whatever he ordered from the general store.

He had noticed that the new courthouse did not even have lightning rods like the old one. Maybe one day lightning would strike, the building would burn down, and they would have to move the county seat back to Two Forks. The county could not afford to be paying for three courthouses at the same time. Well, when it happened, they would find the old one as good as when they had left it. Better even, for Sandy made improvements on it here and there.

But lightning did not strike. Time went dragging on. A windstorm took most of the roof from Sandy's shack. He decided to move into the jail, which stood in the shadow of the courthouse. He reasoned that a building always fared better when someone lived in it than when it stood vacant. They would need the jail again someday when they returned to Two Forks. He kept it as clean as the courthouse.

One by one, his rancher and cowboy friends died or moved away. Cap remained, but he did not often go to town anymore. No longer could Sandy depend on someone else to carry his butter and eggs to town. He had no choice but to walk the six miles to Mathers, carrying his goods in a cloth sack, then walking back with food he could not produce for himself. Most of the townspeople had forgotten about him. Now they talked about him again. He was "poor, feeble-minded old Sandy," who didn't have the sense to give up and quit beating a dead horse.

He became the ghost of Two Forks, a ragged apparition who showed up briefly on the dirt streets of Mather every three or four days, said little or nothing to anybody, and disappeared like a wisp of smoke. A few of the more superstitious even suggested that he had died of lonesome and that what they saw was a wraith, a will-of-the-wisp. Town boys dared each other to visit the Two Forks cemetery after dark and see if the ghost would appear.

He did, on a few occasions. Sandy was as protective of the cemetery as of the courthouse. He was afraid vandals might topple some of the tombstones, especially Ardella's or the baby's. After several town boys hurried home shaking with fright, talking about the ghost that appeared out of nowhere, the nocturnal visits stopped. Hardly anyone except Sandy came to the cemetery anymore.

The few abandoned frame houses gradually succumbed to time and the weather, sinking back to the ground or giving up to the wind which scattered them in pieces across the old townsite. Only the grand old courthouse remained, and the jail. The ghost of Two Forks continued to care for them, to keep up repairs.

Then one day a cowboy happened by on his way to town. It was a hot summer day, but the courthouse windows remained closed. Sandy had routinely opened them each morning from spring into late fall.

Maybe the old man was ill, the cowboy thought.

He rode up to the courthouse and tested the front door. It was locked. He led his horse to the jail and went inside. Sandy was not there. The stove was cold. Sandy's coffeepot sat empty except for yesterday's grounds. Alarmed, the cowboy went outside and called. The only response was the echo of his own voice. A circle through the townsite yielded no sign.

He rode to town and went directly to the office of the new sheriff. A small delegation of townspeople—mostly older ones who remembered the heyday of Two Forks—accompanied him back to the ghost town. They searched every room, every closet in the old courthouse, half expecting to find Sandy dead in one of them. They even climbed up into the clock tower. They did not find him.

"It's like the wind just lifted him up and carried him away," the cowboy said.

"Or maybe he wasn't nothin' but a ghost to start with," a townsman suggested. "Maybe he died when the town died."

So now Two Forks was officially dead. The last person to have lived there was gone. The tall old courthouse stood as silent testimony to the town that once had been, and to the man who had stubbornly refused to accept that it was gone.

But as Sandy had long predicted, the courthouse did not die. It refused to submit to the wind and the rain and the ravages of time. After many years, some former citizens of Two Forks decided it was time to honor the town's memory with a big reunion, a barbecue and dance. Where better to have it than in the courthouse? No one knew where to find the keys, if they even existed anymore, so someone had to pick the lock so the committee could go inside and clean up the place for the benefit of the expected crowd.

To their amazement, the courthouse was as clean as if it had just been swept. Tight windows, they reasoned, had not let the dust in. There should have been cobwebs, yet they saw none. Even the windows sparkled as if freshly washed.

The ghost of Sandy Fuller, some said. He had never given up his job.

The state placed a historical marker beside the front door of the old Two Forks courthouse. The reunion and barbecue became an annual affair, and dances were a frequent event. From time to time the old building pulsed with life as it had long ago. Visitors came often in hope of glimpsing the ghost of Two Forks, but none ever saw him. They knew only that occasionally he still swept the courthouse by night and kept it clean. No one ever knew how Sandy Fuller had disappeared.

Well, almost no one. Cap Anderson knew, for he had found Sandy lying dead beside Ardella's grave. Knowing Sandy's love for the courthouse, and knowing the law would not allow it if anyone knew, he secretly buried him in the basement.

He kept Sandy's keys. He also kept Sandy's broom until he wore it out and had to replace it with a new one.

Kiowa Canyon

James A. Fischer

Shell Green's breath caught in his throat as he reined in his horse. The realization he'd been in this canyon before hit him like being kicked by a mule. If he remembered right, it was about twenty years before.

Stone Knife, the Kiowa, stopped and turned his horse, waiting for Shell to catch up with him. It looked like he had a smile on his face, but that could be the heat waves coming off the high canyon walls.

The thought that something wasn't quite right about the direction they had been traveling had been stuck in the back of Shell's mind for a few days. I didn't like this damn redskin when we met at the border, and I trust him even less now, he thought to himself.

Shell squeezed his horse lightly with his knees and the animal started walking up the canyon. Past the Kiowa and around a bend in the canyon was where the village should be. Twenty years, was it really that long ago? That's over and done with, and I've got other things that are more important to think about right now.

"Mighty hot today, how much farther to the water?" asked Shell as he stopped beside Stone Knife. "I'm out, and my horse could use some." Wiping his brow with a bandanna he put his hat back on.

"Just ahead is water." Stone Knife nodded to his right up the canyon and started his horse in that direction. Shell moved along behind him with butterflies whirling around in his stomach. By resting the right one on the grip of his Colt and holding the reins tight in his left, he kept his hands from shaking.

Shell and his hired hands had brought the herd of mares across the Rio Grande out of Mexico west of the Pecos River. Shell and the cook had ridden into the whiskey trader's place to pick up supplies and found the Indian waiting for them. He was dressed in white man's clothes except for moccasins that Shell noticed were Kiowa, and a buckskin vest with some bead work on it. He gave Shell a letter from Quinn McVey, Shell's boss, turned around and mounted his horse.

The country was in a drought and McVey had hired Stone Knife to find the water holes that hadn't dried up yet. Water was always a problem, and with two hundred head of horses in the hottest months of the year, McVey wasn't taking any chances. They were blooded mares from good breeding stock down in Mexico and a lot of money had been paid for them. So Stone Knife was to be the guide for

Shell Green and the herd of horses till they reached
McVey's ranch.

Shell looked up from reading the letter to the
cook and raised his eyebrows, then turned to the
Indian.

He hadn't said a word till Shell spoke, and then
he spoke very plain but correct English, which surprised everyone.

"What's your name?" Shell looked up at him after
reading the letter.

"Stone Knife." His voice was clear and distinct.

"What tribe?" Shell asked.

"Kiowa," he answered.

Shell nodded and swung up on his horse.

"What way should we be headed?"

"That way." The Kiowa pointed a bit west of
north. "I'll leave trail markers for you." He started
his horse moving, "First water is about ten miles. I'll
be there."

"Nice meeting you." Shell's words were heavy
with sarcasm but Stone Knife was out of hearing
range.

Giving him a guide just sure as hell rubbed
Shell the wrong way. "Damn it! I'm a leader not a
follower and have been most of my life." Shell was
talking to himself again, just like every day since
Stone Knife had become their point man. "Why
I remember when . . . , NO! I don't want to remember. Enough! Right now I have to get these
horses to water, that's all." Shell gave a gruff half
laugh, shook his head, and kicked his horse into
a trot, heading back to the herd. He'd start them

north, again, then he'd head up the trail looking for the markers Stone Knife would have left to show the way.

It was already seventy degrees at sunup and the two hundred Mexican horses started to mill around in the meadow. As the sun broke over the low foothills, the night guard came in to eat and change horses for today's move up the trail.

As they rode up to the wagon where the rest of the wranglers were finishing their coffee, Green asked the night guard. "Any sign of that no good redskin?"

"Nope," said the lead man swinging down. He dropped his reins and walked to the fire, shaking his head as he picked up a cup and filled it from the coffeepot. "I think yer Buck scooted back to the rez to impress the squaws with his newfound wealth."

"Soon as you eat, I want to get movin'." Shell spoke over his shoulder while walking to his horse. "Next water's about five miles I think. Next after is 'bout twelve." Shell swung up into his saddle. "Damn long day if we have to go twelve, so eat quick."

"Everything with you is quick," the lead man replied. "Eat quick, piss quick, ride quick. Hell, Shell, slow down, you're an old man."

"Just talked yerself out a eating, Mister. Dump out the coffee, Cookie, and pack it up, we're moving, now!" Shell spun his horse around and loped off to the herd and started to yell at the cowboys to move out. The ones by the fire just shook their heads and cussed at the lead man for losing them what little breakfast they were going to get. Not so much as a cup of bad coffee. It was going to be a long day.

Shell rode ahead of the horses and wranglers looking for signs from the Kiowa showing him which direction to take the herd for water. Today he rode quite a few miles before he found the sign and then it was not what he had hoped for. The main trail through another canyon to the next water was blocked by a rock slide, so Stone Knife pointed them through this side canyon. The only other route would have been around the foothills region, and ten extra miles of travel. Shell took off his hat and wiped his forehead with the shirt sleeve of his right arm.

No use going back and telling the men we're going farther. They'll read the sign just like I did and keep moving, Shell thought as he headed his horse in the direction the rock sign pointed. Why does that damn Indian make me so nervous? There's something about him and this trip since he's hooked up with us that keeps me on edge all the time. I want to keep looking over my shoulder, behind every thicket, and jump at any loud sound. Sorry I didn't get some whiskey back at the trader's because I sure could use a shot or two to keep the thoughts of calamity from running around in my head.

Coming into the foothills from this direction hadn't registered with Shell until he reached this point and saw the landmarks on the walls of the canyon. Shell recognized the petroglyphs, or ancient drawings carved into the stone, that were on the canyon walls. People had been coming to this spring for centuries and had left their mark with the stone carvings.

This had been the site of one of Shell's early Indian fights after he returned from the Civil War, and his first against a village. He'd been nervous that day, and he was just as nervous today, rounding the bend in the canyon.

On the ground he had to look closely to see that a village had once been here. Only by carefully peering through the grass did you finally see the stone tipi rings. These were the stones that held down the outside edge of the tipi, and in the middle of them he then could make out, in a few places, the fire rings. An occasional piece of charred wood, looking like part of a tipi pole, was scattered around the area, but nothing else was visible to show that this place was once home to men, women, and children.

Shell stopped, but Stone Knife continued riding into what had been the village. In his mind Shell heard the sounds from twenty years ago and a sweat broke out on his forehead and under his arms. The children and women were screaming as Shell and the militia he was with rode through the village, firing at anything that moved and riding down anything that ran. They had been told "No Prisoners!" The Kiowa of fighting age were all away, raiding in Mexico or somewhere with the Comanche. Old people, children, and women didn't offer much resistance, and were soon killed or had escaped into the many small canyons and washes that made up this country.

Riding back through the burning village, Shell saw the men laughing and setting fire to the tipis after taking anything they wanted out of them. Others were scalping the dead, even the babies, because a reward was paid for scalps regardless of size.

As Shell stopped to look over the scene he could hear occasional shots in the canyons around the village that meant some of the villagers had been tracked down. More scalps. Turning to ride back the way he and the other Indian fighters had come, he realized he hadn't fired the pistol in his hand. Quickly holstering the pistol Shell kicked his horse into a lope hoping no one had seen him, but had to rein his horse quickly out of the way. Coming toward him was Louis, an old Indian fighter who had taken him under his wing.

"Damn, Shell. I was just bring'n you a special present. No call to run me down!" Louis was holding something bloody in his outstretched hand.

"Whatever it is, I'm not interested! Now get out of my way or I will run you down." Shell was afraid his stomach was going to come up any minute. He wanted to be out of sight of these men if it did.

"That's all right, Shell. I'll fix it up for ya. I've made these many times," Louis called after Shell.

Shell was brought back to the present by his horse stamping his hooves and tossing its head up and down. The horse then began to dance around, snorting, twitching its ears, and swishing his tail.

Stone Knife had ridden through the village site and was waiting for Shell about a hundred feet away.

Reining his horse's head around, Shell tapped him with his spurs and they started along the tracks left by Stone Knife. When they reached the edge of where the village had been, his horse spooked and shied to the left. Shell barely stayed in the saddle. After getting his horse turned around he started to look over the area to see what had caused the horse to act like that.

Looking at Stone Knife, Shell saw that he still sat waiting for him, as if nothing had happened. Shaking his head Shell brought his horse around and began to follow Stone Knife's tracks again. This time Shell was paying more attention. At just about the same place his horse tried again to turn away from the village site, but Shell was ready this time and stopped him. For the next ten minutes, Shell tried every trick he could think of to get him to walk through the village site. All this time Stone Knife sat on his horse and watched, not saying a word.

Shell was damned if he was going to dismount and lead his horse in front of an Indian.

"Go check the spring." Shell yelled, "I'll be back with the herd."

Shell spun his horse around. Mad because the horse was not obeying him, he gave him both spurs full force and yelled,

"Get-up, get-up!"

Whipping him with the ends of his reins as they raced back to the herd.

* * *

Shell had ridden out to check the first of the night guards and was now off by himself building a smoke. He'd licked the paper, twisted the ends, and was about to strike a match when the Indian's voice floated out of the near darkness.

"Water at the spring is good." The voice was calm and clear.

"Good." Shell answered, hoping the Indian didn't see him jump at his voice. Maybe he'll think I always strike a match that quick, Shell hoped.

Stone Knife rode up beside Shell and took out a small pipe from his vest pocket, filled it, lit it, and sat smoking with Shell. As they looked over the herd in the dying light Shell finished his cigarette and turned to Stone Knife.

"How were you able to ride through that village today and I wasn't?"

Stone Knife was quiet for a few moments, then he reached inside his shirt and drew out a small leather bag on a braided leather thong that went around his neck.

"My medicine keeps me safe from many things."

"Does it protect your horse too?" Shell asked quietly.

Stone Knife pointed to a small leather bag hanging from the brow band of the bridle on the Kiowa's horse.

"He also has medicine," Stone Knife answered.

"Could you make medicine for me, my men, and our horses? I don't know how the hell I'll get this herd to the water unless we have something like that." Stone Knife could hear the desperation in Shell's voice.

"Maybe." The Indian turned his horse and started

to ride away. He quickly became part of the night, but his voice came back to Shell.

"I'll be back tomorrow."

Dawn was a ways off when Shell rode out the next morning. He didn't want the men to find out about the medicine bags 'til he had a chance to ask some more questions about them. Shell just couldn't figure out why his horse refused to go into the village site. No one was there and no animals were in sight. He hadn't seen anything that should have spooked a horse or made it afraid to enter the place. It was all a mystery to Shell and he hoped the Indian would answer some of his questions.

Taking out his bag of tobacco and folding a paper, Shell started to build a smoke. Just as he was about to strike a match to light it, Stone Knife appeared beside him.

"I have your medicine bags," Stone Knife spoke.

"Will you explain what they are to the men so they know why they are wearing them and help put the ones for the horses on the men's bridles?" Shell asked.

"I only have two and they're for horses, not men," Stone Knife said.

"How am I going to get the herd to water with only two medicine bags?" Shell's voice started to climb. "I'll be here a month if I can only take one horse at a time to the water!"

"I'll be at the spring." Stone knife tossed Shell something as he turned his horse to leave.

Shell caught the wad of leather that the Indian had thrown. The two medicine bags had been tied

together with their drawstrings. Looking at them
he tried to think how they were going to help him.
He was so mad that his mind wouldn't work.

Jamming the bags inside his shirt, he rode back
to the cook's fire.

After a couple cups of coffee Shell's mind started
to clear enough that he could start putting a plan
together. With only two medicine bags all the work
was going to fall on him. He would have to take the
herd across the village site without the help of the
hired hands.

Shell mounted his horse and rode out to where
the herd had been held for the night. It was just
getting light and the day riders were relieving the
last of the night guard. He rode up to one of the
day riders and stopped to look over the herd.

"I'm looking for the Bell Mare," Shell told the
rider.

"She's lying down on the other side where that
buckskin is standing." The rider was pointing across
the herd to a couple horses along the outer edge.

Shell rode around the herd to the Bell Mare's location. By the time he got there she had gotten up
and was pacing around with some of the other
horses, looking for water or graze. The herd, or
most of it, would have to be moved today because
the grass in the area was about used up.

Taking down his rope, Shell tossed a loop over the
Bell Mare's head and led her out of the herd a ways
to a cedar thicket. Dismounting, he tied her to one
of the cedars and pulled the medicine bags out of
his shirt. Untangling one, he tied it to the bell strap
that went around the mare's neck. Turning around
he tied the other bag to his horse's bridle. Leaving

the Bell Mare tied he rode to the village site. Shell stopped before he got to the place where his horse had acted up yesterday, dismounting as he dropped his reins. He picked up a couple rocks and laid them on both sides of the tracks the Indian had made going into the village site. Stepping back to make sure the rocks could be seen from a distance, Shell mounted his horse and headed back to the fire.

Getting a cup of coffee, Shell called the men not watching the herd over to the cook fire to listen to him.

"Yesterday, I tried to follow the Kiowa to the spring up ahead, but my horse wouldn't go through where an old Indian village was. Damn spirits, or ghosts, or, hell, I don't know." Shell looked around at the men's expressions to see if any were doubting his word.

"This morning Stone Knife brought me a couple medicine bags that he says will keep the ghosts or spirits away. They're only for a couple horses, and I don't know how well they'll work." Shell took a sip of coffee. He didn't see any questioning looks, so he went on.

"I'm going to have you cut out about twenty head from the herd and I'll try to take them across with the Bell Mare. I put one medicine bag on her and the other on my horse." He was still working out the plan in his head as he went. "If we get a running start from back here a ways maybe we can run the bunch through the village to the water before they can turn back or scatter. At least that's what I think we might be able to do." Shell looked at the quiet men staring at him.

"Well shit, let's see if this works." He threw the rest of the coffee from his cup into the fire and walked to his horse and swung up into the saddle.

"Cut me out a bunch, boys, and some of you ride along on each side of them. I want to get the bunch moving fast and straight into the place where the Indian went." Shell was taking down his rope again to use it to haze the mares along.

"Get the Bell Mare out front so the others will follow her. Johnny, get a short piece of rope from the cook wagon to snub the Bell Mare up close to you." Shell had men moving in every direction and his nerves were calming down.

"Just before you get to the markers turn her loose and get out of the way." With his hands Shell was showing Johnny how he wanted things to work.

Riding up to the cook wagon Shell dismounted, unbuckled his gun belt, and put it in the wagon. Next he pulled his Winchester from its scabbard and laid it in the wagon also.

Anything to help me go faster, Shell thought, anything at all will help. Taking a minute to catch his breath, Shell would have said a prayer, if he had been a praying kind of man.

Johnny had the Bell Mare snubbed up to his horse and the other men had cut out about twenty head. They had worked them over to where Shell wanted to get a start from. The area of the village wasn't in sight from where they all were but Shell wasn't worried about the horses getting away from them because there was no place to go but ahead to the water, or back to them.

"Johnny, you get moving!" Shell shouted from the back of the small herd.

"I'm gone!" He and the Bell Mare took off at a lope.

"Bunch 'em up behind her!" Shell was waving his hat and yelling at the other hands to move the horses in behind Johnny.

"Get-up! Get-up! Yip! Yip!" Shell and the men urged the horses into a gallop around the bend in the canyon.

When they were almost to the markers, Johnny turned the Bell Mare loose and swung off to the left. With Shell pushing from behind and the rest of the men yelling and hollering, the horses headed for the spring on the other side of the village site.

Shell could see from the back of the small herd that they were all running straight and not shying or dodging or acting like anything was bothering them. Then he got to the edge of the village site and his world came apart.

Suddenly, he was surrounded by wailing and crying ghosts. They were hitting him and throwing sticks and rocks at him. He could feel every one that struck him. His horse was acting like it was deaf and blind, giving no indication anything was going on. As he moved through the village site more and more ghosts screamed and assaulted Shell. The dust cleared for a moment and Shell recognized that these were the ghosts of the people who had lived in this village and had died here twenty years ago. They stayed with Shell the whole time he was in the village area but left him at its edge.

Finally leaving the village and reaching the spring Shell again heard loud voices. He spun around, and saw his men yelling and waving their hats on the other side of the village. They were excited he'd made it, but had no idea what he'd gone through.

Now Shell had two new problems. He had to get some of the men over here to watch the horses he had brought over. He also had to get back to the other side of the village. His shirt was soaked with sweat and his hands were shaking. He didn't know if his legs would hold him upright if he dismounted, but he needed a drink of water.

"You did well," Stone Knife's voice scared Shell and he jumped and almost fell down as he was walking to the spring.

"Damn it! Don't you ever give a person a warning you're close?" Shell snapped.

"Guess you couldn't see me in all the dust you kicked up." Stone Knife answered.

Shell just shook his head and continued to a pool of water fed by the spring. He knelt and lifted a cupped handful of water to his dry lips.

Now, what do I do next, Shell's mind was racing. Send some hands over, or keep bringing horses and hope they stay by the spring? I'll need the cook wagon sometime, maybe bring it next in with a bunch of horses. Just slow down and catch your breath, then get the Bell Mare and ride back to the herd. Damn, but I hurt everywhere those ghosts hit me. I don't know how much of this I'm going to be able to take. It's looking like a long day.

* * *

Every time Shell went through the village site, from either direction, he was attacked by the ghosts of the villagers. They screamed, they yelled, and they threw things that hit Shell on the arms, chest, back, and face. He was white as a ghost himself and hollow eyed by the time he had made four trips.

The cook wagon and two of the wranglers went with the second bunch of horses. He sent them in the middle of the bunch and they didn't seem to be bothered during the crossing. Two of the horses from his string along with most of the wranglers' horses went over next.

The Bell Mare was about winded and Shell thought he'd try using one of the saddle horses from the wranglers' horses as a lead horse. The saddle horses were used to being together and one by itself would try to find its buddies. Back and forth, back and forth, he'd lost track of how many times he'd made the trip.

The last time he changed horses Shell's arms hurt so bad he could hardly lift them so one of the men saddled it for him. He couldn't pick the saddle up off the ground after he'd removed it from the horse he'd been riding.

We'll be done before dark, he kept telling himself, we'll be done before dark.

Shell had noticed that when he came back through the village with the Bell Mare snubbed to his horse the ghosts couldn't get to him very well on that side. The next time he came back he put the mare on his other side and the same thing happened. Moving her from side to side helped him keep the ghosts from hurting one side more than the other. Two horses would keep them away, he thought, but got busy getting another bunch ready to go and forgot about it.

Going back through the village for the next to the last bunch of horses, Stone Knife rode up alongside Shell. With the lead horse on one side of him and the Indian on the other, Shell was not bothered much by the ghosts.

When they reached the horses that still had to be driven through the village Shell dismounted and walked into the brush to catch his breath and calm down. When he came back to his horse the Indian was still sitting where he was when Shell left. As Shell swung into the saddle and turned his horse to ride off, Stone Knife stopped him.

"How old were you when you were here before?"

"How do you know I was here?" Shell was looking at the Kiowa with disbelief.

"The ghosts have told me," Stone Knife replied.

"Too young to know what I was doing," Shell snapped and rode off to get another bunch ready to take across.

When Shell returned for the last bunch Stone Knife was still in the same place waiting for him.

"Give me your tobacco pouch, Shell Green," Stone Knife had his hand out.

"What the hell are you talking about?" Shell growled. "Go find the next water hole."

"Those ghosts are from when you were here before. Give me the pouch." Stone Knife's voice was quiet and calm.

"What's that have to do with me?" Shell was about burned out and this was not anything he felt like listening to.

"Those ghosts are from the people killed here and scalped. They can't cross over to the other side unless they are whole so they have to stay here and suffer." Stone Knife was looking Shell in the eyes. "We can hear the pouch crying."

"I didn't kill anyone here that day," Shell answered with a tired voice, "Why are you bothering me?"

"Because your tobacco pouch was made from one of these women's breasts and it needs to be buried so one more part of her is returned." Stone Knife's voice had dropped to almost a whisper.

Shell sat for a couple moments, then dismounted. He unbuckled the strap on his saddlebag and took out a folded piece of cloth. Turning around he walked to Stone Knife and handed him the folded cloth.

"Louis, one of the older fighters back then, gave this to me a few weeks after we were here. He was always laughing about how his pouches would keep you warm at night," Shell said. "I didn't feel right about what happened here. That's why I never used it, and I didn't know what to do with it."

"I'll bury it where some of the people are buried." Stone Knife turned and rode back down the canyon.

Shell took the last bunch of horses through the village site at a walk. Nothing was thrown at him, no yelling, no screaming. From the corners of his eyes he could see things moving around. Quiet ghosts.

About the Authors

Steve Hockensmith's mystery-solving cowboys, Big Red and Old Red Amlingmeyer, first appeared in *Ellery Queen Mystery Magazine* and later starred in Hockensmith's debut novel, *Holmes on the Range*, which was nominated for the Edgar, Dilys, Shamus, and Anthony Awards. Three sequels (*On the Wrong Track, The Black Dove,* and *The Crack in the Lens*) followed, and a fifth book in the series is in the works. Hockensmith's latest novel is *Dawn of the Dreadfuls*, a prequel to the horror/romance "mash-up" *Pride and Prejudice and Zombies.*

William W. Johnstone is the *New York Times* and *USA Today* bestselling author of over 125 books published over the last 25 years, with more than 10,000,000 copies in print. **J. A. Johnstone** is the frequent collaborator of his uncle, Bill Johnstone, and is also the author of The Loner series.

Margaret Coel is the *New York Times* bestselling author of the Wind River mystery series set among the Arapahos in Wyoming. She is widely considered the most accomplished heir to Tony Hillerman's legacy. The fourteenth novel in her series, *The Silent Spring,* was published in September 2009, and her stand-alone novel, *Blood Memory,* appeared in 2008. Margaret is a recipient of the Willa [Cather] Award for best novel on the West. She is also the author of four non-fiction books on the West. A fourth-generation Coloradan, Margaret lives in Boulder with her husband, George.

Johnny D. Boggs has four Spur Awards from Western Writers of America, a Western Heritage Wrangler Award from the National Cowboy and Western Heritage Museum, and has been called "among the best western writers at work today" by *Booklist* magazine. The author of more than twenty-five Western novels, three nonfiction books, and scores of articles for magazines such as *True West, Wild West* and *Persimmon Hill,* Boggs has covered a wide array of subjects in fiction and nonfiction. Recent novels include *Northfield, Camp Ford,* and *Walk Proud, Stand Tall.* A native of South Carolina and former newspaper journalist in Texas, Boggs lives in Santa Fe, New Mexico, with his wife and son. His website is www.johnnydboggs.com.

Bill Brooks has written more than twenty novels dealing with the American West, including *The Stone Garden: The Epic Life of Billy the Kid* and many others. He works as a full-time writer and lives in the Blue Ridge Mountains of Appalachia, the ancestral home of his father's people. He lived and wrote in Arizona for six years, which gave him a chance to explore the West and its history. He hopes that someday the "Western" will make a comeback and that it will be recognized for the true literary form that it is.

Candy Moulton has written a dozen Western history books including *Roadside History of Wyoming* and the Spur-winning biography *Chief Joseph: Guardian of the People.* As a reporter for the *Casper Star-Tribune,* she has written about many Wyoming crimes, including the reinvestigation of the Willie Nickell killing. She writes regularly for a number of magazines and newspapers, and edits the *Roundup Magazine* for Western Writers of America. She makes her home near Encampment, Wyoming.

Louis L'Amour (1908–1988) was the most successful western writer of all time, selling fifteen to twenty thousand books a day at the height of his popularity. He wrote the kind of action fiction beloved by so many generations of Americans, with strong heroes, evil villains, proud, energetic heroines, and all of the excitement and danger that the West represented. His novels include such masterpieces as *Hondo, Shalako, Down the Long Hills, The Cherokee Trail,* and *Last of the Breed.* His most famous series was the Sacketts saga, later made into several excellent television movies.

Sandy Whiting resides along a Kansas section of the Chisholm Trail. Although no cattle currently tread outside the door, an occasional horse and rider will trek up the paved street, and there are buffalo grazing in a pen about a mile and a half away. Sandy's first work of fiction appeared in the *Louis L'Amour Western Magazine.* That story won the Spur Award for best short fiction. In addition, she's published several fiction stories as well as nonfiction articles. She's also reviewed music CDs fresh out of the chute and headed to the public's ears.

Larry D. Sweazy (www.larrydsweazy.com) won the WWA Spur award for Best Short Fiction in 2005, and was nominated for a Derringer award in 2007. His other short stories have appeared in, or will appear in, *The Adventure of the Missing Detective: And 25 of the Year's Finest Crime and Mystery Stories!*, *Boy's Life*, *Ellery Queen's Mystery Magazine*, Amazon Shorts, and other publications. He is also author of the Josiah Wolfe, Texas Ranger series (Berkley). Larry owns WordWise Publishing Services, LLC, and as a freelance indexer, he has written over five hundred back-of-the-book indexes for publishers such as Cisco Press, Addison-Wesley, O'Reilly, and Thomson-Gale. He lives in Noblesville, Indiana, with his wife, Rose, two dogs, and a cat.

Lori Van Pelt won the Western Writers of America Spur Award for Best Short Fiction in 2006 for the lead tale in her short story collection, *Pecker's Revenge and Other Stories from the Frontier's Edge* (University of New Mexico Press, 2005). Her biography, *Amelia Earhart: The Sky's No Limit* (Forge, American Heroes Series, 2005), was one of three in the nation named to the New York Public Library's "Best Books for the Teen Age 2006" list. The author of the Wyoming-based nonfiction Dreamers and Schemers series published by High Plains Press, her award-winning nonfiction articles have appeared in a variety of publications ranging from the *WREN (Wyoming Rural Electric News)* magazine to the *WOLA (Western Outlaw and Lawman Association) Journal*. Lori lives with her husband, Eugene Walck, Jr., on his ranch near Saratoga, Wyoming. She recently completed her second collection of western short fiction.

Deborah Morgan writes in both the western and mystery genres. Her first short fiction appeared in *Louis L'Amour Western Magazine*. Raised on a ranch in Oklahoma, she was named Roundup Club Rodeo Queen in her hometown when she was fifteen. Morgan was managing editor of two national treasure hunting magazines, and later of a biweekly newspaper in southeast Kansas before moving to Michigan. She admits that something western usually finds its way into her antique-lover's mystery novel series. A former Western Writers of America Spur Awards Chair, she's currently writing her first historical western novel.

Former Western Writers of America president **Loren D. Estleman** has written more than sixty novels and a couple of hundred short stories, including the U.S. Deputy Marshal Page Murdock series, many stand-alone historical westerns, and the Detroit Detective Amos Walker mysteries. Estleman has been nominated for the National Book Award and the Mystery Writers of America Edgar Award. He is the recipient of sixteen national writing awards, including five Spurs and two Stirrups from the WWA, three Western Heritage Awards from the National Cowboy and Western Heritage Museum, and four Shamus Awards from the Private Eye Writers of America.

Jeff Mariotte is the award-winning author of more than thirty novels, most set in the contemporary West, including *River Runs Red, Missing White Girl* (both as Jeffrey J. Mariotte), *The Slab,* and the teen horror quartet *Witch Season.* He lives in southern Arizona.

Born in Andrews County, Texas, **Elmer Kelton** graduated from the University of Texas in 1948. He has won seven Spur Awards and three Western Heritage Awards, and his novels have included such critically acclaimed work as *The Time It Never Rained, The Man Who Rode Midnight,* and *Way of the Coyote.* His memoir, *Sandhills Boy,* was published in 2007.

James "Jim" Fischer is an Ohio native and has been around horses most of his life. Both of Jim's grandfathers made their living with horses, one as a farmer, and the other as a teamster. Jim is an associate member of the Western Writers of America and co-author of the book *Custer's Horses,* Wolfe Publishing, 2001. Jim has had articles published in *Buckskin Report* and *Cowboy Magazine,* and his story "Snow Angels" is one of the stories in the collection *Tales from Cowboy Country,* Range Writer, Inc., 2005. Jim belongs to The National Bit, Spur & Saddle Collectors Association, the Single Action Shooting Society, the Custer Battlefield Historical & Museum Association, and is a Life Member of the National Rifle Association. Jim and his wife Candy live in Vermilion, Ohio, on the south shore of Lake Erie.

About the Editors

Martin H. Greenberg has edited more than two thousand books in every genre imaginable, including many western titles, such as *Desperadoes, Texas Rangers, Guns of the West, The Best of the American West,* and The Best of the West anthology series with Bill Pronzini, as well as the Double-Action Western novel series for Tor. He was the 1995 recipient of the Ellery Queen Award from the Mystery Writers of America, the Milford Award for Lifetime Achievement in Science Fiction Publishing and Editing, and the IIWA Grand Master Award, the only person in publishing history to receive all three of these honors.

Russell Davis has edited numerous novels, short stories, and anthology titles, including *Lost Trails.* He is an avid supporter of western literature. As an author, he has written and sold almost twenty novels (under a variety of pseudonyms and in many genres) and over thirty-five short stories. He currently runs his own book packaging company, Morning Storm Books, a western-related blog, and works with his wife on breaking and training Arabian horses for endurance riding. When he's not busy with all of that, he tries to keep up with his kids, coach youth football, and once in a great while, get a little shut-eye.

For more epic stories of the American West,
be sure to look for . . .

LAW OF THE GUN
Stories by Elmer Kelton,
William W. Johnstone *with* J. A. Johnstone,
John Jakes, and Loren D. Estleman

Edited by Martin H. Greenberg and Russell Davis

ONE MAN. ONE GUN. ONE LAW.

He's an American icon: the Western shootist, living by
skill, courage and a willingness to spit in death's eye.
Now the greatest names in Western literature turn this
mythical character upside down, inside out,
and every which way but loose . . .

In "The Trouble with Dude," award-winning
author Johnny D. Boggs saddles a once-famous
lawman with some high-paying New York dudes
in search of Western thrills who get more than they
bargained for; in "Uncle Jeff and the Gunfighter,"
Western master storyteller Elmer Kelton chronicles
a quarrel between a hardscrabble Texas rancher
and a killer for hire—with results that stun a town;
William W. Johnstone and J. A. Johnstone offer
"Inferno: A Last Gunfighter Story,"
featuring series hero Frank Morgan.

From a pistol-packing woman to a freed slave
heading into a Nebraska winter and an education
in gun fighting, *Law of the Gun* is about journeys,
vendettas, stand-offs, and legends that end—or
sometimes just begin—with the roar of a gun . . .

Available now from Pinnacle Books.

Visit us at www.kensingtonbooks.com.

Connect with Us

Visit us online at
KensingtonBooks.com
to read more from your favorite authors, see books
by series, view reading group guides, and more.